MAN
IN THE
SHADOWS

Also by Caroline Crane

Summer Girl
The Girls Are Missing
Coast of Fear
Wife Found Slain
The Foretelling
The Third Passenger
Woman Vanishes
Trick or Treat
Something Evil
Someone at the Door
Circus Day

MAN IN THE SHADOWS

Caroline Crane

DODD, MEAD & COMPANY
New York

Published by Dodd, Mead & Company, Inc.
71 Fifth Avenue, New York, N.Y. 10003
Distributed in Canada by
McClelland and Stewart Limited, Toronto
Manufactured in the United States of America
First Edition

1 2 3 4 5 6 7 8 9 10

Library of Congress Cataloging-in-Publication Data

Crane, Caroline
  Man in the shadows.

  I. Title.
PS3553.R2695M3   1987   813′.54   86-24299

ISBN 0-396-08930-5

For Yoshio

1

The studio was air-conditioned, but the lights were hot. She was covered with a blanket of flowers as though she were dead. As the afternoon wore on, the flowers wilted and so did she. It was someone's bright idea for a perfume ad.

"That should wrap it up," said Paulo, standing away from his camera. "You had a phone call, Denise. A Mr. Reyes. The number's on my desk."

"Thanks. I have it." She tried to extricate herself from the flowers. One of the young assistants hurried over to help her. Wearing only the flesh-colored bikini that was meant to look like nothing under her floral blanket, she went to the telephone in Paulo's office.

"Hi. Is something wrong?" she asked when she had Harlan Reyes on the line.

"Only if you don't feel like joining me for dinner," he said. "That would be catastrophic."

She felt terrible. "I'm really awfully tired. I've been lying on the floor all afternoon."

He laughed.

"The *floor*, Harlan." It was scarcely a bed of roses, for the flowers had been on top of her. As a lawyer, he would not have understood about the lights and the fatigue of endless posing.

"I'm not taking no for an answer, Denise."

"Since you put it that way . . . Let me call my babysitter, okay?" She knew it was an imposition on poor Mrs. Neuberger, although the elderly woman could probably use some extra money.

And dinner with Harlan always had a good effect. If she could love anybody besides Wade, the man she planned to marry, that person would be Harlan. In fact, she did love him, but by now the flame had died down to an even glow, and he was more a father-brother than a lover.

Forty minutes later, after putting on her streetclothes and downing a can of diet soda, she took the elevator to the lobby. He was already there, a tall, elegant figure pretending to study the building directory as he stood waiting for her. Over the years his temples had become grayer and the crinkles around his eyes a little deeper, but he was still one of the most attractive men she knew.

He kissed her cheek. "I'm sorry to hijack you like this, when I know you want to be home with your family."

"Believe me, it's good to have a respite," she said. "I love them, don't misunderstand me. I just need to recharge my batteries."

Harlan would not have known about that, either. He had never had young children, or any children at all, except a teenage stepdaughter for the brief time he was married.

The sun was low, an orange ball behind a screen of high humidity. Denise felt choked after the air-conditioning.

2

"No relief in sight," Harlan remarked. "That's what the radio said."

"I still like it better than winter. It's funny, but I mind winter more in the city than I did upstate. Or maybe my blood is thinning, the way it does with old people."

"Old! Denise, honey, you're a child."

"Not anymore. I was just thinking about it this morning. Do you realize how long I've been here, doing what I'm doing? Ten years."

"I hope this doesn't mean you're planning to move on," he said. "This summing up."

"Oh, no. I'm a permanent New Yorker now, and so is Wade." It made her happy just to say his name.

"Well, I don't believe it's ten years."

"Don't you remember? I was all of nineteen, and I didn't know anything. You called me a green kid that night we met."

"When was that?"

"At a party, my first year here. You really don't remember? I must have made a big impression. That's when Avery was chasing me."

She thought how much better it would have been if she had married Harlan instead. Her life might have made some sense. But Avery's persistence had overwhelmed her. She should have taken it as a warning.

Now at last it was over, and she had Wade. She found it hard to believe that after so many years, things were finally beginning to straighten themselves out.

"You were just opening your own firm," she went on. "That's what the party was about. I was somebody's date, but I don't remember whose. Now you've hit the big time, and I've almost had it as a model."

"That's the way modeling is."

"Thanks for reminding me."

They walked to Lexington Avenue, to a bistro they both liked near Grand Central Terminal. After they had

3

ordered, and she was nibbling on a breadstick, he took a large envelope from his briefcase.

"This is really the reason for my invitation," he said as he handed it to her. "I thought dinner would be more gala than just an office visit. Or worse yet, the mail."

She opened the clasp. "My divorce? Already?"

It was enclosed in a blue cover sheet. "Supreme Court of the State of New York, City of New York," it said, with her name as plaintiff against Avery Burns, defendant.

"Harlan! I'm so happy! Oh, God, I feel guilty."

"It's a little late for that, isn't it?"

"Oh, no, I'm not changing my mind. I felt guilty all along. He needed me so much."

"He didn't need you, Denise, he devoured you. He only used you to make up for his own inadequacies. That's not love."

"I know, but I can't help it. He used to say it was because he loved me too much."

"He may have believed it, but you shouldn't. You had a good case for mental and physical cruelty."

"It wasn't just me. I'm not sure I would have done it for myself. It was the children. He never really wanted them. And then he tried to get custody. Can you imagine?"

"To punish you," said Harlan.

"Yes, I know. He kept saying he wanted me back, but he did it all wrong. He yelled and screamed and bullied me. He—" She put a hand to the side of her face, still feeling the blows. "I assume he got his copy?"

"I assume it's been sent, yes."

"To California?"

"If that's where he is, that's probably where it went. How's he doing out there?"

"I really couldn't tell you. He's living with some

4

woman, and of course trying to get on television, but I don't think— Well, that's the story of his life. Poor Avery."

"He's a good-looking man. I wonder why it doesn't happen for him."

"It's just too competitive. Too many people want the same thing. And they're all good-looking." She blew him a kiss. "You're an angel. I'm going to call Wade as soon as I get home."

"Where is Wade?" he asked in surprise.

She felt herself blushing. How had he known that she and Wade were living together?

"He had to go home. His grandfather died. But this should cheer him up." She stuffed the papers into their envelope. "Harlan, I want you to come to our wedding."

"I'd like that very much."

"You can sit with my sister, since you're practically family. In fact, you're almost all I have."

"What about your children?"

"They're going to be in it. I promised." She brushed away a tear—of loneliness. And happiness. "At least Karen. Rodney's only three, so he doesn't care very much."

Their drinks arrived. She wiped another tear and picked up her glass. "I guess cheers are in order."

"They certainly are. To your happiness," he said. "I hope it all works out for you this time. And will you do me a favor?"

"What's that?"

"Stop feeling guilty."

Harlan took her home in a taxi.

"I really appreciate this," she confided. "I mean, the whole evening, but especially, since it's so late, having you with me."

"Of course I'd be with you. When have I ever sent you home by yourself?" His eyes narrowed. "Why, has something been bothering you?"

"I don't know, exactly, it's just this weird feeling." She clutched at an armrest to keep from sliding as the taxi careened onto her block. "I feel as if I'm not alone. You know, as if there are people— Not just around me, but—"

"Eight million of them," he said.

"No, it's not that. It's more like . . . eyes. Oh, well." She laughed nervously and gathered up her purse and envelope.

As she stepped onto the sidewalk, someone sitting in a parked car switched on the lights.

She stood blinded, impaled. She heard Harlan's voice: "Take care!" and saw him dimly in the brilliance. Waving good night, she hurried into her building.

Even before she reached the third floor, her children's screeches could be heard on the stairs. Mrs. Neuberger, exhausted, was taking a television break. She perked up when Denise came in, accepted her check for the week, and returned to her own apartment down the hall.

Karen waltzed through the living room in her faded pink nightgown. "It's Friday, it's Friday! No camp tomorrow! Mommy, why can't I stay home like Rodney does, instead of going to camp?"

"Because," Denise replied, not thinking, "it would be too much for Mrs. Neuberger. She's kind of old."

"It's not fair."

Denise sighed. The day had been a long one, and the apartment was hot and peculiarly airless. From time to time she considered air-conditioning, but it would have meant a whole rewiring job. Perhaps as a wedding present to each other, she and Wade could do that.

6

She swallowed her impatience. "Don't you like camp?"

"Sometimes," Karen admitted. "But I like to stay home, too. I wish you didn't have to work."

"So do I, if you want to know. I really don't like to go away from you, but working's a fact of life. Now how about getting into bed?"

"Why can't Wade earn the money?"

"He does. It's just—" Why did this always happen? Always at bedtime the chattering began. The profound questions with answers that her children, at ages three and seven, would not have understood in any case. And now she wanted them quiet so she could call Wade.

As though on cue, Rodney piped up from his cot, "When's Wade coming back?"

"Tomorrow night. Karen, get into bed *this minute*."

"But, Mommy, why can't I stay up for a while? I'm older than he is."

"I know, but you both need your sleep."

It was wrong to make them go to bed at the same time, and wrong that they should have to share a room, but in that small apartment there was not much choice. Even before Wade came along, Denise had barred them from her own room as detrimental to their emotional health.

And now Wade was there, sharing her bed. They told themselves it had not been a matter of choice but of financial necessity, in New York's expensive housing market.

The truth was, she needed him. She needed to know that she would never be alone again. At the same time, and with terrible guilt pangs, she worried about the effect that the not-quite-sanctified relationship might be having on her children.

Still, it had been worth the wait, which was now over. They could have a small, beautiful wedding, and everything would be legitimate. And because Wade already lived with them, was already a father to the children, the adjustments would be minimal.

She left their door open for circulation and passed through an archway whose sculpted scrollwork of flowers, leaves, and cupids had been blunted over the years by many coats of paint. It was a rococo touch, but she loved it. She loved everything about the apartment, from its marble-manteled fireplace to the stained-glass window in the bathroom. It was in a pleasant neighborhood, not far from Central Park. She had been very lucky.

A pair of curtained French doors led to her own bedroom, where the telephone was. She dialed his family's home in Lawrence, Kansas, and listened to the ringing. With each ring she grew more impatient, eager to tell her news, but there was no answer.

She would try again later. It was still early in Kansas. Frustrated, she curled on the living room couch next to an open window and listened to the night. The sounds of humans and machines. Voices and laughter on the sidewalk below her. A distant shriek of brakes. A radio playing Latin music. The clink of dishes in a nearby apartment.

She rested for a moment, then put on a leotard and began her exercises, an occupational necessity. There were routines for the thighs, the hips, the upper arms, and abdomen. An exercise to keep her breasts firm.

After her bath and pedicure, the apartment seemed quiet. Unnaturally so, except for the gentle blowing of a hassock fan.

And dreary. There was nothing to do on that Friday night except wait for Wade.

8

"People . . . who need people . . ." she sang to herself as she brewed a cup of Sleepy Time herbal tea.

She took it into the living room and turned on the television. An old Elvis Presley movie was better than silence. Better than those distant dishes, and a beer party on some stoop farther up the block. Besides, he did have a nice, rich voice.

She burned her mouth on the tea when the telephone rang. It made her jump, and she hurried to answer it before it could wake the children.

"Hi, Wade?"

There was no response. Who else? she wondered. "Hello?"

Her ear caught a faint sound. The rustle of clothing.

"Wade, is that you?"

It couldn't be. He would never play such a stupid trick.

A stranger. A random caller, out to get his kicks by tormenting women. She snapped, "Listen, if you want to talk to me, talk. Otherwise, I'm hanging up."

Then it came, faint and breathy. An almost voiceless voice.

"Mrs. Burns," it said, "do you know what time it is? It's late, and it's dark outside. Very dark, Mrs. Burns. Are you sure your children are safe?"

"Who is this?"

She had not meant to ask. It was what he wanted. To involve her and frighten her.

The voice continued. "You're all alone now, aren't you, Mrs. Burns? Tell me, are you afraid?"

She clutched the phone with damp hands. "You'd better stop this, or I'm calling the police."

There was a chuckle like dry leaves, and the line went dead. She pressed the disconnect button.

Her bedroom was dark except for a glow from the

9

living room lamp. The blind was still open. She closed it, then lifted a slat and looked out.

Two couples strolled by on the opposite sidewalk, engrossed in each other. It was silly to think that the caller would be out there. He could have been anywhere.

He or she. From the sound, it might have been either.

But who was it? Someone who knew her name. Who knew she had children, and that Wade wasn't there.

A jealous colleague? But who could be jealous of her? Had she beaten someone out for an important assignment? She tried to remember.

The children.

They were both in their beds, and sound asleep. The window that opened onto the fire escape was covered by a folding metal gate.

Someone could pry it open, or throw something through it. A Molotov cocktail, perhaps.

It would never come to that, not really. The call had only been meant to scare her.

But why?

She examined the gate. It was locked. She could put her fist through the spaces, but it would be extremely difficult to throw anything through it from any distance.

Karen stirred and opened her eyes. "Mommy, I heard the telephone."

"It was a wrong number," Denise replied.

"Why did you come in here?"

"To see if you have enough air. Do you want the fan on?"

"No, it blows too much." Karen sat up. "Mommy, when are you getting married?"

"Very soon. And you're going to be a bridesmaid."

"Do I have to wear a dress?"

"Of course. A beautiful dress. Now go back to sleep. Good night, honey." She kissed her daughter and returned to the living room. The blinds there were down, the slats open, although tilted so no one could see in. She turned off the lamp to make herself invisible.

Her tea was still warm. She drank it in the flickering glow of the television. The sound was so low she could barely hear it. Outside, a car door slammed, and a woman laughed. Peaceful nighttime noises.

The movie had lost whatever charm it might have had for her. She turned it off, washed her teacup, and put on her filmy red nightgown. It was the coolest one she owned. Avery had given it to her. He said he liked her in red, with her cat-green eyes fringed with long, dark lashes, and her nearly black hair.

"Devil colors," he had said. "Red with the black hair. It brings out the devil in you."

She frowned, remembering. It was his old habit of projecting whatever he wanted onto her. Of seeing her as he chose, instead of as she was. If anybody had a devil in him, it was Avery.

She turned off her bedroom light before opening the blind. Again she looked out, hidden by darkness. She saw a man walking his dog. A taxi cruising the street. She did not see anyone watching her.

She had climbed into bed and was arranging her pillows when the telephone rang again.

She hesitated, not wanting to answer it.

But it might be Wade. She picked it up.

The voice said, "You turned off your light, Mrs. Burns. Aren't you afraid of the dark?"

She pulled the sheet over her lace-covered breasts. Her head swam. She moistened her lips, but did not speak.

The voice continued. "Did you go and look in their little beds? Were they safe and sound? It can happen so fast, you know."

Again she pressed the disconnect button. She held it down to keep the phone from springing to life. Finally, cautiously, she released it. With a numb finger she dialed 9, then remembered that it was only for crimes in progress. She used the flashlight to look up her local station.

"Twentieth Precinct," a voice responded. His name sounded something like "Weedy."

"I've been getting crank calls, and I don't know what to do," she told him. "Somebody called me twice tonight. He knows my name, and he asked if my children are safe." She described as much as she could remember of what had been said.

"Are you listed in the phone book?" Weedy asked. "He could have picked out your name. If it keeps up, notify the phone company and they'll arrange a trace."

"That's *all*?" She could not believe they were so impotent, or perhaps uncaring. "He threatened my children! Isn't there anything you can do about that?"

"Best thing to do is to call your phone company business office. In the meantime, keep your doors locked. Usually it doesn't mean anything. A guy like that is a coward, hiding behind the telephone."

"But what about— Never mind." She hung up, then removed the phone from its hook and left it on the night table.

It was easy to tell her to keep her doors locked. But what about Monday, when she had an all-day booking? How could she watch the children then?

She was listed in the directory as "D. Burns," deliberately neuter. How had they guessed that she was female? How did they know about the children?

They knew everything about her. Even which windows were hers.

Again she tried the number Wade had left. *Please be there. Please.*

A figure stood silhouetted in her doorway. Denise gave a cry and quickly set down the phone.

"Oh, Karen! Oh, my God."

"What's the matter, Mommy?"

"You startled me, that's all. What are you doing up?"

"I can't sleep. The phone keeps ringing. Who's calling all the time? Is it Wade?"

"Still the same wrong number. Sometimes they won't believe it's wrong, and they keep trying."

"What did they want?"

"I told you, it was—"

"I mean, who did they ask for?"

"What difference does it make?" She groped for a name. Any name, to stop the questions. "Gregory. Why do you have to know that?"

Karen flopped down beside her on the bed. "Then who were you calling just now?"

"I'm trying to get hold of Wade. I have something to tell him. Come on, I'll tuck you in bed."

"I want to stay up with you."

"I was just going to bed myself," Denise said, "but we'll stay up for a few more minutes. Would you like some sleepy tea?"

She turned on the television, hoping Elvis would distract them both. For a moment she stood staring into the sink, unable to remember what she was doing there.

Of course. She had promised tea. She set a pan of water on the stove and turned on the fire. What if the stove blew up? What if something was rigged somewhere in the apartment?

She had used it earlier, and nothing happened. She

13

mustn't be afraid. That would only give her caller the power he wanted.

Or she. It had been an androgynous stage whisper. But she would show them she wasn't afraid. She would take her children to the playground tomorrow, as she always did on weekends. It was the only real time they could spend together.

"Don't get too interested in the movie," she warned. "I'm not staying up till the end, and neither are you."

Karen snuggled cross-legged into a rattan swivel chair and swung it back and forth. She would probably spill her tea. It didn't matter. Nothing mattered, as long as she was safe.

Again the phone rang. She had hung it up by mistake. Her shock gave her away. She saw Karen's eyes huge with questioning as she went to answer it.

She held it to her ear, but said nothing. Neither did the caller. After a moment, she hung up.

Karen asked, "Was it a wrong number again?"

"I guess so."

"Why didn't you talk?"

"What is there to say? I already told them it's wrong. Did you finish your tea?"

"It's too hot."

"It's cool now. Finish it and get to bed." Denise forced down her own tea.

Karen seemed to move in slow motion.

"Go on," Denise prodded. "If you don't want any more, pour it in the sink."

"I can't drink it fast. Mommy, why can't I stay up with you?"

"I told you, I'm going to bed now, too."

"But it's nice without Rodney."

The child could have written a book on how to stall. Conversation. Slow swallowing. Even loving. All

14

transparent devices, and all difficult to argue with.

"Please? Just put your cup in the sink. We'll wash it tomorrow."

As soon as Karen was in bed, her door left slightly open, Denise tried the Kansas number one more time. She needed him. Needed to hear his voice to get her through the night, and his assurance that he would soon be home to protect her.

There was still no answer.

2

She woke to the sound of the children's voices chatting companionably in the kitchen. Streaks of yellow sunlight shone through the blind.

They had gotten safely through the night. Fragments of bad dreams fell away from her as she reached for her slippers. This evening Wade would be home, and nothing like that telephone scare would ever happen again.

The children were sitting at the table, and they smiled when they saw her. Rodney waved his spoon. Karen had fixed a bowl of cold cereal for him and was eating her homemade granola mix straight from the jar with her fingers.

"If you put that in a bowl with some milk," said Denise, "you'll at least get your protein." Having made the suggestion and knowing it would not be followed, she closed herself in the bathroom for a cooling shower.

When she returned to the kitchen, Karen was eating

16

a slab of bread smeared with apple butter. "Did you get hold of Wade?" Karen asked.

"No, he wasn't in. Why?"

"You don't have to talk to him if he's coming home today."

"I wanted to tell him something."

"About what?"

"Just something." It was for Wade to hear before she told the children. Besides, Avery was their father. In spite of his seeming indifference to them, they could not be expected to share her delight that the divorce was final.

By ten o'clock, when they set out for the park, the air was a hot, damp blanket. Denise wore only a trace of makeup, and a beltless white sundress with large strawberry appliqué pockets. Her shoulder-length hair was tied back with a scarf to keep it off her neck. She carried a tote bag packed with towels, plastic pails and shovels, a magazine for herself, and a lunch of canned soda, carrot sticks, and Vienna sausages.

"That looks like a doll dress," Karen criticized. "It doesn't look grown up."

"When the weather gets more respectable, then I will, too," Denise promised.

She had wanted to braid Karen's hair for coolness, but Karen refused. Nobody wore pigtails, she insisted. Her hair fell down her back in light brown ripples, almost as golden as Avery's. Rodney's thatch was darker, like his mother's. The children wore matching T-shirts that said "I," followed by a big red heart and "Berryville, N.Y." They were a gift from Jill, Denise's sister, who still lived in Berryville.

Cautiously Denise opened the apartment door, half expecting to see someone lurking in the hall. It was filled with sunshine from the skylight, but otherwise

17

empty. She heard the sound of a radio, and someone running a shower. It was Saturday, and people were home. Safe, neighborly people.

"What are you looking for?" asked Karen. There was something in her query that sounded like a glimmer of awareness, but she couldn't really know anything. Denise smiled.

"Just trying to remember if I packed my sunglasses."

At the second floor she glanced over the railing to check the building's front door. Its heavy plate glass, latticed with wrought iron, glowed in the morning light. There were no unaccountable dark shadows.

Where had the caller stood, she wondered, to see her lights go off?

"Wait, Karen." Denise pulled open the door and looked out, to the right and the left and across the street.

"Mommy, what's happening?"

"Nothing, nothing. I just wanted to see how hot it is."

Karen's eyes traveled over her briefly, and there was a slight frown between them. Denise turned away.

The owner of the brownstone house next door stood hosing his section of the sidewalk and watering the ivy beds that grew around his front steps. He diverted the stream while they passed. Denise thanked him, and drew a silent nod in response. Behind her, the hose began splashing again.

As she walked on, she felt the man watching her. Felt his eyes on her back. She had never spoken with him, had never heard his voice. But he lived close enough to look into her windows, and Karen had reported seeing him do it. He could have learned her name without much trouble. He could have found out anything he wanted, even the fact that Wade had gone away for a few days.

18

She felt so vulnerable. And it was all since her separation and move to the West Side. If she had stayed with Avery in their building guarded by a doorman, no one would be bothering her now.

But she hadn't been able to endure it—the temper, the jealousy, and the put-downs because of the jealousy. Once she had had to cancel a booking because he had given her a black eye.

He had insisted it was her fault. She could not make him understand that the loss of income hurt them both. Even then she might have stayed with him, except for the children.

"Why?" Harlan had asked her later. "Why must it be for them? Don't you think *you* deserve anything? Or do you think you're getting what you deserve?"

"But he needs me," she had answered, pleading with Harlan to understand.

And he did. He understood all too well what she herself knew now. That it was only an excuse for her cowardice.

She took Rodney's hand to cross Columbus Avenue, and they walked along a broad, tree-shaded sidewalk past the Museum of Natural History. The trees grew so tall and thick that she could see only bits of the museum's roof and pink sandstone walls.

An abused wife. She hadn't realized it until she talked to Harlan about a separation. He had used the term. At first she had argued, "Avery loves me, and I love him. I just can't take it anymore."

"That's the way it happens," Harlan had replied.

Karen interrupted Denise's thoughts. "What are we doing tomorrow? Can we go to the zoo?"

"We'll have to see. Maybe Wade will be too tired."

"Then he can come to the playground with us."

Upon entering the park, they followed a path that

19

sloped gently toward the playground. Already several families and a few Saturday fathers were there, pushing their children on swings or supervising the seesaws.

"There's Nicole Spitzer." Karen waved to a small figure in bright red shorts. Denise did not see any other Spitzers.

"She can't be here by herself."

"She does it a lot," said Karen.

"Comes to the park alone? I don't believe it."

Nicole galloped toward them. "Hi, Karen. Hi, Mrs. Burns."

"And Rodney," said Karen.

Denise asked, "Where's your mother, Nikki?"

"She's home sleeping." Nicole seized Karen by the hand. "Let's go on the swings."

Rodney took his pail and shovel from the tote bag and climbed into a sandbox. Denise brushed a fallen leaf from a nearby bench and sat down.

She watched the two girls dart from the slides to the swings to the seesaws. A sprinkler in the center of the playground sent out a gentle rain. The girls ran through it, soaking their clothes. Rodney shoveled sand into his pail and dumped it out, forming a cake that quickly fell apart. Following the example of another child, he filled his bucket at the sprinkler and returned to the sandbox to mix a muddy brew.

Denise turned the pages of her magazine but found herself thinking of Wade and gazing up at the treetops that stood motionless in a light, hot haze.

Maybe a wedding at City Hall. They could do it almost right away. But Karen would be disappointed if there were no fanfare. Somehow they must make it a positive experience for the children.

The treetops rippled. A hot breeze blew fitfully over the playground and died. At the other end of the bench, an overweight woman fanned herself with a newspaper and slapped at a fly that tried to bite her leg.

"Some day, isn't it?" she remarked.

"Yes, it is," said Denise. "Very hot."

The woman inched closer. "Did you see the headline?" She paused in her fanning to readjust the folded paper. "I'm telling you, what this city's coming to. A place like that, with a doorman and all. My husband says when your number's up, it's up, so I guess it's all the same."

Denise smiled thinly. She had no idea what the woman was talking about.

Rodney's scream made her jump from the bench. He was engaged in a tug-of-war with a chubby urchin who was trying to wrest his pail away from him. The urchin yanked at Rodney's hair, then pushed him backward against the concrete edge of the sandbox.

"Hey, hey, hey!" said a deep voice. Out of nowhere, a muscular young man in green jogging shorts appeared and crouched beside Rodney, who lay dazed, trying to catch his breath.

"You okay there, kid?" The man helped him to his feet. Rodney found his voice and let out a howl that left him breathless again.

Denise snatched him up and tried to comfort him. "He could have gotten hurt!"

"I think he did," said the man. "Look at his back."

She had meant spinal damage. Rodney's wound was an angry red scrape.

The fat woman seized the urchin's hand and dragged him away, remonstrating. Denise glared after them, then sat with Rodney on her lap, crooning to him, although he drowned her out with his cries.

The man sat down next to her. "Do you think he's all right? Want me to help you take him to a doctor?"

"I don't think so, but thank you."

"It probably ought to be cleaned."

Karen ran to her, looking stricken. "What happened? Did Rodney get hurt?" And then, "We don't have to go home, do we?"

The abrasion scarcely bled. Denise took him to the sprinkler, let the water run onto his back, and applied a Band-Aid for protection. When she returned to her place on the bench, the man was still there.

"You really ought to use an antiseptic," he said. "No telling what sort of germs there might be."

"I want my soda," Rodney said, weeping.

The man patted his arm. "You're a brave little kid. That must have hurt a lot."

Denise said, "Of course it did." Vaguely she wondered why the man thought he was brave, but she was more intent upon listening to his voice. Was it the same? It was hard to tell, because the caller had whispered.

She was sure she had never seen him before. She would have remembered. He had the looks and build of a Greek statue, with a finely chiseled face and sensuous mouth. Dark, wavy hair that curled at the back of his neck. Long limbs and exquisite musculature, so visible in his scanty attire. His eyes were meltingly brown, but he was too friendly. Much too friendly for New York.

"You don't mind, do you?" he asked, and she realized that her stare had been cold. She still could not account for his presence.

"Mind what?" she asked warily.

"I don't usually hang out in playgrounds, but on a day like this it looked nice and shady after a dash around the reservoir."

She stiffened. There were many shady places in the park.

22

"You shouldn't sit down right after running," she said.

He smiled, seeming touched by her concern. She hadn't meant it as concern, but as criticism. He said, "That's okay, it was a while ago. I was on my way home, but it's even hotter there. The name is Cliff, by the way. Cliff O'Donnell."

She noted the unheated face and the pristine white T-shirt. Her eyes traveled down his legs, with their golden, curling hairs. He wore jogging shoes, but if he had just circled the reservoir, he would have been wilted. His shirt would be wringing wet, and so would his hair. His shoes would be scuffed and worn.

"What is it you really want?" she asked.

He met her gaze steadily, but his eyes were soft. "Maybe I want to talk to you."

"I don't want to talk to you. Why don't you leave?"

"I wouldn't blame you if you didn't, but I figured it's worth a try. You probably get a lot of that from guys, don't you?"

"If you won't leave, I will." She began to pack her tote bag.

"No, wait. I'll make it quick. I hate to bother you at all, but they sent—" He paused and studied her anew. "You're Denise, right? The model? Denise Garner? I know your face pretty well, but I never had a name for it."

A process server. She might have known. Avery was suing again for the children. He would claim she was immoral, living with a man. Thank God she could marry now. And that she had Harlan, who would know what to do.

"I never heard of whoever that is," she tried, but she was too frightened to sound convincing. He probably had a picture of her. That was how they did it. Strange that he didn't simply hand her the papers and run.

23

"Do you mind an interview," he asked, "if I keep it short?"

"For what? Nobody wants to know about me."

"You're right, I'm sorry to say. It's not so much you they want to know about, it's Harlan Reyes."

"Wait a minute. I don't know who you are or what you want, but if you have any questions, you can ask Mr. Reyes directly."

"That's just the trouble. I can't. Didn't you hear?"

A prickle began at the base of her neck and oozed down her spine. She felt her lips part, but no sound came.

"I see you didn't." The classical mouth seemed to move in a swirling darkness. "Hey, look. I'm sorry. I didn't mean to spring it like that. You really didn't?"

She shook her head. Vaguely she remembered a newspaper fanning a round, damp face. Something about a number being up.

"Last night," he confirmed. "Reyes was shot. He's dead. I'm sorry."

"He's dead?" The words meant nothing.

"Just outside his building. The police call it a mugging, but my paper thinks there might be more to it. I work for the *Bulletin*. I found out from somebody in his office that he had an appointment with you a few hours before that. You must have been one of the last people to see him alive."

"Who— In his office— On Saturday?"

"Actually, one of the cleaning women let me in."

"On Saturday?" She clung to details, hoping the rest of it would go away.

"Last night," he said. "I work fast. I found out where you live, and I followed you here. I was trying to figure out how to talk to you, and then the kid got hurt—"

"You're insane. Did you try calling me last night?"

"No, why?"

"Somebody—" It might have had to do with Harlan's death. But the thought made no firm connection, and soon floated away. She could not believe he was dead.

"Did it really happen?" she asked.

"I'm afraid so. And my paper wants—"

"Your paper is a *rag*. When I see your headlines in the supermarket, I get sick. And you're going to make something dirty and disgusting out of this, aren't you?"

"Hey, we're not that bad. A little raunchy, maybe, but we mean well. Anyhow, it's my living."

"I really don't care if you starve." She half rose from the bench and looked about for Karen.

Gently he eased her back down. "You don't want to take your kids home yet. They just got here. Couldn't you tell me a little about last night? We know he wrote 'dinner' on his calendar. All I want to know is if he said anything that could be pertinent, and what time he left you. Whether anybody seemed to be following him."

"Why? Why do you have to know that?"

"It's news, Miss Garner. He's a celebrity lawyer. *He's* news. And you're a beautiful model . . ."

"And it's the sort of garbage the *Bulletin* loves to print," she said angrily. "He was a friend, that's all. And he happened to be my divorce lawyer. It was a business meeting."

She had put him in the past tense. She hadn't meant to. He couldn't be dead.

Rodney slid off her lap. As though in a dream, she watched him run to the baby swings and climb into one.

The voice next to her said, almost tenderly, "I won't make up anything, I promise. If you were just friends, that's all I'll say."

"I knew him for ten years. Ever since I came here. I

25

was just a green kid." She pressed her knuckles to her mouth.

"Came here from where?" he asked.

"Berryville, New York." She remembered that he was a reporter. "I don't want you to put in anything about me!"

He studied her hungrily. "You'd make great copy. You look so beautiful and sad. I could paint the most gut-wrenching word picture."

"I'll sue you. My face may be public, but my life isn't." She signaled to Karen and went to lift Rodney out of the swing.

Both children set up a protest. "We're not *going*," wailed Karen. "Why do we have to?"

"I'll explain later," Denise replied.

"But I want to stay. Couldn't I stay with Nikki?"

"Not without an adult."

"Can Nikki come over and play?"

The panic was engulfing Denise, crushing her. At first Harlan's death had been only words. Shocking words, but not real. Now she held it back by force, and the force was crumbling.

"No," she answered. "Not today."

"Why?"

"I said I'll tell you later." Carrying Rodney, she walked quickly from the playground. Karen and the reporter followed.

"Let me help you with that." He reached for the tote bag, which was hooked over her arm. She refused to let it go. She needed no help and would give him no story.

"Do you want me to carry the kid?" he asked.

"No, thanks. I don't need anything from you."

"Look, I'm sorry. I really blew it. But I thought you knew. It was on the radio. And I didn't realize you cared this much—"

"Just leave me alone, please?" The path had taken them out to Central Park West. She stood on the curb, waiting for the light to change.

He said, "You probably want to be alone for a while. But if you decide to set the record straight, will you give me a call?" He tried to hand her a business card. "If I'm out, they'll take a message."

"I'm not interested." The light turned green, and she started across the street.

He trotted after her, still holding out the card.

"As soon as I see a police car," she told him, "I'm going to scream."

He pulled her back as a bicyclist ran the light and bore down on them. "Are you sure you're okay?"

"I'm fine."

"Okay, then." He tousled Rodney's hair. "Glad you're feeling better, little guy. Take care of your mom."

He dashed back across the street and stood watching her. He saw her set down the boy and walk on, holding his hand.

Beautiful chick. As soon as saw her that morning, he remembered her from his television days. She had made quite a few commercials. He hadn't seen any recently, or maybe he just hadn't noticed.

She wasn't going to relent. He knew that. He wished he hadn't said the bit about setting the record straight. It was a form of blackmail, and it sounded sleazy. Just what she already thought of the *Bulletin*. He wouldn't really write anything about her. She was too—he tried to think of the word—sensitive? Sincere? He had never thought of models as having emotions. He had never known one before. He didn't now, but he wanted to.

When she was lost in the crowd, he went back down the path to pick up his motorbike.

3

Denise nearly forgot about Karen, who trailed after her, mournful and bewildered. She forgot about Rodney, whose hand she held, until he insisted upon being carried up the stairs.

As soon as they reached the apartment, Karen asked, "Mommy, what happened? Did somebody die?"

Denise was shocked into awareness. "How did you know?"

"Because you're acting funny. You act like somebody died."

What do you know about death?

"Who was it, Mommy? Is it Wade?"

"No, thank God."

"Is it Daddy? Aunt Jill?"

"It was a friend of mine. Mr. Reyes. You've met him."

"How did he die? Was he sick?"

What words could explain? Was this the end of innocence? But the children were not as innocent as she had been at their age. They were native New Yorkers. And there was television, besides. Mrs. Neuberger let them watch anything they wanted.

"He was shot," she replied, "by a mugger."

Karen did not ask what a mugger was. "Are they going to have a funeral? Can I go?"

"I haven't heard anything about a funeral."

And why would Karen want to go, except out of curiosity? She would not allow it.

Karen helped her unpack their lunch from the tote bag and set it on the kitchen table.

"Mommy, can I have granola?"

"After you eat these other things." Denise considered saving the Vienna sausages, which were still in their can. But she had no interest in preparing anything else.

Damn that reporter. Why must she have heard it from him? The *Bulletin*, of all places.

Would the radio have been better?

When the children were settled and eating, she went to call Harlan's office. Under the circumstances, she thought, someone might be there.

No one answered. Perhaps they didn't know yet. It had happened less than twelve hours ago.

If it happened. She had only the reporter's word for it. And he might not be a reporter. He might be a nut. The city was full of them. Even a nut could be beautifully packaged.

He had offered her his card.

But anyone could print a business card to say anything he liked. She thought of calling the *Bulletin*, but could not remember his name.

She would call Harlan's home. Either he would answer, or the phone would ring and ring. She prepared herself for the ringing, and hoped it would make him answer.

She was not prepared for a woman's voice.

"Police," said the voice.

"Oh, my God."

"Who is this, please?"

"I'm a friend of Mr. Reyes. Denise Ga— Burns." She could not decide which name would be better. "I heard something happened to him. Is—"

"Who did you hear that from, miss?"

"Is it true?"

"Yes, it's true. Who did you hear it from?"

"A news reporter, from the *Bulletin*. Can you tell me what happened?"

"All I know is, he was killed. We're still investigating."

"Was it a mugging?"

"We don't know that yet. You say you're Denise? The person he had dinner with last night? They may be wanting to talk to you."

That meant the reporter was right. The police knew more than they were telling.

"It's all right. Just ask them to call first. Do you have my number?" They had probably gotten it from his files, just as the reporter had.

"They'll be in touch with you," the woman said briskly, dispelling any notion that she might have been part of a hoax. No one could have sounded so efficiently evasive, so professionally noncommittal, as an actual police officer.

Denise had learned nothing, except that it was probably true, and that was not enough. She needed to be doing something. To find out all she could. She dialed Harlan's office again, then looked through the phone book, trying to find the names of members of his staff.

There was Glen Connors, one of the partners. Again

a woman answered, probably his wife.

"He's not in just now. May I ask who's calling?"

"Denise— Burns." That seemed to be how they knew her at the office. "I'm a friend of Mr. Reyes."

"I see. I'll have him call you as soon as he can."

Mrs. Connors had volunteered no information. It gave Denise a flicker of hope. But then, why did the policewoman say he was dead?

"Mommy," shouted Karen, "make him keep his hands out of my granola!"

Denise dragged herself to the kitchen. "Why don't you share it? I'll make you another batch."

"Make *him* some. He's getting mine all dirty. Look at his hands."

"Rodney, wash your hands."

Rodney asked, "Can we go back to the park?"

"Maybe later, after your nap. Right now I'm expecting a phone call."

She was mixing a new batch of granola when the telephone rang. She assumed it was Glen calling her back, and was surprised to hear Wade's voice.

"How's everything?" he asked cheerfully.

"Terrible. What about you?"

"Well, the services are over and I was kind of expecting to leave this evening, but Mom doesn't want me to go yet. I don't get out here very often, so I'm going to make it tomorrow night instead. Okay with you?"

She was shocked. How could he? But, of course, he had every right. She tried to clamp down on her disappointment, and instead, crumpled into tears.

"Hey, what's wrong? It's only a day."

"Everything's wrong." She had not wanted to tell him. She did not want to be manipulative and vie with his mother, but now she had to explain.

"Harlan Reyes is dead. He got shot."

31

"Your lawyer? No kidding!"

"He wasn't just a lawyer. I've known him ten years, and I—" There was no need to go into that. "And last night somebody kept calling, and they threatened—threatened the children."

"Would you say that again?"

She said it again. He whistled. "This is crazy, Denise. Are you sure you're all right?"

Of course she was not all right, but she would never tell him so. She did not want to be like Avery, and try to bind someone to her.

"You're coming back tomorrow?" One more night. She could manage.

"That was the plan," he said. "I already changed it, but I could change it back. Do you want me to do that?"

He was hoping she would say no. Otherwise he would not have asked.

"I'll be all right," she sobbed. "You'd better stay."

"Keep the doors locked, and check that gate on the window. I'll see you tomorrow night, okay?"

She would leave the telephone off its hook tonight. But what if the person was out there, watching?

"Mommy, Rodney wants his granola."

"All right, just a minute." She turned on the kitchen radio, to catch any mention of Harlan. She wished she had thought to ask the reporter which station it was on.

"With a high today of ninety-five to ninety-eight. And now for sports," said the radio.

Rodney stood beside her, watching her stir in the slivered almonds. "What's that stuff?"

"Those are nuts. And there's raisins, and oatmeal, and—"

"I don't think he's going to like it," Karen said. "He just wants to eat mine. Mommy, can anybody get into the apartment if they don't have a key?"

"Of course not. What makes you ask that?" She felt the eyes again. The eyes that had been watching her. She felt them burning into her back.

"I just wondered. Once I had a dream that somebody came in. Do you have to work on Monday?"

"Yes, I do. And you're going to day camp, as usual."

"Do I have to?"

"Yes." Denise sighed. She regretted now that her children could not be raised in a place like Berryville, where she had grown up. A place that was safe, traditional, and sane.

And uninteresting. It was perfect for young children, but dismal for teenagers. She remembered that part of it so well, and how she had longed to get away.

She remembered coming to New York and thinking how alive it was, and that her children, who were then still in the future, would benefit from living there, with all it had to offer.

And now . . .

But it would be different when Wade came back and they were married. They could enjoy the things together that they all liked, and take the children to museums and zoos.

She had forgotten to tell him about the divorce. Her most important news. Harlan's death, and the terror, had knocked it out of her mind.

"Can I have some?" Rodney asked as she poured the granola into a jar.

"A little. And then your nap."

While Rodney slept, Karen played quietly with her paper dolls, then set them aside and wandered about the living room, humming.

"Mom, can I call Nikki?"

"Yes, but I don't want her over here. I can't handle it today."

She heard the sound of dialing, and Karen's murmur.

Then, "Can I go out to Broadway with Nikki and her mother?"

"I don't want you going out to meet them by yourself, and I can't take you till Rodney's awake."

"What if they come and pick me up?"

"I guess so. But let me talk to her when she comes."

As soon as she agreed, she wished she had not. But she couldn't keep the children prisoners, and in spite of her laxity with her own child, Sheila Spitzer was a fairly responsible person. Denise hurried about straightening the living room, putting away toys, magazines, and paper dolls, until the door buzzer rang.

"Find out who it is before you let them in," she called as Karen went to press the release bell. "And remember, I want to see her."

"It's them," Karen assured her, and opened the door. Nicole came in, followed by her tall, lanky mother, who handed Denise an envelope. "This was on the table in your lobby. It must have gotten into the wrong box."

"Oh, thank you." Denise dropped the envelope into the pocket of her dress.

Sheila Spitzer was tanned and leathery, and her dark, frizzy hair showed threads of gray. Denise guessed she must have been about forty, what with two older daughters who were nearly grown. Nicole had been an afterthought, or perhaps not a thought at all.

"I always feel like such a frump next to you," Sheila said, chuckling, and dropped into the rattan chair. "What a day, huh?"

"Miserable. Can I offer you a Coke, or iced tea?"

"Just water would be fine."

Denise brought the water, clinking with ice cubes. She had left the two girls in the kitchen.

"Listen, will you have Karen call me when she's ready to come home? I don't want her outside by herself. There's been some trouble."

34

"Oh? What kind?"

"I'm not sure. And don't say a word to her, will you? Just don't let her out of your sight. I've had some crackpot calls, with threats against the children."

"Good God, did you tell the police?"

"Of course. They said there's nothing they can do."

"Like hell there isn't. You pay their salaries."

"Well, I guess— What can they do, except put a guard on the kids? I'm supposed to call the phone company, but they're not open till Monday. So, please?"

"Of course I'll watch her. Do you think it's anybody you know?"

"I have no idea. Probably just a crank, but you never know. And I was a little concerned this morning," she admitted, "that Nikki was in the park by herself."

"So was *I*." Sheila rolled her eyes.

"I thought Karen said she'd done it before."

"Not if I can help it. I was up all night typing, and I slept late, and she skipped out. And that's what I'd like to ask you about. I have another rush job coming this evening, and I'll be tied up all day tomorrow. I was wondering if she could go to the park with you."

"We'd love it. You've taken Karen so many afternoons."

"Oh, that was just sociability. It keeps Nik out of my hair. But you see, my husband's going fishing—they chartered a boat—and my two older girls have their jobs and their boyfriends— Well, you know how it is." Sheila set down her glass. "Okay, I'm off to Broadway for another ream of expensive paper and some groceries."

"Do you make a lot of money doing typing at home?" Denise asked.

"Not a lot, but it helps. Usually the summer's fairly slow. I just happened to get some TV scripts, and they're a bitch to type. All that formatting."

"I know. I've seen them. My husband used to be an

actor. I mean, he still is, but he's not my husband anymore."

"Did he do a lot of TV work?"

Denise laughed wryly. "Once or twice. He's very good-looking, and he got a few modeling jobs, but he never caught on as an actor. Mostly I supported us."

Sheila nodded knowingly. "And you got fed up."

"Well, that wasn't what I got fed up with, but it made it extra hard."

"Oh?"

"He was very jealous. *Very* jealous. All a man had to do was say hello—" Denise bit off her words. She had had no intention of discussing her marital troubles.

Sheila grinned. "I don't wonder, a girl with your looks."

"He never had any reason. I *loved* him. I don't want you to think it was all bad. It wasn't. We had a lot of nice times together."

"Well, that's what happens. All of a sudden, the honeymoon's over."

Feebly, Denise defended herself. "It was more than that."

"You don't mean what I think you mean. Even *you* had an errant knight?"

"Because of the business he was in. You meet a lot of attractive people."

It satisfied Sheila as an explanation. She did not have to know about Avery's indifference to Karen, his blatant resentment of Rodney.

That was what had really undone their marriage. It was Rodney.

"You never know. Some guys just aren't satisfied." Sheila stood up. "Come on, girls, it's time to get moving. And don't you worry about a thing, Denise."

Denise held her breath, waiting for questions from

36

Karen about that tantalizing assurance, but they didn't come.

She cleared away Sheila's water glass and the puddle it left, and poured herself a mug of iced tea. Thank heaven Rodney had not awakened, with all the noise. Only when she sat down and heard a rustle from her pocket did she remember the letter Sheila had brought.

It had not been in the wrong box. It was not even postmarked. Someone had purposely left it on the table downstairs. Someone who had gotten into the building, or already lived there. She tore it open.

It was a clipping from a magazine. She recognized it at once. She remembered that day by the fountain on Columbus Circle, the black suit with the boxy jacket and the polka-dotted blouse. She hadn't been able to wear a coat, and the day was cold, with a chilly wind.

Someone had cut the picture into little pieces and glued them at random onto a sheet of paper. One cut went through her right eye. It made her look worse than dead. Dismembered.

She ran her fingers through the envelope, trying to find a letter or a note. There was nothing. It didn't need a message.

Again the door buzzer rang. She heard herself exclaim aloud as she dropped the paper and went to answer the intercom.

A voice asked, "Denise? It's Glen Connors, from Reyes, Connors and Durkin. Could I see you for a minute?"

"Oh, Glen. Yes. I tried to call you . . ."

She leaned over the railing and watched him come up the stairs, making sure it was indeed Glen. First his reddish-blond head appeared around the corner from the first flight, and then his glasses. A short-sleeved blue shirt, and his pink, freckled arms.

He panted a little after the two flights. "My wife said you called me. I was driving down Columbus Avenue and remembered you live here. Where'd you hear it, on the radio?"

"No, I was in the park this morning with my children, and a reporter from the *Bulletin* came and tried to ask me some questions. I was hoping it wasn't true."

"I'm afraid it is. I knew you were rather close to him."

"It was good of you to come. Would you like some iced tea? Or a gin and tonic?"

"No, thank you. Well, yes, maybe a gin and tonic. I think I probably need it."

She fixed one for each of them. She needed it, too.

"So the *Bulletin*'s been nosing around," he said. "They would, a paper like that. What did you tell him?"

"Nothing. He told me. It was the first I heard of it. Do they know what happened yet?"

"Nobody saw it. About nine-thirty last night the doorman heard a shot. He went out to investigate and found Harlan on the sidewalk. He must have died instantly."

"Nine-thirty?" Just after he had brought her home. "I still can't believe it."

"Neither can I. On the surface, it looks like a robbery attempt, but nothing was disturbed."

"How could they take anything with the doorman right there?"

"That's the thing," said Glen. "At nine-thirty, there are people around. It's not the best time for a robbery."

"So they don't think it was."

"Let's just say they have to explore all the possibilities. That's one of the reasons I wanted to see you. I understand he was having dinner with you that night. The police may be coming around to ask questions. I thought I'd warn you."

"I'll do whatever I can."

He gulped down his drink.

"If anything comes to mind, Denise, anything he might have said about a grievance or a threat, no matter how farfetched, you'll let them know, won't you?"

"I will."

After he had gone, she studied the picture again.

Hate mail. She had never seen hate mail before. Who could hate her so much?

And Harlan, who would have known what to do, was gone.

Denise had finished tucking her children into bed and turned off their light, when the telephone rang.

Again she considered not answering it. But there was always a chance that it might be important.

At first she heard nothing. She was about to hang up, when a steady breathing began. It gradually became more audible. On purpose, she supposed, to let her know he was there.

Where are you? She fought an impulse to speak. To look out of the window. He might be in a building across the street, or at the phone booth on the corner.

After a moment, her wits returned. She said loudly, "It's him, Officer. This is the one."

The caller hung up. For the rest of the night, she left her telephone unplugged.

In the morning there was no sunshine to awaken her. The day was heavy and cloudy, and the air thickly humid. At ten o'clock, Sheila Spitzer arrived with her daughter.

"Looks like rain," Sheila said. "I wish it would clear away the mugginess. Hon, do you think you could keep her all day? I started the script last night, and it's murder."

"No problem," said Denise. "It's good for Karen to have someone to play with."

As soon as they set out for the park, Denise felt the eyes again. She felt them all around her, piercing her clothes and pricking her skin. At the brownstone next door, a curtain moved in one of the front windows. It was nothing more than a twitch, the curtain falling quickly back into place.

Probably someone dusting the windowsill, she thought. Or watering a plant. Or peering out with normal, human curiosity.

"Nikki, do you know who lives in that house? The one next to us?"

"That's Mr. Pignetti," Nicole replied.

"Do you know him?"

"No. I just say hello and good-bye sometimes. He's creepy."

Karen said, "He stares at me through my window."

Nikki had a solution for that. "You could throw toilet paper into his garden. You have to wet it first."

"Don't you dare, either of you," Denise told them.

"Mommy, can we go to the castle?"

"What for?"

"To play. It's more fun than the playground."

Karen had always romanticized the Belvedere Castle, a miniature turreted, crenellated structure on a rocky hill. No one seemed to know its original purpose, but now it was a weather station, its interior closed to the public.

"I guess so." She must not let her anxiety be contagious, but the playground felt safer. It was fenced, and there were always people in it.

41

There were people all through the park on that summer day. The benches along the path were lined with elderly men and women trying to breathe what they could of the heavy air. A young girl sat in the grass brushing her sheepdog, while an enormous black woman trotted four toy poodles on a pair of brace leads. Mothers pushed their baby strollers, and children zoomed by on skateboards and bicycles. Nicole darted ahead, luring Karen. When they rounded a hillock and disappeared from view, Denise felt a moment of panic, almost a fantasy of fear.

"I want you girls to stay with me," she said when she caught up with them. They giggled, but Karen walked beside her as the path began its steep rise. At the last part of the climb, a narrow flight of steps, Karen took Rodney's hand and helped him up.

They came out onto a terrace next to the castle, which lost some of its romance when seen at close range. It was dark and sooty with blank windows, some of them boarded, and wind gauges spinning like whimsical toys on its turrets. At one side, the ground sloped gently into the leafy wilderness of the Ramble. At the other, the bedrock formed a natural extension of the terrace, one edge plunging sharply down to a small lake and the Great Lawn beyond it, where several ball games were in progress.

The girls dashed about, exploring, almost to the edge of the rocks.

"Get back here!" Denise called. "It's a big drop down there."

They turned and stared at her. "But this is where we want to play."

"Why? One false move and you'll land in the water."

It was a shallow lake. Denise could see the bottom of it, perhaps only three or four feet below the surface at its deepest, all green and gold on a sunny day, now an opaque gray.

Looking up at the sky, she felt it pressing against her. The dark, heavy air added to the strangeness she felt, the unreality, now that Harlan was dead. She seemed to be existing in a dream, and could not shake it off.

She opened her magazine. There were two lightweight stories and a condensed romantic novel with lush illustrations. It hurt to think of romance now, because her own had gone so sour.

But it hadn't always been that way. She remembered the late, loving weekend mornings. Jogging together in Central Park. Dinners at La Luna, where they had subsisted on antipasto. Just the two of them.

What had happened to spoil it? Was it the children? Or Avery? Or her own fault? She sighed and began to read.

Karen looked over at her mother, who had finally stopped watching them and was sitting on the rocks looking at a magazine. Rodney played beside her with his miniature cars.

"We need people to go in the castle," Nikki said. "Find some more ice cream sticks." She had already picked up two, and they were dirty.

"Those are too small for the castle," Karen argued, revolted by the idea that the sticks had been in people's mouths. "Why do we need pretend people? We have ourselves."

"But we can't go in the castle. It's locked."

So it was all going to be an imaginary game, with imaginary people. Karen had wanted it to be her castle.

She tried one more time. "You shouldn't play with those. They've got germs."

"Okay, I'll get something else. You wait here." Nikki crossed the terrace to where the hill sloped down into

43

the wild, wooded Ramble. Karen saw her wandering through the bushes, searching the ground.

She remembered when they used to take walks there with Daddy. He always liked the place. He even called it "Fairyland," probably because it was so secret and green. And he laughed when he said it. She thought it was cute of him. Usually he didn't care about imaginary things.

Of course, there weren't any fairies. She knew that, too. It was mostly men in those woods.

Nikki ran over to her, dancing excitedly. "Bet you can't guess what I found."

"What is it?"

"You have to come and see."

Karen followed her. As they crossed the terrace, she saw her mother look up from the magazine. Karen waved and smiled to reassure her that they were not really going anywhere.

Nikki headed toward a steep slope beside the castle, where the ground dropped sharply to one of the roads that crossed the park. Karen could hear the sounds of traffic, and through the leaves caught a glimpse of a yellow taxi.

A shadow moved behind a bush. She stayed still, remembering the mysterious voice that called sometimes on the telephone and asked if her mother was home. The voice that warned her not to tell anyone and said he would be watching for her.

"See?" said Nikki as a man came from around the bush. He had gray hair and wore a green plaid jacket and sunglasses. He smiled at them.

Karen stared, wondering what Nikki was up to. Was this what she had found? This man?

"He's got something to show us," Nikki said.

Karen edged away. "Nikki, we have to get back."

The man said, "It's right over here. You can see it from here." He put his hand on her shoulder and moved her to one side so she could see around the bush. She pulled away from his touch.

"See that?" he said. "There's a bird over there that's hurt."

She did not know whether to believe him. "How did it get hurt?" She turned and looked at his face, and saw with surprise that he was wearing makeup.

Nikki danced again. "I told you."

"All I know is, it hurt its wing," the man replied. "You seem like nice kids. Maybe you can help take care of it. Come over here. I'll show you."

Karen stood rigid as he reached for her hand. Then she saw it under a bush, a flopping mass of gray.

"It's a pigeon," said the man. "You can see its wing is hurt."

There really was a bird, struggling and in pain. "Oh!" she cried, and hurried toward it. "Oh, it's hurt."

"That's what I said." The man picked up the bird and laid it gently in her cupped hands. It flapped in fear and almost got away. She hugged it to her chest.

"I want it," said Nikki. "You showed it to me first."

"You can take turns," said the man.

"How did it get hurt?" Karen asked again.

"I don't know. I just saw it there, but I can't take care of it myself. I live in a rooming house."

She turned guiltily as her mother called them. "Karen! Nikki! Get over here this instant!"

"That your mom?" asked the man.

"Yes, she—"

"*This instant!*"

The man said softly, "Thanks for helping the bird, kids. Maybe you can take it home and feed it some grain, or maybe some cereal. Good-bye for now." He

45

waved to them and walked away down the path.

"Get over here!" her mother cried. "I told you never to talk to people you don't know."

"But, Mommy, he was only trying to help the bird. Look, it hurt its wing. Can we take it home?"

"I told you so many times, Karen. You've got to listen!"

"Mom-mee!" Karen stamped her foot, because that wasn't what mattered right now. The pigeon flapped and struggled in her arms. "Look, its wing is broken. It can't fly. Can we take it home, just till it gets well?"

"No, honey. Wild animals carry all sorts of diseases, and it probably has lice. Please put it down."

"But it's hurt! It'll die!" She could not believe her mother would be so cruel. "Mommy?" Tears came into her eyes.

There was a moment of uncertainty, and Karen took advantage of it. She smiled through her tears. "Please?"

"Oh, all right." Her mother pulled a towel from the tote bag. "But wrap it in this so your hands don't touch it, and keep it away from your hair and your clothes and from Rodney. And don't touch your hair or your face until you've washed your hands."

Nikki reached for the bird. "It's really mine. I'll hold it, and you put the towel—"

"Wait, Nikki, it'll get away!"

Her mother stood looking down at the bird. "Are you sure it's only a hurt wing? Maybe it has a disease."

"It doesn't," Karen assured her.

Nikki said, "It's my bird."

"But we have to take it to my house, because we're babysitting you. And it has to stay there till it gets well. Then we can both play with it."

"Can I, too?" Rodney asked, trying to see into the towel.

"No. You're too rough, and Mommy said I have to keep it away from you."

"I wanna play with it!"

"You'd better not."

"Then can I play in there?" He tried to pull their mother toward the castle.

"I'm afraid it's locked," she said.

"Can I look in the window?"

"There's not much to see. Karen, don't touch that bird."

"But the towel's coming off."

As they all worked together to get the pigeon wrapped again, there was a bump near the castle, like something falling, and Rodney began to scream.

"Oh, Rodney." Denise picked him up. His knees were skinned and bleeding. "I think we'll have to take him home," she told the girls, and watched Karen sail happily down the steps with her bird. At least today there would be no argument about leaving the park.

The sky grew darker and heavier. Rodney finally stopped howling in her ear, but sobbed long and piteously.

"I don't know why little boys have to do things like that," she said, lowering him to the ground and making him walk, which started a new round of tears. "You could have just asked me. I'd have helped you see in the window." He had probably been jealous of Karen and the bird, and wanted something for himself.

Denise was lost in thought about Harlan, and the pigeon, and Rodney's filthy knees, and wondering how to cope. She did not see the figure sitting on the steps of her building until he stood up, a Greek statue in chino pants and an aqua shirt. He started toward her, but his cheerful look disappeared at the sight of Rodney, who limped beside her, holding her hand.

"Hey, little guy, what happened?"

47

"He fell on the rocks," said Karen. "Do you want to see what we have?"

Denise asked, "What are you doing here?"

"I rang your bell. You weren't home, so I decided to wait."

"But why? I told you I don't know anything, and I still don't. Why won't you leave me alone?"

"When you put it that way, I almost hate myself." He grinned and turned to Karen. "Hey, look at that. A bird? Is it hurt?"

"It's a pigeon, and it hurt its wing."

Nikki held out her hand. "It's raining!"

The few drops quickly became many, and they hurried up the steps into the building. Crowding into the tiny vestibule, they waited for Denise to unlock the inner door. The reporter grinned at her over the children's heads.

"You don't mind if I impose on you, just till it stops?"

"I'll bet you did it on purpose," Denise said. He smiled again, but she hadn't meant to be funny. It really seemed likely that he had.

"Carry me," Rodney whimpered as they started up the stairs.

Denise lifted him. He was getting heavy to tote around, but she did not know how to make him stop injuring himself. Maybe a children's gymnastic class. As soon as they were inside the apartment, she rushed him to the bathroom.

His knees were encrusted with grit. She used a disinfectant soap that made him howl again, and then a spray-on antiseptic. Only when she put on one of the king-size bandages bought when he last scraped his knee did the screams subside. Over his quiet sniffles, she heard the reporter's voice.

She had forgotten. He was there in the apartment,

alone with the girls. With Karen.

They were in the children's room, trying to quiet the pigeon that flapped its objections to the shoebox Karen had given it as a nest.

"Listen, you," said Denise to the reporter. "Just exactly what are you doing in here? I don't even know you."

"That's not for any lack of effort on my part," he replied.

"Yes, but— I don't want you around my kids."

"I assure you, ma'am, I don't do things like that."

She pounced. "Like what?"

"Whatever you're suggesting. I'm strictly a ladies' man." He was cool and dignified, but underneath it all, she sensed his laughter. At her.

"I wasn't suggesting anything. I just don't—"

"He was helping us with the pigeon," Karen explained.

"That's right," he agreed. "I know a little about birds. My mom used to have a parakeet. Now, what you kids want to do is leave it alone for a while so it can rest."

"It doesn't want to rest," Nikki argued.

"It does," the man said firmly. "It's a wild animal. They don't like people around all the time. And neither does your mother, so as soon as the rain eases up, I'll be off." He ushered them all from the room.

"They'll never leave it alone," said Denise, ashamed that he had misunderstood her and vaguely trying to make it up to him. "It was probably better off in the park."

He was very close to her, touching her arm. He had waved off the girls, but was guiding her gently with his hand on her elbow.

She stiffened. "You've been very helpful, but you really don't have to worry about us. My fiancé will be

49

coming back tonight."

There. She had let him know, however clumsily, that she was unavailable.

"The guy with the shoes," he said.

"Excuse me?"

"That pair of size-twelve shoes I saw in the bedroom. I wasn't snooping. Just happened to notice."

He had undoubtedly been snooping. He was a reporter, and that was what they did. But it might prevent him from writing a lurid story linking her with Harlan.

She went over to the window. It was still raining hard, sooty drops pelting through the screen.

"I appreciate this," he said. "And I promise I won't sully your name by putting it in the newspaper."

She was startled. It was almost as though he had read her thoughts.

"Can you do the same for Harlan?" she asked.

"Can't promise anything. He's already in the news, but I'll make it as dignified as possible. How long did you say you've known him? Ten years? You must have been about fourteen—"

"You just finished saying you weren't going to write about me."

"I'm not, I swear. That was for my own information."

"I don't trust you," she said. "You're with the media."

"Where would you be without the media?"

The children trooped into the living room. Karen carried the pigeon in its box. "Mommy, do we have any grain?"

"What kind of grain?"

"For the bird."

"I thought I told you to leave it alone," said the man.

"But it's hungry," Karen insisted. "Do we?"

"Why would we have grain?"

"Oh, I know." Karen disappeared into the kitchen.

"Why don't you take the bird?" Denise asked him. "They're going to maul it to death."

"They're trying. They just don't understand that invalids need rest. You have a nice apartment here."

"Thank you. It's too bad you can't stay."

"Yes, really. You know, as soon as I saw you yesterday, I knew who you were. I don't read the fashion pages, but I used to work in TV. You did a lot of commercials."

"Not so many now. Modeling has a short life." She sat opposite him on the sofa, half wishing he would leave, half wanting him there for companionship. But she could not stop thinking about the phone calls. She shuddered.

"Getting cold?" he asked.

"Not today. Can I offer you anything? A beer?"

"Nothing, thanks. Did you notice that I'm not trying to interview you?"

"Why?" she asked warily. "You already have enough material?"

"You are cynical. No, the truth is, I really don't want to upset you. I did enough of that yesterday when I told you about your friend, and you've been on edge ever since."

"I—" She had been on edge before that. The news about Harlan had finished her off. "I guess so." She twisted her engagement ring. It was more like a wedding band, with only a tiny diamond that was all the more precious to her because it had come from Wade.

"You're perfect," said the reporter, admiring her hands, her careful manicure.

"I have to be. It's what I get paid for."

He laughed. "That's a funny statement. Most girls would preen, or simper, or say thank you . . ."

"I never thought I was good-looking. Never."

51

"You're kidding."

"No, I'm not. I was awkward and ugly. I guess about high school I sort of came together, but I never really believed it. I still don't."

"How come you went into modeling? Doesn't that take a certain amount of vanity?"

"People told me I should try it, and I needed to make a living."

"Doesn't the fact that you're successful at it convince you of anything?"

She shrugged. "I'm lucky, that's all. And I don't know why I'm telling you all these personal things when I don't even know your name."

"Cliff O'Donnell. I did mention it yesterday, but you weren't particularly interested, for which I can't blame you. And then I dropped the bombshell. Or did I do that first?"

In the kitchen, someone gave an anguished shriek. Karen wailed, "Mom-meee!" and Nicole screamed, "What happened to it?"

Both girls rushed into the living room. Karen's eyes were huge and teary.

"Mommy, come and see. I think it's dead!"

Cliff reached the kitchen ahead of her and prodded the inert mass of feathers.

"It's dead, all right. You can tell by its eyes, and I don't feel any heartbeat."

"But how could it be dead?" Karen wept. "It only had a broken wing. Why did it have to *die*? It wasn't sick."

"Maybe it was," said Denise.

"What did you feed it?" Cliff held the shoebox next to the window and studied the bird by daylight.

Karen gulped down a sob. "Just some of my granola."

"And it ate?" asked Cliff. "That's strange. If it was

sick, it probably wouldn't have wanted to eat."

"Karen, don't touch—"

Denise was interrupted by a chair crashing to the floor. Rodney lay half under the table, rolling back and forth as though in pain, and gulping for breath. His lungs were expanded, and he could not take in more air. A jar had overturned and grains of oatmeal were scattered on the table and the floor.

"Rodney," cried Karen, "that's *my* granola."

"Rodney!"

Denise was on the floor beside him.

"Somebody! Get help!"

She heard Karen ask, "What's the matter with him?"

"He's poisoned! Hurry! Oh, my God, the granola."

They had gotten to her children. The caller was serious.

"But that was my granola," Karen protested. "I just had some this morning."

Cliff asked, "Where's your telephone?"

"*Hurry!*"

"But, Mommy, it couldn't be. I just had some this morning."

"Where's your—"

Rodney had gone limp. She picked him up. They were all being dense, and she would have to do it herself.

Cliff called, "Wait!"

She snatched up her purse on the way out.

He hurried after her. "Wait. I'll call an ambulance."

"There's no *time* for an ambulance."

"But what are you—" He turned and ran back into the apartment. She plunged down the two flights of stairs and out to the street.

Then Cliff was there, and so were the girls, and she realized that she had left them alone with him.

What am I doing? she wondered, and glanced down at Rodney. His face was gray. She started toward the corner, trotting clumsily under his weight. Cliff ran ahead of her.

"But, Mommy," said Karen, tugging at her dress, "it couldn't be the granola, because I had some—"

"Please shut up."

Nicole chimed in, "But remember, Karen? We fed it to the pigeon, and it died. Is Rodney going to die, Mrs. Burns?"

She saw Cliff coming toward her, running beside a taxi. He opened the front door and pushed her inside next to the driver. He pushed the girls into the back and climbed in with them. She heard him say something about an emergency room. Thank God he understood.

Thank God the Sunday traffic was light. The taxi picked up speed and hurtled through a changing light. Rodney drew a long, labored breath. She wondered if they ought to have called an ambulance after all, with paramedics, and oxygen . . . Still, it would have meant waiting.

"Emergency entrance," the driver announced. "Hey, thanks, mister," as Cliff handed him a bill. "Have a good day, now."

Cliff helped her out, and she hurried ahead of him, into a roomful of people waiting on benches. A man whose hand was wrapped in a bloodstained towel. An old woman mumbling to herself. A sunburned redhead with two squirming toddlers. People whose eyes were glazed with waiting. She absorbed it all on her way to the desk.

"Please, my child's been poisoned. I've got to get help *now*. We can't wait for all these people."

A pair of brown eyes reproached her through rimless glasses.

"Take it easy, miss. It's quicker that way. Your child took poison? What kind?"

"I don't know, but look at him! It was in some cereal. My daughter fed it to her bird, and it died. Please!"

"Your name?"

"What's that got to do with it?" Denise looked around wildly, but there was no recourse. Only the unflappable woman with lavender hair, and a pen that waited above a printed form.

"Burns. B–u–r–n–s. Couldn't we do this later?"

"You're wasting time, miss. It's going to be okay. First name?"

Cliff stood beside her. He murmured something and tried to take Rodney. Alarmed, Denise clung tightly.

The woman asked more questions. The child's name. Age. Did they have health insurance? What exactly was in the cereal?

"I *told* you—"

"We don't know," said Cliff. "Should have brought some with us," he added to Denise. "I really wasn't thinking."

"Most people don't in a crisis," said the woman. "But it does help. Now, if you'll just take a seat over there."

"But he's *dying*," cried Denise.

"Take a seat, miss, and don't get excited. We'll have someone with you in a minute."

56

She closed her eyes. If she could stop her thoughts, maybe time would stop, too.

A gurney pulled up beside her. Once again, they tried to take Rodney.

"I'll carry him," she said. "I want to stay with him."

"You have to wait out here," a soft voice told her. "We'll take good care of him."

She was young and female. Probably an intern, with wavy, black hair. A Filipino. Her face was pleasant and would have been trustworthy under any other circumstances.

"You don't understand," said Denise. "He was poisoned. I have to stay with him."

And what about Karen, who stood there gaping?

"You brought him here. You have to trust them." Cliff took Rodney and handed him to the intern. "They never let the parents in when they pump a kid's stomach," he explained. "It can be disagreeable."

Cliff led Denise to one of the benches. The girls followed.

Karen whispered, "Look, Mommy, there's a man with only one arm. Is Rodney going to be all right? How come I didn't die when I ate the granola?"

Denise shook her head. There was no explanation. She tried to remember what she had put in it when she mixed it.

"Was it yours or his?" she asked.

"Mine. And I ate some—"

"Why wouldn't they let me in? How can they take a child—"

"You'd probably faint," said Cliff, "and then they'd have to deal with that, too."

"Nobody understands. They were threatened."

"Who, the kids?"

"Yes."

"How do you mean? Who threatened them?"

"I don't know. If I knew, I could . . . do something."

"Want to tell me?"

"No."

He was silent. Thoughtful. Then he said, "You don't trust me, do you?"

"Why should I?"

"I didn't threaten your kids."

"How do I know?" she said angrily. "I don't know who it was."

"Was it a letter? A phone call?"

She felt a prickle of alarm. He was coming too close.

He said, "You have to trust somebody."

"I do. And he's coming back tonight."

"Ah, yes, the shoes."

How many hours? She looked at her watch, and then she thought of Rodney. How many minutes?

"Look," said Cliff. "Blame it on the weather, but I'm a little bit involved with your family now, and I care about your kids. And you, but that's a different story. Why don't you want to tell me what happened? This is not for publication, I assure you."

"All right, it was phone calls. It started Friday night. The night . . . Harlan was killed."

"What happened?"

"They asked if my children were safe. And they saw when I turned my light out."

"Somebody watching, then. Any problem with the neighbors?"

"I don't even know most of my neighbors," she said. "And I don't know of any problems."

"What about your ex-husband?"

"How do you know I have—" Had she told him? She could not remember.

"I know you were getting a divorce," he said. "I, uh,

58

found that out in your lawyer's office. And sometimes there are problems."

"But he's in Los Angeles. And even if he didn't have much use for the kids, he would never hurt them."

"Are they his kids?"

"Of course."

"And he had no use for them?"

"I'm not going to talk about it anymore."

But she thought about it. Avery? He could have called from the West Coast, but how would he know about her lights?

Avery?

He couldn't be here. In the city.

"He wouldn't do that," she said.

"Okay. You know him better than I do."

Did she know him? Apparently not when they first married, but gradually she had found out what he was like. She had come to know what to expect. The worst. Always the worst.

"But he wouldn't— It could be my next door neighbor. The girls think he's a creep. He stares at Karen through the window."

"That's not good."

There was the picture, too. Hand-delivered. She thought of telling him about that, when a door opened and the intern came back. She did not have Rodney with her, but she was smiling.

"We found traces of cereal and raisins," she said. "We can't tell what was in it without an analysis. You didn't happen to bring any with you?"

"No, we didn't. I wonder if it could have been something on his hands. We came in from the park not long before that. But there was the pigeon . . . My daughter brought home a bird with a broken wing. Maybe it had a disease. Could Rodney have caught

59

something?"

"When was that?"

"This morning. Just before— But a disease wouldn't work so fast, would it?"

She felt something enclose her. It was Cliff, reaching both his arms around her, to hold her hands.

He said, "We do know the bird ate that same stuff. I'll bring some over. Just tell me where to deliver it."

Denise pulled away from what was almost an embrace. If there was poison in the granola . . . Cliff was the only outsider who had been in the apartment since that morning. Except Nicole and, briefly, Sheila. But she had been with Sheila the whole time, and as for Nicole, that was ridiculous.

She couldn't look at him. She could not believe it, but he was the only one . . .

Mr. Pignetti? How would he get in?

And even if Avery had come back, he did not have a key. He had never lived in that apartment.

"Where's my son?" she asked.

"He's still pretty weak," said the intern. "We'd like to keep him here overnight."

"By himself?"

"Oh, he won't be alone. He'll be in a semiprivate room, and there are nurses all over the pediatric wing. They'll be checking on him constantly. If you'll go over to the admitting office, you can see him after that."

Denise stole a look at Cliff. Was he satisfied? Disappointed?

It couldn't have been Cliff.

What would he do next?

Why?

Was he doing it for someone else?

"Thank you for everything," she told him mechanically while her brain tried to figure it out. "How much do I owe you for the taxi?"

60

"Nothing. That's my small contribution."

His eyes lingered on her. She did not know what to think.

But she didn't have to. Wade would be home in only a few hours.

"Come on, girls," she said. The intern opened a door and pointed down the corridor.

"Go through there and make a right, and then a left—"

She looked back. Cliff was still there, watching her.

By the time they walked home from Broadway, the rain had ended and the sky was clearing. Warm, weak sunlight drew moisture from the sidewalk in another wave of steam.

She could not stop thinking of little Rodney alone in the hospital. It would be his first night away from her since he was born. She missed him terribly, although for his part, he had seemed too sick to mind that she was leaving him. The doctor had told her that if all went well, she could take him home the next day.

As they approached their building, she noticed two men lurking by the front steps. One was in shirt-sleeves, pacing back and forth, glancing at his watch. The other, old and heavier, perspired in a corded jacket. She had never seen either of them before.

Warily, she slowed her walk and put a restraining hand on Karen's shoulder.

Karen stiffened in alarm. "What's the matter? Who are those people?"

"I don't know."

The men had seen them coming and heard Karen's question. They started toward Denise. The jacketed one held something in the flat of his hand. "Are you Mrs. Denise Burns?"

She hesitated. If she denied it, Karen would blurt the truth, and so would Nikki.

"Who are you?" she asked.

"Police. We'd like your help for a few minutes, Mrs. Burns, if you don't mind." The thing in his hand was an identification. She saw that much, but no more. He put it away, took out a handkerchief, and mopped his face.

"I don't understand," she said. "How did you know?"

"Call it a lucky guess. This is your address, isn't it? We'd just like to ask a few questions. Only take a couple of minutes."

"Did the hospital call you? Already?"

Or could it have been Cliff? Had she misjudged him?

The man had no answer for that, and it dawned on her that they were not talking of the same thing.

"Oh. This is about Mr. Reyes."

"What about Rodney?" Karen demanded.

Denise wished she had studied the identification. Really looked at it. She was afraid to trust anyone, but this was not wholly unexpected.

"Come on upstairs," she said.

Without waiting for them to begin their questions, she led them to the kitchen. There was the granola scattered on the floor, and the dead bird in its box.

"This is what happened. My son was poisoned. He was eating that stuff in the jar, and he nearly died. And the bird died from the same thing. I can tell you who was here. And somebody's been calling me and threatening—" Good Lord, now she had said it in front of Karen.

63

The detectives cleared everyone out of the kitchen. "You'll have to call your local precinct on that, miss. They'll send somebody over. Where's your phone?"

They called the precinct for her, and then talked about Harlan. About their last evening together. Had she seen anybody watching or following?

They asked about her relationship with him.

"We were good friends." It sounded trite and evasive. "He was handling my divorce. It just came through. That's why he wanted to see me Friday, to give me the papers. We used to date a little, but this wasn't a date. I'm engaged to be married."

"Where's your fiancé?"

"He's in Kansas. I guess he's on his way here."

A few minutes later, two patrolmen arrived from her local precinct. She showed them her kitchen, described what had happened, and reluctantly gave them Cliff's name.

"He says he's a reporter for the *Bulletin*. He wanted to know about my friend who was shot, and he came again today. He's . . ." Not exactly bothering her. For a while, she had even enjoyed his company.

"Was he here when your son took the poison?"

"Yes, and when the pigeon died. That was just before. I only let him in because of the rain. My son had a skinned knee, and I was taking care of it. There was plenty of time for him to poison everything in the apartment. How do I know the rest of my food isn't—"

"But, Mommy, he was helping us with the bird," Karen said indignantly. "And he was nice!"

"Of course he was. Like that man in the park. They're all nice. That's how they get away with it."

"This reporter fella," one of the officers said to

Karen. "Was he with you the whole time your mother was busy?"

It was the girls' turn. They had been with Cliff, and had fed the pigeon and seen it die. They chattered at high speed, interrupting each other in their excitement.

"I had some for breakfast this morning, and nothing happened to me," Karen said.

Denise felt lost. She didn't want it to be Cliff, but who else could have gotten in?

She remembered his warm brown eyes, and the strong arms slipping around her in that crowded emergency room when she so badly needed reassurance. And she had pulled away from him.

"Does anyone besides you have a key to this apartment?" asked one of the men.

"Well, my boyfriend, but he's away right now. And my babysitter down the hall, and the building super, but they wouldn't— I just can't think of anybody."

Both would have to be questioned about their keys. Mrs. Neuberger would probably have a heart attack, and the super would tell everyone in the building, but they would all know sooner or later.

"I can't understand it. It was the same stuff I always make for Karen."

"And I had some for breakfast . . ."

The police checked her apartment. They tested the gate on the window where the fire escape was. Denise had a chain and a police lock on the door.

"If there's any trouble, give us a call," they said. "We'll be right over."

They gathered sweepings from the floor and took the tainted jar and the dead bird away with them. As they were leaving, the doorbell rang.

Denise stood without moving. One of the officers

told her, "Find out who it is."

She picked up the intercom.

"Florist, delivery," said an Hispanic accent.

Wade had sent her flowers. How did he know about Rodney?

Or maybe it was Cliff.

A slight young man with a mustache brought up a long white box. A box, not the usual paper-wrapped bundle. The officers waited while she opened it.

Inside lay a dozen long-stemmed roses of deep velvet red. Exquisite. Expensive. The only person who would do such a thing was Harlan.

She opened the card. "To my sweetheart with love, from Avery," it said.

"Oh, my God!"

She leaned over the railing. The delivery boy had gone.

"My ex-husband," she told them. "But he's in California. He must have . . . had them—"

"Do you mean it's from Daddy?" asked Karen, removing the flowers from their box. "Can I put them in water?"

"Yes. Please."

It was the loving message that destroyed her. He couldn't, after all that time. Not when their divorce was final.

The officers muttered something about getting back to her and went to find the building super.

By then, the sun was fully out. Although no less hot, the day had acquired a sparkle. Denise was exhausted. The girls were lively but hungry, having missed lunch. She took them to a Mexican restaurant and then to the Planetarium.

When they returned home in the late afternoon, the

telephone was ringing. Her first thought was the hospital. They were calling to tell her—

"*Finally*," said a voice, with an attempt at a valiant laugh. "I've been trying to get you all afternoon. Where the hell were you?"

Denise sat down on the bed. It was unreal. A whole unreal day.

"Avery. Where are you?"

"In New York. Where do you think? Did you get my flowers?"

"Yes. Thank you."

"How are the kids?"

Did he really care?

"Rodney's in the hospital," she said. "He got poisoned."

"What are you talking about?"

"I'm talking about your son. I don't know how it happened. The police are investigating."

She described the day's events. He said, "Well, that's a fine way to welcome me back—"

"Avery, do I have to spell it for you? Your son almost died! Can't you, for once in your life, think about something besides how *you* feel?"

"Here we go again." He sighed, then caught himself, and was charming again.

"It must have been hell for you, baby. I wish you'd called me. But, of course, you didn't know where I was."

She, too, made an effort. "How long have you been back?"

"Couple of days. I had an audition for a part on a soap. It could be steady."

"That's wonderful. When will you hear?"

"Soon, I hope. How about getting together?"

"I—"

67

"You're home, so why don't I just come over? I want to see my kids. And you, of course."

"I told you, Rodney's in the hospital."

"Then Karen and you. My girls. I'll hop a cab right now."

She couldn't stop him. He had every right to see Karen.

He had added "And you" as an afterthought, with Karen first. Could he possibly have changed? A little?

No, he hadn't. Karen was only a pretext. Denise paced the floor, feeling icy one moment and feverish the next. It should have been over, but of course it never would be, because of the children.

He arrived with more flowers, wrapped in pink paper. She thought he looked older and perhaps thinner. His face, always beautiful, still had no lines, but it seemed to have planes that had not been there before. His golden brown hair was impeccable as usual. He smiled as he came up the stairs, and she remembered that he had done several toothpaste commercials.

"That's my darling," he said, handing her the parcel. "Gorgeous as ever."

She lowered her head to avoid meeting his eyes or being kissed, and distracted herself with unwrapping the flowers. It was a bouquet of pink carnations and baby's breath.

"They're beautiful. Karen, Daddy's here." The words rushed out, and she heard a tremor in her voice.

Karen hurled herself into her father's arms, which belatedly opened to welcome her. Nicole was introduced, and the two girls babbled about Rodney. Avery played at showing an interest, but gradually edged Denise away, toward the bedroom.

When they reached the French doors, she caught his arm. "What are you thinking of? Not with the kids here."

68

"I just want to see you alone," he said.

"I am not closing these doors. We can talk in the living room."

She glanced back to be sure she had hidden Wade's shoes under the bed. Avery mustn't find them, or any evidence of Wade. Karen must not say anything. She could not get over her dread of what he might do, even though he had no claim on her now.

She managed to maneuver him to the living room couch, and she sat in the swivel chair so there would be no chance of their touching.

"Would you like some iced tea?" she asked.

"No, I just want to hear how you've been doing."

"Not very well. You know about Rodney. And somebody's been making threatening phone calls, and— You know Harlan Reyes?"

"Better than I'd like to." He seemed to want to say something more, perhaps a reference to the divorce. "What about him?"

"He's dead. He got shot outside his building Friday night. And I just—"

The papers. Still on their way to California. Avery didn't know it was final.

"Did you hear from your lawyer?" she asked.

"What happened to Reyes? Tell me."

"He got shot. They think it was a mugging, but they're not sure."

"No kidding? It doesn't pay to have too much money, does it?"

He sounded almost exultant, but perhaps it was natural. After all, Harlan had been representing her in the divorce.

"Anybody can get mugged," she said.

Karen brought in the second vase of flowers and set it on the television set. Avery stood up to rearrange a few. Another pretext. He moved to the back of Denise's chair and began to massage her shoulders.

She squirmed away from him. "Please, Avery, the children are here."

"Are you crazy? What's wrong with this? It's not as if we're jumping in the sack. And you're still my wife."

"No, I'm not. It's over." She felt a blinding flash of fear at having said it so directly.

"It can never be over." His hands eased down toward her breasts. "You and I were made for each other. Don't you know that?"

She squirmed again, but knew better than to remove his hands. "If we were made for each other, then you'd be able to consider my feelings as well as your own."

He chuckled. "Your feelings are wrong, darling, at least right now. If you come back to me, I'll prove that to you. Or should I say *when* you come back to me."

She shook her head. He returned to the sofa and tried to pull it forward, closer to her.

"You don't seem to understand," he told her earnestly. "It's different now. I'm ready to listen to your problems and try to help you."

She was still unable to meet his eyes. "You know what my problem was. You know how you tried to own me so completely that you were even jealous of your own kids. I don't think you ever saw me as a real person, Avery, with actual human rights."

"What did I see you as, a giraffe?"

"I told you, as your possession." There was more to it than that. She did not know how to express it.

"You cast me in a role that you invented," she went on. "I was a prisoner physically, and in your imagination. And you tried to get me to stay by hitting me. That wasn't calculated to make me *want* to stay with you. It was just to force me, like punishing a runaway slave. And that shows what you really think of me."

70

"What do I think of you?" he asked with that annoying, superior smirk of his.

"You'll never understand, will you? I don't think you want to, even to get me back. But I have a right to myself."

"This is yourself?" With a wave of his arm, he included the whole apartment. "Living in two little rooms, wiping kids' snotty noses, working your butt off, and getting too old to model? What's in it for you? Tell me."

"It's four rooms," she whispered, wilting, because his arguments always wore her down. "And at least I'm free to make a few choices of my own, and have my own friends. And the kids don't have to be afraid in their home, because their father—"

"What are you talking about? Those kids were never afraid of me."

"They were. But they loved you, too, which is more than you did for them."

"Now who's projecting?" he demanded.

"Avery, I know what I saw. There's no point in discussing it."

"You know what you interpreted. You saw it the way *you* wanted to, and you had your reasons, which I'm very well aware of."

She stiffened, waiting for the blow to fall. He would accuse her of wanting the divorce so that she could, as he would delicately put it, screw around with other men.

"I thought you came to see Karen," she said.

"Both of you. I said both of you, didn't I? Okay, look. I agree that we should let bygones be bygones. Do you know what I came here to tell you? How'd you like to go to California?"

"Not really."

"You don't know what you're talking about. It's just the place for you. I can help you meet a lot of influential people—"

They hadn't done him any good, she observed.

"And I've got an apartment you'll love, just for the two of us. We can live in heaven."

"What about—" Her head began to throb. "Do you remember that we have two children? What were you planning to do about that?"

"I was thinking we could leave them with your sister. It'd be better than dragging them out there. And you can't be tied down if you're going places, which you will with these contacts I've got."

"But Jill's having a baby of her own. She's pregnant. And you can't just dump your kids on somebody. It's not like— I mean, they're our children. Our family."

He shrugged. "So we'll bring them with us. But I think it would be a mistake."

He had not really given in. She knew that. Even if she agreed to his plan, he would never dream of taking the children.

"What about your friend?" she asked.

"Who?"

"Your girlfriend. Trish, or whatever her name is. I thought you were living with her."

"I was. That's finished. It's you and me forever."

Denise sank back in her chair. She had never met Trish, but welcomed her involvement with Avery. "For her sake, I hope it was you who broke it off."

"It was both of us. What difference? Anyhow, you think about it."

"Avery—"

His eyes narrowed, alerted by her tone.

"You wouldn't know," she said. "You wouldn't have gotten the papers. They were probably sent to California."

72

"What papers?"

"It's final. The divorce. We're officially finished. And I think it would be a lot easier if you'd just . . . try to make a new life."

He stared at her long and hard, his mouth tight.

"So it's final, huh?"

There, she had told him. On the surface it had gone smoothly enough, but she did not feel relieved.

"Yes, and that's the way I want it. It doesn't make sense to keep this up. This—"

"So you want it, huh?"

"Yes. For once in our life together, I'm going to have what I want."

"Looks like you've already got it."

There was something eerily flat in the way he spoke. She held herself rigid, trying not to shudder or cringe. If only Wade were there. Maybe she ought to tell him about Wade.

Not yet. She was grateful that Karen hadn't talked. That Karen, in fact, kept well out of his way.

He stood over her, his arms folded, and spoke woodenly. "You really mean that, don't you?"

She nodded. Her fear of his anger warred with pity. He couldn't help being the way he was. Needing her so much.

"Aren't you afraid?" he asked.

"Of what?"

Of him. Of the way he had behaved when she first announced her wish to be free of him.

Again he flung out his arm in a wide sweep. "What about Rodney? And those threatening phone calls. Aren't you afraid to stay here by yourself?"

Now was the logical time to mention Wade.

"It's all right. The police are—"

He shouted, "All right? Is it all right that my son took poison, and you don't even know how it got into this

73

apartment? And what about those calls? Somebody's after you, baby. It's a wicked city, and you're all alone. If you don't care about yourself, think of the kids. I could bring a suit against you if you let anything happen to my kids."

It flashed through her mind that he might have made the calls himself, to convince her that she needed a protector. Would he do that?

She could stand it no longer, but this was not the right time for any more statements of finality.

"I'll think about it." She started toward the door. "But I can't make any decisions right now. I'm too tired and upset."

He took the hint. At the door, she patted his cheek.

"It was nice of you to come, Avery. And thanks for the flowers."

He kissed her very lightly on the mouth and went downstairs.

She closed the door and leaned against it. She saw what she had done. And now she realized that she had done it before, when they first broke up. Because of her own guilt feelings, because she hadn't wanted to hurt him, she had left the impression that there might still be hope.

Instead she hurt him more, by letting him go on hoping when there was no basis for it. All because she could not bear confrontation.

And for that, she would never be rid of him.

She was afraid of her own kitchen. Afraid of the boxes and jars, the cupboards, and the refrigerator. Anything that was not factory-sealed. She took the two girls to Burger King for supper, and from there delivered Nicole to her home.

She said nothing to Sheila about what had happened that day. Nicole would be sure to tell her, and Denise left quickly before the account could begin.

As they returned to their own building, Karen asked, "When's Wade coming back? Did you tell Daddy you're going to marry him?"

"No, I didn't think he'd want to hear it."

"Why not?"

"Because your daddy doesn't like to hear things like that. He doesn't like love stories."

"But you're not a love story. You're real."

"Thank you. And I will tell him, but only when I think it's the right time."

Their apartment was hot and quiet. Too quiet, without Rodney. And they had come so close to losing him.

Karen noticed it, too, and it disturbed her. "I wish you didn't have to go to work tomorrow. Are you going to keep working when you marry Wade?"

"I think I'll have to. Life is just too expensive these days."

Besides, they were her children, not his, although he loved them. To Harlan's annoyance, she had not asked for child support. She told him it would be futile to expect any money from Avery. She did not tell him that it was really because of her guilt feelings. He could never understand why she felt so guilty, after the way Avery had treated her.

"Well, I wish you could stay home and be a real mommy," Karen sulked.

"I'm sorry, but that's the way it is. And I'll bet most of your friends have mothers who work. Even Nikki's mother works at home. It doesn't mean we're not real mothers. It's just life."

She listened, hearing someone on the stairs. She recognized his particular way of climbing them, that little shuffle before his foot hit the step.

"He's *here*!" she cried, pulling open the door as Wade stood ready to insert his key. "I missed you so much!"

He held her, smoothing his hand across her back. "I missed you, too, sweetheart. I missed all of you, but it's okay now."

"Rodney ate poison," Karen volunteered.

"What's that?"

"Rodney ate poison and he almost died."

Wade looked at Denise.

"It was an accident," she explained. "Just this morning. There wasn't time to call you." She was amazed to realize that she hadn't even thought of it.

"What happened? Tell me!"

She started to tell him, but Karen took over, concluding with, "And we all went to the hospital, and Rodney had to stay there, and some policemen came."

"Is this for real?" He turned from Karen back to Denise, who nodded. "And those phone calls. What in hell's going on?"

"What phone calls?" asked Karen.

Wade pushed back his hair. "I'm sorry. I wasn't thinking."

"The wrong numbers," Denise said quickly. Karen stared at her in silence.

"What a weekend." Denise tried to smile. "At least it's over." Meaning that he was there. She rested her head against his chest. He felt solid, bigger than Avery, but without the striking good looks. When he smiled, a slight gap showed between his two front teeth. She had always liked that gap. She did not know why, but it added to his sex appeal.

"I should have come Saturday, after all," he said.

"It wouldn't have made any difference. We still don't know what happened. He ate some of Karen's granola, and the next thing he was writhing on the floor."

"And I had some for breakfast," Karen said, "but nothing happened to me."

"How can you be sure it wasn't appendicitis or something?"

"Because of the bird." It had been part of Karen's narrative. "The police took it away for testing. But it wasn't all bad. I mean the weekend. My divorce came through. It's final!"

"Hey, great!" Again he swept her into his arms.

"When did that happen? How come you didn't tell me?"

"I tried to. I kept trying to get you Friday night, and when you called on Saturday, I guess I was too upset about you not coming. I just didn't think of it."

"You forgot a thing like that?"

"I don't see how, but—"

He interrupted her with a tender kiss. "You really must have had it rough. But I'll make it up to you. I won't go away again, and maybe we'll get an unlisted number. I'm going to keep you safe."

"There's something else. I just found out this afternoon. Avery's back."

"Here? In New York?"

"Yes. He sent flowers. All those flowers are from him."

"Did you talk to him? How did he seem?"

"He came over. And he seemed— I don't know, he's still living in a dream world. He wanted me to run off to California with him, and leave the kids with Jill. I didn't tell him about you, of course. And neither did Karen," she added proudly.

"That's good." He sounded genuinely relieved. "But if Avery's here in the city, he'll keep tabs on you. He's bound to find out."

"What can he do? It's finished. He'll just have to deal with that."

As they snuggled together on the couch, her head began to swim with fatigue.

"Let's get Karen to bed," she suggested. "You must be tired, too."

"Good idea."

Karen did not want to go to bed. "What if a person really sneaked in and put poison in my granola, and what if he comes back?"

"Honey, I don't see how anyone could have gotten in. I really don't. I'm sure it must have been that reporter." She flinched as she said it, but it seemed true. It certainly hadn't been Mrs. Neuberger or the super.

"It wasn't him," Karen grumbled. "Anyway, I can't sleep without Rodney here."

"I'll leave your door open, and we'll be right—"

The telephone rang. She caught her breath, thinking of the hospital.

Or the caller . . .

She reached it before Wade did. The voice was Avery's, rich, theatrical, and teasing. "How's my darling? I hope you got hold of your sister and set something up. I'd like to get back there as soon as possible and follow up on some leads I have."

She tried to call his bluff. "What about the soap you auditioned for?" It was all bluff. She knew it. Even those "leads" in California. Poor man.

"I don't want to get stuck in a thing like that," he said. "That's all you are, is stuck. There's no diversity. But I have a couple of projects for both of us out on the Coast—"

"Avery, please be realistic."

"What do you mean? This is perfectly real. I'll even give you the guy's phone number. You can ask him yourself."

"I'm not talking about that. I mean us. You don't seem to understand."

"I understand you better than you think," he said. "You're afraid to make changes. But you'll be crazy about it when we get there."

She groaned. "This is really my fault. I didn't make it clear before, but I'm kind of involved with someone now."

There was silence. She could imagine her words

reeling through his head.

Then he asked, "How involved?"

She would have to say it. Make a clean and final ending. It would be bad for a while, but then it would be over, for both of them.

"Well, actually, I'm planning to marry him."

Another silence. She thought he coughed, or made some kind of noise.

"Anybody I know?" His voice sounded raw, its theatricality gone.

"It's nobody you know, and I'm not going to tell you his name. I'll send you a wedding announcement. It will be soon now."

"Have you been sleeping with this guy?"

His belligerence frightened her. She felt herself cowering. She looked back at Wade, in the living room. He was listening to everything she said.

"I don't think it's any of your business," she answered.

"It is my business! You're my wife!"

"I'm not your wife. I told you that. You'll have to wake up and face reality."

"That's no reality! It's all in your mind, baby!"

She had expected it. The shouting. He had done it before, every time he felt her slipping away.

She steeled herself. "You always did live a fantasy. You made me into some dream that had nothing to do with who I am, and you tried to wish the kids right out of their existence. I stood it for a long time because I cared about you. I still do. I want you to be happy and learn to make your own life, instead of clinging to me. You're thirty-six years old. It's time you grew up."

She put down the phone before he could speak, then lay on Karen's bed for a moment, trying to regain her strength. Wade stood in the doorway.

"I think that was the best thing you could have done," he said. "Telling him off like that."

"It killed me. I should have done it sooner, but I couldn't. Where's Karen?"

"In the shower. Why?"

"I didn't want her to hear that. She's entitled to a few illusions about her dad, but I'm glad he won't be their role model."

Wade joined her on the bed, running his hands over her body, under her dress. He unfastened her bra. She listened for Karen to turn off the shower.

He kissed her long and hard, then raised his head. "What did Avery ask that was none of his business?"

"Whether we slept together."

His touch on her body slackened. She saw him staring pensively down at the bedspread.

"You see," she explained, "he still thinks of us as married. He didn't know the divorce was final until today, when I told him. It'll probably take him a while to get used to it."

"He's not very adaptable, is he?" said Wade.

"Not very."

After Karen had gone to sleep, they went back to their own bed. It didn't matter now about Avery. He couldn't see them. She even managed not to think of Rodney as Wade slipped the straps of her nightgown over her shoulders and kissed her breasts.

"Turn the light off," she whispered.

"I want to see you."

"Just this time. What if Karen wakes up?"

He switched off the bedside lamp, and she removed her gown. They embraced, in spite of the heat. He kissed her shoulders, her neck, her ear. She held him tightly, feeling the hardness ready to enter her, when, beside them, the telephone rang.

"Oh, no!"

She struggled out from under him, needing to answer

81

it, since it might be the hospital. He rolled away from her.

There was no response to her "Hello?" She said it again. Then a third time.

She knew someone was there. The line was open, and she sensed a presence. She pushed the receiver toward Wade. He shook his head and motioned for her to hang up.

She did, but she felt let down. "Why wouldn't you say something? Maybe if he heard a man's voice, he'd stop bothering me."

"You don't know who it is or what his problem is," said Wade. "A man's voice might only make it worse."

"You don't think it's Avery!"

"I don't know what to think. But after what happened to Rodney, you've got to consider that it probably isn't just somebody who picked your name out of the phone book."

"You're crazy if you think Avery would do that to his own kids."

"I didn't say it was Avery," he reminded her. "I said I don't know."

"It couldn't be. Not the poison. He never cared much about the kids, but he tried to get custody. He just wouldn't."

"Forget it, sweetheart. The police'll figure it out. Damn, I seem to have— Damn that phone call, anyway."

"It's all right. Just hold me."

He pulled her close to him. She thought how blissful it would be if they could spend the entire night in each other's arms. He said he couldn't sleep that way, but he would learn. And so would she.

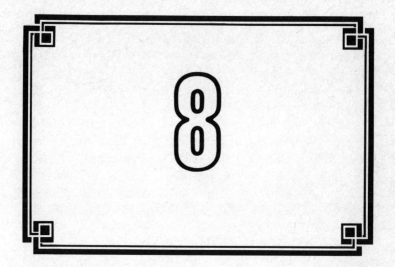

8

On Monday she traveled to Weehawken, New Jersey, to pose for a fashion spread on the crest of the Palisades, with Manhattan as a background. The session was over by four o'clock. A car brought her back, dropping her at the hospital so she could pick up Rodney.

She had to wait nearly forty minutes for a doctor to come and discharge him, but finally he was free to go home. He walked sturdily beside her down the corridor and out the door.

"I got sick," he said as they waited for a taxi.

"You certainly did."

"I got sick in the park, when I fell."

"No, I think it was later. You probably don't remember it happening. Do you remember about the bird?"

"What bird?"

She was glad he would not be traumatized by the kitchen, as she was. In the morning, she had bought two cans of corned beef hash and one of mixed vegetables and carried them with her all day. That would be their dinner. She fully expected complaints. They could go out later to Broadway and buy fruit from a stand, for vitamins and dessert. And if nobody fussed, she would treat them to ice cream.

The taxi took them to Seventy-seventh Street, where they waited on a corner for the camp bus. It horrified her to think of the chances she had taken, allowing Karen to walk home by herself.

Karen broke into a smile when she saw Rodney. She leaped down from the bus and ran to hug him. "I'm glad you didn't die!"

As soon as they were home, Denise did a quick check of the apartment to be sure no one was hiding. She looked in the bathroom and in the cleaning cupboard next to the refrigerator. She looked under the children's beds.

"What are you doing?" asked Karen.

"I thought I dropped something out of my purse."

"Oh." Karen sounded unconvinced. "I wish I had my granola now. I'm hungry."

"We'll have supper in a little while, when Wade gets home. But don't eat anything that's in the kitchen. We'll just have to be careful until they find out what happened."

She went to her own room and looked under the double bed. Wade's shoes were no longer there. He must have worn them to work.

Rodney toddled after her. "When's Wade coming back?"

"Any minute now."

"He came back last night," said Karen.

"I think Rodney means from work." Denise opened the closet and stood still.

His clothes were gone.

All of them—gone. She could see the wide space next to her own clothes, which were pushed to one side.

I'm dreaming, she thought. It's just a dream. He took them all to Kansas.

He had taken only a carry-on bag when he went to Kansas.

She stared, waiting for her eyes to stop playing tricks and the clothes to reappear.

She pulled open the top bureau drawer. It felt light, and sounded hollow. A layer of clean white paper gleamed up at her.

She checked the closet again, still not believing, and then the living room. The children clamored, "Where's Wade's clothes? Did a burglar come and take them?"

His stereo was gone. His record collection. He had moved over a rubber plant to cover the bare shelves.

His books.

"Was it a burglar, Mommy?"

"Please! I have to think."

A burglar. That was it. While they were both at work. She would have to call him.

There was nothing to say. He knew what he was doing. She only wished it had been a burglar.

Karen showed her a piece of paper. "This was on your dresser."

She hadn't seen it. She had been too intent on opening the drawer.

". . . better for both of us, I think," it said. She started again at the beginning.

"Obviously our being together is causing some problems, and this is better for both of us, I think. I won't leave an address because, first of all, I don't know where I'm going, and second, it would be defeating the whole purpose. I wish you the very best in the world.

Don't forget, darling, I love you."

"Love me!" she screamed, hurling the paper away. It fluttered to the floor. "Damn you! Coward! I hate you!"

The children stared at her, stricken. She sat down on the couch, dizzy with shock.

How could he? She had thought she knew him. Had thought they could stand together against anything, because they loved each other.

Karen tried to snuggle next to her. "Why did he take his clothes?"

All of them. Everything he owned. He must have packed this morning after she left. Loaded everything into his car and driven off. She wondered when he planned it. She wondered where he had taken it all if he did not know where he was going.

He could have told her. At least he owed her that.

But where could he have gone? He had a job.

A job! It wasn't over yet. She felt herself quivering, partly with excitement, partly with rage, as she dialed his office number.

There was no answer. It was after six o'clock.

She hung up, frustrated. She needed to talk to him *now*. But if he hadn't quit his job, she could get him in the morning. It was better than nothing.

"How could he?" she wondered aloud. Who was he? Not Wade. Not the man she thought she knew. It had all been a sham.

Had she invented someone, as Avery had? Or did people always misunderstand each other?

Rodney, sensing something, asked again hesitantly, "When's Wade coming back?"

"He's not." She held out her arms to him, and he burst into hoarse cries.

"I want Wade!"

"What are we going to do if he doesn't come back?" asked Karen.

"Do about what?"

"But we need him."

"I know we do."

"Then why don't you call him and tell him to come back?"

The question made her angry. At Wade. At Karen, for not understanding.

"I don't know where he is. And that's not the problem."

"Then why—"

"He doesn't want to get involved. He doesn't care. He doesn't give a *damn* what happens to any of us." She twisted off her engagement ring and flung it across the room. She did not see where it landed, and didn't care.

The telephone rang.

"Maybe it's him!" Karen exclaimed.

It had to be. A misunderstanding. She tried to think what she would say.

It was not Wade's voice that purred, "How's my precious darling?"

She felt sick with disappointment. And sick because it was Avery. She wanted to hang up, but couldn't.

After a moment, he said cautiously, "You are there, aren't you?"

"Yes."

"You sound a little down. Are you feeling all right? Kind of lonely, maybe?"

"Lonely! How could I be lonely? All you did was ruin my life, so what have I got to be lonely about?"

"Wait a minute, wait a minute." Avery could sound so calm and reasonable. "You say I ruined your life? Was I the one who broke us up?"

"It doesn't matter. It's all part of the same thing. You drove me away with your insane jealousy, and now *he's* gone."

She should not have said it. Should not have let him know he'd won.

It took him a moment to understand. Then he said, "Is that right? He's gone, and you're all alone?"

"I'm . . . not—"

"Aren't you afraid, Denise? All alone, with only your children to keep you safe? Who's going to look after the children?"

The words. The breathy voice.

"Avery, did you make those calls? And you sent the cut-up picture, didn't you? What are you trying to do?"

She did know. She was playing into his hands.

"You're mine, Denise."

"I'm not. You can't own me."

"Nobody else wants you. He screwed you, and he's gone. That's all he wanted, a free piece of ass. You thought he was going to *marry* you, a cheap slut like you?"

Her tears blurred the children's faces watching her from the doorway. Too frightened to come into the room. Frightened of her gulping sobs. She didn't care that they could hear her.

"You . . . can't . . . do . . . this."

"You wore the red nightgown, didn't you?" he said. "You let him pull it down over your shoulders, over your tits . . ."

How could he see? *How could he have seen it happen?*

"All that belongs to me, Denise. It's mine. And you let him touch you, filthy bitch. You let him touch—"

She dropped the telephone into place. A few seconds later, it rang again.

Karen said, "Mommy, answer it."

She shook her head. It rang, splitting the air. Karen picked it up and handed it to her.

"You'd better not hang up on me!" Avery barked. "Listen to me, you dirty bitch. I'm going to take those kids of yours. You won't know when or how. It might be tomorrow, it might be a year from now. You'll never know, but I'm taking them. No slut is going to touch my kids."

"You don't want them." Her voice sounded watery and timid. "You never did, and you have no income. You'll never—"

"You won't know when it's going to happen, you filthy piece of garbage. It could be tonight. Next week. Next month. Maybe Christmas. There's nothing you can do. You'll have to buy a gun and stand guard in front of your door. Or get yourself another prick to screw you."

"I'm calling the police," she said. "Right now."

She dialed her precinct, but as she expected, the two patrolmen who had seen her yesterday were not on duty. She talked to someone who looked up the case.

"I just found out that he did make those calls," she explained. "And he sent me the picture. I don't know about the poison. I don't see how— I can't believe he'd do that, and he doesn't even have a key."

Again she thought of Cliff. Maybe Cliff worked for him. He could have done something subtly and quickly that Karen, busy with her bird, failed to notice.

"If you're worried about childsnatching or bodily harm," said the officer, "I suggest you get in touch with your divorce lawyer. He can get a court order to keep the guy away from you and your kids."

"But that won't keep him away! A court order won't keep him away!"

"That's the only thing I can tell you, ma'am. We can't lock up a guy who hasn't done anything."

"This is right back where we started. Isn't there something about harassment and intimidation? Isn't that against the law?"

"You want to file charges? You can do that, but keep in mind that you gotta be able to prove it."

"What about in the meantime? What do I do *now*? He'll—"

The children were still there, watching her. "Thank you," she said, and hung up.

"Is Daddy going to kidnap us?" Karen asked. "What's going to happen?"

"Nothing's going to happen. You just don't go with Daddy, understand? If he tries to take you, scream for help."

"Why?"

It was a valid question. He was, after all, their father. She had to be brutal.

"Because he doesn't really want you for yourselves. I'm sorry, but he doesn't love you. He never wanted children. All he cares about is hurting me."

"He does love us." Karen kicked at the door frame.

"He's an actor. He's good at pretending. He'd grab you off the street and maybe hurt you, too, and he'd never let you see me again."

Karen began to cry. "I want you and Daddy to get married again. I want both of you!"

"I wish it didn't have to be this way, but I can't live with your father. He has too many problems."

She had never before talked against Avery to the children. Now it seemed she had no choice. Somehow she must make them understand.

"Do you know what he said to me yesterday? He wants me to go and live in California with him, and leave you kids with Aunt Jill. That's how much he loves you."

They regarded her, Karen stubbornly and Rodney with his mouth turned down. She imagined Avery charming them away in spite of her warnings. He could do that.

"And you," she said to Karen, "you won't even listen to me about not talking to strangers. You were deep in the woods with that man yesterday in the park."

The sullenness disappeared. Karen almost smiled, remembering. "Mommy, do you want to know something? I think that was Daddy."

"You what?"

"That man. Daddy can make his voice do lots of things, and that man was wearing makeup, like Daddy does when he acts."

"Oh, God."

Why hadn't she paid more attention to the man? But she hadn't guessed. She hadn't even begun to guess.

"Oh, dear God."

Cliff O'Donnell paced back and forth on the sidewalk. He had been ringing her doorbell since six o'clock, and now it was after seven. He had no idea what sort of hours a model would keep, but she was also a mother with young children, and they didn't seem to be home either. Where would a family like that go on Tuesday night?

Almost anywhere. They could be at a birthday party, or a movie. Maybe a funeral. She could be working, with the kids parked somewhere.

He rang again, then scanned the street in both directions. There were plenty of people around, but no slender figure with long dark hair. He fidgeted, and paced again.

An executive type, walking with a busy stride, approached the building and turned up the steps.

"Excuse me, sir. Do you know Mrs. Burns in Three A?"

"Why?" asked the man.

"I've been looking for her. I thought she'd be home by now."

"Why don't you leave a note?" The man trotted up the last two steps and into the building.

She would never answer a note. He knew that. When the inner door had closed, he went back inside and rang a doorbell at random.

A voice squawked over the intercom, "Who is it?"

"I'm looking for Mrs. Burns in Three A," he said. "Would you happen to know where she is?"

"Sorry."

More carefully this time, he selected a bell on the third floor. After almost half a minute, a woman answered. When he asked about Denise, he heard a click. She had hung up on him. He made a note of the name. E. Neuberger.

He rang another bell. There was no answering voice. Only the sound of the release buzzer. Careless. Very careless. Before the buzzer could stop, he pushed open the door.

He climbed to the third floor and knocked softly on 3A. When no one answered, he knocked again more loudly. He put his ear to the door and listened. It sounded dead. No bright childish chatter. He thought of the little boy who had been poisoned, and felt a shiver of apprehension.

Back at his post on the front steps, he noticed someone across the street who looked familiar. A child. At first, in a confused way, he thought it might be Karen Burns, then realized it was the other kid, her friend. He dashed over to intercept her, startling a flock of pigeons that were pecking at something in the middle of the street.

She was with an older girl, nice-looking, but on the

pudgy side. Probably a sister or a babysitter.

"Uh—" He could not remember the kid's name. She stared at him with no sign of recognition.

"I'm looking for your little friend Karen. Actually, her mother. They don't seem to be home right now. Do you know where they are, or when they might be coming back?"

"Nope."

"You don't know where they are?"

"Nope. She goes to camp."

"Who, Karen? She's away at camp?"

"No, *day* camp."

"What time does she get back?"

"Huh?"

"What Nikki means," said the older girl, dimpling like a doll, "is that she doesn't see her friend during the week, if her friend goes to day camp, because Nikki doesn't."

"Oh, is that it? Well . . . okay. Thanks, anyway. Have a good evening." He nodded to the older one.

She looked back at him over her shoulder and gave her hips a little twitch. He grinned, managing to look attentive, but his mind was not on her. Instead, he saw a pair of wide green eyes with thick, dark lashes. He saw them frightened.

And no wonder. First there was her friend's getting shot, and then her son's being poisoned. There were threatening phone calls, too, that terrified her. Could she have gone somewhere to get away from it all? Taken a hotel room for a while, or even left town?

All you really needed was an unlisted number, but that didn't help if they knew your address. And maybe it all tied in together.

Maybe the boyfriend had taken her away to keep her safe.

Or maybe they got married. He shuddered.

Unfastening his motorbike, which was chained to an iron tree guard, he rode off toward Broadway.

Two hours later he returned.

By then it was dark. Her blinds were open, and he saw no lights on. Not even the glow of a television set.

It didn't necessarily mean anything, even with young kids, and in the middle of the week. It didn't mean she was away. This was New York, and it was summer. A relaxed time, and the city kept going all night.

He rang her doorbell and waited. Then he tried E. Neuberger again. This time she actually replied to his question, saying she did not know anything.

He received the news with skepticism. She had hung up on him before, and it made him suspicious, but there was nothing he could do about it.

He rode away again and returned at eleven. The windows were still dark, the blinds still up. He waited for an hour, sitting on the steps in a light, misty rain, questioning anybody who went in or out of the building. No one seemed to know about her or care.

As he had remarked to himself earlier, this was New York.

10

"Then I tried calling him at his office," Denise told them, wiping away a tear.

"And?" prompted Jill.

"He wasn't there. They said he took a leave of absence. Just like that. He probably went home to Kansas."

"He probably told them to say that," was Jill's opinion. "As soon as they heard a weepy woman's voice—"

"I wasn't crying then."

"Okay. But did you actually try going to his office?"

"No. I thought about it, but I . . . didn't want to. I think I was scared."

"Just as well. He's not worth the cab fare. That's how *I* feel."

"Me, too, I guess." Denise dried her eyes. It was almost true. She had no use for someone who disappeared as soon as she needed him. Really needed him.

After all, she had not made so many demands. Almost none. Maybe, in time, she would be able to forget the love she had had for him.

Jill sat opposite her in a pool of golden lamplight, youthfully glowing and obviously pregnant. Her costume never changed. The jeans had a maternity panel now, and the crisp gingham top was a smock instead of a shirt.

"How does it feel to be home again?" she asked.

"It feels like home." Denise listened to the rain on the apple trees. In the city, on Sunday, the rain had been steamy hot. Here in Berryville it was so cool they had had to come in from the screened porch that looked out upon the bean fields in back of the house and a woods over at the side. This had been her home. She had grown up here. Now it belonged to Jill.

And Jill had earned it. She was the one who had sought approval. There was always one, Denise reflected. Jill, five years younger, had stayed home and been a dutiful daughter, studying business and agriculture at Community, and seeing both parents through their final illnesses. She and Virgil kept up the farm, as Dad would have wanted. Virgil Dorfman was a nice, steady, plodding sort of person. . . . She shuddered, thinking of Avery.

"Are you cold?" asked Jill.

And Wade.

"No, I just can't get over it. The whole thing."

"I could loan you a sweater."

"I have one, thanks."

"Care for a beer?" asked Virgil, coming in from the kitchen. He was a big-boned man, his rather ordinary face now enhanced by a blond mustache.

"No, thank you."

"Sure?"

97

"She probably drinks champagne," said Jill. "Probably French champagne. What do you drink, anyway? I never saw you with a beer."

"French champagne," Denise replied.

"Do you like it?"

"I'm kidding. When I drink, it's more apt to be gin and tonic, and that's not often."

"Sounds nice."

"Oh, no you don't." Virgil popped open his beer can. "Not while you're carrying that kid."

"So you're just going to abandon your apartment?" Jill asked.

"I don't know what to do. I suppose I could go to Houston or someplace. But the only thing I know how to do is model, and if I were modeling, he'd find me."

"Why Houston?"

"It's sort of a boom town, isn't it?"

"If he wants to find you, he will," said Virgil. "He'll look for your social security number, or look for the kids in school. That's how they do it. He might hire a private detective."

"Thanks."

Jill asked, "How do you know he wasn't just bluffing?"

"Avery doesn't bluff. And Harlan told me that if people like that threaten violence, they should be taken seriously."

"But did he?" asked Jill.

"Snatching the kids is violence. He doesn't really want them."

Virgil gulped down his beer and went to get another. He brought Denise a can of orange soda and Jill a glass of milk.

She opened the can and took a sip. For a moment, the artificial odor drowned out the smell of home, that faint settled smell, which she could not identify. It was home, and so was her maroon velveteen armchair with the stain on the seat, where someone had dropped a turkey leg years ago. And the high-backed sofa where Jill and Virgil cuddled together in a field of faded roses. And the patter of rain on leaves and the smell of wet greenery.

The city was home, too, but she didn't want to think about that now. It was all gone. Everything she had ever loved was gone. Except the children.

"I'm beginning to think my whole life stinks," she said.

"Oh, Dee, you have a terrific life," Jill exclaimed. "Think of all the glamour and excitement. He *was* exciting. I thought." Jill glanced at Virgil, and her animation subsided. "Anyway, you're not even thirty yet."

"All I want is to keep my kids safe and have some peace and quiet."

"What's thirty got to do with it?" Virgil asked.

"Jill's right. For a model, it means plenty. And in six months I'll be there."

"Do you mean you get laid off?"

"No, it more sort of dwindles away."

Jill giggled, then nestled against her husband. "You could model old-lady fashions. And vitamins, and Metamucil and stuff."

"It's not only age, it's faces. They start wanting new faces."

"Then why don't you retire? You must have stashed away plenty by now."

"Not exactly. Not with Avery."

"That's right. You had to support him, too."

"He was pretty expensive. Clothes and stuff, and entertainment for the contacts. All the things to get himself established."

Jill stroked her ballooning gingham. "Dee, I sort of think you let him take advantage of you."

"But we were working together. We were a team. That's what I thought."

"That's how it should be, but there are limits." Jill thought for a moment, then smiled to herself. "It must have been pretty heady, having a man suffocate you with his love. It's so romantic."

Denise did not know whether she was being sarcastic.

"It's not a bit romantic. It's a prison."

"A gilded cage."

"I'm not kidding, Jill. He tried to cut me off from everybody. All my friends. Even the kids. Especially Rodney. Maybe because he was male. Can you imagine being jealous of your own infant son?"

Virgil said, "I can't wait for our kid. Boy or girl, it doesn't matter."

"And my work, too. It's what we lived on, but he never wanted me to go, even though half the guys you meet are gay. He used to try to keep me— He tore up some of my clothes to keep me home. Some of my nicest things. They were expensive."

She would not tell them about the black eye. That was too shameful.

"Maybe he was jealous because you got more money," Jill suggested.

"That might have been partly it. But he really wanted me to devote myself to him a thousand percent. He never got enough attention, no matter what I did. And I was a good wife."

"Of course you were. But there are some men—"

"Women, too." Virgil began collecting the empty cans and Jill's glass. "Better turn in, sweets. You have to take care of yourself."

100

Denise watched them go upstairs together and thought of all the times in her childhood when she had kissed her parents good night and climbed those same stairs, believing that the world was hers for the taking and she had it all ahead of her. Now it was nothing.

She heard a bathtub running, and thought: This is their life, their whole life, right in this place. They don't want anything else. Just each other, and their children, and the farm. And to make a decent living.

It was all she wanted, too, in her own style. Her pleasant New York existence instead of the farm. But there was no "each other" for her. And there was the fear of Avery . . .

The bathtub drained. The footsteps and the soft conversation subsided, and she was alone.

At least she had her children. No matter what she had to do, she would keep him from getting the children.

Even if she had to give up New York and modeling, and work in a boutique somewhere, or a doughnut shop. Lose herself in the mainstream of life. She might have to do that, for it would not take him long to think of Berryville.

After a while she became aware of an odd prickling on her face and arm.

But only on one side, she noticed. The side that faced the window.

She rubbed a cooling hand over her skin. It was not a rash, not even an actual irritation, but more a consciousness.

It was the eyes again. Those unseen eyes. They were watching her. Now, at this moment.

She looked toward the window. It was black with night, and raining. Who could be out there?

She had been stupid, very, very stupid, to come to Berryville.

Feeling trapped in the lamplight, she got up and checked all the doors and windows to be sure they were locked. Then she turned off the light and went upstairs to bed.

"You said we could go swimming," Karen reminded her mother.

"I think it's a little chilly after the rain." She was afraid to go anywhere away from the house. But if she kept the children cooped up, they might do something desperate. They didn't understand.

"But Rodney and I want to go swimming. Can't we?"

"Maybe we could think about it later, if Jill comes with us."

"She's busy. She's always busy. You said we could do nice things if we came here, and go swimming in the pond where you used to swim when you were a little girl, and go to the county fair—"

"That's not till August."

She was glad of that. What a perfect place for the children to be snatched, if he happened to think of it and happened to find her there.

"Then can we go?"

"Swimming, yes. We might not be here for the fair."

The early-morning clouds broke up, and by eleven the day was warm. Denise packed sandwiches, then walked the children through a woods and down a dirt road past the Paysons' farm, to the old pond. Some years ago, the Paysons had bought the land where the pond was, but they still allowed neighbors to swim there.

The sunshine was white and clear, and Gladys Payson was out at her clothesline when they passed by. Denise waved, and Gladys ran down a little knoll to say hello.

"Dee! For heaven's sake! Jill didn't tell me you were coming." Gladys was blonde, with a heavy face. She and Norman were in their forties, and looked enough alike to be brother and sister.

"I just came up for a little visit. Karen and Rodney, do you remember Mrs. Payson?"

Gladys beamed at the children. "Good to get them out of the city for the summer." Like most people, she did not understand what an enchanting place the city could be, even for children.

Without waiting for an answer, Gladys asked with a meaningful twinkle that was almost a leer, "You going to be here for the big event?"

Karen clapped her hands. "The county fair?"

"I don't think we can stay that long," said Denise. "It's not due until September."

"You said August!"

"Mrs. Payson is talking about the baby."

"You'll be here. You wouldn't miss it." Gladys started back up the knoll. "Enjoy your swim, now."

The pond was around a bend, out of sight of the Paysons' house. A young boy of about ten had just packed up his fishing gear, ready to leave. No one else was there. Denise perched on a rock where she could

104

see in all directions. What if he came? There would be little she could do except scream.

He's not here, she tried to tell herself. But he knew where her roots were, and that Jill still lived in the house. He had been there for Jill's wedding.

That was the only time. He had even been jealous of her family.

"There's fish!" yelped Rodney. "Mommy, I saw a fish!"

"Can we go fishing?" Karen begged.

He would hear their voices. "Please don't shout."

"Why? Nobody can hear us. There's nobody here."

She lied feebly. "I'm getting a headache, and it bothers me."

While the children looked for fish, Denise's head actually did begin to ache. She would ruin their lives, keeping them quiet and out of sight. She had already done so, and ruined her own, by marrying Avery. It should have been obvious what he was like from the way he courted her: a blitz of constant phone calls, flowers, and gifts. Too much attention. It simply wasn't real. But in her ignorance, she had been swept off her feet. Someone wanted her so badly. He said he needed her.

He did, but he did not need her for who she was. It had nothing to do with her. As Harlan said, he only used her to answer his own needs. His insecurities. He was back in the infant stage, wanting someone to belong to him totally, and vice versa. When she stopped playing that role for him, he hated her with a monumental, terrifying hatred. He could never bear to be thwarted or rejected.

"Rodney, watch out. That mud can be slippery." She climbed down from the rock.

"Can we go fishing sometime?" Karen asked again.

105

"I guess so." It didn't matter what she said, because they wouldn't be here. She had felt the eyes, and she trusted her feelings.

After two hours, she took the children home. They were slightly sunburned, even though she had tried to keep them in the shade of a willow grove. She had forgotten how much clearer the air was in Berryville, and how much stronger the sun's rays.

While Rodney took his nap, she and Karen did the laundry, hanging it out in a fresh breeze, as Gladys had done.

"I like it here," said Karen. "I like it better than going to day camp. So why can't we stay?"

"We'll find some place, I promise."

"Why can't we stay and work on the farm, and take care of Aunt Jill's baby?"

If Wade hadn't left them, they could be happy in the city. She wondered how he felt about it now. Guilty? Ashamed? Or fully justified, and relieved that he was out of the mess?

"Can I go with Jill when she goes shopping?"

"No," said Denise. "I can't ask her to watch you."

"I can watch myself. I won't get lost."

"That's not what I'm worried about."

"You're worried about Daddy, right?"

She no longer wanted her children to call him that. He didn't deserve it. "Daddy" was someone like her own father, who had been a silent man, but a dear one. She had taken him for granted.

And the only daddy she had given her children was Avery. It wasn't fair. But they had to call him something.

"If he kidnaps you," she said, deliberately using the word, "I won't be able to find you again."

"I'll tell him to bring me back."

106

"Karen, you don't understand. He wouldn't do that. He's—Something happened to him. He's not reasonable anymore. That's why we have to be careful.

Again Denise stayed up after Virgil and Jill went to bed. She was used to later hours than they, and she needed time to unwind. Restlessly she switched television channels, and finally found a mystery that she hoped would keep her interest.

All around her, the house creaked and settled. She listened for other sounds. Anything besides the house. She tried to feel whether the eyes were there, watching her.

It was gone. She didn't feel it now. Whatever had watched her was gone. It might have been a deer, or something from the woods. Avery hadn't found her yet. Maybe he was not even bothering to try. After all, he had a career to pursue. It would be stupid to blow the whole thing just to get even with an ex-wife.

Or maybe she had done right in coming to Jill. Maybe it never occurred to him that she would do anything so obvious.

The show ended, and she watched the news, then part of a movie. Her eyes kept closing, and she missed bits of the film, until it no longer made sense. She turned off the set and went upstairs to bed.

The sun and the laundry had tired her. She fell asleep almost at once.

Sometime later she woke, oddly disoriented. After a moment she remembered that she was at home, her childhood home. She heard strange thumps, and people shouting. But it couldn't be morning, because it was still dark.

The door burst open and light from the hallway flooded her room. Karen stood above her, screaming.

107

"Mommy, the truck's on fire! Uncle Virgil's truck is on fire!"

She raised her head. "Is Virgil in it?"

"Come and see!" Karen tried to pull her from the bed.

The clock said a little after two. Suddenly she was wide awake. Jill must have gone into labor, and they had started off in the truck, and it caught fire. She raced out to the hall.

Jill and Virgil were there in their nightclothes.

As soon as Denise appeared, Jill cried, "What happened?" and Virgil asked, "Did you see what happened?"

"Oh, you're all right, thank God!"

Jill paid no attention. "How could it start burning like that?"

"Can't," said Virgil, slipping his large feet into a pair of zori. "I didn't drive it since this afternoon. It must have been set." As he rushed toward the stairs, a white light exploded below him.

"The house!" Jill shrieked. "The house is on fire!" She stumbled into her room and picked up the telephone. Virgil unsnapped a fire extinguisher from the wall. *Get out! Get out!* Denise thought, and realized she was screaming it.

She hustled the children into their bedroom and fumbled at the hook that fastened the window screen. "Jill! Virgil! Never mind the fire. Just get out!"

Then Jill was beside her, distraught and unwieldy, and Virgil said something about the whole extinguisher, and Denise knew the fire was still burning.

"You go first." Virgil pushed Denise toward the window. Out onto the porch roof. Would it hold? It sloped toward the ground, and there was a drop of ten or twelve feet. They could stay there, unless the porch caught fire.

I'm scared, she thought.

108

But burning was worse. And she was the only able-bodied adult besides Virgil.

She crept out onto the roof. It was nearly vertical. Miles above the ground. Her fingers dug into the shingles, but she had to let go and help Karen, who was climbing out under Virgil's relentless pressure.

Then Rodney. He felt so small leaping into her hands, and he had no fear. She sat him down firmly. "Don't move, now."

Jill leaned from the window. "Oh, my God."

"You can do it. Put your foot out first," Virgil said. He lifted her under the arms.

"I'm going to fall. I'm so heavy." Jill was more frightened than Denise had ever seen her. Easygoing Jill.

Denise stood up to help her. Facing the window. She could not look back at the drop.

"Come on, dear. Up and over."

"I'm too big. I won't go through."

"You will. Think of the baby." She clasped Jill's hands and helped her through. As Virgil followed, they heard a siren in the distance. Then another.

Jill said, "Maybe they'll put out the fire and then we can go back in instead of down." Her teeth chattered.

"That's pretty fast for Berryville," Virgil observed.

Karen said, "Mommy, what's going to happen? All our clothes will burn up."

Denise remembered the eyes. She had not been wrong. And it wasn't a deer. Nothing so harmless.

Rodney screeched with excitement as the fire trucks roared down the driveway. She caught his pajamas to steady him.

Maybe someone had it in for Virgil. That was it. In a small town, you could make enemies. People couldn't get out of each other's way.

One of the trucks had a ladder, and the firemen were

109

intent upon rescuing them. Climbing down was worse than the roof. Jill moaned and sobbed until she was on the ground. Then she lay gasping in a patch of crabgrass.

A car pulled up and the Paysons jumped out, hastily dressed. Norman wore his pajama tops with a pair of jeans.

"What happened? Somebody smoking in bed?" He glanced at Denise.

"She doesn't smoke," said Virgil. "It was a firebomb."

"Hey, fella. Your water heater, maybe? The stove? Gas line?"

"A firebomb," Virgil repeated. "It just exploded in the front hall. There's no gas line there. And just before that, my pickup was burning."

Norman whistled his amazement at the news. Then he stood frowning, trying to puzzle it out.

Gladys said, "You're all coming to our house for the rest of the night. Are you okay, Jill? Maybe we should get you to the hospital."

Jill struggled to sit up. "What for?"

"We don't want you to lose the baby."

"It's all right. I can feel it kicking. I'm sure it's a boy, and he's having as much fun as Rodney with all this." Her voice quavered, but she was trying.

Denise sat down beside her and watched as silhouetted figures drenched the flames.

When there was no more fire to be seen, the men stood around talking.

One of them told Virgil, "There'll be a lot of water and smoke, but the fire damage isn't too bad. It was mostly confined to the front hall. Looks like an inflammable liquid of some kind."

"I don't get it," said Virgil. "I just don't get it." He turned a swift glance at Denise, then looked away as though embarrassed.

110

So his guess was the same as hers. But maybe they were wrong. They had to be wrong.

Gladys rounded up the women and children and led them to her car, while Norman stayed and discussed the fire.

For the rest of the night, lying on a sofa in the Paysons' house, Denise could not sleep.

12

A phone call to the hospital elicited the fact that her little boy had been discharged on Monday afternoon. By Tuesday, she had gone, and was still away when Cliff went to check her apartment on Thursday morning.

She could not have left permanently. There were the plants hanging in the window, and some knickknacks on the sill. But she had been afraid of something, and that made him anxious, too. He wished she could have trusted him.

His first thought was elopement. But tracking down the boyfriend, with zero information, wasn't easy. A bribe to the building super gave him a name, but no occupation. No place of work where he might be found, and his home address was the same as Denise's. Back to square one. Where would they go if they eloped, and what had they done with the children?

Now was the time to get in there and dig. At least he knew what Denise did for a living. He called the various agencies, pretending to be a photographer, until he struck gold with Hegger Models. But when he asked her present whereabouts, a figurative door slammed in his face. "We don't give out that information," he was told.

Was there something he had missed? Something she might have said? He didn't think so. He was pretty good at remembering pertinent details. Things like names and places.

And he had another name, if he cared to approach the matter from a different angle. With the cleaning woman's help, and his generous expense account to cover such help, he had managed a brief look at Denise's file in the lawyer's office the night of the shooting.

Avery Burns. An address in Los Angeles. He had made a note of it, and his friend Pete Mandelbaum, who worked for a wire service there, was obligingly checking it out.

Most of Wednesday had been wasted on a man-bites-dog assignment, although he periodically stopped by her apartment and rang the doorbell. After handing in his story on Thursday morning, he looked through the phone messages that had piled up. Dentist and stockbroker could wait. His mother . . . He'd get back to her that evening. Pete from L.A.

Pete had been waiting to hear from him.

"I checked out that address, the apartment," he said. "It's still in Burns's name, but nobody's there."

"Any idea where he is?"

"They think he went to New York. . . . Hello?"

Cliff had been plunged into immediate thought, and had forgotten to speak.

"Hello," he said huskily. "So he's here?"

"That's what they think. The guy next door said the police are looking for him."

"Any particular reason?"

"Seems they've got a mystery on their hands. He was living with a woman, but she disappeared. He told everybody she went back to Michigan, but her family hasn't seen her. They kept trying to reach her here, and finally filed a missing person report."

"Well . . . maybe she didn't go back to Michigan."

Maybe she ran off with another guy, he thought, and maybe she didn't want to tell Burns. From what he had read in Denise's file, that could be something of a problem.

". . . might have been dried blood in the crack," Pete was saying.

"Blood?"

"Yes. You see, there are these vinyl tiles in the kitchen, and when the building manager went in to check, he noticed a place where it looked like somebody spilled bleach, so he told the police, and they poked around between the tiles, and came up with some stuff that might be dried blood."

"You found all that out?"

"It seemed pertinent. I talked to the manager, then went to the police. Nobody's drawing any conclusions yet, but they're testing the blood."

"When did this happen?"

"A couple of days ago. That's when they found the blood. A neighbor said the woman might have been seeing someone else."

"Are they following that up?"

"They're trying to, but nobody has a clue who it might be. It seems Burns is a real jealous type."

"I know."

"You do?"

"That's what I heard, anyway." His mind raced. There was that murdered lawyer. The threatening phone calls. And they thought Burns was here, in New York. Did she know it, too?

"I'll keep you posted," said Pete. "What are you doing, a story on this guy?"

"Not exactly, but he's moving into center place. Any idea what he does?"

"You mean professionally? Not much. He's kind of on the fringes of acting, modeling."

"Probably TV commercials. It'll give me a place to start. And if there's anything you want from New York, I'll gift wrap it for you."

Again he tried the modeling agencies. He tried the theatrical talent agents. He called the entertainment unions. Finally he found an agency that had formerly handled Burns, but they thought he was still in California.

So maybe he hadn't come East after all. But then, where was he?

Or if that really was blood on the floor, he might be lying low. If he was in New York, he might have come for only one purpose. Denise.

And where was she? Had he gotten to her already, or was she running from him? Did she know about the bloodstain?

Maybe she didn't have to be told. Maybe knowing Avery was enough.

Or she might have been safe in the arms of her boyfriend. But he needed to know that for certain. He would have to try her agency again, and this time he would do it in person. Sometimes it worked better than the telephone. Cliff knew he was good-looking, and he knew how to pour on charm.

He made a quick trip home for a clean shirt and tie, then rode across the park and down to the East Fifties.

It was a new luxury office building on Third Avenue,

115

with canned music in the elevators. Behind a pair of glass doors, a receptionist sat at a large semicircular white desk, talking on a pink telephone. Next to her was a vase of pink flowers.

As soon as he saw her, his heart lightened. She was young, a wholesome-looking blonde with a naive smile and cowlike eyes. Probably new to the city. Probably a nice family background, but no streetwise sophistication. Exactly the kind he could twist around his finger.

She grinned at him over the receiver, murmured a giggly good-bye, and hung up.

"Yes, sir, may I help you?"

Quickly he decided on the best approach, and went for broke.

"You certainly may," he said, his smile widening. "How about lunch?"

"You're kidding."

"No, I'm not. I'd really like to take you to lunch, and I guarantee I'm harmless." He stood against the desk and gazed down at her tenderly.

He saw her waver. She checked her watch.

"I can't go till my relief gets back, about ten minutes."

"I can wait." He made himself comfortable on a pink sofa.

The girl watched him for a moment, then said, "By the way, I don't know your name."

"I'll give you my card." He slid it across the desk. "Keep it under your pillow. Don't let the boss see it. People usually aren't crazy about newspapermen."

She glanced at the card and put away in her purse. "Are you after a story or something?"

"I'm always after a story," he admitted. "I'm doing one on the modeling business and the people who keep it going, such as yourself. I'd be interested in talking to

116

a couple of models, too, if you could help me. Do you know a Denise Garner?"

"Oh, yeah." The girl nodded. "People always want to meet models. But I think Denise is engaged."

"She's working? Right now? She's in the city?"

"I mean she's getting married soon."

"Oh, that kind of engaged. Yes, I know that. I told you, I'm doing a story. This isn't just a gimmick to meet women. If you take a look at my card, you'll see that I write for the *Bulletin*."

"I saw that. Oh, good."

The door opened, and a small woman with dark frizzy hair came in carrying a paper bag.

"Doughnuts," the woman announced. "I'll leave some for you."

"Thanks," said the receptionist. "I'm glad you're early. I have a lunch date with this gentleman here. Excuse me a minute while I run to the powder room."

He did not expect her to reappear, but she did. Because she worked for Denise's agency, he treated her to an Italian restaurant that was out of his usual price range.

Her name was Sandi. She was twenty-two, and this was her third job since junior college. She loved it, but it was not a good place to meet men. There were some male models, but they were usually married, or gay, or too full of themselves. He tried to get the conversation back to Denise.

"I don't know," Sandi said. "She told them to cancel her bookings for the next couple of weeks, and not make any more till we heard from her."

"Do you think she might have run off and gotten married? Would she tell you if she were doing that?"

"Not if she wanted to keep it secret. I didn't think of that. I figured she was just tired. But you know, if a

117

photographer wants a particular model, and he's got her booked, then he doesn't necessarily want somebody different. But what can you do?"

"Do you mean people don't cancel very often?"

"Well, sometimes they do. But if you're going to send a substitute, it has to be the same size and coloring. And the same type. They go a lot by types, often. But if it's clothes, then the coloring is important, too."

"Yes, I see. Did she have a lot of bookings this week?"

Sandi watched his face, and her lips moved with his, but he had the feeling that she wasn't really listening. He repeated his question.

"I couldn't tell you." She sighed. "I don't handle that. I just sit at the front desk."

"And look beautiful."

She blossomed. "*You* could model. You're so gorgeous."

"Thanks, but it isn't quite my dish of coffee."

"You'd probably make a lot of money. Do you like writing for the *Bulletin*?"

"I consider it a very excellent entry-level job."

"You want to work for *The New York Times*."

"Doesn't everybody?"

"I don't." She smiled fondly, and he began to wish he hadn't tried so hard. He almost hated himself for using her. Not only that, he wasn't any closer to finding Denise.

He started to speak, but she beat him to it.

"What did you do before the *Bulletin*?" she asked.

"Television. Nothing glamorous. I'm not an actor. I dealt with commercials."

"Before that?"

"I tried the army for a while."

She looked surprised. "I didn't know anybody did the army anymore."

"No, it's not an 'in' place these days. But it got me through school. That's the main thing."

She took her time over spumoni and coffee, and they started back to her building.

"Is there an actual person named Hegger?" he asked. "I mean, if it's Hegger Models?"

"Oh, sure. You mean Claire?"

"Is she the head of it?"

They had just passed a flower shop. He turned back, bought two small bouquets of something pink, and handed one to her.

"I know you already have a bunch of them on your desk," he said.

"Oh, those aren't mine. They're just for looks. This is *so* sweet. Thank you."

She was still cooing over the flowers when they reached her office. He asked rather offhandedly if she could arrange for him to have a few minutes with Mrs. Hegger.

"Oh, sure. I can ask, anyway."

She disappeared into the back reaches and returned almost immediately.

"What is this in reference to?"

"For the article I told you about, the one on the modeling business. It's not for my newspaper," he added, remembering what Denise had said about the *Bulletin*. "I'm doing it for a magazine. If this isn't a convenient time, I could make an appointment."

Claire Hegger said she could give him ten minutes. He had his notebook with him. He never traveled without it.

She was a slim, elegant woman, expensively dressed,

and with a finishing-school accent. Her office was done in pink, gray, and glass. She asked him what publication he was writing for.

"Uh— It's an Italian magazine," he said, aware that she would know all the American ones, and probably the British and French, too. "*La Romana.*"

There were pictures of models on the wall. He did not look all the way around to see if Denise was there, but thinking about her stiffened his resolve. He managed to ask relatively intelligent questions as to how the agency had started and how it worked, before he turned the conversation to his objective.

"I met one of your models the other day. Denise Garner. I met her in the park with her kids. She wouldn't happen to be around here now, would she?"

"Denise is away for the week," Hegger said with a drop in inflection that implied the subject was closed.

"Oh, is she? Too bad. But she'll be back next week?"

"Possibly. She left it open."

"Taking a few days off, huh?" At least she had planned her departure. She hadn't simply disappeared, leaving blood in a crack on the kitchen floor. "You said she went away somewhere."

"I said she's away from work."

"But she's in the city."

"Young man, we don't give out our models' home addresses."

"I know her home address. I've visited her there, but she's not there now. She must be out of town."

"I wouldn't be surprised."

"But you don't—"

No, she didn't. He knew she did not know where Denise was, and even if she did, she wouldn't tell him. He asked a few more questions to calm her suspicious nature, and left.

Sophie Burger didn't like the man's looks. He was rough and unkempt, but her revulsion went beyond the shaggy eyebrows and missing tooth. The hair that looked as if it had been chopped off with a knife. There was something in his manner, but she couldn't tell what it was. Just a gut feeling she had.

She sat with her elbows on the counter, trying to read the day's paper, while he browsed through the store. She could hear him tramping up and down the wooden aisles.

He carried a long, thin package that was clearly marked as to its contents. She wished her father would come back. He had gone to the bank for change. It was getting near three, so he probably had to wait in line.

She tried to make herself take it easy, but her eyes kept going to the package. It still had a price tag on it. The man took two six-packs of beer out of the refrigerator and headed toward the door.

"Hey, you!" she called.

He turned to face her. He had blue eyes and strangely tanned skin that didn't look natural. His eyes blazed with an odd light. She opened her mouth to tell him he had to pay for the beer, but no words came. Probably Dad would have said to leave him alone. She wished she had just kept quiet.

"It's . . . okay," she managed, and quickly looked down at her paper. He wouldn't want to be stared at. She tried to focus on the print while she listened for him to tear open the box. At any moment she would feel a slug burning through her head.

Instead, she heard the door open and close, and when she dared to look up, he was gone.

She sat still, her mouth dry. He would come back.

When he didn't, she hurried over to the door. It made a squeaking sound, but he was nowhere in sight to hear it.

She pulled out the telephone that was under the counter. There was a special way you were supposed to call the police, but she couldn't remember what it was. Dad . . . Dad . . .

Call the police over a dozen beers?

It wasn't that; it was the rifle. And the way he looked. She had never seen him before in Berryville, which in itself didn't prove anything. But he looked so *odd*. And he hadn't been at all embarrassed about taking the beers. He knew exactly what he was doing, and he meant to do it.

The door burst open, startling her.

"Oh, Dad!"

"What's the matter, Sophie? You saw a ghost?"

"Dad, a man was just in here and he took some beer without paying—"

"Why didn't you stop him?"

"He had a gun."

"He threatened you? Did he take anything else?"

"No, just the beer. He had the gun in a box, but I was scared. It was the way he looked at me. He might still be around somewhere. I think we should call the police."

Her father started toward the door. "What was he, a tall man? Short? Fat?"

"Not too tall. Dad, get the police! Don't go by yourself!"

Bitch, he thought. Stupid bitch. It was the way she had looked at him. She was probably calling the police right now.

He swatted at a fly that zoomed toward his arm. His hideout was a small abandoned structure in back of an empty house. From the outside it looked like a miniature barn. It smelled like one, too, and the flies loved it.

Besides, it was stiflingly hot. The only way he could get relief was by pillowing his head on cold beer. One six-pack to drink and one to keep him cool. When night came, with some relief from the heat, he would drink the second one.

Maybe he should have paid for the beer, but he couldn't spare any more cash. It was the last of Trish's money that was seeing him through. After that, he had nothing.

Another fly buzzed at his face. He struck at it furiously, but only knocked it through the air.

Midafternoon. It was a long time before dark, and the barn was getting hotter every minute. He felt the old familiar pain in his chest, the hurt at having to go through this when he should have been happy and comfortable.

He wasn't going to hurt anymore. It was someone else's turn now. He knew exactly what to do, and it was all her fault.

Tears came into his eyes. "Mommy, Mom—"

Where the hell did that come from? He couldn't believe he had said it. He didn't mean *her*. Alarmed, he hammered on his chest to drive out the pain. It made him angry to hurt like that. He banged until he thought his heart would stop.

Then he lay still, feeling every breath, afraid of what he might have done to himself. What if his heart really did stop? What if he had an attack? He placed a hand lovingly over his ribs and rocked back and forth.

"Yeah, a white T-shirt," said a voice outside.

God. He stared down at his shirt. They were right there, only a few yards away. She had called the police after all, stupid bitch.

He lay against the beer. It was too late to get away. He had a minute, maybe two minutes, and then they would find him. He was finished before he even started.

He began to move very slowly, rolling over without making a sound to reach the bag where he kept his handgun. If he could get it out and load it before they came . . .

"We gotta go down over the—"

They were farther away this time. The voice faded altogether in midsentence. He listened, expecting them to regroup and come back. But time ticked on. He heard it ticking in the gold watch on his wrist.

She had given him that watch. She had loved him once, the shallow bitch. Like all the others, she couldn't be trusted. He hated women. Yes, really hated them. Men, too.

124

Fifteen minutes. They really were gone. He couldn't believe his luck. Dumb small-town yokels.

The heat made him sleepy, and his makeup was starting to melt. Such heat could kill a person, but if he lay still, which he planned to do anyway, he would probably pull through. It was only a few hours.

Stealthily he opened another beer and settled down to wait for evening.

14

Cliff slapped his forehead and turned back. He had reached the lobby before discovering that he still carried the second bouquet of flowers, which had been meant for Mrs. Hegger. He managed to catch the elevator as it was closing.

"Can I see her again?" he asked Sandi. "Just for a second?"

She was about to admit him without question when Hegger came out to the reception room, purse and briefcase in hand.

"For you." He bowed. "And thank you for your time."

"You're a dear. Sandi, would you put them in water?" She left at a brisk pace, probably late for whatever it was.

He watched the models go in and out, the platinum blonde with the sooty eyes and a poodle tucked under her arm, the elongated one with the funny eyebrows, and the one who chatted endlessly into a coffee-table phone, promoting herself in drawn-out Brooklyn tones for some TV job.

When Sandi was back from her errand with the flowers, he tried again. "Look, Mrs. Hegger had to cut it short. I wonder if you can help me."

"Of course!"

"We were talking about Denise Garner, you know, for my article. I want to put in something about the different life-styles, and she's one I know who has a family."

"She has two little kids," Sandi volunteered.

"Yes, right. I wanted to ask what she does with her kids while she's working. I mean, is there a relative who takes care of them? Or a neighbor? A day-care center?"

Sandi looked blank. "I really don't—"

Something brushed his elbow. It was the poodle's wet nose.

"Hi there." He scratched the dog's chin. "Do you like my fabric softener, or did I put my arm in the mozzarella?" He grinned at the sooty eyes above the poodle. The model did not smile back.

"You don't happen to know Denise Garner?" He was growing desperate. "I was in the middle of interviewing her, but we had to stop, and now she's on vacation."

"Interviewing her for what?" The eyes stared at him coldly. All of these women, he thought, had probably heard every line in the book.

"For an article I'm doing on the modeling business. I got to the part about who takes care of her kids while she's working, and she took off, and I have this deadline—"

The girl held the dog up to her face and nuzzled it, then turned away with a shrug.

He stood surrounded by beauty, and felt lost.

127

"Are you talking about Denise?" asked a voice.

This one had big blue eyes and russet hair that matched her dress.

Cliff wanted to kiss her. Instead he repeated the question. "Do *you* know who takes care of her kids while she's at work?"

"I really don't. Some neighbor, I think, when they're not in school."

"Somebody in the building?"

"I think so. I don't know." She turned to the desk. "Are there any messages for me?"

He no longer wanted to kiss her, but it wasn't her fault. Waving good-bye to Sandi, who was suddenly deluged with people and phone calls, he set out for the West Side.

Again he checked her windows and rang the doorbell. He turned cold at the thought that she really might be on a wedding trip. He had to expect it sooner or later, unless she could be talked out of it, but this was too soon.

He studied the names on the mailboxes, each with a doorbell beneath it. There was only one other apartment on her floor, 3B. The E. Neuberger one.

But Neuberger was cautious, he recalled. That would not help. He tried to remember which party had pressed the release buzzer without asking who he was.

This time it didn't work. It was the middle of a weekday afternoon. Probably most people were out earning their livings.

He biked up Broadway until he found a stationery store that sold legal forms, and then a florist shop. He went back to the building and rang Neuberger's bell.

It was a long time before she answered. He had almost given up.

"I have some flowers for Three A," he said. "Will you accept it?"

128

"She's not home."

"I know that. Will you take the flowers and keep them for her?"

"I don't know when she's coming back."

"Ma'am, can you please accept the delivery? If I take it back to the store, I'll lose my job."

"Put it down in the lobby," he was told, and the buzzer sounded.

He had gotten into the building, if not the apartment. It was time to implement his backup plan. He climbed the stairs and rang 3B's doorbell.

"Who is it?" Neuberger demanded testily.

"Reyes, Connors, and Durkin," he said.

"What's that?" Her voice sounded right against the door. He knew she was looking at him through the peephole.

"I'm from Mrs. Burns's attorney. I have some papers for her to sign about the divorce, but she's not home."

The door opened a crack. There was a chain across the crack.

"I thought you were the flower man," she said.

"I was." He produced the flowers. "They're for you."

"What's going on here?"

He smiled disarmingly. "You wouldn't have let me in if I told you right off I was from the lawyer, right? Now, I have some papers here . . ." He rummaged in the folder he had also bought.

"She's not here, and I can't sign anything for her," snapped the woman. She was small and gray-haired, with gray eyes that might have been kindly. But they were not kind toward him.

"Can you tell me where to reach her? It has to be done right away."

"No, I can't." She tried to close the door. He blocked it with his foot.

"Look, I'm from her attorney, her friend Harlan

129

Reyes. I just want to know where she is. It's important. It's for her sake, not mine."

"I can't tell you where she is, because I don't know, and that's the truth." Mrs. Neuberger was still cautious, but he detected sincerity in her statement.

"Okay. Can you tell me who looks after her kids while she's at work?"

"I do, but they're not here, either. She took them with her. That's all she said, except I'm supposed to water her plants."

So she thought it might be for a while. Would she have taken the children on a wedding trip?

"Can you tell me about the gentleman, uh—"

"What gentleman?"

"The one who lives there. Did he go, too?"

"He split. And I wouldn't call him a gentleman."

"Oh, really?"

So the man had left. Had she gone away to forget him, perhaps?

Or was it something more sinister? There was the lawyer, after all, murdered either for handling her divorce or having dinner with her. Or maybe both.

"Mrs. Neuberger?" He thrust the pointed end of his wrapped bouquet through the crack in the door. "Have a wonderful day and a wonderful weekend."

"Are these really for me?" she asked.

"They're for you. We appreciate all you've done for Mrs. Burns."

So that was that. The mighty O'Donnell had struck out. He unchained his motorbike and headed back to the office.

15

"I can still smell the fire," Karen exclaimed when they returned to their house on Friday.

"The smell I can deal with," Jill said crossly. "We're just lucky to be alive."

Denise put an arm around her sister. The props had been pulled out from under Jill's world, both physically and emotionally. They had spent all of the previous day cleaning up the mess and assessing the damage, and Jill was exhausted.

"Can't understand it," Virgil muttered, looking around the blackened front hall.

Denise tried not to think. Tried to make her mind a blank. There was no reason, she told herself, to imagine that it had anything to do with anyone but Virgil. He even speculated that it might have been Norman Payson trying to burn him out and get his land.

"For God's sake!" cried Jill. "Are you crazy?"

"They got here awfully fast," Virgil said.

"Of course they did! They're right next door. And they were good enough to take us in for two nights."

"Guilt."

"You'd better stop that, Virgil."

He ran his finger over the charred door frame. Someone had cut out a piece of window glass to throw in the firebomb. Probably he had taped it first, the investigators concluded, since evidence of tape remained, and the cut-out piece could not be found.

"It wasn't Norman," Jill said again.

Karen did her usual stalling that night on her way to bed.

"Mommy, you know the person who started those fires? What if he comes back?"

"He wouldn't," Denise said quickly. "Nobody who did a thing like that would come back. He might get caught."

"What if it's the same person who put the poison in my—"

"Karen! That's enough!"

"But what if it is, Mommy? I'm scared."

"I'm scared," echoed Rodney. "I'm scared of the fire."

"Can we sleep downstairs?" Karen asked. "Then we can get out easier."

"But downstairs is where the fire started," Denise reminded them. "Just close your eyes. It won't happen again."

They refused to sleep unless she stayed with them. "All night," Karen insisted. Virgil brought a folding cot from the basement, and Denise made it up for herself. She stayed with the children until they were asleep, then went downstairs to join the others.

"I'm really sorry about it," Jill said. "You came up here to get away from one bad thing, and then we—" She stopped, frowning thoughtfully. Had it really not occurred to her before?

Virgil looked away quickly when Denise caught him watching her.

"At least we all got out," she said.

Jill clutched at her gingham smock. "I could have lost the baby."

"You probably wouldn't lose it," Denise assured her. "It's too far along. Even if it came prematurely, I'm sure it would live."

Why was she talking like that? Chattering, trying to distract them from what they might be thinking.

"You were very brave, Jill," she added.

"I wasn't. I was scared to death. The only thing that scared me worse than climbing out was the fire."

"I've always been worried about that in the city. Especially when we lived in a high rise." With Avery. "And we were at the back of the building. They can't get those ladder trucks around to the back. There weren't any fire escapes, just an enclosed stairwell. But what if you can't get out to the stairs?"

Still chattering. She couldn't stop herself.

"At least we have fire escapes where we are now, and some front windows. But they have window guards so Rodney won't fall out, and that gets in the way."

She saw that they were not interested in her city problems. Jill looked dejected, and Virgil was rubbing her back with the flat of his hand.

"It's so awful," Denise went on. "It's not my house anymore, but it still feels like home. I hate to see it damaged. It's like a personal attack. I'll get busy on the curtains tomorrow and wash out that smell."

"Slipcovers," said Jill. "Rugs."

"Everything. You just take it easy. I'll do it."

Virgil studied her with interest. "Do you really know how to clean a rug, Denise?"

"Watch me. I'm no hothouse flower. I have a cleaning woman at home, but I may have to let her go. The jobs aren't coming in the way they used to, and now with Wade gone—"

It's over, she thought, still amazed. It's *over*. "With Wade gone, I guess I'm on my own."

Neither of them said anything. She realized, belatedly, that they may have thought she was angling to stay with them. She would show them it wasn't true. She did not want to live under someone else's roof, even though it felt safe and homey.

She wanted Wade. She wanted . . .

Oddly, she thought of Cliff, and the way he had put his arms around her at the hospital. She fought with herself, recalling her suspicions, then remembered that he had helped save Rodney, collecting the girls and finding a taxi, keeping a level head when she had lost hers.

Cliff, she repeated to herself. Cliff what? He had said his last name once or twice, but so much had happened. Could she call the *Bulletin* and ask for Cliff? Would she? What would she say?

"Denise, you look positively sappy," said Jill. "What are you thinking about?"

"Oh . . . just . . . something."

"Wade?"

"Absolutely not."

Again the suspicions rolled back. There had been no one else in the apartment.

Or maybe one of the ingredients had been spoiled, farther down in the jar from where Karen had eaten.

134

Or maybe . . .

Nicole was in the kitchen. But Karen had been with her.

Karen had been with Cliff, too.

Mrs. Neuberger had access all the time. But she loved the children.

Jill said, "I like you better with the sappy look. Now you're letting it get to you again." She yawned. "You'll have to excuse me, folks. I'm turning in before I conk out on old smokey, here."

"Who's old smokey?" asked Virgil.

"The sofa. Don't you smell it?" Jill went upstairs, carefully avoiding the first step, which was badly burned.

Virgil crushed his beer can and scowled at the floor. He was working himself up to say something, and Denise dreaded it. How would she answer? She really had no ideas about the fire. None at all. She would tell him that.

But when the question came, it was not as bad as she had feared.

"Uh— I know we asked you this before, Denise, but, uh— I just want to get an idea, you know, how long you might be staying here. You know, with the baby coming, and all the stuff we have to do . . ."

She started guiltily. "Oh, I know. I never meant to stay more than a couple of days."

And if she wanted to be literal about it, more than two days had already passed.

"I'm still trying to plan my— I guess my future," she said.

"I'm not trying to kick you out. I just wanted, you know, to get an idea."

"Yes, I understand. I would like an idea, too. What do you think I should do?"

He agreed that, under the circumstances, she should not go back to the city.

"You said something about Houston," he reminded her.

"I really don't know a thing about Houston."

"You could check it out. You could even leave the kids here for a while if you want to go down there."

"I . . . don't know. Maybe someplace nearer. Rochester or something.

"What made you think of Rochester?"

"I don't know. It's not really very near, is it?"

"Hardly. And it's cold."

"Maybe Washington, D.C. What would I do there? Or Atlanta. I've got to think of something."

She thought of her apartment in the city. Her work, and her life there. It had all been taken away from her. Even Wade.

Thinking his name again, she waited for the pain to come back. But there was no pain. Only anger. Why would she want a person like that? Perhaps he had always been weak, or unconcerned, and she simply hadn't known because there was no crisis.

"I suppose I can thank Avery for that much," she said as Virgil fiddled with the television set.

"For what?"

"For making Wade show himself up like that. I really pick them, don't I? All these people look so good in the beginning. Do you think I'll ever . . . find anybody—"

"I don't know, Denise. I guess that's sort of up to you."

"How do you mean?"

"Well, maybe— It's not my business."

"Tell me, Virgil. You're a man. What do you mean?"

"It's really not my business, but . . . maybe you sort of have to . . . not need anybody so much."

136

"How can you not need anybody? Everybody needs people."

"Well, sure, for companionship, maybe for sex, but not to lean on. You can lean on yourself."

"I don't know what you're talking about."

He turned off the set. "I guess I mean you're a pretty strong person. But I don't know if you know it. You're independent, you can support yourself, and maybe you don't need a guy as much as you think. Maybe if you felt more independent, you'd be able to see them clearer. I don't know what I'm talking about either."

"Well, I certainly don't."

He rose from the chair and stood bouncing on his toes for a moment. "Guess I'll turn in now. Good night, Denise."

"Good night."

It's not true, she thought. Everybody needs somebody.

She could not imagine having to spend the rest of her life alone, with no one to depend on but herself.

But she had been alone for a while, and it was not so bad. Of course, she had considered it a temporary thing, not for a lifetime. But while it had lasted, she could call her soul her own. And after Avery, that had been a relief. Perhaps she was still getting used to it.

Once more she checked to be sure everything was locked, then went upstairs to bed.

When she entered the room she was to share with the children, Karen rolled over.

"Mommy, are you going to sleep now?"

"Yes. Don't wake Rodney."

"Can I talk to you?"

"Could it wait until morning?"

"I just remembered something. About somebody who went in our apartment."

137

"Who was that?"

"A man. Once when we were at Mrs. Neuberger's, a man came and said he had to fix something. Electricity or something, in our apartment."

"Electricity?" There had never been any problems that she could remember.

"He said he had to have a key, and Mrs. Neuberger gave it to him."

"*She did?*"

"Because the super wasn't there, and the man said if he didn't get the key he'd go away and not fix it, and she got scared. But he brought it back."

"When was this, Karen?"

"It was— I don't know. When did Rodney eat the poison?"

"Do you mean it happened recently?"

"I think so. But he brought it back. And then she got even more scared, and said not to tell you."

"I see."

"So don't tell her I told, okay?"

"I'm glad you did."

"Why? Because maybe that's the person who put the poison in my granola?"

"I don't know."

But somebody had. And maybe it wasn't Cliff.

"That was before Rodney got poisoned," said Karen. "So how come I didn't get poisoned?"

"He probably copied the key and went in later."

"Can you do that?"

"Yes. It's very quick and very cheap to copy a key."

"But why did he want to poison Rodney?"

Karen suspected, but didn't know she suspected. Her own father.

And I did it to them, Denise said to herself.

"Why, Mommy?"

138

"Maybe only the pigeon," Denise managed to say.

"Are you crying?"

"Not really. I'm just tired."

"You're crying. Is it because Rodney got poisoned? But he's all right now. Isn't he?"

"Yes, he's fine. If I'm sad, it's because I want to go home."

"Why can't we?"

"Maybe, in a while. Maybe he . . ."

Maybe he would go back to Los Angeles. She wondered how she would know he was gone.

"Try to sleep now, Karen. You seem to get your brightest ideas in the middle of the night. I'll be along in a few minutes."

Karen was still awake, waiting for her, when Denise returned from the bathroom.

"Mommy, you won't tell Mrs. Neuberger I told?"

"Not a word. But I wish she'd been a little more careful."

Maybe it was not Mrs. Neuberger who had given him the key. Maybe it was Karen herself.

In any case, it was done. Now she knew how he had gotten in. But the solution was far more complicated than simply going home and having the locks changed. A lock was only one thing; there were many ways he could reach her. Too many ways.

16

Denise's eyes opened to darkness. She hadn't dreamed it. Someone was screaming, on and on.

Someone in the house. It sounded like Jill. She heard pounding footsteps, and shouts.

Another fire?

The children woke, adding their own screams. Denise sat up.

Karen leaped into her bed and clutched at her. "He came back! Mommy, he came back!"

Jill, having her baby. Already at the screaming stage. Denise started across the room and bumped her toe on Rodney's bed. She groped for the light switch.

"Police!" Jill was shrieking. "Get the police!"

The light would not go on. She tried it again. And again. It was like a nightmare. Something horrible waited in the darkness.

She knew there was a lamp on the dresser. Feeling her way around her cot, she reached it—

"The lights are off!"

She opened the door. A flashlight moved through the hallway.

"Virgil?"

The beam shone in her face. She put up a hand to shield her eyes. He came toward her, lumbering and bearlike, and she realized he was limping.

"What happened?"

"Somebody attacked us in our room," he said, panting. "Had a knife."

Jill came out of their bedroom. "Did you get him? I called the police."

"Didn't even see him." He looked down at his arm. The glow from the flashlight showed blood on his pajamas.

"You're hurt!" cried Denise. "You'd better lie down."

"It's okay. Just a scratch."

"What about your leg?" asked Jill.

"It's *all right*." He slipped his other arm around her, flashlight and all. "You okay, baby?"

"I'm fine. He only hit me."

"Only hit you!" Denise exclaimed.

The children swarmed around her. Rodney clung to her leg. Karen butted her elbow and demanded to know what had happened.

Virgil limped across the hallway and tested a switch. "They're out all over the house."

"A burglar?" Denise asked. It had to be.

"A maniac is more like it. He jumped us in our sleep."

"What would a burglar get from this house, anyway?" asked Jill.

Karen tried again. "What happened?"

Denise said, "You ought to do something about that, Virgil. Let me see it."

He removed his pajama top. Blood oozed from a gash on his arm.

141

"A fire engine!" Rodney yelped as lights flashed on the wall.

It was the police. The door chime rang, and Jill admitted a fatherly, gray-haired officer whose name was Stowall. He heard their account of what had happened and was shown the blood-spattered bed. Denise tried to keep the children out of his way while he examined the rest of the room.

"Didn't come in through the window, that's for sure," Stowall noted. "Screen's fastened on the inside."

"It's getting so we can't even get a night's sleep," said Virgil. "Never know what's going to happen. We could wake up dead."

"Did anybody hear anything?"

"Not till Jill started screaming," said Denise.

Jill rubbed the side of her face. "I woke up, and I thought he was killing Virgil. Then he hit me, and he kept hitting me, but I managed to get the pillow over my face."

"Maybe you folks ought to think about going away for a while," said the officer.

"Hell, no," Virgil replied. "I'm not leaving my home."

"Maybe the women and kids—"

"I'm staying with Virgil," Jill said, putting her arms around him.

"Did you see anything? See what he looked like?" Stowall continued.

"He had something over his face," Jill said.

"Smaller than me," Virgil remembered. "Soon as I got my feet under me, he ran."

"Which way did he go?"

Smaller than Virgil . . .

"Downstairs, I think. I tried to go after him. Beats me how I lost him. I should know my own house, even in the dark."

"You were hurt," said Jill.

"He moved pretty fast."

Denise slipped over to a corner of the room and sat down in a rocking chair.

Someone who knew the house. Who had seen it before.

Who had been here for Jill's wedding.

Why would he do that? Why Jill and Virgil?

The officer started downstairs, and everyone followed. He led them to the basement.

Karen asked, "Is Uncle Virgil going to die?"

"No, of course not," Denise answered.

"Just a loose fuse," she heard Virgil saying. "They're all loose. That was no accident."

Of course it wasn't.

"When we had the fire, I thought it might be Norman Payson."

"You on good terms with Payson?"

"Sure, but you never know."

"You wouldn't be if he could hear you talking," Jill said. "It was not Norman, Virgil."

"I know, I know."

They knew.

The policeman had taken Virgil's flashlight and was shining it over the windows.

"Here's the place. He cut out a screen."

"How could anybody get through there?" asked Jill.

"He was small," said Virgil. "Not a midget. But, you know, wiry type."

Five feet seven. And all lean. A wiry type.

The policeman tramped outside to study the ground. Jill was feeling her baby, and smiling. It had just kicked.

"I think you ought to go away," Virgil told her. "You and Denise."

"I'll go," Denise offered. "I'll leave tomorrow morning. Then . . . maybe . . . everything will be all right."

There was silence. No questions as to what she meant by that. They simply accepted it, and she felt as though she had brought a curse on their house.

"Where will you go?" asked Jill.

"I'll think of something. Maybe Lawrence, Kansas."

"What's there?"

"Nothing. Just talking to myself."

The officer returned. "Anybody hear a car or anything before it happened?"

"We were all asleep."

"Must have come in a car," said Stowall. "It's pretty isolated."

That was her mistake—one of them, Denise thought. It was too isolated here. But she had no one else.

Where will I go tomorrow?

They had tightened the fuses, and the house blazed with light. She felt vulnerable. In a showcase, or a goldfish bowl.

The officer finished his inspection and was ready to leave.

"Try to get some sleep, folks. I'll drive by every now and then and make sure you're okay."

"Thanks," said Virgil. "Maybe we should put up some floodlights outside. But we never had trouble before."

Where will I go?

She could go back to the city. If he was here, then she could sneak back—

He might be watching. He might be out there right now, watching from the woods. How could she get away without his knowing?

144

But she would have to go somewhere, and it might as well be the city. At least she could earn a living there.

"Good night, Jill. I—don't know what to say. Come on, kids."

"Mommy, what if it was the same person who put poison in my granola?" Karen whimpered.

"We just don't know."

But she did know, and so did the rest.

Even the children.

17

He thought it was me.

The realization woke Denise abruptly. Somehow she had managed to sleep after the attack, and now it was morning.

It all made sense—for Avery. He had found a woman in bed with another man, and his obsessed mind jumped to its only possible conclusion. He hadn't even stopped to think that this was Jill's house. He had seen Jill married, but had forgotten about Virgil. All he knew was Denise.

She sat up in bed. It was early, but the sun was up and the birds were calling. She heard Virgil clumping down the stairs in his heavy shoes, still with a limp.

She lowered her feet to the floor. It was a warm, dewy day. In the city it would be steamy again. She preferred the steaminess. The city was her home, and today she was going back.

She combed her hair, washed her face, and put on a

light cotton duster, then went downstairs to the kitchen, where the family ate breakfast.

Jill was alone at the table. "You're up early. For you," she said.

"I'm going back to the city, remember?"

"Why the city?"

"Why not? I decided it couldn't be any worse than here."

Jill poured a cup of coffee for her. "Do you really think it was him last night?"

"I don't know, but it's possible. I guess." She did not want to believe it, but there seemed no choice. It was possible.

"What are you going to do there? I mean, to keep him away from the kids?"

"Well, for one thing, it's harder to get in." She would have her locks changed, and warn Mrs. Neuberger not to trust anyone.

"I think you should go somewhere else," said Jill.

"I can't just take off and go somewhere. I have to be able to earn a living, and I can do that in New York. I have my contacts. Even if I could model in another city, it takes a—"

Jill started wildly, her hand to her chest.

Denise felt her own heart lurch. "What was that?"

"It sounded like a shot." Jill peered out through the screen door.

"Probably hunters."

Jill turned and looked at her. It was not the hunting season, and Denise knew it.

She cried out as a second shot was fired, and then another. They were coming closer. Jill ran out to the hall and up the stairs. Denise followed her, thinking of the children. Jill was going to rescue her children.

Instead she went to the master bedroom and opened

the big clothes closet. Denise saw her tugging at something in the back.

"What's that?"

"Dad's old hunting rifle."

"You're not— Jill—"

"If the police can't stop him, I'm going to do it myself. I have a right to protect my home."

Jill felt along the closet shelf, took down a cardboard box, and headed back toward the stairs.

Denise went to check on the children. Incredibly, they were still asleep. From the window, she noticed something flopping along the ground. She was about to warn Jill, when she saw that it was Virgil.

Hurt. The second time. She ran down the stairs, past an anguished Jill, and opened the kitchen door.

"Keep back!" Virgil called, waving her away. She realized he was not hurt, but only trying to reach the house. She started toward him, crouching low and holding out her hand.

"I said get back! Are you crazy?"

A shot struck the outside wall just above her head. She tumbled backward into the kitchen.

Virgil burst through the door. Jill tried to give him the rifle.

"Hell with that," he said. "Can't even see him. Get the police."

Jill reached for the wall phone and started to dial. Then she paused, looking baffled, and jiggled the switchhook.

"It's dead."

Virgil snatched it from her and listened. He rattled the hook, and they both looked at Denise.

She felt a sinking, as though the earth were dissolving from under her. "Maybe I should . . . go out there."

"Don't be stupid," said Jill. Then she added, without conviction, "Maybe it's not him."

"I know it's him. And I'm putting you all in danger."

"Stop being so damn noble. You're stupid," Jill told her.

"He wouldn't shoot me." *He loves me.*

She remembered their last conversation, on the telephone. She remembered the hatred in his voice, and the things he had said.

That was his love. He would kill her as easily as he would kill Virgil.

Jill sat down heavily. "What are we going to do?"

Denise said, "I was going to leave here today."

"How? He's got us pinned down."

"He'll get tired," said Virgil.

"How will we know?" Jill asked. "Maybe we could make it to the car, do you think?"

"Don't you dare try it."

"I've got to get away," said Denise. "If I'm gone, he'll leave you alone."

Virgil replied angrily, "We don't know that. Just sit tight. Somehow we have to get word to the cops."

Another shot. They heard it hit the house. Then Karen came racing downstairs.

"Mommy, I looked out the window, and there was a man with a gun, and he shot at me!"

Shot at . . . *Karen?*

"Did you see him?" asked Jill.

Denise said, "Karen, you've got to stay away from the window. Rodney, too. Did you see what he looked like?"

Karen stared at her dully.

"If you didn't, that's okay. We don't want a made-up story."

"I don't know," Karen said. "He was kind of far away."

"What color was his hair?"

"I don't know. What color is that?" She pointed to the refrigerator.

"Coppertone," said Jill.

"Brown," said Virgil.

"It was that color, that kind of brown. And it looked funny."

"What do you mean funny?"

"It was all messy."

He might have worn makeup. Even a wig.

It might have been someone else.

Denise went up to the children's room. Rodney was just waking. She carried him downstairs, warning him to stay away from the windows.

"Why?" he asked sleepily.

"Because you might get hurt. And don't argue. Just listen to me, okay?"

Virgil was pacing back and forth, darting angry looks at the window above the sink. "Hell, we can't stay in here. I've got work to do."

"You'd *better* stay here." Jill tried the telephone again. It was still dead. "What are we going to do?"

"It's psychological warfare, that's what it is." Virgil rubbed at his injured leg. "I guess we wait until nighttime. That should do it, if we can hold out. Then we'll get in the car and go to the police."

Jill asked, "What if he tries something else?"

Virgil patted the rifle. "This was good thinking, baby. There's no way he can come near the house without being seen, so we're okay. All we have to do is keep a lookout and not lose our heads."

Jill winced. "Good choice of expression, dear."

It was an unreal day. As unreal as the day after Harlan's death. They were a family of five, held prisoner by one man. Jill looked out of the window, trying to see him, her rifle by her side. A bullet struck the shingles only inches from her face.

"Damn it, don't you have any brains?" cried Virgil, throwing her to the floor.

"He's in the woods," she said as he helped her up and hugged her. "Maybe we could get out on the other side."

"What other side? There aren't any doors on the other side."

"A window? Then we could run through the orchard—"

"Not enough cover."

Denise listened. It was her fault. All of it was her fault. The first mistake was marrying him. But she hadn't known. How could she know?

She pretended to pack her suitcase, pulling out a pair of moss-green slacks and a lime-color shirt. A terrible match, but they were green.

"Mommy, what are you doing?"

"Getting dressed."

"But why, if we can't go anywhere?"

"Because I feel like getting dressed. Karen, I want you and Rodney to go down to the basement. You'll be safer there, and I'll come in a little while."

"The basement's yucky. I want to stay with you."

"That's an order."

"Why? What are you going to do?"

"Don't be such a wise guy. What about the attic, then? It might be more fun for you, and I'm sure it's all right with Jill." It would be hot, but the kids were heat-resistant. "Just don't look out any windows."

151

She pulled down the attic stairs and helped Rodney up. She was tempted to raise the stairs again and trap them, but they would yell and scream.

Besides, it might be dangerous. What if he threw another firebomb?

Jill and Virgil were in the kitchen. She smelled coffee. They would be calling her soon to join them. She unhooked one of the living room screens and climbed out.

Crouching, as she had seen them do in war movies, she darted among the apple trees. Acres of them. Far beyond was another wooded area. If she could—

Something zipped past her. She threw herself flat on the ground. A shot made the earth explode in front of her face.

How could he? Where was he?

She began to inch backward. Back to the house.

Another bullet flew past, barely missing her hand.

She sobbed, and dragged herself through the grass. He would kill her there in the orchard. Then he would take the children.

She heard a voice screaming her name.

"I'm coming!" she called. "Jill, stay there! Don't move!"

18

"You nut!" cried Jill. "You crazy, dumb nut! What were you trying to do?"

"I thought I could get out. Maybe get help." Denise looked down at her green outfit, now streaked with earth stains. "I even tried to camouflage myself."

"But where is he?" Jill peered around one of the window drapes. "How could he be everywhere at once?"

"Where did the shots come from?" asked Virgil.

"I don't know. He must be in the woods. And when I got out far enough, he could see me."

"Then we're stuck here," said Jill. "What are we going to do?"

"We're not going to do anything," Virgil replied. "Quit asking that. We're just going to wait him out."

"But what if there's more than one? I mean—what if it's not what we think?"

How carefully they avoided mentioning his name, thought Denise.

"What if," Jill went on, "it's something like a . . . a Mafia burying ground? That's happened, you know, on farms."

"Farms that belonged to the Mafia," said Virgil. "I think you're getting a little carried away."

Denise added, "We've lived here all our lives."

"Don't let him psych you out," Virgil told his wife. "That's what he's trying to do. We'll just wait for dark, and hope the moon isn't too bright." He set out on a tour of the house, trying to see what he could see.

Karen appeared at the top of the stairs. "Mommy, I heard shooting."

"It's all right, honey."

"But who is it? Why are they shooting?"

"I don't know, but stay away from the window. It's going to be all right."

Jill caught her eye.

When Karen had gone, Denise explained, "You have to lie a little. I'm only trying to keep them from getting scared. And I really don't know what he wants."

"Is this lesson number one in child-rearing?"

"No, because it usually doesn't come to this. It's not going to happen to you."

"Maybe not," Jill said bitterly. "Maybe it'll be all over before my child even gets born."

"Don't talk like that!"

Virgil had reached the kitchen, when they heard another shot.

"Get back—" he started to call, and then, "Oh, shit!"

Jill ran to him. "What is it?"

"Norman."

They crowded at the window above the sink. A green pickup truck stood askew, tilted off the driveway into the weeds.

"It's Norman!" Jill exclaimed. "What happened?"

154

"I don't know. I saw him coming up the road, and he must have been hit."

"Oh, God." Jill moved toward the door.

Virgil seized her arm. "You want to get your head blown off?"

"But we can't just leave him!"

"Don't you understand? The guy's trying to isolate us. He's already done it. You go out there, and you'll get killed. Do you think he's playing games?"

It's Avery, thought Denise. I can't believe it's Avery.

But she could. It was Jill who could not believe it. She didn't know his temper.

And now even Norman had been dragged into it. Perhaps killed.

"We can't just leave him," Denise said, echoing Jill.

"What are you going to do?" asked Virgil. "You'll get picked off before you even reach him, and that's no help."

"Then . . . what?"

"Nothing. I told you. We're safe enough in here. We'll wait."

They saw the truck begin to move. Jill gave a cheer.

Another shot blasted the windshield. Again the truck jolted to a stop. Through the shattered glass, they could see nothing.

The children came pounding down the stairs.

"Mommy, there's a truck out there and it got shot!" Karen cried.

"I told you to stay away from the windows."

"But what's happening?"

"A sniper. There's somebody out there with a gun."

"But who is it?"

"Some crazy person. That's why I want you to keep out of sight, do you understand?"

"But what about the person in the truck? Is it Mr. Payson? Is he dead?"

"I don't know. We can't go out there."

"Is it really happening?" Karen looked puzzled. "It's like a television show."

"I'm afraid it's real. And it's dangerous, so you have to do what I tell you."

They stared at her, Karen in bewildered alarm, Rodney with no comprehension at all. As they started toward the stairs again, Denise stopped them.

"You'd better stay down here where I can see you."

She wanted them with her. It was the only way she could be sure.

Jill stood at the window, her hand going slowly to her mouth. She began to bite on her fingertips.

A shot exploded.

"He's alive!" Jill cried. "I saw the door move, and then they shot him again."

Virgil went to watch over her shoulder. "He'll roast to death in that sun."

Jill screamed, "No, Norman, stay in the truck!"

Virgil pulled her from the window. "Don't *do* that, baby, please. Norman's got brains. He'll figure it out."

"Why don't you go and lie down?" said Denise.

"How?"

"Go ahead," Virgil agreed. "There's nothing else to do."

There was nothing to do but watch. After several hours, it had become the longest day of their lives. The children were restless. Rodney asked to go swimming.

"That's so stupid!" Karen exclaimed. "Mommy, he's stupid. He doesn't understand anything."

"He's very young." Denise felt too apathetic to

156

reprimand her. And Karen was under a double strain. The adults she trusted were helpless.

In the early afternoon, Virgil spotted a car turning into the driveway.

"Damn, it's Gladys! She probably called here and couldn't get through."

"Can you fire a warning shot?" asked Denise.

"No way. It'd only alert him."

Jill got up from the sofa, where she was trying in vain to rest, and joined them at the window.

Almost at once, they heard Avery fire. Gladys's car sagged as the right front tire collapsed.

Jill whimpered, "*Please* do something."

Virgil pounded his fist on the sink in a steady drumbeat. Then he snatched up the rifle.

"No!" cried Jill, pulling him back as he reached the door. "I didn't mean it!"

A bullet crashed against the house.

Virgil's face turned red, and he steamed like an angry bull. Denise backed out of his way. It could kill a man to feel impotent. A man like Virgil.

It could kill a man to feel rejected. . . . Unwanted. . . .

"You tell me not to do dumb things. What about you?" screamed Jill.

Denise said, "I don't understand why we can't see him. If he's close enough to hit those—Look!"

Gladys's car began backing toward the highway, faster and faster, flat tire and all. As she reached the road and turned, they saw her right rear window shatter. They saw her speed away and disappear behind the trees.

"She did it!" Jill clapped her hands.

"Now we'll be hearing from the cops," said Virgil. "It won't be long."

Denise asked, "What if she didn't understand? They

157

might think it was us doing the shooting."

"They'll find out as soon as they get here. Where'd he learn to shoot like that, Dee?"

"I don't know. When he was a kid, I guess. It's all about wanting to feel powerful."

"Who are you talking about?" asked Karen.

No one answered her.

"Do you mean that person out there? Does Mommy know who it is?"

"Not really," said Denise.

The children would find out sooner or later. Someone would say something, or . . .

She couldn't bear to think of his being captured or killed. But it was his fault. *Why do I care?*

If she had stayed in the city, he could not have done this.

It might have been worse. He would have snatched the children, then tortured her with their being gone.

"Here they come!" Jill hugged her husband as two police cars turned into the driveway.

"Can I see?" Karen pushed toward the window.

Denise caught her and held her. "You stay away from there!"

They heard the crack of a shot.

Virgil opened the window screen and braced his rifle on the sill.

Something gray flashed among the trees and then was gone. Virgil moved the gun, trying to follow it.

"Sonofabitch," he muttered.

Karen struggled to see what was happening. Denise tightened her grip.

Another shot.

"He got a cop!" cried Jill. "He was just getting out of his car."

A pile of blue lay in the weeds at the side of the driveway.

They saw Gladys's car return and park on the highway. They heard an exchange of shots. Something that looked like thin smoke rose from behind a large rock. Then a police bullet struck the face of the rock, leaving a mark.

Jill said, "We could get out now on the other side, while they're keeping him busy."

"Go!" Virgil pushed Jill toward the living room. She looked back at him, then rounded up the children.

"Come on, Dee."

The police were shooting at Avery. Denise remembered bits of rock flying up in the air.

She remembered Norman. And Harlan.

It was Avery who did that.

Without noticing, she had reached the ground outside the window. She helped Rodney and Karen, and then Jill. Crouching, they started through the apple trees.

Then she was lying on top of the children, while bullets flew wildly, not hitting. And Karen cried, "Mommy, Mommy, you're hurting me!"

"Get back," said Denise. "Back. And keep low." Shielding both children, she herded them toward the window.

Virgil was there, reaching out his arms for Jill. "Baby, I'm sorry. I shouldn't have told you to go." He helped the children in, and then Denise, and told them, "He got another cop."

Jill huddled on the sofa. "Are you sure it's only Avery? How could it be just one person?"

"Do you mean it's *Daddy*?" Karen asked.

"Oh, Dee, I'm sorry."

"Why is Daddy shooting at us?"

159

"Because he's angry," said Denise. "He's sick."

"Then why isn't he in bed?"

"It's a different kind of sickness."

"Did he shoot those policemen?"

Rodney said, "I don't like that shooting!"

"Mommy . . . when Daddy told me to take home the pigeon and give it cereal, do you think he put that poison in the cereal?"

"I don't know."

"Did he know Rodney was going to eat it?"

"He couldn't have known that."

"Rodney almost died."

Jill paced the floor. "Stop it. Stop it!"

Karen said, "I don't want those men to kill Daddy!"

Two more police cars arrived and parked on the highway. A voice spoke over a bullhorn. There were shots and answering shots. The police tried to enter the woods and were driven back.

"He can't hold out forever," said Virgil. "There's limits."

The two police cars that had been caught in the driveway started to back out. The first one was trying to turn when it suddenly veered, its windshield broken. The second car backed into it.

"What are we going to do about Norman?" Jill asked again.

"Nothing," said Virgil. "We can't."

It would be hours until nightfall. Even the season was on Avery's side. The cover of trees, the long day.

More cars gathered on the highway. Sunlight glanced off chrome and glass and figures moved about, but they were not all policemen. Some were people who had come to watch.

The police tried to clear away the onlookers. A shot popped distantly and the crowd scattered, disappearing behind cars.

"Maybe they should set fire to the woods," said Jill.

"Oh, great," Virgil replied. "Here we are, just yards away."

Karen clamored to see, but Denise sat both children in front of the television and turned it on. She found a movie, a cowboy picture. The shots on the screen would mingle with those outside, and they would not know the difference.

"There goes more cops. They've got the state police now," Virgil called from the kitchen.

Against her will, Denise went and looked out. She saw a flash of something bright disappearing behind the trees.

"They'll get him from the other side," Virgil said. "It's about time. One guy holding off all those cops."

Jill pushed in between them. There were more shots, and then silence.

Was it over? Denise looked out through the screen door.

A car started down the driveway. She thought it was Gladys. The car stopped short under fire.

"He's still there," said Jill in amazement.

Virgil stood poised, his rifle on the windowsill.

"What are you going to do with that?" asked Jill.

"If he tries anything—"

A volley of fire crackled from the woods. The children left the television and ran to their mother, Karen in tears.

"It should be all over now," said Virgil.

"No!" Karen shrieked.

There were more shots. Another volley. Denise looked out, keeping the children away from the door. She could see nothing. Only a cloud of smoke, or perhaps she imagined it. She though she could smell it.

There was silence. The smoke cleared away, drifting from the trees.

161

Virgil set down his rifle. He turned to Jill with a fond smile and started to reach for her.

They jumped apart as a bullet shot through the window and into the kitchen wall.

Shivering, Avie reloaded his rifle.

Avie. The name startled him as he remembered it. That was what *she* had always called him. His mother. Not as a pet name, but only because it was shorter.

He tried to stop his teeth from chattering. He had never imagined it could be so cold in the summertime. There was not enough humidity to retain the heat after sundown.

In that respect, it was just like home. His old, cold home, with stark pine trees against a cold moon. He could never think of home and feel warm. Never.

He looked up through the trees. There was the moon again, almost full. He saw it shining on the bean fields. He could see each row, but there was no color. No color in the bean fields.

He huddled into a tight ball as his teeth began to chatter. Planning what he would do after he got the kids, he tried to imagine jumping out of a plane.

It made him sick. Better at night. A solid black, when he couldn't see the emptiness ahead of him. He would have to take the children with him. He would start out carrying the kids, and what he did with them on the way down, no one would know, if it was night.

She'd never get over it, would she?

He listened to the forest around him. There was a steady sound that he hadn't noticed before. High-pitched, like a ringing in his ears. Probably insects. Far off, he heard a dog barking.

The police were still there. He could see their lights out on the road. A couple of times they had come into the woods and tried to get him, but he had driven them off. They did not know how much noise they made crashing through the underbrush.

Again he looked up at the moon. It had a strange schedule, the moon did. There was no telling when it might set. He couldn't wait forever, or he would lose his advantage.

He got up and began to move toward the house.

"He's wearing black," said Denise.

"Huh?" Virgil stirred in his chair.

"Black. That's how he stays hidden. I thought I saw him this afternoon. It looked like gray, but that was the sun shining on it."

The sound of their voices woke Jill, who had been asleep on the sofa. She rubbed her face and sat up. "Are we there yet?"

Virgil reached out a soothing hand. "Get some rest, hon."

"I want to see."

"There's nothing to see."

"She's not really awake." Denise wished Jill would go back to sleep before she remembered Norman Payson,

164

still out there in his car. It did not seem possible that he could be alive. All day, Gladys had maintained her vigil. Even as the sun went down and darkness gathered, her car had been parked on the highway.

The police were there, too, for all the good it did. At least they kept Avery from approaching the house.

Would they really be able to see him? The moon was bright that night, but there were misleading shadows. Denise wondered why the police didn't bring in a searchlight. Maybe they had their reasons.

Her mind drifted, and she imagined an attempted rescue. She imagined Virgil unwilling to leave his house. Would Avery set the place on fire? The house where she had grown up?

"Do you think," she asked, "if we all dressed in black, maybe we could get out of here?"

"No way," said Virgil. "Not with that damn moon. He'd see us moving."

"I guess so. But it works the other way, too. If we can't get out, at least he can't get in."

Inching across ten feet of open space, Avery crouched behind the woodpile. He had been moving so slowly that they hadn't been able to see him. It took discipline not to make a dash for it.

He looked up at the second floor and tried to figure out where the children might be. Was everybody asleep?

The porch door was closed. Probably locked. He would have to get in through the basement again.

Or maybe there was a better way. And he thought he had found it.

Something moved in the living room. A torso with a blond head crossed in front of the window. It was a rather massive head, and male. The one who was in bed with her.

No, it wasn't her. That had been his mistake. It was the other one, the sister.

The head disappeared through a door. He remembered that the kitchen was there. Probably their vantage point. It looked out toward the driveway and the road.

They were watching for him, but they hadn't seen him. No alarm had been raised. He left his shelter and started across the next patch of silvered earth.

Again Denise felt wide awake. "Did you hear something?"

"What?" Virgil looked in from the kitchen.

"I thought I heard something." She did not know whether she had been asleep or only dozing.

"Where?"

She waved him to be quiet, and listened. There were no more sounds.

"We'd better check," he said. "Where was it?"

"I'm not sure."

Her first thought was the children. But if she had heard anything, it probably came from the basement. She opened the door and listened.

It was silent, but she felt a draft. Was the window open? The one where he had climbed in before?

"Virgil . . ."

He was looking out of the kitchen window.

"What is it?" She asked.

"Just want to see if anything's going on out there."

"Is anything?"

"Doesn't seem to be. I can see their cars, but nothing's happening."

"Did we leave the basement window open?"

"He cut the screen, remember?" Virgil replied.

"Yes, but the glass part. Is it open?"

166

"We'll fix that." He took one of the dinette chairs and tried to brace it under the knob of the basement door.

Karen's voice wailed, "Mom-meee!"

Virgil abandoned the chair as Denise started up the stairs.

"Probably just a nightmare," he told her. "It's not too surprising."

"Mommy!" Karen came running, ghostly in the gray light. "Rodney's not in his bed."

"Where is he?"

Of course he was in the bathroom. Something like that.

"I had a dream that a man came in and took him out of his bed, and now he's not there!"

"He's gotta be here somewhere," Virgil said, dashing up the stairs behind Denise. They turned on a hall light and began their search, first in the bathroom. It was empty.

"Hey!" Virgil called from the children's room. He was by the window. The one that opened onto the porch roof. Denise noticed a faint, odd smell in the room, but quickly forgot it.

"Will you look at that?"

She looked. The screen was raised. When Virgil lowered it, she saw that a hole had been cut, large enough for a man to reach his hand through and unfasten it from the inside.

20

Crouching, Avie ran through the shadows. The child felt limp in his arms. He might have been dead. His own son.

He felt nothing, either for the child or the fact that he might be dead. He wondered what he was supposed to feel. No one had ever told him.

He set the boy down in a patch of weeds and readied his rifle. Even from there, he could hear Denise screaming.

Let her, he thought. Let her scream for her boy. It was all she cared about.

There was something unhealthy in that. He had tried to tell her, but she wouldn't listen. She never did. That was her trouble.

Somewhere, a twig cracked. Then silence.

He was fully alert. They talked about a person's hair rising. It really did. He leaned forward and gave the kid another whiff of chloroform.

Then a faint rustle. It had started moving again, whatever it was. Somewhere in front of him, he thought. It might have been an animal, but he doubted that.

He sat with his back against a tree trunk and his knees doubled. He rested the rifle on one knee, its barrel pointing ahead. Not that he could hit anything in the dark. For in spite of the moonlight, it was dark there in the woods.

Another branch snapped back. You couldn't walk quietly through the woods, especially at night. He wondered if they guessed where he was.

The kid breathed heavily. More chloroform. He kept the plastic bag over his hand like a tent, so the odor would not betray his presence.

There was another stealthy sound, a gentle crunching. Footsteps on dry leaves. Whatever it was would pass somewhere to his right. He aimed the rifle, pivoting it on his knee. When he thought he had the sound about right, he pulled the trigger.

As the explosion cleared from his ears, he could hear something crashing away through the underbrush. He hadn't expected to hit it, but at least he'd scared it off. Probably a cop. The only problem was, now they knew his exact location. He snatched up the boy and began moving away, as silently as possible. But there might be more . . .

The kid whimpered. "Mom-my."

"Shut up," Avery said, and covered its mouth with the chloroform-soaked cloth.

The child gagged and tried to push it away.

"Doesn't smell too good, does it?" He wondered if the boy remembered him at all. It had been almost a year. They were pretty stupid at that age.

He could make his move now and go out where the

169

cops were. But they would blind him with lights. Better to wait until morning, and until he had both kids.

He was so close to the house that he could see in the windows. This time they blazed with light. He saw people running back and forth.

He could hear her screaming.

Jill tried to comfort her. "It's his own child, for heaven's sake."

"You don't understand. He hated Rodney." She glanced at Karen, who sat on the sofa with a blanket pulled up to her mouth.

It didn't matter now that she knew. All illusions were gone.

His own child.

He would do anything to get back at her. It was *Medea* in reverse.

"I've got to find him," said Denise. "I have to."

Jill said, "You can't go out there."

"What do you expect me to do?"

Clumsily, Virgil patted her shoulder. "This can't go on forever. He's only one man. How long can he hold them off?"

"You've been saying that all day and all night!"

"Yes, but really."

Denise could not think practically. Instead, her mind echoed with what Virgil had just said.

Only one man.

Was he a man? She wondered what had happened to her, that she had stopped thinking of him as a mere man. He was full of failings, perhaps more than most people. But she had given him all that power over herself, her destiny.

She had done it. She had let him get away with it, because she was dependent, too.

"If I go out there . . ." she began.

170

"He'll kill you," said Jill. "And that won't help Rodney."

Denise paced the floor, clenching her hands. What would Avery do? Run off with him? Was he running already? She wondered how he could slip past the police.

"They'll shoot him. They don't know he's got Rodney."

"Well . . ." said Jill.

"We could try signaling," Virgil suggested. "Flash a lantern in code. Does anybody know the Morse code?"

Jill said, "It's in the dictionary. I saw it once."

"Where's the dic—"

Jill had already found it and was turning the pages. " 'International Morse Code.' We have to think up a message. 'Be careful. He took child prisoner.' Do you think they'll understand that?"

Denise said, "What if they don't know the Morse code?"

"Somebody will. Okay, hon?"

Virgil had a large, bright lantern, which he set on the windowsill above the sink.

"I'll start with a couple of SOS's to get their attention. At least I know that much."

He flashed the light. After a moment, an answering flash came from the road.

"They're reading us!"

Jill began to dictate the code.

Denise watched from the doorway. They were treating it like a game. But in all fairness, maybe they were glad to be doing something.

Jill screamed. Virgil jumped back as bits of plaster fell from the ceiling.

"Jee-e-e-ez!" Virgil exclaimed, crouching in front of the sink.

Jill knelt beside him. "Are you okay?"

"I'm fine. But I felt that. I felt it go right by my face."

"He's watching everything we do."

Denise turned away. "Why was I so stupid, leaving them alone in that room?"

Virgil stood up and helped Jill to her feet.

"For heaven's sake," Jill said peevishly. "Nobody thought he'd get into the house."

They had not been able to finish the message. "Be careful, he—" was as far as they had gotten.

"It might be enough." Jill put a cool hand on Denise's arm. "At least they'll know to be careful. Okay? He'll be all right."

"You don't know that!"

Jill withdrew her hand and stood listening.

"What is it?" asked Virgil.

"Maybe nothing."

"I wish you'd get to bed, hon. Get some rest."

"I can't leave Dee."

"I'll stay with her," he offered.

They didn't care about Rodney. Only her. Jill started up the stairs and then turned back. "I don't know if I want to be up there alone."

Karen still lay on the sofa with her eyes open. She seemed rigid.

Denise touched her lightly. "Why don't you move to the easy chair and let Jill lie down?"

Karen sat up. "Did a bullet come in here?"

"The kitchen ceiling. It didn't hurt anybody."

"Was it Daddy?"

"I don't know."

"What's he doing to Rodney?"

"Probably nothing. Maybe it's just . . . so he can get away safely."

Maybe. But she did not believe it was only that.

"How's he going to get away? I want Rodney, Mommy."

"So do I." Denise helped Karen into the chair and tucked the blanket around her. "Maybe when the sun comes up the police can do something."

"I don't want them to hurt Daddy!"

"Nothing's happening right now. Why don't you try to sleep, like Jill?"

"I very much doubt that I can," Jill said from the sofa.

"I'll be right here." Virgil settled into another chair with the rifle between his knees.

Denise sat on the floor next to Karen. She heard a breeze rustling the leaves of the apple trees.

And Rodney was out there, with that same breeze blowing through the ice-colored moonlight.

Or maybe he was already dead.

21

He seemed to watch himself from somewhere outside his body, as though Avie were a separate person.
He liked that name, Avie, but he didn't want to think
of *her*.

Pleased with his cleverness, he saw himself inching
toward the house again. This time he would have to go
through the basement. They would be watching that
upstairs window. They might even have locked it, or
the door to the room, and there was no other place
accessible from the porch roof.

So far, it had worked out pretty well. He could get
back and forth without anyone seeing him, in spite of
the moonlight. And oddly enough, they had not made
any attempt to escape—at least since Denise tried it that
morning. It showed he was doing something right. He
had them all scared. Right where he wanted them.

He slipped feet first through the basement window
and dropped to the floor. He used to wish he were a
tall man, big and imposing, but there were times when

that could be a disadvantage.

He crept up the stairs without making a sound. The door at the top was closed. He stuck his long knife under it and felt around to be sure the way was clear.

The knife touched something. It was solid, but not very wide. Probably a chair leg. He pushed it and it moved. They must have tried to brace the door but couldn't make the chair stay in place. It wasn't as easy as people thought.

Very slowly, he turned the knob. After a moment it made a clicking sound, and then a louder *proing*. He stopped and listened for voices. Either they were asleep or they hadn't heard him. He didn't see how they couldn't. Maybe they were lurking in ambush. The thought pricked him with a delicious fear and started his adrenaline coursing.

He waited. He had all night to wait. A minute or two later he turned the knob again. It clicked once more, but that was all. And then the door was open.

He pushed it far enough to reach his arm around the edge. The thing that blocked it was a chair, as he had thought, with metal legs and silent rubber feet. He caught its back and lifted it out of the way, then stepped into the hall.

So far, perfect. He took a moment to orient himself. There was a dining room between him and the living room, where they were, but he could see them. He saw the brother-in-law sprawled in a chair. Something against his knee gleamed faintly in the moonlight.

He saw what it was. He could see them all. He didn't think they were sleeping. There was something unquiet about the feel in the room.

Silently he withdrew into the kitchen. He remembered that there was a walk-in pantry. That would be a good place to wait for his chance.

"Mommy?"

Denise, resting her head on Karen's chair, looked up.

"I thought I heard something," Karen mumbled.

Virgil opened his eyes. "What did you hear?"

"I don't know. Just something."

"Where was it? Upstairs? Downstairs?"

"I don't know. I think it was . . . over there." She pointed toward the dining room.

"Maybe we should keep the lights on," Denise suggested.

"Then we'd be sitting ducks." Virgil picked up his gun and moved toward the dining room. As he reached around the doorway, Denise braced herself, waiting for the light to go on and reveal Avery.

"Hey," Virgil said.

Denise heard the switch clicking vainly, then tried the lamp beside Karen's chair.

"This one's off, too."

"He must have loosened the fuses again, or pulled the master switch." Virgil started through the dining room.

"Don't go down!"

He hesitated, looking back at her.

Jill sat up. "What's happening?"

"Lights are off," said Virgil.

"But they were on just a while ago."

"Could it be a power failure?" Denise ventured.

"On a night like this? It takes more than a little breeze to knock down the lines," Virgil said.

"Then he's in the basement."

Virgil pulled over the chair that stood crookedly by the basement door and braced it under the knob.

"May not be there now," he said, "but that's one way he's not getting in."

Denise stood at the window and looked out at the

woods. Was Rodney there? Or maybe in the basement with Avery.

She turned, feeling a shiver. He was there, in the basement. And the lights were off to lure someone down.

To see—what? Was Rodney alive? She took a step toward the door and stopped.

"Uh-uh," said Virgil, watching her.

"I have to find Rodney."

But even she knew better than to let herself be trapped.

A cold wind blew through the woods, and Rodney whimpered. He was freezing and afraid, because the night was full of monsters.

The man had tied him to a tree and told him not to move, or it would be "curtains." He couldn't move anyway, with his hands pulled around in back of him and in back of the tree. And he didn't see any curtains, or anything except cold, scratchy trees and bushes. Even his winter pajamas didn't keep him warm.

He cried, softly humming to himself. The man had said he would kill him if he made any noise, but he didn't think the man was there anymore. He had been alone for a long, long time.

He heard a noise that didn't sound like the wind. It was something walking. He huddled by the tree roots, trying to stop his crying.

Then he saw a light. He tried to make himself even smaller. They were probably from a spaceship, and they would take him away and never let him come back.

A voice called softly, "Anybody there?"

He thought he had heard the voice before, but he didn't answer. It was a spaceman. From outer space.

"Anybody—"

The voice stopped, and the walking stopped, and he knew the light was shining on him. He kept very still, too frightened now to cry. If he was quiet and didn't look at them, maybe they wouldn't see him. Maybe . . .

But the walking started again, moving quickly toward him. He felt something crouch down next to him. And then it touched his arm.

22

"I don't care, I have to do something."

"Don't be an idiot," said Jill. "Please?"

"You don't understand. We're talking about my *child*."

"What do you mean I don't? I'm almost a mother myself."

"It's not the same. You don't really see it as a person till it's born. And you don't know Avery. You don't know what he can—"

"I'm beginning to get an inkling, which is why I think you should stay right here."

"But Rodney—"

"*Do you hear me?*"

Jill wanted them together. All of them. It was safer that way, and more important to her than Rodney.

That was not fair. It was only that Jill could see how pointless it was to try to find him. Denise, drained and hopeless, collapsed into a chair.

"I always thought— He was so domineering. I thought— When somebody's like that, you think he's very strong."

"Hell," said Jill. "Strong people don't have to be like that. Don't you know?" She beamed at Virgil as he started out to the kitchen.

"He was scared," Denise went on. "All the time, he was so scared I'd leave him that he drove me away. And I never realized—"

Jill said, "I don't know why you didn't, the way he acted."

"Maybe I didn't want to. Maybe it was important for me to lean on him. And if I'd had more guts, and could have confronted him like an adult, maybe all those people would be alive."

"What people?"

"Harlan Reyes. I know he killed him. I know he saw us together. He turned on his headlights, and then he followed him home. And Norman Payson out there. And Rodney . . ."

"Mom-mee," wailed Karen.

"He's all right!" Jill said fiercely.

In the kitchen, Virgil gave a yelp of alarm. It was quickly muffled, and his rifle clattered to the floor.

Jill jumped up. "Virgil?"

There was silence. The two women looked at each other.

"Don't—" Denise began.

Jill whispered, "He can't be there. How would he get in? The door's locked."

Denise began to back, very slowly, toward the porch door. It was their only escape. But what if she was wrong, and he was outside, waiting?

Jill seemed to have frozen. Only her eyes moved, toward the kitchen, and then to Denise, questioning.

Wouldn't we hear something else? Denise wondered.

She tried to think. All the doors were locked. They would have seen anyone coming down the stairs. They had blocked the basement steps.

"No!" Denise whispered as Jill started toward the kitchen. Jill came back and clutched at her hand.

"Mommy?" said Karen in a faint whimper.

"Sssh."

Again they were silent. They heard Virgil moan.

Jill raced to the kitchen, and when Denise and Karen followed, a man in a black mask stood pointing a rifle at them all.

23

Rodney shrank from the spaceman's touch. He kept
his eyes closed and sat very still, wishing the spacemen
would go away. Wishing the light would go out, so they
couldn't see him.

"What's all this?" asked the voice, almost in his ear.
"What's he got rigged up here?"

Rodney felt a pull on the wire. It made him remember what the man had said when he tied him up. Something about curtains if he moved. Now they were making him move.

"Want to go home," he murmured, in case they really
didn't know that he belonged somewhere. But of course
they knew, and they would take him to their spaceship
anyway, and he would never see his mother, or Karen,
or Wade, or his toy cars, or that castle in the park . . .

"Hold still, kid," said the spaceman. "One false move
and you're pie in the sky."

He knew it. He knew they meant to take him away
as soon as they untied the wires.

"I want the man," Rodney choked out. "I want the man to come back." And he began to cry with great big sobs that shook his whole body.

A cloud passed over the moon. For a moment Denise couldn't see the others, who were tied up as she was, but they were gagged. Both of them. Jill moaned, whimpering with inarticulate protests.

"She's seven months pregnant," Denise said. "Can't you be a little careful?"

Her warning had a feeble sound. She was back where she had always been. Her one thought was to keep him from getting angrier.

Again the kitchen filled with silver light. She could see Jill and Virgil bundled on the floor like bales of cloth. Jill was trying to move her hands. He had tied her too tightly.

Denise saw him reach toward Karen. When Karen didn't move, he seized her arm and dragged her out through the door.

Not her, too.

"Avery!"

A moment later she heard his voice. It was some distance away, his trained theatrical tones projected out toward the highway.

She tried to stand, to see what was happening. She could not brace her feet.

The words were indistinct. She caught only a few. She heard him say "children." And something about "wired with explosives."

The house. She looked over at Jill, whose head was turned toward the door.

He had wired the house with explosives. To force them into letting him take the children. She managed to rise to her knees.

The door opened, and he came in with Karen.

Denise cowered as he raised his foot. He kicked her back down to the floor.

Karen said, "Don't do that to Mommy!"

He slapped Karen's face, making her head snap to one side.

Again Denise struggled to rise.

"Listen, you don't really want them. They'll only slow you down. Why don't you just kill me? And if the house is wired with explosives, they'll let you get away."

Jill shook her head violently.

"They would," said Denise. "But first they'll make sure the rest of you are alive."

Jill shook her head again and mumbled something. Denise could not understand. Was it because she had offered to die? But that was better than all of them dying. Better than letting him have the children.

"Avery?"

He whipped off the mask, then folded his arms and leaned back against the counter. He was smiling—that twisted little smirk that she hated so much.

At the edge of the woods, a figure in a black jacket and dark blue jeans stood surveying the distance to the house.

Thirty yards?

About that. Thirty yards of bare moonlight. And there was no telling whether someone might be watching. He would have to take a chance.

No, there was a better way. It would be a little longer, and there wasn't much time, but it seemed like more of a sure thing. He would have to get out to the road, somehow past the police, and go in among those apple trees.

He froze as a voice blasted through an amplifier.

184

"Mister? You there with the kid. We've got a telephone here, if you'll come out and bring it in. It's a direct hookup to the police. You can use it if you have anything to say."

He waited to see if there might be an answer.

There wasn't. Sometimes it worked, if the hostage-taker was confused and frightened. But this dude was as cool as ice. They would never talk him out of it.

"Please?" she begged. "It's silly to throw it all away, your whole life, just to get back at me."

She might as well have been talking to the air in the room.

"Avery, listen. This is no way to get known. You could still have what you always wanted."

He had already killed; it was too late for him. But she tried to keep the doubt out of her voice.

"You could get away and you'd still have a chance, but if you blow us all up—"

Jill stared at her fixedly over the top of her gag and shook her head. Trying to tell her something.

Had she been wrong about the house? He had said something was wired with explosives, and what else—

"Jill?"

Denise glanced at Avery to see if he was listening. He was standing at the door, looking out.

"It wasn't the house?"

Another shake of the head.

"Then what? It's not—"

Jill nodded, slowly and significantly.

"Oh, my *God*."

"Mommy?" said Karen, who had seemed in a trance until then.

Avery took her arm in one hand, his rifle in the other, and pulled her toward the door.

Karen called over her shoulder, "Mommy, it's Rodney. He made it so if they don't let us go, Rodney's going to die."

The moon was still high and bright, but at least the apple trees made shadows. The man in the black jacket decided to take a chance. If he moved slowly enough, he would be just another shadow. With the utmost care, he left the shelter of one tree and edged his way toward the next.

Good thing it was summer, and they were in leaf. He wished he had thought of this sooner, but he really didn't know the setup at all. He wasn't even sure how to get into the house.

He heard a voice faintly in the breeze. It sounded like a child. "No, no, don't!"

He stood still. He was between two trees, and there was no way to move without being seen.

He tried to figure out where the voice had come from. It sounded near the house, but that side was in deep shadow, and he could see nothing.

Then he caught a glimpse of something light. It seemed to float above the ground. Perhaps a white shirt or blouse.

"Don't!" the voice cried again. The white thing jerked, and he knew the child was in trouble. He crouched down and rushed forward as silently as possible.

Something struck his shoulder and spun him backward. He thought he had run into a tree. Then he felt it burning, and knew he was shot.

His legs stopped moving. He stumbled and fell.

His head whirled, and he lost his sense of direction. He was drowning in a deep black sea . . .

Denise heard the gunfire. "Oh, my God, Karen!"

Both children. Both. He couldn't . . .

She fell back against the cabinets. Now it didn't matter. Nothing mattered anymore.

The screen door opened. She did not look at him. She only remembered her silly idea that after they were born, he might love them.

"Mommy."

Karen's voice. Karen stood above her in the moonlight, her face shadowed.

"Mommy, there was somebody running through the apple trees, and he shot them and they fell down."

The police. Trying to reach the house. It was no use; he could patrol all around it. But Karen was alive.

"Honey, come and sit with me."

"Get over here!" It was the first time he had spoken.

Dragging her feet and hanging her head, Karen went to stand next to her father.

Denise felt a flicker of hope. Maybe he did not mean to kill them. He would not be exactly good to them, but if they were alive, then sometime after they grew up . . .

In the fading moonlight, she watched him lash Karen's wrists together and heard her cry out, "It hurts!"

Then he left for another tour of the house and grounds.

He was lying with his face in wet grass. Wet and cold. He felt the moisture seeping through his black jacket, and pushed himself to his knees.

Gently he probed his shoulder. All around it, the jacket was sticky with blood. There was a slug, all right, and the thought of its being embedded in his flesh made him queasy. He tried to stand, but could not stay on his feet.

The police amplifier blasted.

"Mister? Mister Burns?"

How did they know? he wondered.

"Mr. Burns, there's a dead officer out here, and several wounded. You have a kid endangered in the woods, and some people held hostage there in the house."

He was glad they had not forgotten the kid in the woods.

"How many murder counts do you want against you,

188

Burns? Come on out, before it gets worse. Maybe we can make a deal."

What deal? he wondered grimly. Burns was too smart to buy that kind of garbage.

Creeping along, he remembered all that had gone on just before he fell. He remembered the kid crying "No, don't." What had happened to her?

He thought it seemed darker now, or maybe he was blacking out again. He pulled himself through the dew, soaking his clothes.

It was taking hours. At least it felt like hours. His arm had gone numb. The bullet could have hit a nerve. He thought it was just a shoulder wound. What was he going to do? Thank God it was his left shoulder, for he was right-handed.

Suddenly he became aware that he was not alone. There was something out there. Something human.

He flattened himself on the ground, but it was too late. He felt, rather than saw, the figure standing over him. He sensed the gun being raised and pointed at his head. He closed his eyes and braced himself, clenching his teeth.

All this, he thought, for nothing.

Again Denise heard the gun being fired.

But it was not a gun. It shook the whole house.

She waited for aftershocks. For a secondary roll of thunder. It was thunder.

"It's thunder," she said aloud, seeing Virgil raise his head and Jill turn to look at her with huge, shocked eyes.

And then she knew.

Karen leaned against her. "Mommy, it hurts."

It hurts. Rodney.

189

She mustn't think of it. Think only of Karen, who still had a chance.

"Honey, do you know that rack over there? Can you go over and reach in backward and get me a knife?"

"I can't. He tied up my hands."

"Yes, I know. Do the best you can. Don't get one that's too long."

Don't think of Rodney.

"Why? What are you going to do?"

"I'm going to try to cut this rope."

Karen groped, whimpering, and muttered, "Ouch." Finally, she brought a fillet knife.

"What will you do if he comes back?" she asked.

"I'll push it under the refrigerator."

Karen snuggled next to her. "What was that noise?"

"It was thunder."

"But there isn't any rain. Mommy, I'm scared."

"We'll manage."

Denise could barely move her hands. The strain of trying to get the knife into place made her sick and faint.

"What's explosives?"

"Karen . . . Please."

At last she managed to insert the point under one of her bonds. She tried to get a grip on the blade.

"Do you mean it's something that explodes?" Karen asked.

"Don't talk about it, honey. Don't think about it."

Denise sawed at the ropes. It would take all night, and more.

"Is Rodney dead?"

"He's all right."

Don't think about him. Not now.

Jill gave a low moan and doubled over.

"What is it? Your hands?" He had tied them all so tightly. Denise kept working at her ropes.

"Mm-mm," groaned Jill.

"It's not— It can't be."

Virgil, who had been hunched apathetically, shot upright.

"It can't be," Denise said again. It was two months early. She could barely see the clock. Then she realized it had been stopped anyway when Avery pulled the fuse. They would have to time the contractions by counting.

Jill sat up, testing herself, and blinking in surprise.

Denise said, "Maybe it's just an isolated cramp."

She remembered being pregnant with Rodney. It almost made her give up. She thought of Karen instead, and struggled furiously to cut her rope.

It was hopeless. She couldn't move.

And then Avery was back. She barely had time to slip the knife out of her hand and cover it with her body.

Jill gave another cry.

"Avery, you've got to untie her! She's having her baby!"

He stepped over Denise's legs and went to look out of the window.

So close to her. If she leaned a few more inches to her left, she could touch him.

But he was not paying attention to her. He wouldn't, since she had told him about Jill. She thought of the torture Jill would have to endure before she died.

Slipping the knife out from under her hip, she backed up to the refrigerator and continued cutting. Taking a chance, since he wasn't watching. And it was dark. If she could get through one strand . . . Just one . . .

Jill rolled on the floor, groaning. Virgil fought to pull his arms free, mumbling through his gag. Avery left the window, and Jill cried again.

"Avery!" Denise called as his footsteps padded away through the dining room.

She looked at Jill, who had turned to watch him leave. It occurred to her that Jill's cramps were much too fast for early labor. Especially the first time.

"You okay?" she asked. Jill nodded.

It hadn't worked. Nothing would work, she realized. Avery had no pity. He had killed his own child.

"The only person he ever cared about," she said, "is himself. And he really hates himself, so you can imagine—"

Suddenly her hand broke free. She brought it around and looked at it, pale and barely visible in the darkness.

"Karen, get over by the door and tell me when he's coming back."

Denise hacked at the ropes tying her feet. In her frantic haste, she accomplished nothing. She tried to work with more purpose, holding the knife at an angle and cutting deftly.

"He's coming!"

She hid the knife and wound the rope loosely about her ankles just as he entered the kitchen.

She sat staring at the floor, feeling her heart pound. He would certainly hear it. He would know.

One kid left, thought Avie. He gazed out of the window to keep from looking at the people in the room.

One kid. The stupid boy had blown himself to pieces. Or maybe somebody found him there and tried to get him free, and they both went up.

A police voice thundered through the darkness.

"Mr. Burns? Listen to me. In another hour, the moon will be setting. We can move in then. You want to go easy on yourself, come out now."

Go easy on himself? Did they think he was stupid?

What did they plan to do when the moon went down? He would still be able to see them.

Or would he? He had been thinking of the driveway, but they could come in from any side.

He wondered if they were all over the woods. Probably, by now, but he would have to take a chance. There were no other places he could hide, especially while trying to keep the girl hidden. For a moment he thought of taking them all with him, but that would be unwieldy. He could shoot them right now.

His eyes traveled over the husband and the sister. Maybe it was better to make them all suffer. He might threaten to come back for the sister's kid sometime, and they would know he could do it.

He looked down at Denise. She sat motionless at his feet, her head bowed. Did she know her precious boy was dead? Had she figured that out? She would when they found what was left, if anything. When daylight came.

He put out his toe and prodded her hands. She gave a little gasp and rolled to one side. He thought he heard a sound, a faint clatter. He pushed again.

"Mr. Burns?" bellowed the voice. "We're going to give you five, Mr. Burns. Five minutes to get out here and give yourself up. We've got reinforcements now, and we can move in any time. You've got a five-minute grace period, Mr. Burns."

What reinforcements? They were bluffing. He hadn't seen anything happen out there.

But he couldn't count on it. He slipped the mask back over his face, grabbed the kid by her hair, and pulled

193

her, stumbling, after him, out the door and toward the woods. Behind him, Denise gave an anguished cry.

"Say good-bye to your mom," he told the girl. " 'Cause you aren't going to live to see the sun rise."

That was really all that mattered. Let them take him, as long as the kids were dead. Then he could enjoy Denise's suffering for the rest of his life, even if he spent it in prison.

"Virgil, help me!" Swiftly Denise cut through the ropes that bound his arms and legs. He could take off the gag himself. With the knife still in her hand, she scrambled toward the door.

"Wait!" he called.

He was trying to untie Jill.

"Virgil! Help me get Karen!"

He looked up, his face a blob in the moonlight, and reached for a knife from the rack. She couldn't wait for him.

Outside, she scanned the darkness. Karen wore a white shirt. She ought to have been visible, but there was nothing.

At the end of the concrete walk, Denise remembered the telephone the police had put there. She wished she had a flashlight, but it too late to go back. She began to grope, trying to remember where the voice had come from when the officer brought the phone.

Something pale caught her eye, near the small embankment that led up to the woods. At the same time, she heard a faint voice: "Daddy, Rodney isn't dead, is he?"

Karen— oblique, as always. *Are you going to kill me, too?*

Denise hurried toward them. He had a gun, but could he see her? She looked down at her clothes, still the stained green outfit from that morning. She tried to run silently. He did not know she was free of her bonds.

A cloud scudded over the moon, blacking it out. She continued toward the woods, glad of concealment. She knew every inch of that land.

Somewhere far in back of her, she heard Virgil call, "Dee, where are you?"

She dared not speak and give herself away. She would have to do without him.

The moon reappeared. She had reached the edge of the woods, but could see nothing. Sickly she remembered what had happened in the woods. Would she stumble across it? *Oh, Rodney.* Her heart seemed to rise up and break, and she made a small, involuntary sound.

Something moved through the brush nearby. She froze.

She had done it. Betrayed herself. She tried to keep silent, but she had been running, and her breathing was hard.

Another sound. Closer, this time. She backed against a tree and held her breath, choking on the heaving of her lungs.

He was there. She could feel him. His fingers brushed across her arm.

She tried to move away. He grabbed her wrist, pulled her toward him, and clamped his other hand over her mouth. She gave a frightened, muffled cry.

196

The hand slipped from her face. "Denise!"

"Who—" Something about that voice. She couldn't think.

"Cliff? Are you Cliff?"

"That's me. Where did he go?"

"I don't know. He has Karen."

"What's that in your hand?"

"A knife. I've got to help Karen."

He stumbled beside her. He, too, was breathing hard. She wondered vaguely how he had gotten there. But, of course, this was even better than Harlan's death for his newspaper. Her children. Oh, God, her children.

Cliff whispered between gasps for breath, "He's probably headed that way, toward the police. He'll use her to try to get away."

"He's going to kill her. He killed Rodney."

"No . . . he didn't."

"He did. The explosion."

"I got Rodney out of there and reset the charges. Glad I did. It saved my life."

"Rodney's alive?"

"He's fine."

The words were wheezed. He seemed to be in pain. But Rodney—

He stopped, holding her back, and again put his hand to her mouth. She could hear other sounds. She thought she heard a voice. Someone walking, rustling through the leaves.

A light snapped on in Cliff's hand. A flashlight beam, dancing over the trees. It caught two figures and went out. Cliff pushed her, and they both stumbled as Avery fired at where the light had been.

She managed to scream, "Karen, run!"

Cliff rolled her over, and they hit a rock. There were more shots. "Karen!" Denise wept. "Karen."

The woods crackled with gunfire. There were lights.

197

And people. And then a policeman stood over them.

"We got him. The kid's okay."

"Karen?" she asked fearfully. It would be Avery's last desperate act, to kill Karen as she tried to run from him.

"Both kids." The officer reached out a hand to help her up.

Cliff did not move.

"He's hurt," she said, and remembered Karen talking about a man who was shot as he came through the apple trees.

He couldn't be dead. After all he had done. Tried to help her.

Even for a story.

They were back at the house. Someone had fixed the fuse, and the lights were on once more. Nervously, Denise looked toward the window. It was still hard to believe that the eyes were not out there, watching her.

Karen, resting against her, asked, "Is he dead, Mommy?"

"I'm afraid so."

"No, I'm not," said Rodney sleepily.

"Mommy, *you* know who I mean."

A waste of life. A sad, failed life. Was Karen sorry because he was her father, or glad that the danger was gone? She would have to help them work it through, but not now. They were all too tired.

"He's at peace," said Jill from her corner of the sofa, next to Karen.

"You could put it that way," Denise agreed, but it still hurt. All of it.

She looked over at Cliff, resting in the easy chair, his

shoulder bandaged. He had come all that way, risked danger and death, not for a story, but for her.

Virgil came in from the kitchen, where the police had been taking their statements.

"Payson's alive," he told them. "He nearly got heat stroke from the car, but he's alive. They took him to the hospital."

"Oh, thank God," said Jill.

"But one of the cops got it."

"And the girl in Los Angeles," muttered Cliff.

"Trish?" asked Denise, in shock. "His girl?"

"Looks that way. There was blood on the kitchen floor."

"Oh, my God."

It was so close. It might have happened to her.

"And *I* almost got it," said Karen. "And Rodney. And Mr. O'Donnell."

"How come you knew what to do when . . . when you found Rodney?" asked Denise.

"Uncle Sam," said Cliff. "It was a tough course, but I passed."

Virgil asked, "How come you didn't just dismantle it?"

"I don't know. Some vague idea about letting him think he succeeded. It must have been my guardian angel talking. He was about to give me the coup de grace when the lid blew off, and he ran. It probably startled him, because it was sooner than he expected."

"I can't believe he's dead," said Karen.

Denise held her closer and patted her shoulder. "That always happens when somebody dies. It takes time."

I didn't believe Rodney was dead, and he wasn't.

"Jill, I don't know what to say. Bringing all this on

you. And Virgil. And even my kids. I just . . . didn't know."

"I guess not," Jill agreed, somewhat reluctantly. "How could you, really?"

"Maybe I kidded myself. I don't know. But I'm really sorry. And there's another thing. Cliff? I'm sorry I didn't trust you. From now on, I will. I promise."

A slow smile brightened his face. "You couldn't have known that either. I must have been pretty obnoxious. It's my *Bulletin* training. I'll try to get over it. But I like that phrase you used."

"Which one?"

" 'From now on.' I like that."

"I'm glad."

She did not say more. Too many people were around, and Jill was beaming at her foolishly over Karen's head.

But once they were back in the city, there would be plenty of time to get to know him better.

Twayne's English Authors Series

EDITOR OF THIS VOLUME

Kinley E. Roby

Northeastern University

James Bridie

SO-CUD-289

TEAS 293

James Bridie

JAMES BRIDIE

(Osborne Henry Mavor)

By TERENCE TOBIN

TWAYNE PUBLISHERS

A DIVISION OF G. K. HALL & CO., BOSTON

Published in 1980 by Twayne Publishers,
A Division of G. K. Hall & Co.

Printed on permanent/durable acid-free paper and bound
in the United States of America

First Printing

Frontispiece photo of James Bridie,
courtesy the Hulton Press, London.

Library of Congress Cataloging in Publication Data
Tobin, Terence, 1938–
James Bridie (Osborne Henry Mavor)

(Twayne's English authors series ; TEAS 293)
Bibliography: p. 170–178
Includes index.
1. Mavor, Osborne Henry, 1888–1951 —
Criticism and interpretation.
PR6025.A885Z89   822′.912   79-27828
ISBN 0-8057-6786-X

12.50

3-31-81

For
Violet

Contents

About the Author

Terence Tobin has published numerous articles on Scottish dramatic writing and theater history. He edited *The Assembly* by Archibald Pitcairn (1972) and *Letters of George Ade* (1973). *Plays by Scots 1660–1800* appeared in 1974 and "Plays by Scots 1800–1850" is to be published.

Preface

Osborne Henry Mavor, a Glasgow doctor, who took the pen name, James Bridie, is one of the leading dramatists of the twentieth century. He wrote more than forty plays, which have entertained generations of British audiences: *The Anatomist, A Sleeping Clergyman, Tobias and the Angel,* and other works are revived continually. *The Queen's Comedy* and *The Baikie Charivari* are masterpieces, which have not been recognized, because they are modern plays. Had they been written in Shakespeare's time, they would be accorded universal public acclaimation. Bridie also wrote autobiographies, essays, children's books, and newspaper columns. Despite his prolific work, which shows a distinctive sense of humor as well as profound thought on God and man, this writer has received less critical attention than he deserves.

This study is a consideration of the Scots writer's multifaceted output. Study of his plays, some briefly, others in more extended fashion, has been made in a critical textual manner. Analysis of characteristic aspects aids in grasping the elements which make Bridie distinctive, and on occasion, unique. Historical lights necessary to illumine the works, the author, and his period have been included. Text plus background, as Ronald S. Crane observed, puts literary works in a broad-based perspective, that helps students gain detailed and panoramic insights.

The arrangement of chapters is designed to show specific aspects of Bridie's interests. Each section is arranged chronologically to show the author's maturation. The divisions for discussion of his writings are arbitrary in the sense that a miracle play may be treated as a satire of the estates. The spirit of the playwright, who detested compartitionism, has guided the arrangement. Selected minor writings exhibit the scope and variety of James Bridie. His drawings also aid in understanding the author's thought.

Bridie could make people laugh. He could make them think. He used this rare combination of abilities to lead men to find the Truth within.

TERENCE TOBIN

Acknowledgments

To Rona Locke Bremner Mavor, and Ronald and Sigrid Mavor I am deeply grateful for the hospitality they extended and the information they shared. Grants from the Penrose Fund of the American Philosophical Society made research in Scotland possible. For permission to quote from unpublished works I wish to thank the Mavor family. Permission to quote from published works was granted by Curtis Brown Ltd.

Barbara Sherman typed the manuscript with skill that makes reading one's copy a pleasure.

Staffs in Scottish and American libraries, namely, the Mitchell Library, Glasgow; the National Library of Scotland, Edinburgh; the Newberry Library, Chicago; and the University of Glasgow Library have labored in my behalf.

Many people are always involved in the production of a book. To all who helped: "Here's tae you. . . ."

Chronology

1888   Born in Glasgow, Scotland, January 3.
1913   Graduated from Glasgow University, M.B., Ch.B.
1923   Married Rona Locke Bremner.
1926   *Some Talk of Alexander.*
1928   *The Sunlight Sonata* first staged.
1929   *The Switchback; What It Is to Be Young.*
1930   *The Anatomist; Tobias and the Angel; The Girl Who Did Not Want to Go to Kuala Lumpur.*
1931   *The Dancing Bear.*
1932   *Tobias and the Angel; Jonah and the Whale; The Amazed Evangelist.*
1933   *A Sleeping Clergyman.*
1934   *Marriage Is No Joke; Colonel Wotherspoon; Mary Read* (with Claud Gurney); *Mr. Bridie's Alphabet for Little Glasgow Highbrows.*
1936   *Storm in a Teacup.*
1937   *Susannah and the Elders.*
1938   *The King of Nowhere; Babes in the Wood; The Last Trump.*
1939   *The Golden Legend of Shults; What Say They? One Way of Living.*
1942   *The Dragon and the Dove; A Change for the Worse; Jonah 3; Holy Isle.*
1943   *Mr. Bolfry.*
1944   *It Depends What You Mean; The Forrigan Reel; Tedious and Brief.*
1945   *Lancelot; The British Drama.*
1947   *Dr. Angelus; John Knox.*
1948   "Gog and Magog".
1949   *Daphne Laureola; A Small Stir; Letters on the English* (with Moray McLaren).
1950   *Mr. Gillie; The Queen's Comedy.*
1951   Died January 29.
1952   *The Baikie Charivari.*
1954   *Meeting at Night* (revised by Archibald Batty).

CHAPTER 1

Prologue

THE drama in Scotland as in other countries of Western Europe emerged from ancient pagan rites. Remnants of these rituals were adapted by Christians. The extant information about these early folk entertainments comes mainly from ecclesiastical edicts suppressing the festivities.

Medieval religious ceremonies developed into plays of a more literary character, such as representations of St. George and Robin Hood. *Guisards,* or players who performed on various holidays, were familiar figures in sixteenth-century Scotland. They danced, sang, played bones and bells, masked and donned costumes. Mock King ceremonies, May plays, and feasts presided over by Fools were popular Scots entertainments.[1]

The figure of the Fool is central in the earliest known Scottish dramatic records. He, who functions as destroyer of old order and overseer of new confusion,[2] gave way to craft guild dramatizations of Bible stories and lives of the saints. Of the sixteenth-century theatrical presentations inspired by the new Protestant religious thought, Sir David Lyndsay's *Ane Pleasant Satyre of the Thrie Estaitis, in Commendatioun of Vertew and Vituperatioun of Vyce* is the best known. The fearless attack upon abuses which incorporates pawky humor and satire is a dominant characteristic of Scots literature.

It is likely that other Scots wrote plays during the Reformation era, in addition to those authors whose works are recorded, but many manuscripts were destroyed during the religio-political frenzy. Under puritanism, which lasted for centuries in Scotland, drama was held in disrepute. By the seventeenth century drama was a court appendage rather than a popular entertainment.

There is no definite indication that a play by a Northerner was staged until after Charles II ascended the throne. In 1663 William Clerke's *Marciano, or the Discovery* was presented in

15

Edinburgh. In his preface, Clerke compares the position of the drama in his native land to that of a "City swaggerer in a Country-church." Thomas St. Serf (Sydserf) wrote *Tarugo's Wiles, or the Coffee-House,* which opened in London in 1667. This comedy is an imitation of the fare that entertained England during the Restoration era. St. Serf is the first Scot to obtain a London premiere. His play marks the beginning of Northern dramatists' seeking English rather than Scottish presentations. Playwrights endeavored to gain recognition in the South throughout the eighteenth century, when modern commercial theater developed. Because the position of the drama in the North remained precarious for generations, Scots had to seek fame abroad. They followed English models; this militated against the development of a distinctive Scottish drama.[3]

Although Scots produced hundreds of plays during the 1700s, most of these efforts are British in form and feeling. Those who struck out in new directions achieved greatest success. Allan Ramsay published *The Gentle Shepherd* (1725). This comedy was the most popular pastoral on the eighteenth-century British stage and spawned numerous imitations. As a result romantic adventures of rustics who speak dialect became the popular estimation of the Scottish play. Robert Heron, who wrote *St. Kilda in Edinburgh* (1798), strove to transcend this confining stereotype, but he did not succeed in his early attempt to devise a national drama.

By the end of the eighteenth century the Scottish language had ceased to be used for intellectual expression. It was chiefly a spoken tongue, variously transcribed. Playwrights who used Scots fashioned intentionally quaint products. Their striving to be provincial may be the result of disappointed nationalism. It is more likely that the humorous, mocking, and homely dialect dramas, which evoke superiority of rural virtues, are manifestations of the romantic fantasy of the peasant.

Writers of serious drama wrote in English. The choice of language was necessary if their work was to gain general acceptance. Traditional qualities of Scots expression, personal and direct statements simply put forth to convey character, were foregone by playwrights who exerted the greatest influence. James Thomson's plays entered the repertory because of the romantic elements he inserted. His most famous tragedy.

Tancred and Sigismunda (1745), pointed the direction neoclassical tragedy was to take. John Home's *Douglas* (1757), proved that Scottish national material could succeed on the stage. Harold William Thomson has called Home's best remembered play the "Scottish Declaration of Literary Independence," because the tragedy, based on a Scottish ballad, first produced in the North, won all Britain by its merit.[4]

The sense of national achievement and the success Home experienced with *Douglas* inspired playwrights to create dramas on national subjects. Many of these were poetic exercises included in a volume of *Miscellanies*.

In 1792 the Theatre Royal in Glasgow opened. This first permanent playhouse outside Edinburgh signaled the development of theatrical circuits. During the 1800s dramas were presented in a number of Scottish towns on a regular basis for the first time since the Reformation.[5]

In the early nineteenth century the chief spokesman for glorification of Scotland's past was Sir Walter Scott. *Guy Mannering, Rob Roy,* and other novels were adapted for the stage and achieved popularity as dramas.

Despite the retarded development of the theater, interest in national drama persisted. Robert Louis Stevenson drew a portrait of one of his country's most notorious characters in *Deacon Brodie* (1880). It was James Barrie who combined the sentimentality and impishness, for which Scottish writing is noted, with competent craftsmanship to establish himself as the most significant dramatic contributor since John Home. *The Little Minister* (1897), *Peter Pan* (1904), and *Mary Rose* (1920), are examples of plays which show his varied capabilities. As had most of the better Scots dramatists who preceded him, Barrie sought recognition in London. Abrogation of the theater as "the de'il's wark" persisted well into the twentieth century in Scotland.

A decade after William Butler Yeats and Lady Augusta Gregory started the movement which would produce Dublin's Abbey Theatre, the Glasgow Repertory Theatre began in 1909. During the five seasons of operation this group, under the direction of Alfred Wareing, produced several Scottish plays. The best of these was John Ferguson's one act tragedy, *Campbell of Kilmhor*. The troupe expressed its intention in a prospectus.

They wished to cultivate "a purely Scottish drama by the production of plays national in character, written by Scottish men and women of letters." This company was forced to disband because of World War I. Its work was sufficiently impressive to inspire the St. Andrew's Society to launch the Scottish National Players in 1921. During the fifteen years of its activity this group fostered productions of native dramatists. They presented Scottish life from varied perspectives as created by over thirty Scottish playwrights whose works premiered at the Athenaeum Theatre in Glasgow. They mounted productions of plays by John Brandane, Joe Corrie, Neil Gunn, Robins Millar, and James Bridie. The last named writer was destined to make the outstanding contribution to the stage.

Bridie endured the difficulties inherent in presenting plays in a country notoriously suspicious of the theater. The playwright who succeeded in Glasgow and in London was familiar with his nation's drama. In his choice of genres, topics, characters, and diction he followed many Scots traditions. It is his distinctive treatment of the matter of Scotland that made him a contributor to rather than an inheritor of tradition. Bridie was individualistic in method. In this he may be said to follow the best in traditional Scottish thought. In using his own lights Bridie produced works of striking originality, which are replete with conflicts that arise from the writer's search for an acceptable epistemology.

J. B. Priestley wrote a tribute to his friend and fellow playwright in the Citizens' Theatre program (1956). It is an accurate assessment of James Bridie's position in literature. "First, in terms of the World Theatre, that of all the nations, he still seems the most undervalued dramatist of his stature known to me. . . . Secondly, he must be included in any short list of the English-speaking Theatre's leading dramatists of the century. . . . Thirdly, he is Scotland's best dramatist."

CHAPTER 2

Enter Osborne Henry Mavor

JAMES Bridie wrote plays which were performed in the Gorbals, Glasgow's worst slum. Like the "common auld workin' chap" of the song, the chief contributor to the Citizens' Theater belonged to Glasgow. Bridie exuded the spirit of his home city and possessed a sense of romance and fantasy which those born north of the Grampion Hills have in abundance. These qualities frequently have been linked to Scots sentimentality. Bridie's intelligence enabled him to transcend the excess of feelings. He was not given to emotional pyrotechniques on or off stage. The writer who labeled sentimentality cruel and self-indulgent liked to mask as the Puck of modern British drama.

To illustrate the method Bridie used to confound the Scottish stereotype in his life and works, one might use a newspaper from the day of his birth. On January 3, 1888, Queen Victoria was preparing a speech for the opening of Parliament in which she would recommend further development of the Land Act of 1870 "in a manner comfortable to the special wants of Ireland." Henry Irving and Ellen Terry were entertaining London audiences in Shakespearean revivals. The English steamer *Herelda* ran into the Spanish ship *Leon*.

The political story couched in diplomatic euphemism to hide serious implication takes place the same day crowds are entertained by genteel cuttings of the bard. An accident at sea calls into question man's ordering of the world. How can one make sense out of these disparate incidents, which are related by time, and should therefore tell us something of the day on which Osborne Henry Mavor was born. Such questioning would lead Bridie to regard the world as a sphere of glorious variety, and, by turns, "an eel pit."

Shortly after Osborne was born at Pollockshields, Henry A. and Janet Osborne Mavor moved to East Kilbride near Glasgow.[1]

19

They reared three sons in a prosperous Victorian household. Henry Mavor was a talented engineer, who founded the first electric lighting plant in Scotland and invented electric devices.[2] Mavor earned his comfortable living in Glasgow, the second city in the United Kingdom.

Glasgow, the town reputedly founded by Mongah, or St. Mungo, in 560 on the banks of the Clyde was noted for steel, iron, and chimneys by the late 1800s. From George Square to the shipyards Glasgow was gray. In 1883 the authors of *Picturesque Scotland* apologized for the city's lingering smoke, few trees, and heterogeneous crowds. Londoners stayed in their proper neighborhoods and suburbs. Glaswegians, affluent and destitute alike, mixed in a cosmopolitan hodge podge.[3] Jacobite longings for a regal and independent past were suitable for towns that looked like steel engravings. Glasgow had little time for poetic memories. Its financial moorings were anchored in reality.

Henry Mavor was as practical as his neighbors. He had wanted to be a doctor, but had been forced to drop out of medical school because he lacked money. Osborne's father, who resorted to engineering as a second choice, also possessed writing talent and artistic ability. He fostered his son's interest in creative endeavors, as he would later encourage the boy to study medicine. Osborne wrote his first play, "King Robert the Bruce," when he was four years old. His father took him on excursions to the Glasgow Art Club. The boy met Macaulay Stevenson, the artist, at an age when his contemporaries were learning cricket.

As with many offspring of successful parents, Osborne was shy. Dr. J. C. Scott, one of his school masters at Glasgow Academy, recalled the lad being lazy, frail, and not very popular. His teacher admitted that his stature increased after Osborne combined his writing and cartooning talents to create *The Kernel*, a school lampoon, which shows that, by 1895, the pasty-faced boy with glasses had learned that entertaining others provided *entrée* to acceptance. Mavor wrote and illustrated "Peter/ A Tale of the Boer War/ of Robin Thrush" for his *Kernel* at thirteen.

None of us thought much of Peter. He was a cracked half witted fellow at the best and seldom, or never entered our company. There were seven of us up in the most desolated part of Rhodesia cattle farming.

There were, Simon P. Lincoln, Sandy Scott, Patrick McShane, Dick Anson, our chief, John Saunders, Esquire, or Babs, and your humble servant Bob Thrush or the Microbe (John and I were called Babs and Microbe on account of my being 6 foot 2″ and Tom 6 foot 4.). Babs was a very giant in strength and stature. I saw him once seize a charging bull by the horns and fling it on its haunches. . . .

Mavor edited *The Tomahawk*, another underground school magazine, which Dr. Temple the rector of the academy stopped in 1904, when the lithographed periodical poked fun at him. The author recalled the rector's reprimand as the proudest moment of his life. "There was born in me the ambition to annoy others and in a larger field." The observations Mavor made in his autobiographies, *Some Talk of Alexander* (1926) and *One Way of Living* (1939), indicate that in evaluation of the man and the mask one must, as D. H. Lawrence advised, trust the tale rather than the teller.

The youth matriculated to Glasgow University in 1904 to fulfull his father's ambition to become a doctor. During his eight years in college, Mavor's pace was leisurely. Perhaps to disguise his inhibitions Mavor gained a reputation as a wit and a prankster. He wrote for the *Glasgow University Magazine*, became contributing editor of the *G. U. M.* (1908-1909), and wrote plays for student performances. All that survives of these efforts is a string of bizarre titles: "The Son who was considerate of his Father's Prejudices," "No Wedding Cake for Her," "Ethics among Thieves," "The Duke who could sometimes hardly keep from Smiling," "The Baron who would not be convinced that His Way of Living was anything Out of the Ordinary," and "The Young Man to whom Romance was The very Breath of his Being." These comedies helped to make his reputation at the university. *The Quincentenary Year Book* stated that O. H. Mavor was to the university what Victoria was to Victorians.

Dr. Mavor graduated in 1913, and joined the staff of the Glasgow Royal Infirmary. In 1914 he entered the service and doctored troops in France, Mesopotamia, Persia, India, and Turkey. His five years experience overseas later provided source material for dramas and paintings. When he returned to civilian life at the end of World War I, Mavor set up practice in his home city. He enjoyed his duties as a member of staff at the Victoria

Infirmary. Former patients remembered his concerned bedside manner as well as the stories he told to amuse them during convalescence.

The drama of the hospital was not enough for the physician. Despite a full schedule he managed to write *The Switchback*. Mavor asked Alfred Wareing, the former director of the Glasgow Repertory Theatre, to read his play in 1922. Wareing admired the cleverness of the three-act piece written by the man who had attended his theater in costume, while in medical school, but Wareing thought its appeal too limited for production. Mavor put aside the play with the medicinal taste.

In 1923 Dr. Mavor wed the attractive Rona Locke Bremner. Mavor, who later confessed that women terrified him, was equal to taking on other challenges simultaneously, despite his assessment that he was shy and indolent. The year he married, Mavor made other significant changes in his way of living. He sold his practice, became a consulting physician at Victoria Infirmary, and taught at Anderson College of Medicine. Mavor also became a member of the board of the Scottish National Theatre Society. The Scottish National Players, who had been in existence two years, would present the doctor's first professional dramas by the end of the decade.

Mavor wrote a number of pieces during the early 1920s. He said that he was turning out copy for money, but he realized a mere seven pounds in three years. The need for creative expression was far greater than the craving for pence.

In 1926 he published his first autobiography, *Some Talk of Alexander*. The title of his initial book he borrowed from the old military song, "The British Grenadiers." Like the seventeenth-century tune, the account of his experiences, which transpired while he was in the Royal Army Medical Corps, is light.[4]

When he was forty, O. H. Mavor realized an ambition he had long nurtured. The Scottish National Players performed *The Sunlight Sonata*, 1928. The doctor because of himself turned dramatist.

CHAPTER 3

The Doctor in the Playhouse

THE season O. H. Mavor was born the *Scribners Magazine* critic reported that London theater lacked lustre: "Madame Modjeska is the attraction of the hour; but it only points the moral of these desultory remarks that the principal ornament of the English stage just now should be a Polish actress performing in a German play." In 1888 Modjeska appeared in Friedrich Schiller's *Mary Stuart*. The reliance upon performers and emotionalism to create catharsis vitiated Victorian drama.[1] The concept of playwriting was about to undergo a profound change.

The great architect of plays, Henrik Ibsen, was building dramas which realistically reveal the deceit and parochialism of small town life. *A Doll's House* (1878-1879), *Ghosts* (1881), *Hedda Gabler* (1890), and other substantial contributions to world theater would change the course of British drama.[2] Radically new approaches usually produce squalls of protest. George Bernard Shaw defended the Norwegian dramatist against the European storm in *The Quintessence of Ibsenism* (1891).

Shaw launched his own playwriting career in the last decade of the nineteenth century. He used the stage to provoke thought on serious subjects. *Arms and the Man* (1894), *Mrs. Warren's Profession* (1902), *Man and Superman* (1905), and other dramatic works in the Shavian corpus introduced controversial subjects such as satirization of the military, prostitution, and the battle of the sexes in which women are the aggressors in a propagandistic yet entertaining manner. Intellectual stimulation began to replace emotional titillation.

The problem play or drama of ideas exemplified in the work of Ibsen, Shaw, Galsworthy, and others featured representation of social issues confronted by the protagonist. The realism which playwrights in the forefront of change espoused gave health to

23

the invalid stage after its long lapse into sentimental and romantic languor.

The Celtic Renaissance had exploited Irish folk materials. Synge had gained recognition with *Playboy of the Western World* (1907), and *Deirdre of the Sorrows* (1910). The Irish National Theatre Society was experimental and vital. John M. Synge, William B. Yeats, Padraic Colum, Sean O'Casey, and other dramatists were producing plays which employed the local to express the universal.

O'Casey's *Juno and the Paycock* (1924) combined tragedy and comedy. With a bow to Oscar Wilde, W. Somerset Maugham and Noel Coward were writing comedies to please audiences that Evelyn Waugh would characterize as the bright young people. While London laughed, New York admired the psychological plays of Eugene O'Neill. Theater was flourishing in Dublin, London, and New York. With the advent of James Bridie the place where man speaks to man about man became exciting in Glasgow as well.

Glaswegian first nighters received their programs in the aisle of the Lyric Theatre, March 20, 1928, and settled back to enjoy *The Sunlight Sonata, or To Meet The Seven Deadly Sins* by Mary Henderson. This was Mavor's first pseudonym. The doctor used the feminine pseudonym only once more after *The Sunlight Sonata*. He attributed the playlet within *The Dancing Bear* (1931) to the woman he cast as a dottering matron. When he abandoned this masquerade, Mavor combined the names of his grandfather, James Mavor, and his great-grandfather, John Bridie.

Anonimity when writing secular materials was necessary for centuries in Scotland. By the Waverley era it had become customary. Scots reticence and his first profession prompted the author to change his name. Medical colleagues would have scorned the failure and questioned the success of a playwright in their ranks, who might be neglecting patients in order to contribute to the stage. Mavor was mature when he embarked on his theatrical venture. For a forty-year-old physician a change of professions was not a transition made blithely. In his speech "The Prize Giving" Bridie advocated multiple careers for those who possess sufficient talent and interests, but such options were not generally open to bourgeois Scots born in the Victorian period.

In *Colonel Wotherspoon* (1934), James Bridie created the character of Archibald Kellock. He used the name of the emotionally immature character as pseudonym, when he brought out a domestic comedy set in Glasgow, "The Pyrate's Den" (1946).[3] Three years later he resurrected the name for ascription of *The Tintock Cup*.

It is perilous to psychoanalyze the dead, but the comedic talents and the flip pronouncements of the playwright indicate a different dimension of personality contained in the doctor who continued to practice medicine after he had succeeded on the stage. His ability to pursue two demanding careers, by their natures mutually exclusive, shows that Mavor did not schizophrenically substitute one guise for another. The caution that makes Celts loathe to part with everything from pence to poor photos steered Bridie to use the Kellock pseudonym for pieces he considered inconsequential.

Ambition, dignity, and slow accomplishment were his hallmarks. Bridie possessed farsightedness unusual among dramatic writers. The practical author exhibited shrewdness in marketing his plays. The man, the doctor, the dramatist was determined. He worked diligently.[4] Mavor, Henderson, Bridie, Kellock set high and occasionally unattainable standards, resented criticism, and possessed a sense of right which compelled him to maintain honorable professional relationships.

Throughout his playwriting career Bridie investigated the honor of relationships, for these show the moral sense. Truth is written in the hearts of men, but the longer he lived, he discovered an ever-increasing variance from Truth in human action. To find and portray and question the truth became his artistic mission.

I   The Switchback

James Bridie, the name Mavor would use throughout most of his playwriting career, appears on the title page of *The Switchback*. The drama makes use of Dr. Mavor's medical background, as do Bridie's better early plays.

During the seven years between its writing and production the author revised the script. *The Switchback* is flavored with long marination. Throughout his career the playwright continually worked on pieces, stuck them away in drawers and cupboards, then pulled them out much later to polish.

John Brandane recognized that *The Switchback* has a complexity early dramatic works rarely exhibit. Bridie's mentor, who was then directing the Scottish National Players, thought the drama sufficiently good to submit to Sir Barry Jackson, the director of the Birmingham Repertory Theatre. Jackson, a handsome man with manners as beautiful as his acumen was shrewd, recognized the power of the play and produced it on March 9, 1929. The work was revived at the Malvern Festival in 1931, where it was performed by a strong cast which included Cedric Hardwicke and Ralph Richardson. It met with no better reception than when it opened. The critics railed against Bridie's last act, which reviewers felt did not fit the first two. The press would continue to decry the dramatist's treatment of part of nearly every play he wrote.

The unpredictable, which was to become a Bridie trademark, rankled those who had been inundated with well-made dramaturgy. Critics went to see dramas that followed rules. When the playwright deviated from prescriptions, he was upbraided. What concerned the reviewers of *The Switchback* was the resolution.

What engrossed the author is the tension within the protagonist. Bridie wished to dramatize conflict on more than one level of consciousness. The first acts portray the conscious; the last act draws the subconscious. The difference in the acts is that of the waking and sleeping states of mind.

The Switchback tells the story of Dr. Mallaby, a Scots doctor who is in the process of finding a cure for tuberculosis. A car full of important men breaks down near the physician's home. One of the party, Sir Anthony "Toad" Craye, the President of the Royal Academy of Medicine, discovers Mallaby's research. Viscount "Bubbles" Pascal, the newspaper mogul, and Moses "Ikey" Burmeister, the financier, are enthusiastic about the cure. They offer their host a clinic. The doctor's wife, Dorothy, who longs for prestige, cajoles her spouse to accept. Mallaby is tempted by the proposition made by the cartel that would profit financially by his work. He takes the offer. In the final act Mallaby has been drummed out of medicine, for his cure is ineffective. His wife has run off with one of the benefactors. The doctor retreats to the bottle. Mallaby's Aunt Dinah Bullfinch (a fitting name for an explicator of myth), sees through the prophesies of success. She possesses truth, but the daft psychic encourages Mallaby's further retreat into anthropology. The man has listened to others rather than relying upon his own judgment. Mallaby continues to walk the treadmill that stirs the muddy waters of recidivism.

In a prefactory note to his second revised edition Bridie summarizes the plot. The story line is of less importance than the manner of presentation and the lesson to be learned. The dramatist states that the play is intended to demonstrate "the Vanity of Human Wishes, the Importance of Being Earnest, the Inevitability of Fate, the Economic Law, the Immortality of the Soul and the Pleasures of Hope." The old phrases indicate the antiquity of human temptation. Bridie's choice of worn words to describe a work that possesses much newness continues to puzzle critics.

Helen Luyben explains *The Switchback* in terms of the Adam myth.[5] If, as she asserts, Adam falls after being tempted by the sham of civilization, his rejection of the tempter by going to Palmyra to dig in ruins is doubly unsatisfying. Bridie is then ambiguous with regard to the restoration to be affected by Mallaby's going backward, neglecting the research which could improve man's condition. Mallaby says that he is as mad as a thunderstorm. The doctor is emotionally unstable, egotistic, stubborn, tactless, and gullible. Miss Luyben does an admirable job of textual substantiation in discussing Mallaby's character. These qualities do make the man human rather than despicable.

The Switchback is neither a conundrum nor an indictment of twentieth-century society. Mallaby is tempted by greed. The prominent visitors offer to bring the doctor's method of treating tuberculosis to public attention. Pascal is the pride of life. The hellish lord's sensational coverage of the cure in his newspapers does not bring fame but censure for breech of ethics. Burmeister is the lust of the flesh. He seduces the Faustian Mallaby's wife with a string of pearls. The gems produced by irritation bring the unfaithful woman consternation.

Mrs. Mallaby first appears in a black and gold kimono, which represents the glitter of darkness. When Bridie specifies the color of costume it is invariably symbolic. The woman who is susceptible to sins that do not lure her husband knows him well enough to cast artificial pearls of wisdom to abet his fall.

The third visitor, Sir Anthony Craye represents the principles

of the medical profession. If his traditional responses are
sometimes short of right reason, he alone gives Mallaby sound
advice, and twice offers the protagonist ways out of snares.
Mallaby listens to all others but Craye.

Only Aunt Dinah recognizes Pascal and Burmeister for the
hounds they are. She tells Mallaby in the course of their third act
card game that he does not pay attention. Rather than sobriety,
vigilance and common sense Mallaby chooses flight to the city of
Palms, for a "martyrdom" that is no more rational than his
heeding the suggestions of a press lord and a business man rather
than a fellow physician.

The immature sinner says, "Mankind has many inventions, but
only three ways of happiness—Make-believe, Curiosity and
Irony. The first two ways I have travelled hopefully on aching
feet. They are finished. I'll see what is in the third." The irony of
the speech is that Mallaby's description of Palmyra, where men
dispute "about the best advice to give to the Almighty,"
indicates that he is still going on the curious route of fantasy. God
listens to reason, but not to men's advice.

The protagonist believes he has rejected the temptations of
Pascal and Burmeister. Mallaby says, "I'm an altruist. I want only
the kingdom of heaven. It is within me, and, by heaven, I'll be
king of it!" The soul of the man who would be the Deity is in a
worse state than the mortal who thought himself "the most
original worker since Pasteur."

Man rides the switchback or roller coaster when he abandons
his own reason in favor of others' propositions. In this state he
falls off the steep grade by positing that God is made in man's
image and likeness.

II   The Anatomist

Bridie's first major success came the year after his insubstan-
tial comedy, *What It Is to Be Young* (1929), was produced in
Birmingham and Glasgow.[6] Bridie based *The Anatomist* on a
cause célèbre that created a furor in Edinburgh. In lectures at the
University of Glasgow Bridie had heard of Burke and Hare, a
pair of body snatchers, who were tried for murdering at least
sixteen persons.[7] The 1828–1829 proceedings implicated Dr.
Robert Knox, a famed specialist in anatomy, who created the
demand which the culprits supplied by making cadavers.

Bridie's treatment of the macabre case opens in the drawing room of Amelia and Mary Dishart. One of the Dishart sisters is engaged to Walter Anderson,[8] who works in the thrall of Dr. Knox. The doctor comes to dinner. He is blustering and egocentric. These qualities the dramatist frequently assigns medical characters. Amelia admires the intelligent scientist who has lost esteem because of allegations that he has trafficked with ghouls. Mary provides the opinion of a foil. She regards Knox's dedication as fanaticism and fears his influence upon Anderson, her fiancé. The stage crackles with the flames of argument as Knox and Mary present their divergent points of view about his profession in a potent first act scene.

KNOX It is a religion. It is a passion.
MARY It is a very horrid sort of religion.
KNOX My dear young lady, it is less horrid than the religions of most of mankind. It has its martyrs, it has its heresy hunts, but its hands are clean of the blood of the innocent.
MARY Do you call the hands of a resurrectionist clean?
KNOX Of the blood of the innocent.
MARY Grave-robbing is worse than murder.
KNOX Madam, with all respect you are a pagan atheist to say so. If you believed in an immortal soul, why should you venerate the empty shell it has spurned in its upward flight? And with a false veneration too. The anatomist alone has a true reverence for the human body. He loves it. He knows it.[9]

Walter Anderson goes to a tavern after Mary Dishart breaks their engagement. While getting drunk with Mary Paterson, a red head of the evening, Knox's assistant learns than Daniel Paterson, his idol's porter, is in league with Burke and Hare. The proposition—Knox, demon or prophet—is restated by implication. The doctor's need for corpses is greater than his concern about his source of supply: His research is imperative if accurate medicine is to advance.

The next day at the laboratory, Walter sees Mary Paterson's red hair sticking out of the casket. He is horrified when he discovers that he knows their next anatomical subject. Dr. Knox exhibits no hint of chagrin that the girl has been murdered to provide him with a body: "The life of this poor wretch is ended. It is surely a better thing that her beauty of form should be at the service of divine science than at the service of any drunken buck with a crown in his pocket. Our emotions, Walter, are forever tugging at our coat-tails lest at any time we should look the truth in the face."

When Walter suggests reporting the crime, Knox excoriates him with, "You poroncephalic monstrosity!" Bridie's use of the epithet is masterful. He brings to Celtic imprecation the ability to delineate character and combines heritage with technique to reveal speakers' inner emotions in a phrase.

The last act transpires in the Dishart home. Walter affects a reconciliation with his fiancée and defends the doctor's actions. Knox comes in wounded by a mob that now seeks to destroy the anatomist. He is more anxious about continuing his work than he is fearful of the crowd's vengeance. Students come to protect their instructor along the route to the lecture hall. Amelia suggests that Knox teach the class in her living room. The play ends with Knox orating on the structure of the heart. "I shall not profane the sacred gift of human speech by replying to these people in any other language than that of the cudgel. With you I shall take the liberty of discussing a weightier matter . . . 'The Heart of the Rhinoceros.' This mighty organ, gentlemen, weighs a full twenty-five pounds, a fitting fountainhead for the tumultuous stream that surges through the tangled verdure engirdling his tropical habitat. Such dreadful vigour, gentlemen, such ineluctable energy requires to be sustained by no ordinary forces of nutrition. . . ." The single-minded practitioner is not a hero; he is not a villain; he is not a martyr. Knox is the energetic rhino. Bridie uses the rhinoceros as a symbol of egotism and power in other plays as well. The anatomist then, is a man of serious faults who makes major contributions. His accomplishments are, by their nature, melodramatic. Bridie averts cliff-hanging skillfully.

Good versus evil is the struggle that preoccupied Bridie in serious conflicts. The audience is forced to come to grips with the question: Can good come from evil. The practices of the body snatchers are wicked. Knox provides a market for the corpses. He uses the bodies to advance science, and argues that end justifies means.

Bridie puts the proposition to his audience that there are rarely clear-cut cases of right and wrong. Humans do not regard an action as evil and decide to proceed with it. They submit that the deed, under particular circumstances, is good for them. Bridie's insights into the psychological labyrinths created to justify actions are acute. The author says in *One Way of Living* that *The Anatomist* is a consideration of the scientist as dictator. When Knox makes his own rules he falls from grace. There are for Bridie objective standards of morality, which must be upheld, but showing obfuscation of those standards makes theatergoers aware that moral choices are fraught with difficulty.

Critics who attended opening performances of the play seem to have longed for melodrama or savagery or both. Bridie says in a note on the play that if *The Anatomist* "illustrates anything, it is the shifts to which men of science are driven when they are ahead of their times."

James Agate in his *London Times* review asked, "Must not the ideal drama have concerned itself between the conflict of the man of science determined to admit no bar to the prosecution of research even if it means conniving at murder and the man of normal conscience and responsibility."[10] Agate, as well as other contemporary critics, judged on the basis of what they wanted to see rather than what was presented.

The tension of *The Anatomist* arises less from man versus society than from man versus himself. Suspense is maintained by the question, What manner of man is the protagonist. In the last act the doctor says "Do you think because I strut and rant and put on a bold face that my soul isn't sick within me at the horror of what I have done?" Knox is also capable of rhetoric which indicates that he can contain and live with the horrid. "Do you imagine her life was so significant that we must grue at her death?" he asks Walter, when the young man is shocked at seeing the body of Mary Paterson. The diverse facets of the character in control elevate Knox above a Jekyll-Hyde. Dedication is not in conflict with dementia. The two may coexist.

To the consternation of critics, whom Bridie once characterized as "vermin on the mantle of Thespis," the playwright explores problems, but offers no comforting solutions packaged in tidy containers. The characters who search won the respect of the best actors of Britain, because the roles admit of variation in interpretation.

Bridie originally conceived the part of Dr. Knox to be performed in the tradition of the "barnstorming tenor." Henry

Ainley, who first played Knox, did the role in this manner. Alastair Sim, who later portrayed the anatomist, wrote Winifred Bannister his analysis of the character. "He was an intellectual giant of his community and time, and knowing this, he made a hobby of practising his wit and sophistry on mental inferiors. Yet his stature could not but be founded on a deep humility in the search for truth through knowledge."[11] Sim's conception is arguable, but the actor added shades of subtle complexity to the role. Bridie admired his friend's new interpretation.

The Anatomist opened on July 6, 1930, at the Lyceum Theatre, Edinburgh. Bridie's first play to be presented in London opened at the Westminster Theatre in October, 1931. This production also introduced producer Tyrone Guthrie to the English capital. The play has been staged a number of times at the Citizens' Theatre, Glasgow, and continues to be revived on stages throughout the English-speaking world.

III   A Sleeping Clergyman

The Switchback and *The Anatomist* both present ethical and moral concerns. In 1933, after he had begun his biblical plays, Bridie completed *A Sleeping Clergyman*. Again he drew from his experience as a physician. The medical story of success and its concomitant hazards engrossed the dramatist.

If Mallaby has failed in scientific research, he may grow as a man. Knox accomplishes professional attainments at risk of becoming monstrous. In *A Sleeping Clergyman* a physician lives to see the vindication of his belief that eugenics is fallacious. One may consider this work as representing the completion of a cycle of the playwright's thought.

In a letter to actress Flora Robson, February 2, 1933, Bridie summarizes the play he had labored over for two years:

A young medical student, (drunken) seduces his benefactor's sister, discovers the germ theory before Pasteur and dies in a slum lodging — all in the first scene! His illegitimate daughter falls in love with an industrious apprentice-blackmailer and poisons him with prussic acid. *Their* twins (!!) grow up into blazing benefactors of the human race by virtue of the nasty characteristics inherited from their ancestors being turned into effective channels by pure chance. It is called "Nunc Dimittis" [i. e., *A Sleeping Clergyman*], because Benefactor No. 1 lives all through it—Mr. Hardwicke, for a ducat—and dies, a bit muddled, but feeling fine at 95.[12]

A Sleeping Clergyman, which has a first act that Bridie predicted would make an elephant sick, opens in a Glasgow club. In this contemporary setting two doctors discuss the Marshalls and Camerons. Flashbacks to the club provide requisite exposition. This Scottish family is as brilliant as the Jukes and Kallakaks are dull. The families studied by eugenists in the early decades of the twentieth century are the inspiration for Bridie's dramatic argument against the pseudoscience then enjoying a vogue. The clergyman in the club, who is God, sleeps through the entire account of the family, whose history is replete with crime and depravity.

After the introduction in the nodding presence of the divine representative, the scene shifts to the cheap digs of Charlie Cameron, a medical student, who is dying of galloping tuberculosis. It is apparent that the bacillus, which travels through the bloodstream causing high fever, pulmonary disturbance, and rapid respiration, will prove fatal to Cameron. The tuberculer is smoking and drinking as he researches the disease with which he is stricken. Cameron longs for time to prove his medical discovery, but refuses Dr. Marshall's offer of proper care. Bridie draws the compulsive, short tempered, and sarcastic Cameron in a few sure strokes. He limns a distinctive portrait of a man who has not time for self-pity.

Women are irrelevant to Bridie's medical characters. Thus, when Harriet Marshall visits her lover soon after her brother departs, Cameron shows more interest in the germs he has isolated than in giving the child Harriet carries his name. Cameron flings an epithet at Harriet, which capsules the antifeminist attitude. The dying man calls her "the recreation of a warrior."

After a compelling fight scene, that includes Harriet's smashing the tubes of tubercle cultures, the pair reconcile. Cameron dies before his marriage to Harriet can take place the following day.

In the next scene Wilhelmina, the orphan whom Cameron and Harriet Marshall produced, is about to celebrate a birthday in the home of her uncle. Dr. Marshall dotes on his niece. Other relatives are not as fond of his ward whom, they are convinced, will be wicked because she is the product of an illicit union.

The third act shows a wild, intelligent, and sensual Wilhelmina. The young woman has been seeing her uncle's handyman, John Hannah. He is the son of her father's landlady. Hannah is working his way through medical school. Wilhelmina taunts her lover in a manner reminiscent of Charlie Cameron's treatment of Mrs. Hannah. She announces that she will marry another man. Hannah rages, because marrying the doctor's niece would further his own career. He threatens blackmail; she poisons his wine with prussic acid. Hannah has had too much to drink and does not notice the bitter almond taste of the lethal beverage. Wilhelmina regains the incriminating letters and gives them to her uncle. Love prompts Marshall to perjure himself at the trial. Wilhelmina is free to deliver her bastard twins, Charles and Hope. When the children are infants their mother commits suicide.

Dr. Marshall raises a second generation of Camerons. Hope exhibits none of the negative qualities of her forebearers. The intelligent and well-balanced girl goes to Geneva to work for peace. Charles sustains suspense in the accuracy of the eugenic theory. He has some of the quixotic traits of his ancestors. Genetic inevitability may prompt Charles to fling one of his war medals to a prostitute, when she asks for a souvenir. The rake matures to become a physician, who finds a cure that prevents a universal epidemic. The environment Dr. Marshall has provided for three generations of Camerons is stronger than their heredity.

The play, which takes sides in the nature-nurture controversy, provides choice roles. Marshall's progress to serene octogenarian helps to draw the long span of events together. The doctor is a taxing part, as is the female lead, who plays Harriet, Wilhelmina, and Hope.

The many necessary scenes of the drama were handled better in the 1947 revival, when the theater had advanced technically. In 1930 and 1931, when A Sleeping Clergyman opened at the Malvern Festival, played Edinburgh, Glasgow, and ran 230 performances in London, the ten scenes dragged. The Theater Guild did the play in 1934. Ruth Gordon played the Cameron women in New York, in the first production of a Bridie play in America.

IV   Dr. Angelus

During the 1947 London revival of *A Sleeping Clergyman*, Bridie's new play with a medical backdrop opened at the Lyceum Theatre, Edinburgh, June 23. *Dr. Angelus* was a showcase for the talents of Alastair Sim, the Scottish actor.

Dr. Angelus is drawn from a nineteenth-century Glasgow murder case. Bridie set his version in the 1920s. The playwright is creative in his use of the historical source.

The felonious physician is the quintessence of the dignified hoodwinker. In much the same manner touring charlatans inveigled gullible Scots to purchase panaceas from temporary stages set up in the wynds and closes during the seventeenth century, Angelus deceives the people in his world. He makes his assistant, Dr. Johnson, an associate. Angelus then persuades his partner to sign victims' death certificates.

Angelus kills his wife to be rid of a partner who has grown intolerable. The wife who is poisoned lacks the color her husband possesses in abundance. This contrast of personalities is like that used in portraying the Mallabys.

That Angelus desires his loose housemaid is presented with such detachment, his motive superficially is ludicrous. The comic flavor of much of the play makes it difficult to take seriously the doctor who prays, "Jesus tender shepherd," when arraigned.

Bridie's peculiar comic treatment eases the audience into another world. Angelus is a macrocosm who is completely self-absorbed. For him reality cannot be objective. To heighten the protagonist's destructive personality by contrast, the dramatist exaggerates the idealism of Johnson, the extraordinarily easy mark.

When speaking to the seductive Mrs. Corcoran, Johnson compares his profession to the Holy Grail: "I mean, you were after something. It might even be a way of saving mankind. And although you didn't believe in God or any of that sort of rot, you were really a kind of priest; with high standards and self-discipline and fine, simple rules and so on."

One is reminded that Parsifal means perfect fool. But is not, Bridie asks, Angelus the greater fool than Johnson. Angelus, who strews Christian clichés about with the ease of a fraudulent evangelist, captivates the defender of the Hippocratic Oath. Those who use trite expressions in Bridie's plays are never on the side of truth. "I have lost all that is dearest to me in life. It will take me many months to gird up my loins and once again march breast forward. The married state is a blessed one, George. It will be the happiest day of my life when I see you standing at God's altar taking those solemn vows which can only be dissolved by death. Alas, death has dissolved my vows and there remains an emptiness that can never be filled. A great void, George."

The agnostic idealist lives with the pious amoralist. Their world is held up for the audience. The mirror of this ironic microcosm glints reflections of the real world, but those who look and see are continually urged to make judgments about which elements are real by a series of comic and serious devices.

The title character's name is the sort of contradiction Birdie delights to employ. The murderer shares the title of a prayer. Angelus is diabolical in action, but he wears an angelic mask and appears to believe he is what he seeks to show the world.

The set description stipulates a consulting room photo of Angelus with a hippopotamus he has bagged. The trophy represents Elizabeth Taylor, the doctor's mother-in-law, who has been given enough poison "to kill a hippo." The symbolism is the crowd pleasing sort used in situation comedy. Other examples of techniques include Angelus' gesture of untying the maid's apron to indicate his lust, which is reminiscent of French farce. Mrs. Corcoran's attempts to interest Johnson during his examination of her are in the tradition of the comedy of manners. Through a variety of methods stock in light entertainment, Bridie shows a world upside down. In such a place a man whose profession it is to preserve existence can be bent on taking life.

The comic elements persist after Angelus has committed murder. The protagonist's world view is completely distorted, which is evinced by the platitudes he utters. "You must not shake my faith in human nature. . . ." But what kind of faith can a slayer have in human nature?

To rule his sphere Angelus uses insinuation and intimidation. His ability to hector Johnson into signing the death certificates of the victims shows that such methods aid achievement of Angelus' main purpose: "realisation of oneself as the aim and object of existence."

Angelus claims that his wife and mother-in-law tried to mold him to their concepts of right thinking, thereby preventing him from gaining his objective. Mrs. Angelus appears incapable of affecting anyone's thinking. Unless we take the sphere of Angelus as a mad state, the motive for the crimes—the wish to marry the maid—is unsatisfying. In the perverted reality of the character, who shows how smooth the insane can be, absence of comprehensible motive heightens realization that this is a world of Angelus' making, that turns around him.

One can be more comfortable in seeing Angelus as demented. If the sane with whom he deals represent the world of reality, this world is little better than Angelus' conception. Johnson is immature. He feels has has been treated as a colleague, although we see him solely as a tool. The police inspector tells the young assistant he does not know the difference between good and evil. Johnson has the use of reason, but fails to implement the faculty in time to save the second victim.

Sir Gregory Butt is reason itself. This doctor's unvarnished speech contrasts to Angelus' florid garrulity. Butt long suspects the madman, but when Johnson enlists the physician's help, the more experienced Butt refuses to become involved. Stupidity and diffidence permit Angelus to function.

Johnson gains the truth in a dram-induced dream sequence. This segment parallels Bridie's last act of *The Switchback*. Johnson, like Mallaby, gets drunk. This condition allows suspension of reality to depict a heightened state. Bridie explains in *One Way of Living* that he has characters become intoxicated to reveal their feelings because of Scottish reluctance to display emotions. In *The Dancing Bear* and other works Bridie asserts that the truth of poets, which transcends knowledge acquired from a compilation of facts, comes from trance or dream.

The world the inebriated Johnson sees becomes a means of conveying another perspective. The dream shows that phantasm can be more reliable than reality. In the sequence which functions as a manifestation of conscience, Butt becomes a barrister, who censures Johnson for complicity in the murders.

When the peculiar reality of the drama returns in the last act, Johnson is about to go to the police, but this proves unnecessary. Johnson has become caught up in Angelus' world, and it is more fitting that one from without should be the instrument to bring him to objective justice. Mrs. Corcoran supplies the authorities with evidence that incriminates Angelus.

Angelus' announcement that his wife is dead is anticlimactic. The doctor's final manifestations of fear shade into howling lunacy. Poetic justice as regular as verse satisfies theatergoers, but it is Dr. Butt's indifferent behavior which is the genuine surprise. The reasoner is as flawed as the protagonist and the antagonist. This points out the conflict of man versus self in a world of his making.

The arrival of the inspector, who functions as the most objective representative of the actual world, enables the dramatist to comment upon how Angelus was able to make his world turn. "You did your best and it wasna very good and that's a fair epitaph for most of us," the policeman tells Johnson.

Bridie hints in *Dr. Angelus* that the way to certitude and truth may be found in altered states of consciousness, but upon awaking man does not make use of the truth he has been given.

Although farcical proceedings and clever dialogue do not hide Bridie's position, it was the humor, which ranges from portrayals of Scottish eccentricity to satire of medical foibles, that entertained London audiences. They came for seven months to see *Dr. Angelus*, after it opened at the Phoenix Theatre in July, 1947. The footlights shone on a play of admirable facility. Bridie's stagecraft had developed to the extent that he could weave the laugh pattern, shuttle the pace of emotional moments, and be sure of the reaction his "Berlin Persian" would produce.

CHAPTER 4

Literary Properties

W HILE writing a serious piece Bridie could turn his flexible
mind to concocting light comedies. Throughout his career
he managed to achieve a difficult balance in writing. *The
Anatomist* was produced during the same season as *The Girl
Who Did Not Want to Go to Kuala Lumpur.* A revised version of
The Switchback was performed six months after *The Dancing
Bear* opened.

I   The Girl Who Did Not Want to Go to Kuala Lumpur

The Girl Who Did Not Want to Go to Kuala Lumpur was
presented on five November nights in 1930 at the Lyric Theatre,
Glasgow. The burlesque of Highland drama and romance was
produced by Elliot Mason, who contributed to the sprightly
invention by pacing the comedy at breakneck speed.

Bridie's satire is warmhearted, for it is born of his love of
Scottish writing. Rather than poking fun at specific authors or
works, the playwright spoofs conventions of eighteenth- and
nineteenth-century Scots literature. He also lays bare contemporary foibles, inserts outrageous one-liners, and ranges from
physical business, to malapropism, to bright repartee to keep a
Northern audience laughing. If, at times, the effort appears
frantic, one must remember that Scottish theatergoers have a
reputation for being dour.

While having tea with a lady painter and a witty law student,
who paints wood jewelry, Margaret Unthank confides that she is
desperate. Her wards are about to take her to Kuala Lumpur,
where the young girl fears she will wither on the stem.

Tom Garscadden, an eighty-five-year-old painter of the
Glasgow School, who is a plain-speaking eccentric, arrives
shortly before Margaret's uncle and aunt. Tom reveals that

Unthank is a confidence man, who probably must leave the country to escape the police. The artist's presence affords opportunity for a sally on art criticism.

To prevent the "abduction" of Margaret to the Malay States, her friends see marriage as the only solution. A postman arrives, who is a fighter, a poet, and single. The mail-carrier, John Sobieski Stewart, is of royal lineage, and spouts rhetoric as lofty as it is lengthy when he sees Mary's expressionist portrait of Margaret: "Her hair is like the golden web that is the canopy of a fairy's barge; and her eyes are like two of the Pleiades reflected in the dark waters. Her little mouth is full of loving. To look on her makes me think of my own glen in a day of sunshine with a far-off piper on the sea-shore playing faint songs of loves long ago."

The Celtic preoccupation with family as well as the high flown language spoken by unlikely characters, who appear to be peasants but are noble, are elements found in Scottish drama since *Douglas* astounded Edinburgh. And John Home used an old ballad as his source.

As the second act begins, Margaret and her snobbish aunt tearfully pack for the journey. Mrs. Syme, as canny a landlady as Sir Walter Scott could desire, wants her rent. Margaret explains her situation to Syme. She tells ingenuously how the Unthanks kept her "after they spent all the money that Father left me." The hapless ward, dear to writers of tragedy, pastoral, and comedy, is told by Syme to marry, but Margaret has only twelve hours to find a husband.

Dick Unthank brings the very drunk Mr. Smellie to his digs to extract the rent money from his pigeon. Before Dick writes a bad check, the uncle tells his neice: "Greater than a serpent's tooth to have an Unthank child." The travesty of the line from *King Lear* is in the tradition of nineteenth- and twentieth-century pantomime.

Margaret asks Smellie for money to relieve her plight, but the penurious Scot, who would rather be bilked than be charitable, refuses. Margaret tries to prevent the skinflint from hurting her uncle. Dick seizes this opportunity to try blackmail. The suggestion that he pay a large sum sobers Smellie instantly. The incident has the savor of a Sir Harry Lauder variety routine.

Margaret's friends gain entry and introduce the postman to the heroine. In the stilted, florid, antique diction of the old heroes, Stewart threatens Unthank, then proposes to Margaret. She demurs demurely. This sequence of events follows the established pattern of the novels that employ the sensibility of Henry Mackenzie.

In the third act the postman rescues Margaret from Smellie by entering through the window. Such an action is as obligatory as a haunting in Scottish gothic novels. The hero then embraces Ellen, the servant rather than the heroine. Stewart and Ellen are from the same part of the country; they burst into Erse. This device has been used since the late eighteenth century, when Archibald Maclaren wrote comedies that introduced the use of the Celtic language on the Scottish stage.

Bridie compounds the mirth provoked by the aged gambit. He has Stewart explain that he is a fairy and a student for the ministry. A leap from the fey to the likes of Barrie's *Little Minister* in one bound is as incongruous as the plot itself. In such a vehicle one can have a heroine agree to wed a hero before learning his Christian name, without apology to Oscar Wilde.

Bridie adds flourishes to the resolution by a series of other proposals. The octogenarian Tom offers marriage, and tells Margaret, "I can still walk my twenty miles a day." The author sends up Celtic embellishment, even as he uses it in Unthank's rejoinder: "You've been forestalled, I think, even in pedestrianism. The postman!"

The Girl Who Did Not Want to Go to Kuala Lumpur is farce. The satire of literature expands its comic dimensions and adds meaning to the antics.

II   The Dancing Bear

The season after the Scottish National Players presented *The Girl Who Did Not Want to Go to Kuala Lumpur* Bridie wrote *The Dancing Bear* for them. In February, 1931, they presented the romantic comedy at the Lyric Theatre.

In his preface to *Colonel Wotherspoon and Other Plays* Bridie said "*The Dancing Bear* is an unsuccessful experiment in chorus work. The chorus has oozed in the front and swamped the leaders." In this play the author satirized facets of provincialism, literature, and criticism. The individuals he created to show his annoyances do overshadow the lovers. Subsidiary characters such as Professor Nish, the mannered pedant, Miss Soulis, the lady novelist, Tam Kilgour, the hypocrite, and other traditional and modern Scottish types, at times obstruct one's view of Colin, the Scots poet, whom Bridie made the hero of the piece. *The Dancing Bear* is out of focus, but it does provide some clear pictures of the dramatist's thought.

The comedy begins with a parade of characters who stroll about a Scots village in summer twilight. Betts suggests that Kitty play him "a spot of Chaminade," while he eats chocolates. She wants to sit outdoors on Betts' copy of *Vogue.* "It's thick and soft and doughy."

Wit and wisecracks seem to matter more than plot development. Betts proposes marriage in such a casual manner that the breaking of this engagement to create suspense at the end of the first act sticks out as a ploy to create interest in the proceedings to follow.

The second act consists of a literary soiree. The main event of the evening is the presentation of Mary Henderson's "St. Eloy and the Bear." The author describes her effort as a symbolic, expressionistic, festival piece. The host thinks "St. Eloy" a "Tchekovian little thing with a rather pretty touch of old-fashioned sentiment."

The play within the play becomes a contretemps to parallel the action of the main events on stage. In "St. Eloy" Mirabel (Kitty) and Gaston (Betts) argue about whether the Bear (Colin) has a soul. Other characters play these roles. Thus the audience may see the reactions of Kitty, Betts, and Colin to a situation which is like their own.

St. Eloy is roused from slumber on a haystack. He gives the animal a soul. The Bear asks why he could not "be spared these mysteries," for now he sees the haystack has "bitter beauty." It is no longer merely a source of food. Gaston tells the Bear to "dance down the road and think." This exhortation is a leitmotif that Bridie would continue to play in light works.

During the course of "St. Eloy" the interplay between prompter and actors intrudes upon the reality of Miss Henderson's work, even as "St. Eloy" intrudes upon the reality of *The Dancing Bear.*

The Bear feels that he is now the "strongest of mankind" and wants a "righteous deal." The bruin hugs Gaston, and Mirabel stabs the bear in the arm. Miss Henderson remarks that if Gaston had killed the bear it would have destroyed the *meaning* of the play. Her real intent was to have the bear eat the others.

After the performance Professor Nish reads a poem about mud, i. e., criticism that obfuscates. The last line of the verse contains Bridie's thrust: "What are we looking for in this mud? / Can it be we shall find a Star?"

Colin is asked who is judge of a poet's work. The poet himself Colin answers, and states Bridie's view of the creative process. "It comes to you, and you just say it. You can't quite explain why you come to the conclusion that what you say is, in a way, true. Though you know fine somehow that it is."

Colin leaves the dais before he finishes reading his poem, for he feels freakish in the midst of those who do not share his vision. In this state Colin proposes to Kitty, and she accepts.

The third act is set in the garden where the first act took place. The structure is cyclical, and Bridie attempts to reinforce this idea by a seduction scene. Miss Soulis tries to get Nish to take her to Paris. Rather than strengthening the play, this business remains another comic turn. The irony is heavy-handed. The married professor protests. The critic says he is a gentleman, but he is rapacious in reviews. Nish is contrasted to Pringle, the padre who relishes an affair. Such twists and turns place the hero too far left of center stage.

As the parents of the engaged couple bicker over money, the now bossy Kitty leads the wedding party from a dress rehearsal. Betts asks the bride-to-be if she noticed that the vermillion of Elijah's robe in the stained glass window clashes with the burgundy of the bridesmaids' dresses. Kitty agrees that this will spoil the whole show.

The church window depicts Elijah being fed by ravens. The prophet's situation with the scavengers is somewhat like Colin's.

Jean, the realistic servant, who has waited on those who attended the soiree, comforts the dejected poet. She tells Colin the kind of woman a poet should wed. "She couldna see onything in you but a queer mix o' a man and a wean and an angel and a devil." Colin and Jean elope, as do the reconciled Betts and Kitty.

The Dancing Bear devolves on choice. Whether selecting partners or discriminating what is good in art, the characters do not give much thought to the choices they make. This is the supreme irony in their dance down the road.

III   Colonel Wotherspoon

On the title page of *Colonel Wotherspoon or the Fourth Way of Greatness* Bridie explains the subtitle: "Some are born great; some achieve greatness; and some have greatness thrust upon them; while some write Best Sellers." The character mentioned in the title never appears on stage. Colonel Wotherspoon is the authority cited by the hero's uncle. Uncle Tom is as obtuse as Dr. Watson and as bumbling as Colonel Blimp. The title is an admonition to consider the source, when relying upon others' opinions to reach a conclusion.

Archie Kellock, an uneducated and unoriginal sort reads to his cousin Emily excerpts from the novel he is writing. The girl tries to point out that Archie's effort is riddled with clichés. Kellock thinks a cliché is a "cliesh."

Emily's intellectual manuscripts are rejected. Archie's *Madder Music* becomes so popular that Archie, his over-protective mother, Emily, and Mrs. Kishmul, his American agent, gather at Uncle Tom's cabin to hear the novel discussed on B. B. C. radio.

Critic Derek Putney assesses Kellock's book shortly after the reviewer has returned from the dentist. "One had read so many books recently by young people who take an almost corpse-like view of life that one feels—how can one express it?—as if one were strolling in the catacombs and as if suddenly a large and healthy and Lido-bronzed Mr. Kellock had burst his cerements and asked one to have a drink." It is Putney's state of shock as a result of his tooth repair that prompts the favorable comment. Helen Luyben believes Putney resembles J. B. Priestley.

The now emboldened Archie has proposed to Emily, who turns him down. It is not the closeness of the degree of kinship that prompts the reaction, for marriage of cousins in Scotland was not uncommon, but Archie's unwitting literary dishonesty.

Miss Luyben points out that the fantastic invention of Kellock parallels Bridie's, and that the dramatist uses the name Kellock as a pseudonym to substantiate that the playwright is satirizing himself in *Colonel Wotherspoon*.[1]

Emily is the only "accurate" judge of objective literary merit

in the play. Her estimation of what a book should be is at odds
with aspects of Bridie's writing.

A book should be about real things and real people. A book that does
nothing but reflect the silly, sluttish day-dreams of a lot of morons is a
crime. It's pandering to the filthiest kind of vanity. It's making them
think their rubbishy systems are fit for a decent world. It's bolstering
up their conceit by making them thrill with horror at what their
imaginary opposites do. And it's making the horror delicious to them by
smearing it with smut—smarmy, hypocritical, leering, winking smut.

Even as Kellock embellishes situations in his own life to
manufacture popular fiction, Bridie inserts his own mannerisms
and the criticism these brought forth to produce comedy. The
dramatist says less about his own writing than he does about the
literary climate of the day.

By the beginning of the third act Kellock is in London and is
romantically involved with his opportunistic married agent. The
achiever of the fourth way of greatness is acting out the fantasies
he used in his second book, *Stronger Wine.*

Bridie develops the temptation of the newly acclaimed author
more fully in *Babes in the Wood.* In both plays blandishments
are overcome by the heroes' reversion to puritanical Scottish
upbringing, which stays men from traveling the lengths of
wayward paths.

The critical condemnation of Kellock's second novel draws
him to seek collaboration with Emily on a play and for life. The
plot is as Bridie described it: "bare simplicity."

The literary satire entertained Glaswegians when *Colonel
Wotherspoon* opened at the Lyric Theatre, March 23, 1934.
After a three nights run the play was staged at the Arts Theatre,
London, for three June evenings. The critics were amused.

James Agate said that Bridie had found the fourth way to
greatness. To pillory literature and one's own writing can
entertain and divert for an evening. It is the characterization of
Mrs. Kellock that points the way to the creation of long-lasting
dramas.

Archie's mother is hovering. domineering, and self-righteous.
With all her faults, one is sympathetic with Mrs. Kellock, when
Emily points out her interfering, critical, and sniveling behavior.
The older woman is a person; the younger one is a type who

states facts without care (see the prologue to *What It Is to Be Young*).

When characterization predominates, Bridie's plays become more substantial. Both *The Dancing Bear* and "Gog and Magog" deal with Scots poets. The earlier work features satire of literary concerns. The superficiality of this approach is apparent when one considers the more mature study of an untalented poet who has the dimensions of a rounded character. In *Colonel Wotherspoon* a critic says: "Personally one considers it intolerably in the Papa-Potato-Prunes and Prism School, coloured infrequently with schoolmasterish bursts of bad temper." After seeing the play Agate wrote in the *Times:* ". . . the penny whistle screamed rather painfully over the sentimental passages which some imp of frustration tempted him [i. e., Bridie] to try."[2] It is difficult to distinguish newspaper impressionism from satirical exaggeration.

CHAPTER 5

The Hero, Stage Left

BRIDIE'S protagonists as well as his minor characters are flawed individuals. They are products of the Calvinist tradition. Those whose fortunes are of chief interest are tempted.

Similarities in the relationship of character to action occur in a number of Bridie's plays. The same ideas continue to surface. They are of an order which admits variation on a theme. When paradoxical concepts hold the center of the stage, the hero, as a spokesman of ideas, cannot tell it all in a single play.

The romantic and adventurous hero of Scottish tradition possessed mystery and dash. With the death of Sir Walter Scott in 1832, this figure, who stood larger than life on the craigs, vanished into the mists of the grouse moors.

Bridie, perhaps inadvertently, created a new Scottish hero. He is, as we learn in *The Dancing Bear, The Anatomist, John Knox,* and other works "part angel and part devil." He has a puritan conscience, yet performs cavalier actions. If this is contradictory, it is that which makes him more "a man for a' o' that."

Many of Bridie's heroes are adolescent. It is innocence and ignorance that prompts juvenile behavior. And why not have it both ways, Bridie says repeatedly, as he explores ambiguity personified in men who can accomplish much in one area yet lack judgment in other matters. In showing the foolishness of heroes, Bridie entertained. In making figures more true by leading playgoers into the worlds of their psyches, the dramatist frequently sailed over the heads of the audience.

I   Marriage Is No Joke

Marriage Is No Joke opened on February 6, 1934, at the Globe Theatre, London. The play, featuring Ralph Richardson, closed after five performances. Bridie knew that the piece would not succeed, but he liked parts of the comedy he called the greatest of his failures.

MacGregor, the hero, is a hard-drinking Calvinist who is studying for the ministry. While on one of his drunks he marries Priscilla, an innkeeper's daughter. On his wedding night MacGregor abuses Hogbins, a hotel servant.

From the Highlander's feelings of inadequacy at Glasgow University to vague recollections of what he did while under the influence of rum, Bridie draws an alcoholic. MacGregor seeks illusion in liquor, but, he says, "drunk or sober we're always our real self, and that's the tragedy of it." To this Priscilla counters, "I don't see any tragedy about it. You'll do just quite well as you are." Those who see life or events as tragic in Bridie's works are invariably wrong in this assumption.

It is their marriage which will give MacGregor, who finds "predestination even in illusion," a new beginning. Bridie evinces his fondness for new beginnings in the hero's statement of the author's philosophy. "Och, it's all beginnings and beginnings and beginnings anew; and if it's not every time what we thought it would be, what was it promised us anything different but our own daft whimsy-whamsies and imagination and nonsense? Life's dozen lives, and they're all fine."

The next start for MacGregor is war. He is stationed at the same Persian post as Hogbin. From this point farcical improbabilities build to the outrageous conclusion. MacGregor has taken the pledge at his wife's insistence, but he drinks arrack punch with Hogbin. It is drink that operates as a springboard to the hero's involvement in romantic adventure. MacGregor rescues Nastasya, even as he rescued Priscilla. He goes off with the exotic former mistress of Mirzah Khan to take over the dead leader's troops. As king of Jangalistan[1] MacGregor's conscience abides. He tells Nastasya, the temptress he has kissed but once, of the perils of leadership. "When you're a king and a general, your job is to rot and break and ruin the immortal spirit of a people to the third and fourth generation. And it runs in my mind that the Lord'll forgive you for being a hunting beast, but not for being a Devil." The Scot at home, in Persia, or in England remains the same in thought, word, and deed.

Ten years pass and MacGregor dwells in Antariksha, the region of air between heaven and earth. The speaker on the radio, who discusses the *Rig-Veda,* refers to this cloudy place. Priscilla turns off the wireless in her London home, shortly before she admits Motherwell, the leading elder in MacGregor's kirk. The slum lord complains about the minister's lectures on substandard housing.

MacGregor tells the elder, "I'm a Highlander; and well, a Highlander's a sort of a mystic; and well, you see, I'm maybe even more of a mystic than most of them. And when you're, in a way, living in another world, I think it does you good to try now and then to pull the two together. . . ."

Bridie pulls MacGregor's worlds together by contrivance. Hogbin arrives with the message that Nastasya, now a stage performer, wants to see MacGregor. The minister drinks once more and goes to the theater, where Nastasya informs MacGregor that she wants him to accompany her to Paris. Before the Russian can offer many blandishments, Priscilla arrives:

MACGREGOR. . . . A devil woke up in my stomach just now that I thought was dead.
PRISCILLA. But you surely wouldn't think for a moment of going off on a mad jaunt with the like of that?
MACGREGOR. I wouldn't think it for a moment, but there's something more than thinking in it all. We do because we must.

Motherwell, who has been seeing Nastasya, enters, and a mêlée ensues. MacGregor overcomes the temptation to be king and will begin to be king of his own castle and kirk.[2]

The author based the compulsive MacGregor on a seminarian he had known at the University of Glasgow. In his second autobiography Bridie tells of opening night of *Marriage Is No Joke,* when he heard his "lovely lines falling like cold porridge on a damp mattress." The author admits that others did not think the drunken divinity student as funny as he did, but he used the same formula again for Hector in *John Knox.*

For all of the antic farce, the reasons behind the drinking are serious. MacGregor imbibes because reality is commonplace. He wants to be heroic and adventurous, and he succeeds while under the influence. But his success is illusory. The minister preaches responsibility, but its opposite lures him. He sees the temptation as heroism rather than irresponsibility in an altered state of consciousness.

In his preface "The Anatomy of Failure" Bridie discusses his
use of intoxication. "The actor must unbosom himself rapidly and
all of a heap if he is to establish the philosophy underlying the
motives of his two hours' traffic. In the old plays a confidant was
used. To a drunken man, all the world is his confidant." This
applies to Lady Pitts, but with Drs. Mallaby and Johnson and, to
some extent, MacGregor, the altered state of consciousness is a
step along the way to the acquisition of truth. The drunk, the
dream, the Highland second sight are approaches for Bridie to
show what he himself seeks. This is a total grasp obtained
simultaneously without the pitfalls of reasoning. For Bridie this
becomes the only thing worth having. It is angelic intuition.

The playwright noted that *The Girl* is a "burlesque forerunner
of *Marriage Is No Joke.*" *Meeting at Night* and other works also
feature rescues, but the similarity of plot devices does not make
the writing repetitive, because the thought elevates the plays
from farfetched situation farce, which they often seem in critical
discussion.

II   The Black Eye

In *The Black Eye*, as in *Marriage Is No Joke*, Bridie used
improbability to reach a place where the dramatist could treat
issues that transcend the mundane. Bridie had taken characters
in and out of the real world in previous plays. From the outset of
The Black Eye he dispensed with that which exists independently
of ideas concerning it.

George Windlestraw meets the Serious Person, who speaks
poetry, for he is on a different plane. The Serious Person says
that he conforms to unreasonable rules to live in his aunt's house.
He trades rationality for comfort. This figure is the antithesis of
the protagonist in some ways, yet like him in others.

The Serious Person has no time to listen to George. Young
Windlestraw, who must tell some one of his experience, takes the
audience into his confidence. George unveils what Bridie terms a
"hypothetical universe." Theatergoers receive the story from
George's point of view, but the hero never learns what has
happened to him. The reason for this does not become apparent
until one considers *The Baikie Charivari.*

Bridie, who frequently questioned the reliability of narrators
in life, uses the storyteller who does not have all the "facts," to

demonstrate that human knowledge is incomplete. Man's inability to know the truth is one of the messages that finds many deaf ears. In fairness to those who did not perceive the message, discovering truth from one who does not know he possesses it taxes the most astute of advocates.[3]

The action of *The Black Eye* is interspersed with George's explanatory speeches, which are justifications of a confessed sinner rather than soliloquies. The story, which Bridie called a fairy tale, is deceptively simple. George Windlestraw has failed to pass the accounting exam a sufficient number of times to settle for a clerical post in his father's company. After having too much to drink, George becomes infatuated with Elspeth, his brother Johnnie's girl. The protagonist is tempted to run away.

An accident puts the head of the Windlestraw family in the hospital and George at the helm. The brothers quarrel over Elspeth. George discovers negligence on the part of his "dutiful" brother in the management of the firm. Love and financial disaster strengthen the impulse to escape responsibility, but George determines to be heroic.

The younger Windlestraw brother meets Samuels, a gambler, who functions as a guiding spirit, in much the same manner as Mallaby's Aunt Dinah. While drinking George and Samuels play roulette. The lucky number George chooses is seventeen, because he believes it is that day of the month. The game takes place on the eighteenth, but the ball stops at seventeen. What men think chance, Bridie asserts, is controlled by unseen Force. This Force George never recognizes, and so one must take more account of the actions than the protagonist's words.

After the game George and Samuels meet Elspeth in the hotel lobby. The girl who would rescue George has the potential to destroy him. She preaches "stability," but the one who has easily transferred affections from one brother to another does not know the meaning of the word.

Mrs. Windlestraw plays patience and gives a traditional fortune teller's reading of the cards: "Oh there's a Queen of Diamonds [the fair, worldly Elspeth] for that King of Spades [the older, brooding, darker Johnnie]. It's going to come out all right. I hope Johnnie fixes things up with Elspeth tonight, She'd suit him, I think."

Connie, the Windlestraw daughter, so like Elspeth that she dislikes her, says, "There's a Jack of Clubs [the younger,

chancetaking business man, George] underneath that pile of
things. You can move him to the Queen of Diamonds." To this
Mrs. Windlestraw answers, "Should I? Well perhaps," as she
gathers the cards. "Such a pity! It looked as if it were going to
work out." The irony of the reading is that George's mother does
not know her final interpretation is accurate and for the best.

George and Elspeth return home. The brothers fight; George
receives a black eye. Elspeth leaves the Windlestraws, whose
fortunes are bettered by the windfall from roulette, and the
wind that bounced the female "balloon" from their midst.

George resembles other Bridie characters in that he is
independent, and this brings him into conflict with those around
him. The immature youth, who admits he has no sense of humor,
does not see himself as funny. This increases the incongruity.
Other eccentrics, e.g., Mallaby and Dr. Knox, are equally
earnest.

George's life, like Mr. Gillie's, is a product of apparent chance,
but success, material or spiritual, is the result of divine guidance.
When selfish man uses his own dark thoughts, he fails.

George says, "We can't live for ourselves." Later he observes
that "Living one's own life is all very well when one knows
exactly the sort of life one would like. But who does?"

George claims he has "a sort of sixth sense," but he does not
see what Bridie states in the "Author's Note": "that we are not
justified by a catalogued series of sensible, social acts but by
something very much more extraordinary."

Bridie wrote Stephen Haggard, who played the lead, that the
protagonist "muddled through to a fortune by doing everything
the wrong way. The play brought back the soliloquy to the
London Theatre. The young man George Windlestraw was
desperately anxious to justify himself to the audience, and at
intervals throughout the play came down to the footlights and
explained."[4]

In Bridie's use of the word "justify," he links the play to
justification by faith, the central emphasis of the Protestant
Reformation. George tries to justify himself, because he has not
yet leaped to faith. The state of George's soul is as the condition
of the Serious Person's life. The Serious Person sings:

> I care not for the leaping stars.
> I clutch the cold, triumphant bars,

> For, one by one in regular row,
> They lead me where I want to go.

Bridie shows a man with good intentions who is visited by the extraordinary, but fails to see Who is responsible for his good fortune.

Like Tobias, George receives help to enable him to aid his parent. But Tobias recognizes the supernatural forces and cooperates. If a protagonist is blind to the Truth, how can he correspond with grace. It is the spiritual blindness of man which robs him of heroic stature, however he might succeed. But the fact remains that George has been aided and does succeed. The criticism of Protestant thought is implied. Bridie's dissatisfaction with traditional theological explanations becomes stronger as his comedies become more ironic, and as the author continues to explore the realm of truth.

The Black Eye opened at the Shaftesbury Theatre, London, on October 11, 1935. On the first night of the play George Bernard Shaw sat in one of the boxes. He laughed with the rest of the audience but remarked to the author, "It'll never do." In *One Way of Living* Bridie supposed that Shaw was right.

During the six weeks run, critical reaction to *The Black Eye* ranged from James Agate's "trumpery" to Ivor Brown's label "immoral fairy tale." Bridie stretched domestic comedy to its limits to convey the dismissal of convention. The experimental form he carefully constructed to ask profound questions is a major achievement. When a comedy is too brilliant, it is easy to mistake a gem for paste.

III   The King of Nowhere

The King of Nowhere starring Laurence Olivier opened at the Old Vic on March 15, 1939, shortly before the Munich crises. The comedy about dictatorship was ill timed. The author's rational approach contrasted sharply to the violent temper of the period.

Although Adolph Hitler's Third Reich was tilting the globe to World War II, Bridie's play was less intense than actual events. From Charlie Chaplin's burlesque, *The Dictator,* to Leni Riefenstahl's beatifying Nazi propaganda films to postwar documentaries on the Hitler regime, the enormity of the actuality was larger than the scope of media. The tyrant was inadequately portrayed as hero, anti-hero, or clown.

Bridie's king of nowhere believes that stagecraft and statecraft are sisters under the skin, a premise that has more currency in the age of television, than when the play appeared. The playwright makes the protagonist a neurotic clown. Bridie puts explosive material in a more objective perspective by showing dictatorial designs as small patterns surrounding a portrait of a sick thespian, who cannot control himself, let alone a very small domain.

In the Introduction Frank Vivaldi, who has become paranoid over a theatrical failure, is brought home from the theater by the doctors who will commit him to an asylum. The unstable actor first appears in the makeup of Pierrot. Bridie uses the French version of the *commedia dell' arte* character Pulcinella (i. e., Punch), because Pierrot is a naive, clumsy, childish figure who rejoices one moment, and despairs the next. This should be Vivaldi's best role if type casting makes a *succès fou*.

Bridie would use a full complement of Punch and Judy characters in *The Baikie Charivari*. He did not make other roles correspond to *zanni* in *The King of Nowhere*, although Mrs. Vivaldi, a former actress and the fourth wife of the actor, is the female counterpart of the protagonist. Bridie describes her as a "vacuum."

The note at the beginning of act 1, an apology for the setting, is a sole reminder of Opinion, a character based on critic James Agate. Bridie dispensed with Opinion before opening night.[5]

In the lounge hall we meet Miss Rimmer, a repressed spinster, who does not know what to do with her inheritance. Vivaldi seeks refuge with the woman, who has written a Manifesto for dictatorship that will improve Britain.[6] Miss Rimmer is impressed with the actor's voice and manner, and wants him to be the spokesman for her ideas. She introduces the man she sees as sent from God as "Mr. John Roland Henry Lancaster Gaunt. My Aunt Boadicea's son." The woman, who devises the role that is too big for Vivaldi, becomes Britannia of this England in which dictatorship is possible.

Rimmer's menage includes a loutish John Buller (i.e., John Bull—England) and nurse Charlotte Appleby, whom Vivaldi calls Charlie (i.e., Bonny Prince Charlie—Scotland).

As the second act begins, the clacking of a typewriter underscores that adherents are organizing the movement. Vivaldi shows Charlotte how to curtsey: "When I am Dictator, people will do things beautifully . . . perfectly, or not at all." The actor wants to direct illusion. Rimmer's vision is impractical, but Vivaldi does not see others' perspectives. In "sleeping and dreaming and waking up and reading" he has not "soaked up" the manifesto.

Dr. McGilp[7] comes looking for his escaped patient and tells Miss Rimmer that Vivaldi is sane but unreliable. How reliable the psychiatrist's opinions are is moot. The spinster who has fallen in love with her leader cannot see McGilp's point of view.

Vivaldi speaks to Rimmer of love by inverting St. Paul's discourse on charity. The performer fails with the individual, but he succeeds when addressing a crowd: "What the people of this country want they shall have." Bridie uses Sophoclean irony to comment on politics.

McGilp confronts Vivaldi with reality. The actor can stir emotions, but he has no knowledge of government. Bridie has shown a man whose lust for power is confined to the boudoir. The womanizer who dislikes the opposite sex has no idea of the consequences of any of his actions.

Miss Rimmer has no notion of what her rhetoric will produce. Buller and his Myrmidons (i. e., the fierce Thessalian troop who accompanied Achilles to the Trojan war) physically abuse Kitchin, Miss Rimmer's lawyer. The idealist, who wants to build a new Jerusalem, cannot bear the ramifications of her scheme. She throws Buller out. Yet her faith in her spokesman and in her ideas persists.

The Epilogue opens with Vivaldi playing Chief for other inmates of the asylum. He prefers this audience to pleasing London crowds. Vivaldi says he is an "automaton." McGilp attributes his behavior to the "atavistic impulse."

The protagonist with no personality of his own, who speaks others' lines, often at inappropriate times, is mad and sane by turns. To convince Sarah Rimmer that he is too unbalanced to escape from the institution and resume the role in which she has cast him, he feigns madness. This brings on real symptoms of derangement.

Vivaldi, like MacGregor, is immature; both seek kingdoms, but

they are more contrastive than comparable. Self-absorption
leads man to irresponsible behavior. When this results in
disorder that involves others, the result is chaos.

Bridie provides a sound psychological portrait of a performer
with delusions of grandeur. According to the doctor Vivaldi is
harmless. The protagonist summons pity, for he holds no terror.
Yet the ramifications of his actions are chilling.

MacGregor sees his folly. Vivaldi mistakes his foolishness for
divinely inspired wisdom. The actor refers to Dr. McGilp as
"Beloved Physician," i. e., Luke. At one point he implies that he
is Samson. Such inversion is diabolical. Vivaldi tells the inmates:

I have tried to apply to the problems of domestic and foreign politics
the simple doctrines of Christianity. I humbly describe myself as a
practising and practical Christian. It is only in that spirit that the world
can be saved. And I am going to see that it is saved, and in that spirit. If I
receive no reply to my letter by midnight, I shall be patient. I shall send
another letter. It will be borne by five thousand troop-carrying
aeroplanes and accompanied by ten thousand ton of incendiary bombs.
I'll teach them a Christian spirit!

Vivaldi has no way of implementing his designs. He is entertaining the inmates with his rhetoric. Yet we hear more of Vivaldi's
ideas than of Miss Rimmer's. Belligerents have justified themselves by proclaiming that God is on their side. Persistence in
such folly is insane.

Vivaldi cannot grasp new ideas. Bridie's heroes can be
identified by their ability to see things in new ways. They are
liberal, and tend to be left rather than right wing. When they are
involved in politics, e. g., Sir James Pounce-Pellott, they see the
ineptitude rather than the wisdom of governmental systems, and
rebel against constrictive man-made order, as they search for the
way God intended man to live.

IV   Mr. Gillie

Mr. Gillie opened at the Royal Theatre, Glasgow, on February
13, 1950. The play directed by Alastair Sim, who also starred in
the title role, was well received. It went to the Garrick Theatre,
London, on March 9 of the same year and ran four months.

The Prologue consists of a conversation between the heavenly
Judge and the Procurator. The use of the word "procurator"

suggests the jesting Pilate figure, who functions as prosecutor. William Wotherspoon Gillie is a candidate for immortality. The Judge (God) asks, "What is success?" This question is the premise of the play. The answer serves as theme: true success is spiritual betterment.

Bridie frequently gives the theme early in the play, then develops the side of the question he has chosen to explore. His manner of presentation of the argument more than turns of plot provides suspense.

The Black Eye is a companion piece, in that it treats of earthly achievement. *Babes in the Wood*, whose academic hero, Gillet, has something in common with Gillie, is another variation on the theme, but it is in *Mr. Gillie* that Bridie offers his most profound thoughts on the subject. The protagonist who is a celestial success reaches higher heroism than any other person in Bridie's dramas.

From the perspective of the eternal now, where Truth is known, Judge and Procurator look back on scenes from the life of the man who was killed by the van that took the Gillies' furniture to auction. The seeming chance in the impoverished Gillie's demise is not a trick to get rid of the hero, but an indication that the man has fulfilled his purpose.

Both acts take place in Gillie's study. People in his life parade through the book-lined room. The parade device is a pat solution to character interaction, but in this play it is expertly managed. Careful preparation and subtle dialogue elevate the play to a naturalistic drama of the first rank.

We first meet Gillie, a schoolmaster, in a coal mining village, tutoring a sleeping Tom. The dominie defines genius as "Possession by a god." Gabriel Marcel points out that Bridie incorporates his artistic creed in this play. In reading Carlyle, Gillie makes his own pronouncements on creativity, perfection and drama. "In the Drama, there's all the more need for that meticulous carefulness. Every line must be loaded with significance and pull its weight. Every moment counts. Every article of furniture on the stage must mean something. . . ."

Tom Donnelly beats Gillie at chess "played to a Fool's Mate." Mrs. Gillie chatters throughout their game, and her husband loses the contest of skill. Later he wins at cribbage, a game of chance. The ironies which function on several levels begin to pile into patterns.

After Tom leaves, Gillie expresses his faith in his student's literary abilities. Gillie fosters creativity in those whom he believes show promise. This relieves the drudgery of his life's work.

Mrs. Gillie says, "you might have been headmaster of a high school in Glasgow if you'd paid attention to your cards." Her husband answers, "But for the grace of God I might have been." The slight twist of a familiar line indicates that the hero, who is not a player of vain games, knows he is in the proper place.

Dr. Watson, a drunken physician, next visits Gillie. Watson wishes to keep Nelly, his daughter, at home for his convenience. He cares nothing for her musical ability, which the school master has encouraged. Watson is concerned only about himself. He assesses what his daughter thinks: " 'there he is, slaving his soul out for a lot of bloody higher-grade apes, who can no more win to an appreciation of what he does for them than they can win to the Kingdom of Heaven.' She never says much, but I can read her thoughts."

Bridie uses the man's estimate of others to reveal the speaker's character. When Tom and Nelly announce their secret marriage, her father's lack of self-knowledge, selfishness and subsequent inability to know others becomes more apparent. Watson denudes himself with Sophoclean irony.

In arguing about his daughter with Gillie, the doctor tells the teacher that he misjudges those whom he believes have creativity, as does Mrs. Gillie. Those who have no vision can see things which Gillie does not.

Mrs. Gillie becomes vexed with her husband, after he encourages Tom and Nelly in their impractical marriage. Gillie sees it as the rescue of the girl from her boorish father. The wife, who does not understand her spouse, says, "Self, self, all through." This is an irony Bridie employs in play after play. Characters accuse opponents of qualities which they do not possess, but which the accusers have in abundance.

Those who boast of good deeds perform few. When Watson discovers that Nelly has gone he asks, "Am I to be left in the tragedy of my loneliness with nobody . . . nobody. . . . Me that has broken myself in the service of the sick and dying. . . ."

The next visitor to Gillie's study is Mr. Gibb, whom the stage directions describe as *"A Personage."* The parson does not bring consolation. He is the instrument by which the hero's dreams

turn to nightmares. Gibb has come to tell Gillie that his services
are no longer required, because the school is being closed.

The unsuccessful novelist tells about his time as a teacher, and
shows his power to stand alone against all adversaries.

MR GILLIE. . . . I've been a turnkey in a children's prison. It's been my
business to baulk and thwart their bouncing energy and tie
them to their hard benches for hours at a time. I've seen
their wretched eyes, day after day, staring at me in stony
hatred till the bell sounds at four o'clock and lights them
up with joy and relief. The unutterable joy of getting out of
the reach of my hand for a few hours. I've pumped
ditchwater in at one ear and watched it come out at the
other. As for myself, I've spent every minute of my spare
time groping blindly for a way to escape, like a lavatory
attendant filling football coupons. If I hadn't had a decent
wife, keeping me fat and fed and comfortable—
anaesthetising me—I'd have shot myself long ago.

GIBB. You haven't got a vocation for teaching. That's the trouble.

MR GILLIE. Wait a minute. I knew one way of escape.

GIBB. Yes, I know. Escape, escape, escape all the time. Escape
from your duties. Escape from your responsibilities. That
was all you cared for.

MR GILLIE. Well, suppose it was? What kind of duties? What kind of
responsibilities?

GIBB. Responsibilities to the Community.

MR GILLIE. I know what you mean. I know the Community. The
Community nowadays means Parliament and the Civil
Service. We pay them to look after us, and so they do. In
return we have to do what we are told, like the wretched
brats in my school. We can't blow our noses without their
high and mighty permission. There's only one kind of man
who isn't ordered about from the cradle to the grave, and
that's the artist. He's bullied like the rest; but he's under
nobody's orders. He's responsible to God and, perhaps to
his neighbors. But not to what you call the Community. I'd
be an artist myself if I could. If I can't, I'll help others to be
that. And you and the rest of you can do what you like
about it.

When a man is at odds with the fools who surround him, and
yet persists in helping fellow creatures, he resorts to irony. God
Himself is ironic.

Gibb is apprehensive that Watson, who has accused the teacher of being a meddler, will make trouble.

GIBB.   . . . Parents still like to have some small say in the arrangement of their children's careers. . . .
MR GILLIE. I know. Not many generations ago they had them helping in the pits before they were ten years old.

Irony is a shield, but it is not a protection from reality. To overcome the shock of being fired, Gillie starts another novel. He tries to make a new beginning.

In the Interlogue the Judge says that labor at one's calling is not enough. Man must *do, produce,* and *create.* Yet intentions and effort rather than accomplishment finally win Gillie his seat next to John Wesley in heaven.

In act 2 Tom and Nelly return. He is a film critic. She is "going places" with Tom's employer. Again those in whom Gillie has believed disappoint him. Gibb has accused Gillie of sending students into the maelstrom. In this instance it proves true. But the man who has no illusions about his literary gifts, yet thinks he can inspire by teaching, is not shattered by this apparent failure. After scolding Tom, Gillie offers him a drink. The teacher lives in "forlorn hope."

When Gillie sees a sketch of Nelly, which one of the village girls has done, he persists in fostering talent. Nothing any one says or does can dissuade him. The stubborn quality, which is annoying to others, is a virtue in the eyes of the only Judge Who can hand down a just verdict. In the Epilogue the Procurator argues that Gillie's effort is misdirected. The Judge finds that in freeing people Gillie succeeded: "I find most good men occupied in designing and strengthening cages. I do not like cages. I think that the few minutes between the door of the cage and the jaws of the cat make life worth living."

V   Meeting at Night

While working on *Meeting at Night* Bridie asked Priestley to read the play, because the author thought he should bring it out under another pseudonym. The fellow playwright assured the writer that the comedy was worthy of James Bridie's by-line.

Bridie was suffering from a vascular condition. He was unable to shape *Meeting at Night* into a final form that satisfied him. The play was revised by Archibald Batty, before Bridie's death on January 29, 1951, and eventually was produced at the Glasgow Citizens' Theatre in 1954.

Meeting at Night is worth consideration, because in reading Bridie one is tempted to "improve" his plays. There is so much that is good in his scripts that the annoying loose ends seem to be easily remedied. Batty's revision is an example of the results of such temptation. Bridie's satire of isms becomes obscured by sitcom.

Batty tied up the plot to make a fashionably tight knit structure. Insertions such as the postal orders and the antique desk incidents are sentimental strands which put the confidence man in a soft, audience-pleasing fabric. Batty's knots result in situation comedy. Bridie's loosely woven material, which lets thought breathe, is a more suitable backdrop. Improbability in the action forces one to examine what the playwright is trying to say.

Helen Luyben says that *Meeting at Night* is an explication of *The Girl Who Did Not Want to Go to Kuala Lumpur*. Hector Maclachan's attempt to rescue Connie Triple from her father, George, a swindler, who is about to be taken into custody, resembles the plot of the 1930 comedy. It is the very similarity that indicates the subsidiary place plot holds in Bridie's comic writing. What the author says within the frame of the story makes his works distinctive.

Hector has rescued Connie from an amorous drunk, before the action begins. She brings the hero home. There he learns her name.

HECTOR. There's nothing wrong with Cornelia. It's a kind of precious stone, isn't it?
CONNIE. Yes. It's red. I was born during one of my father's swings to the Left.
HECTOR. He's a Socialist?
CONNIE. Not now. Are you?
HECTOR. I suppose I am in a way.
CONNIE. I'm a Civil Servant.

Bridie uses names for humorous purposes in a number of plays. The serious question which is tumbled by a frivolous answer is another favorite device. These methods help to establish the tone and to provide comic distance. From this vantage one can observe the satire clearly.

Hector meets George, who explains his philosophy of business. The swain does not like the crook, who is a confirmed capitalist. George runs a mail-order healing racket. In the course of airing his financial views, Triple discourses on a hundred pounds.

A hundred pounds is never a hundred pounds. It is a crime to own it if you've earned it in dollars and a crime not to own it if you owe it in income tax. It may represent ten thousand ping-pong balls or a single share in a defunct gold-mine. It will buy a hundred square miles of land in Alaska or a pair of boots in Chungking. In hard cash it would drag any swimmer to the bottom of the sea, and in post-war credits it builds him a castle in Spain. A man can earn it by washing dishes for a year or smiling at a camera for three seconds. A horse, of course, can do far better.

The tangents introduce Hector to George's world, but they do not quite succeed in revealing the speaker's personality as conceived by two writers. Hector wishes to rescue Connie from George. With his offer to take them to his mother's inn, Hector brings the Triples to his sphere. At the end of the first act Hector successfully evades Inspector Flatt's questions. In fending off the policeman who seeks Triple, Hector shows that he can function in George's world.

The second and third acts take place at Mrs. Maclachlan's inn. The proprietress is, in fact, a capitalist, but the eccentric woman, who dabbles in spiritualism and New Thought, is an avowed communist. After a "prayer meeting," during which Mrs. Maclachlan reads from *Das Kapital* in a satire of the substitution of communism for Christianity, the woman explains to George how she heard a voice that prompted her to partake of the Universal Consciousness. The Universal Consciousness is the Emersonian Over Soul as interpreted by practioners of New Thought. It is akin to the Collective Unconsciousness of Carl Jung. If one can tap this source, he may get the answer to anything.

Mrs. Maclachlan is the embodiment of misplaced faith. Soon after she meets George, she accepts his bad check for half interest in the Hammer and Sickle Inn.

Sandy the servant has flashes into the future. His visions are genuine, but he does not know what they mean until after events have occurred. He seems to have been intended as a foil to his employer, but the relationship is not developed.

Ideologies can coexist, because man is a contradictory creature who tailors beliefs to suit his own purposes. The idea gets lost in the shifts of youth versus age. The parents are against Hector and Connie's marriage, even as the offspring oppose their parents' merger.

In a satire of the play itself George describes the situation as a conventional sentimental comedy. Connie sees it as a tragedy, for she is Electra, Hector is Oedipus. But both handle their own and each other's parents adroitly.

Flatt arrives to seek his Jean val Jean, as the second act closes. This entrance signals the contrived denouement. The policeman buys a Sheraton desk from Mrs. Maclachlan for a pittance. George, who is a picker of antiques, among other things, confronts the policeman with his greed. George's bad check, postal order, and letter are artificial respirators used to jerk laughter and suspense into the final act.

The worlds of the characters come together, and chicanery is common. Early in the play Bridie's satire points to symbolic characters, but the play remains literal. The shift in focus causes one to question who is the protagonist—rescuer or rogue.

Bridie's protagonists are frequently immature, always flawed individualists. They have strong egos which they need to come up against matters that cause them to consider what truth is. When they are most earnest, they are often most entertaining. Some realize they cannot find truth in this life and become ironic. They are consciously and unconsciously ambivalent. The heroes revert to adherence of the moral law, which is as absolute and universal as the principle of gravity. With *Meeting at Night* the Bridie hero slips into the grouse moors.

CHAPTER 6

The Heroine, Upstage

IN *One Way of Living* Bridie speaks with a familiar—the eighteenth-century dramatist, Mrs. Aphra Behn—then launches into "A Lecture on Women."[1] In writing familiar essays Bridie often strikes a pose. The facade is well constructed and difficult to penetrate.

The man who enjoys the all male preserve of the British club finds women in general perplexing. The individual woman is a particular enigma: "If we select a specimen for intense study we quickly find ourselves oscillating between extremes of love to hate, irritation and rapture; very clouding and embarrassing to the judgement."

The differences between men and women's psyches fascinate Bridie. In some matters women are too like men, in others they are too different. In his irritation with the dissimilarities, Bridie echoes Professor Higgins in Shaw's *Pygmalion.* In asking, as Higgins does in *My Fair Lady,* "why can't a woman be more like a man," Bridie replies that, when this happens, it degrades.

In treating women's imitation of male behavior, the Victorian, who had been taught to put the fair sex on a pedestal, comes up with one of his frequent and striking similes: "It is like an Angel strapping his wings with elastoplast to make himself fit to associate with an income tax collector."

In his discourse on women Bridie offers an explanation of his frequent use of the rescue: "In stage plays no heroic or unselfish act by a male used to be thought valid unless it was performed on behalf of some pure and desirable woman. This was because stage plays always have been written for women. They destroy by their indifference any play which does not conform to their peculiar, and perhaps temporary ethic. The truth is, that no act performed in a state of erotic frenzy is an heroic act." The "Lecture" betrays an attitude that may be stated as beware of female. It is not misogyny but Bridie's wariness on a venture into the unknown.

I   Mary Read

The playwright was cautious about focusing on women. In his first attempt to create a female protagonist he undertook to foster the career of Flora Robson, an actress whose outstanding talents seemed doomed to be wasted in secondary parts, because her features did not conform to the common concept of a heroine. Bridie created an extraordinary female lead in *Mary Read*. The title character is sufficiently masculine that the use of the word "heroine" becomes a reference to gender rather than sensibilities.

Bridie's source is Charles Johnson's *General Histories of Robberies and Murders of the Most Notorious Pirates* (1724). In Johnson's account Mary Read was dressed as a boy to hoodwink a wealthy grandmother. The girl continued to pass as a man when she reached adulthood. She became a soldier, a sailor, then a pirate. The prototype was twice married. She was tried for piracy, but died of fever before her sentence was enacted.

Bridie had a taste for swashbuckling adventure and a sure feeling for Georgian setting and dialogue. His correspondence with Miss Robson indicates that he was enthusiastic about the project.[2]

After rewriting the romantic pageant more than ten times, Bridie was not satisfied with the script. He asked Claud Gurney to collaborate. Gurney trimmed some of the scenariolike leaps, and changed the two lovers of Mary into one part. As a result the role of Edward Earle, with its combination of characteristics, is an unconvincing pastiche.

Bridie was a soloist rather than a team player. He quarreled with Gurney by letter and in person. In his preface Bridie termed *Mary Read* "nobody's play." In *One Way of Living* Bridie described the fiery collaboration, and said that the drama was "a hideous conglomeration of nothingness with this to recommend it, that it had a simple coherent story and a part for Flora."

After tryouts in Manchester, *Mary Read* opened in London at His Majesty's Theatre on November 21, 1934. Thirty-four characters enacted a picaresque tale before nine sets.

As the play begins Mary's mother is dressing her in breeches to meet her grandmother. The mother, her suitor, and most of the subsidiary characters are as poignant as Hogarth thumbnail sketches. They show the effect of environment upon Mary.

The girl enters womanhood, but has mannish traits and abilities. As soldier and pirate she is aggressive, emotionally cool under fire, and able to argue with the same skill with which she wields a rapier. Mary falls in love with Earle, a painter who is her opposite in character. The man of feminine instincts lacks courage. He follows Mary into her life, then deserts her.

Earle returns as a spy for the Governor of Jamaica. The heroine duels with another pirate on her love's behalf. She slays her adversary, then kills the one she loves to spare him torture at the hands of her brigands. After a battle with the governor's ship, Mary dies in childbed fever.

The breeches part of a rootless creature without friends, love, or understanding has pathos. Mary's long act 2 speech about love, marriage, conception, and parturition has a masculine perspective.

Mary Read is a compensatory woman. In addition to the maze of sexual complications through which the actress must wend, she needs great stamina to perform the physical feats required. From shipboard to tavern, the historical tableaux diminish all but the most powerful and resourceful of players. Like the historical paintings of Sir David Wilkie, the individual tends to be dwarfed in the grandeur of the scene.

Opening night critics pointed out that *Mary Read* is comparable to opera. The montage ran 105 performances. Miss Robson's superb acting of a challenging role and Robert Donat's portrayal of Earle, which in its way is equally exacting, prolonged the life of the play, that is better suited to film than stage.

II Mrs. Waterbury's Millenium

The year after *Mary Read* was produced by Tyrone Guthrie, Bridie published *Mrs. Waterbury's Millenium* (1935). This one-act comedy, which was designed to make a political statement, satirizes the English manner of coping with the Depression. Mrs. Waterbury, an indomitable matron, gives a breakfast for liberal and conservative members of Parliament, a Man-on-the-Dole, and his mother. The wealthy hostess questions her guests and finds the government works to provide idleness. The woman decides not to bother visiting the prime minister to offer help on the problem of unemployment. The caricature of the strong willed individual, who does and yet does not understand, is a shared characteristic of Bridie's men and women.

III   Daphne Laureola

Winnifred Bannister calls the woman who holds the center of the stage throughout *Daphne Laureola* a "masculine female," Helen Luyben sees Lady Pitts as "a symbol of disillusioned innocence, a symbol of England after the Second World War, and by extension, of Western civilization."[3] The heroine is of such complexity that the play becomes another example of Bridie's cutting into brocade to make pocket lining.

Bridie had witnessed a brandy-drinking woman burst into song in the *fin de siècle* confines of London's Cafe Royal. In his second autobiography he notes that as a medical student he met a woman who worked in a shop by day and by night ran a shelter for prostitutes in Glasgow's Gallowgate. He combined elements of a number of women he knew to forge a character that admits inclusion of mythic dimensions.

Daphne Laureola opens in a Soho restaurant. The patrons range from spivs—those who live by their wits—to young people, whose conversation shows that graciousness has gone from England. The floor of the eating establishment is ready to collapse, but the management cannot obtain the steel girders necessary to prop it up. With Lady Pitts' singing Massenet's *Elegie* and the Fat Man's mouthing the line from François Villon—"Where are the snows of yester-year?"—Bridie establishes that Britain is at the end of a cycle.

As Lady Pitts downs brandy she tells parts of her life. Piecemeal revelation is Bridie's usual method of providing information. The audience must put the puzzle together. The lady tells a personal anecdote in which she questions the Adam and Eve legend; she asserts that "Even God is unreasonable." The woman is ready to trade new myths for old, but this new Eve is no more honest than the old one, and it is necessary to consider her actions more than her words.

In her remembrance of things past, the woman, who says she drinks to forget loneliness, also states that men are brutal, and that she loved a doll given her by a wife-beating gardener more than anything in her life. The woman is drunk and feeling sorry for herself. How seriously is one to take her account? And yet in her noting that the gardener's wife enjoyed being beaten, she says something of herself.

Lady Pitts speaks her thoughts aloud. She posits a cyclical world with its periodic decay, then launches into an explication of *The Tempest*. This reinforces her estimation that God is unreasonable.

The woman, who glides across the dangerous floor to invite strangers to tea, engages a young Pole in conversation.[4] Ernest Piaste is a humorless, melancholy idealist, who desires to be Lady Pitts' champion. Her chauffeur Vincent knocks Ernest down. Lady Pitts says she loves Ernest, but Piaste is no more able to understand hyperbole than he is capable of comprehending that this woman does not need his kind of rescue.

Part of Ernest's difficulty in obtaining objectivity is his inability to laugh. Bridie carefully shows that this is not a foreigner's linguistic difficulty. Ernest understands an intricate English statement on probability.

The second act takes place in Sir Joseph Pitts' garden. The octogenarian husband is hard of hearing, which is a convenience, for he listens to what he wants to hear, and becomes deaf to things he can or will do nothing about. He says he cannot understand his wife, but his comments about the woman thirty years his junior are more objective than those of the woman who lies to herself and others.

Lady Pitts, who hisses invective without provocation when drunk, is the gracious hostess to unwanted guests, when sober:

LADY PITTS. . . . I want to hear about you. You must have led a very exciting and dangerous life.

ERNEST. Perhaps. I don't know. Strange things have happened to me; but they have been like a dream. I feel safe in my waking world because I hold fast to the Church of my mother. All other things have been of great irrelevance.

Formal religion and education are Ernest's anchors. He relies upon old myths and outmoded conventions, such as courtly love. School and church mean little to Lady Pitts, who, like her fellow puritan, MacGregor uses liquor to escape reality. The dream-worlds Ernest and Lady Pitts inhabit are illusory, not prescient. She has seen life and retreats from it. Ernest refuses to see reality. When he does perceive that his ideal love is a mask for lust, he too retreats to brandy.

Lady Pitts tells her guest that she wants danger, and although her exit from the restaurant over the unsafe floor, which the infatuated Ernest sees as passing "from the room like a ghost," indicates that this is true, she was intoxicated. Her subsequent behavior belies love of risk.

Others from the restaurant arrive for tea. They have the grace to be embarrassed, and one apologizes to his hostess. Indications of civilized society persist in individuals. Ernest tries to throw these people from *Le Toit Aux Porcs*, whom he considers interlopers, from his goddess' temple, but again his rescue is thwarted.

Ernest professes his love for Lady Pitts, who spurns him with a speech that has the resonance of Dr. Knox lecturing his students.

It's calf love. You think I'm your poor damned Presbyterian mother, or something. You come bleating to me because you've lost your way. I'm not a Presbyterian and I'm not your mother. And I've lost my way too. You've made a mistake. . . . You were right about only one thing—I'm a bad woman—as bad as I knew how to be. As bad as be 'damned. I've been bad all over. Europe and most of America—North *and* South. Now when I'm burned out and more than half mad, I'm playing at respectability with all the fervour I put into the other thing. I'm even the Chairwoman of a Marriage Guidance Clinic. I could tell them something! And now I'm a kept woman. Kept in more senses than one. Vincent, there, is my keeper, among other things. His job is to keep me out of mischief when I have the impulse to dash out and say to the first beggar in the street: "For God's sake, speak to me. Tell me I'm not the only creature in this damnable dead universe. . . ." *(quietly)* I can only say that when I'm tight you see. I think I told you that already.

Piaste takes this mixture of truth and fiction as a sign of hope, and kisses her. Sir Joseph sees them embrace.

At the beginning of the third act, Sir Joseph Pitts notices the laurel his wife had planted in November. He is concerned that setting the plant out too late in the season is an indication that Katherine's mental problems are recurring.

Ernest comes to see Lady Pitts. He encounters her husband. Sir Joseph tells Piaste his wife's history: her education, first marriage, and occupations, which include working as a secretary by day and running a shelter for prostitutes at night:

> SIR JOSEPH. . . . She has outbreaks. One can't really be surprised. It's all this emancipation of women. They think they can do what they like but it's not in their nature to do what they like. They just wallop about with the tide until they're caught in some new form of slavery. I found her plenty to do to keep her mind occupied but there's more than the mind has to be kept occupied and she has outbreaks every now and again. . . . I wouldn't mind her amusing herself with young men, but the trouble is she doesn't know how. She has the misfortune to be a dyed-in-the-wool Puritan.

This explanation is not intended to satisfy those who seek the cause of Lady Pitts' behavior. It is a reiteration of the playwright's thought that no one knows why certain things happen.

The callow Ernest explains his feelings for Lady Pitts to her husband. He envisions her as Beatrice to his Dante, then recounts the Daphne and Apollo myth. Pedantic, stuffy Ernest is giving his point of view.

In the final moments of the third act Sir Joseph dies. In a stream of consciousness speech he links his wife to the Daphne Laureola, for both are better behind glass. The plant is a symbol of the intimation of mortality.

In the fourth act the same characters are once more in the House of the Pigs. They discuss Sir Joseph's death. When Ernest hears his feminine ideal has remarried, he faints. Bridie intends to show how foolish the humorless are, but such comic intrusions hinder the mood of the drama.

Lady Pitts enters with the chauffeur, whom she has married, although she knows him for the boor he is. When Ernest and Katherine meet, she defends herself with the accusation of selfishness, a stock tactic of Bridie's women. The protagonist asserts that all men are in love with themselves and care nothing for women. Since this is the case, she has "settled down in a nice clean pig-sty."

Katherine Vincent tells Ernest a new myth: "You wanted to save the distressed lady from the ogre, didn't you? But the lady was too old to play these games, and she married the ogre and settled down. They all do, Mr. Piaste. . . ."

Lady Pitts is a survivor. She needs to be kept, but although she marries, her true needs remain ambiguous. Vincent knows her. He says she is the "cyclothymic type."

The drama, like the lady, is cyclical in structure. The message that comes from it is that man is bound to repeat his mistakes, although the slight variations make them seem ever new.

Critics in London and in New York were misled by the symbolism of the play, because they did not realize Bridie was working from the perspective of dream. They assigned too much importance to Ernest's story of Daphne, Apollo, and aged Ge. This is the symbol of one character's dream, rather than the allegory of the play. Although Bridie was not a Gestaltist, in this instance he followed the theory that the dreamer's image of the personality is not the person himself. The symbolism functions as a dream of contraries: it tells us what the characters are not, rather than what they are.

The placing of the laurel on stage for the third act is intended to make the audience ponder whether the Daphne will survive. When a symbol becomes a stage prop it tends to become ineffectual. It is as the Chinese proverb: a dream much discussed loses its power.

The play opened in London at the Wyndham Theatre on March 23, 1949, and ran for a year. Dame Edith Evans' performance helped the play achieve good box office receipts, but, as Bridie observed, she was miscast. The original leading lady played the part as an intellectual exercise: she emphasized the evergreen toughness of the Daphne, but it has a fragile flower also.

Bridie's women fall into patterns. Older women, such as Mrs. Gillie and Mrs. Maclachlan, are inclined to bustle, give unsolicited opinions, which frequently show contrastive perception to that of their men. Personal eccentricity makes them distinctive. Mrs. Hangingshaw, Aunt Dinah, and Lady Dodd are each bizarre in their own fashion.

There is not a love story in Bridie's entire output. Characters become romantically involved in relatively few lines of dialogue. Propinquity and proximity draw them together. What keeps couples together is largely the province of the woman.

Wives put up with much from their husbands. Some are common sense, hospitable souls, such as Mrs. McCrimmon and Mrs. Windlestraw. Margaret Gillet, who tells her husband she is glad she is not intellectual, has the same perspective as Mrs.

McCrimmon. Mrs. Gillet's practicality is similar to Priscilla
MacGregor's. They do not share their husbands' visions. This
objectivity enables them to lead their spouses out of temptation.

Wives tend to be martyrs, who do not understand their mates.
One is inclined to ask the question Shaw raises in *Androcles and
the Lion:* do all martyrs go to heaven? Angela Prout endures an
artist's tantrums; Mrs. Vivaldi, an actor's neuroses. Yet these
women are self-indulgent in their own ways.

The female as temptress can lead men astray within and
without marriage. Susan Copernicus and Mrs. Kishmul offer
adultery. Mrs. Mallaby and Mrs. Gillie propose that their spouses
do things in conflict with the divine intention. Bridie's women
are most interesting when they are unwitting temptresses.
Susannah is one of these.

In the preface to *Susannah and the Elders* Bridie says that the
play is "a tribute to womanhood." The heroine is chaste,
intelligent, and charming. The biblical character speaks of love,
peace and good sense to men who do not know the meaning of
these qualities.

DIONYSOS.   What do *you* think that love is like, Susannah?
SUSANNAH.   Why should I say what love is like? It is like nothing. It is
            like itself. It is a sister of birth and of death, but it is not like
            them. We know it as we know God. We can deny God if we
            are so wicked that He makes us unhappy; but we know that
            He is there.

In Susannah's short speeches she displays no internal conflicts.
We see only the surface. Bridie does better with quick sketches
of character parts than with leading ladies. Thus, women are
identified by relationships. They are wives, mothers, daughters,
or sweethearts. Those who have jobs are nurses or actresses, the
two positions Bridie mentions in his "Lecture on Women" as
those at which females excel. The nurse who provides necessary
exposition in *The Last Trump,* as she displays officiousness, is
typical of Bridie's *besoms:* "I think a man like you ought to have
more sense. How do you expect to get well if you never do what
you are told? And you might think of the people who're
responsible for you. I don't know whether I'm standing on my
head or my heels. Of course, you won't be interested, you think
of nobody but yourself. . . ."

CHAPTER 7

The Devil, on Proscenium

DREAM has been associated with drama since the ancient Greek priests of Asclepius encouraged pilgrims at Epidarus to cleanse themselves by experiencing catharsis while watching tragedies performed in the amphitheater. If the world portrayed on the stage did not succeed in producing the desired purgation, the patients, who had dreamed of the god of medicine, were assigned places to sleep in the snake-infested porticos. In the *abaton* those in need sought visions in which they would be visited by the god once more. Asclepius would cure them in the dream or guide dreamers to the right remedy.

Of the large number of creative works that have been inspired or influenced by dreams, Robert Louis Stevenson's *The Strange Case of Dr. Jekyll and Mr. Hyde* is among the best known. Stevenson's use of dream parallels that of Bridie's. When the nineteenth-century author was a boy, he was troubled by nightmares. These grew in intensity during the period Stevenson studied medicine at Edinburgh. He consulted a doctor about them.

When Stevenson effected a change in his dream life, he was able to tell himself stories, then dream of their continuation. He came to be able to dream in serial form. This he attributed to "Brownies," who aided him "to find a body, a vehicle, for that strong sense of man's double being, which must at times come in upon and overwhelm the mind of every thinking creature."[1] The result was the famous psychological tale of the scientist who becomes a monster.

In *One Way of Living* Bridie describes a recurring nightmare he experienced as a child. He would seek the light in the hall and find his mother and father. They would appear in the corridor as "malignant strangers. They made fierce hideous triumphant faces at me. The passage gradually filled with simulacra of my brother, my uncles, my aunts, my nurse. . . ."

That the boy's subconscious regarded the people around him
as obstructions is less informative than his pictorial and verbal
formulas to dispel nightmare: "Before I went to sleep, I shut my
eyes tight and saw a number of red devils in blue jackets dancing
round a cauldron surrounded by leaping flames." He would
repeat a couplet he had learned in a dream, which was "an
invocation to birds, beasts, flowers and Jesus."

The structures of Bridie's plays have much in common with
dreams. Some are episodic and frequently leap from one locale
to the next, e.g., *Jonah*. The cyclical pieces are designed to show
that matters recur, e.g., *Daphne Laureola*. Segments of plays
feature dream visions, e.g., *Dr. Angelus*. Characters in altered
states of consciousness, usually induced by drink for theatrical
purposes, reveal things which they would not normally say, e.g.,
Lady Pitts. Events are linked by intentionally improbable
situations. A fantastic segment or atmosphere is thrust into
conventional proceedings, e.g., the reenactment of the Prouts'
first meeting.

Symbolism, such as McCrimmon's chasing the devil out of his
life with a knife, is the kind one finds in books on the meaning of
dream. Bridie uses symbols in the manner they occur in dreams
as well. They are flashed before the beholder, not explained, and
prima facie they are not justified. Upon closer consideration, the
symbols do add to the play. Those who see the symbols are free
to take the meaning. Bridie's imagery, notably the seeing of
similarities in dissimilar things, is comparable to the kind one
experiences during sleep.

When one has been dreaming, he often awakes remembering
only half of what he saw or heard. Bridie's variations on themes
which he cannot capture to his satisfaction are related to efforts
to convey the meanings of dreams, rather than what has been
called the Scottish flair for repetition.

Bridie garnered a number of themes, perspectives, and
thought forms from his dreams. He desired to take his audience
into another world, where one can attain greater truth than one
can find while awake. He rarely explained this course he
followed, because the most frequent responses to a man's
account of his sleeping visions range from boredom to doubt of
the narrator's sanity.

At the end of his 1939 autobiography Bridie tells more about
his general method and aims in playwriting than in his prefaces

and essays. If many of his dramas fail to satisfy completely, many dreams do likewise, for visions are meant to whet, to lead man on to keep searching. They are rarely designed to make him complacent. Bridie's arrangement of materials is *sui generis*. His use of dreams and other sources to create more than ordinary significance makes his writing worthy of being called art.

"I make patterns. I'm a carpet playwright. I weave. If you cannot follow the lines of my design; if you cannot read the Great Names of Allah woven among the olive trees and the scorpions and the stags, at least I hope you will like the gaiety of the colours and the variety of the shapes. Tread lightly on my Berlin Persians, on my quaint linoleums, for you tread on my dreams."

"That is all very well," said the Recording Angel, when he had read my plays, "but. . . ."

"Just a minute," I said. "Listen to this. 'She came downstairs. She went to an office and sat there all day. She went back to her divan room at six-thirty and stayed there reading library novels. She had no friends and no money to spend. . . . If I make her alive then I have told a story, a story out of which you can take your own meaning, a story you can round off with your own moral. If I put in a murder in the next flat, a love affair with her employer or any such miserable incident I put it in because otherwise no one would buy this story. But they are not the story. The story is the girl herself, coming to life, reaching to you over the footlights and telling you that you are not alone in the world; that other human beings live, suffer, rejoice and play the fool within the same limitations that bind you. And all this nonsense about last acts. Only God can write last acts, and He seldom does. You should go out of the theatre with your head whirling with speculations. You should be lovingly selecting infinite possibilities for the characters you have seen on the stage. What further interest for you have they, if they are neatly wrapped up and bedded or coffined?"

One of Bridie's favorite sayings was the line from a popular song: "If you want to do something big, go out and wash an elephant." The manner he chose to express the grand design has the same tone. The problem of good and evil in the world is the most ambitious theme in literature, and it remained Bridie's abiding concern.

The force of evil is universally depicted as a demon or devil. The man, who as a youth was frustrated in the Free Church of Scotland, where he daydreamed through lengthy Sunday sermons, had long outgrown the anthropomorphic conception of a blue-jacketed creature leaping about a large pot. For dramatic purposes, however, he relied upon traditional depiction, because for all Bridie's efforts to expand what a play might contain, he was limited by a proscenium arch, and by what the audience would accept.

I   The Sunlight Sonata

Tyrone Guthrie liked *The Sunlight Sonata* and produced Bridie's first professional play to be mounted at the Lyric Theatre, Glasgow on March 20, 1928. The comedy was experimental. Neither the *Glasgow Herald* critic—who wrote a review that became Bridie's favorite as an example of misunderstanding[2]—nor a number of the theatergoers comprehended the stuff his dreams were made of.

The Sunlight Sonata, or To Meet the Seven Deadly Sins, "a Farce-Morality in A Prologue, An Interlude, A Demonstration, An Apotheosis and An Epilogue," indicates a departure from traditional genre and structure. The morality-farce, a near contradiction in terms, is indebted to dream in form and content.

The title, which is a play on Beethoven's "Moonlight Sonata," refers to Phoebus Apollo, the sun god who never appears on stage. Apollo's intervention does not really change the course of the action. The play might be more accurately described as the devil's sonata.

Giuseppe Tartini used the title, "The Devil's Trill Sonata," for his early eighteenth-century violin composition. Tartini had heard the devil play the violin in a dream. Later he tried to retain the sounds and write them down. Although Tartini considered the sonata his best, he lamented that it was far inferior to what the devil had played. An account of this phenomenon is to be found in Havelock Ellis' *The World of Dreams* (1911) which Bridie had read.

For *The Sunlight Sonata* Bridie uses the devil of his boyhood nightmares. In the "Description of Characters" the playwright stipulates that Beelzebub is to be dressed in dark blue doublet and hose. The prince of devils gives the Prologue, as he stands near Loch Lomond. The "de'il," whose favorite haunt is said to be Scotland, talks in Doric verse. Beelzebub's hexameters and the verse which other spirits speak place their speeches on a different level than the prose sections assigned to mortals. The devil, who can crawl into men's souls, does this by the thoughts, which are the "living heart of a man." The evil one claims to be able to prevent man in all his ways, then cites a prayer. The petition for the wrong things, i. e., "Prosper our cheating and let us be!" may be addressed to God, but it is the devil who listens to such requests. From the beginning of the drama Bridie stresses the idea that matters which are commonly thought to be good may have bad aspects in particular circumstances.

To aid the author of confusion and to help emphasize the point that there are two sides to every condition, the seven deadly sins are brought forth. Superbia (Pride), Ira (Anger), Accidia (Sloth), Avaricia (Covetousness), Gula (Glottony), Invidia (Envy), and Luxuria (Lust) are capsuled in exchanges with their master.

SUPERBIA. I am Lady Superbia. The first of the Seven Deadly Sins. Those are the others. I forget their names.

BEELZEBUB. It was you got my excellent crony, the Son of the Morning, the sack. Ye Inferiority Complex! . . . Get ower. Get oot o' my sicht.

That pride lurks behind timidity is illustrated by a minister in the Apotheosis. The Sins use their wiles on each other in the same manner the humans do during the Demonstration. The Prologue functions as a statement of propositions which will be shown in the action.

In the Interlude Faith, Hope, and Charity are introduced. The graces, whom Bridie describes as "uneventful Pantomime Fairy Queens," are personifications of what passes for virtue. The dramatist sends salvos at the midsection of bourgeois morality. This area is a lacuna filled with socially acceptable behavior. Hope, who lisps, asks: "How are thothe darling Deadly Thinth?" Charity, who loves too well, responds: "Busy as bees, the dears. Quite happy too. /How can they realize the harm they do? /I love Luxuria. She is such a child. /Gula's good-natured. Ira's a little wild."

Bridie links love, lust, and anger to show that from one human impulse different emotions can spring. He explicates this idea in the Epithalamium: At the close of the Interlude Charity says:

> I'm hoping to inspire a profiteer
> (Such a nice man) to give a pound or two
> To help a most deserving kangaroo
> Who sprained his ankle yesterday, in the Zoo.

Here the wordplay on "charity" is incongruous, but it is more than a device to provoke laughter. The lines point out that a popular misconception may be corrected by providing the contrary of the intended meaning. Calling attention to charity in this way is a technique from dream. Bridie makes the virtues inadequate in order to let the audience see what they should be.

The Demonstration consists of a Highland picnic. The Groundwaters, the Carmichaels, and Pettigrew illustrate how the deadly sins work in man. The seven mortals also function as representatives of the estates, which the author satirizes.

Gluttonous Mrs. Groundwater says, "I think it's so nice to sort of prolong the picnic. I mean it's so nice to see the things still lying about as if we were going on and on and on, like as if it was some beautiful dream of eternity."

Matters progress to the nightmarish with the aid of the infernal, as minister, business man, artist, and others reveal their besetting sins and display the interrelation of one fault to another. Mr. Marcus Groundwater, who parades his greed as virtue, tempts the Reverend Carmichael with pride, even as his son Hamish lusts for the wrathful Elsie.

MARCUS. Gifts to the Lord! You know perfectly well that I'm as generous as my neighbor. I practically put in the new organ myself. But there's a limit. There's the Economic Law, and that's God's Law—you can say what you like. Supply and Demand, and fair, untrammelled competition. This offer of Wyllie & Symington's is sheer damned foolishness. Of course they'll put the loss down to advertising expenses, but that isn't business. . . . See here, Mr. Carmichael, you've said yourself I'm a very valued member. We've been more like friends than a minister and Elder, the pair of us. And there's Hamish taken a notion to Elsie. It's like we'll be closer connected still, before very long. And now I've been put on the University Court it'll be bad luck or bad guidance if I can't get my spiritual adviser made a Doctor of Divinity before the year's out. I'll tell you what, I'll make you a fair offer. I'll cut down my price £500 and count that as a wedding present to the young folks, and you'll put your foot down on this Wyllie & Symington business. After all, you're the shepherd of the flock.

Beelzebub is unsatisfied with the job the Sins have done. He spreads his hand over the sun and casts a gloom over the picnickers. The picnickers awake from dreams in which they have indulged in their favorite sins. They accuse each other of faults, and attribute their own repeated transgressions to their neighbors.

Through Charity's intercession Apollo intervenes. The sun god bites the hand of the devil, who has hidden the source of warmth and light. All of the picnickers save Elsie depart. She asks Charity to give her the Sins, rather than put them away in an institution. Charity, who can refuse man nothing, complies. The graces then picnic on what the mortals have left.

By definition "apotheosis" is the elevation to divine status or the perfect example. One can assign both meanings to the Apotheosis of *The Sunlight Sonata*.

The curtain opens on the drawing room of Sir Marcus Groundwater. Five years have passed since the picnic. Beelzebub is now guising as the knight's gardener, Macpherson. Faith, Hope, and Charity are Groundwater's house servants. In dreams, when one entity functions in two or more capacities, the dual role serves to expand consciousness.[3] Here the natural and the supernatural come together.

The Groundwaters have invited the Carmichaels to lunch. As the sun is at its highest point, Sir Marcus has pangs of conscience about his business dealings with Wyllie & Symington.

Hamish, who is now in Holy Orders, enters. Young Groundwater's vocation provides opportunity for a satire on the first estate. Hamish, an Episcopal divine, has had breakfast with his bishop. His father, a United Free Church member, does not hold with bishops. Lady Groundwater says that the "Pope lives in the Vacuum in Venice." In this and other examples of malapropism, irony in the misusage or in the response adds substance to the comic device.

In an exposition of Scotland's sectarian squabbles, Bridie says, as he does throughout his writing, that the dismay of the religious establishments is the product of power hungry men, who seek their own advancement not the things of God.

The Carmichaels arrive. The stage directions state that the minister "has grown a beard and an inferiority complex." The preacher confesses that he has had a nervous breakdown and has lost his ability to deliver homilies. He asks his host for a job as

hod carrier. False modesty is a sin too. The point becomes lost in
laughter as Carmichael timidly gives his qualifications.

> CARMICHAEL. . . . I know a little Greek and Latin and a little Hebrew.
> MARCUS. The Hebrew might help you in a commercial
> career. . . .

The comic intrusion, which causes the audience to lose the
thread of the thought, is rare in Bridie. The author gives voice to
prejudices of his audiences, then reduces the bias to the absurd.
How effective this is to dispel erroneous opinion is questionable,
for a crowd tends to laugh at rather than with a minority, when it
is merely the subject of a one-liner.

While the Sins wait in the garden, Elsie enters. The now
successful novelist, who lives with Pettigrew, the painter, has
become a vamp. The realistic becomes fantastic once more. The
temptress does not recognize her former love, who is now a
minister. When Hamish refuses to kiss Elsie, she lures him by
asking for salvation. The guests exit to the dining room.
Beelzebub and the sins enter, and the devil lights a Hand of
Glory with a petrol lighter.

According to Richard Cavendish in *The Black Arts* (1967), the
Hand of Glory is a hanged murderer's extremity. It is dried in the
heat of the sun during the Dog Days. The influence of the sun is
intended to contribute to the dazzling quality of the hand's light.
If the sun's heat is not sufficient, the hand is heated in a furnace.
The magician uses the hand, which holds a candle made of
human fat, by lighting it, for this enables the practioner to rob
people's houses with impunity by rendering the victims immobile.

The mixture of light and dark imagery this stage prop calls
forth is clever, but arcane. The devil attempting to use that
which the sun god shaped to further his evil ends is bright, but
the general audience is left in shadow.

After delivering a curse, Beelzebub plays the piano, while the
Sins perform a ballet in which they act out their negative
qualities.

Faith disposes of the Hand of Glory, and the representatives of
evil are scattered. Groundwater gives the devil severance pay.
He makes a cross on the check. It burns in Macpherson's hand. In
a twist that illustrates that *The Sunlight Sonata* is indeed a

morality-farce, Sir Marcus also fires Faith, Hope, and Charity. He sees them as vampires and remarks, "I feel as if you'd sucked the soul out of me."

Faith has burned the food. To be servants is not the function of the graces. Faith, Hope, and Charity have been catering to the whims of man. Yet Faith, who stamped out the fire from the Hand of Glory, has enabled Groundwater to make his move.

After Hope and Charity leave, the mortals are soon back to their old ways. Hamish proposes to Elsie because he needs her money. She accepts. Faith remains and recites an Epithalamion.

> IF EVIL SPIRITS COME (AS COME THEY MUST),
> AS REVERENT SERVITORS LET THEM ATTEND,
> UTTERLY PURPOSED NEVER TO OFFEND.
> LET AVARICE KEEP THE WOLF-PACK FROM THE DOOR
> AND ENVY POLISH UP THE PARQUET FLOOR.

Accidia speaks the Epilogue. Sloth claims authorship, but gives Beelzebub credit for inspiring the play about old fashioned British vices.

The devil's hand separates imperfect man from light. The sun god bites the devil's hand to dispel the darkness. The devil uses the Hand of Glory, a combination of human element and artificial light, to spread darkness once more. Man's imperfect faith intervenes, and the devil is thwarted for the moment, but the struggle of light against darkness continues.

II   The Amazed Evangelist

The Mavors went on a jaunt to Kilcreggan. The Devil's Bowling Green at Loch Goil gave him the idea for *The Amazed Evangelist*. The one act companion to *Jonah and the Whale* was first performed on December 12, 1932, at the Westminster Theatre, London.

Aggie and Will, a young Scottish pair, find lodgings presided over by a witch and a devil. The couple are confronted by mythic characters who are as polite as they are evil. The atmosphere abuilding early in the piece promises memorably weird events. Aggie's desire for her Bible precipitates a storm, that chases away the unearthly creatures.

In *The Sunlight Sonata* the devil sends thunder. In *The Amazed Evangelist* it is lightning that dispels him. That one phenomenon can have two opposing aspects repeatedly comes into play in Bridie's dramas.

Aggie and Will, who are far less entertaining than the devil and his consort, have stepped into another world. The mortals finish the play outside the house, unaware of what has taken place. The abruptness of the ending is not the pat "and then I awoke" conclusion, but rather an attempt to express the wonder and frustration entailed in trying to remember a dream.

III   Babes in the Wood

Bridie identifies *Babes in the Wood* as a "Quiet Farce" on the title page. The drama is a morality laced with comedy to make the sermon more palatable. Laughter is produced by domestic situation, satire, parody of the Faust theme, and the decoction has substance. What makes the play distinctive and original is the implementation of dream processes.

Bridie's adroit use of foreshadowing and expository devices of the well-made structure should have convinced critics of his capabilities in handling techniques, which were the reviewers' criteria for judging a play. Bridie understood that these are merely tools. He used these methods to prepare the audience for the leap into the world where matters of the soul are the chief concern. That which pertains to the soul is like nothing else, the playwright says in *Mr. Gillie,* and he designed *Babes in the Wood* to convey this.

Babes in the Wood opened at the Embassy Theatre, London, on June 13, 1938. Ivor Brown wrote in the *Observer* that the last two acts did not fit with the first. (There are only two acts.) James Agate of the *Times* saw the inhabitants of Brewer's house outside London as nasty versions of Maugham's and Coward's bright sophisticates. Agate attributed showing evil for what it is to the Scot's estimate of the Sassenach. Newspaper copy fades; printed plays remain. Forty years after the premiere the thought of *Babes in the Wood* stays striking and relevant. Its shape stands out as a subtle blend of the real world and the heightened experience that is of the psyche.

The first scene takes place in the living room of Robert and

Margaret Gillet. The schoolmaster is frustrated by the students' papers he is correcting. The opening lines illustrate the sure strokes with which the picture is drawn.

GILLET.   O Lord! O Lord! O Lord! O Lord!
MARGARET. What's the matter, Bob?
GILLET.   All Life is frustration and devilry.
MARGARET. Oh? Is it, dear? Why? What's eight and seventeen.
GILLET.   Twenty-five. This young infantile anthropoid ape Walker.
MARGARET. Nice boy. What about him?
GILLET.   The microcephalic idiot translates, "They say that the city will be captured," as "Dicunt urbem capturum iri."

The use of the word "devilry" is the first in a series of clues that indicate Bridie will raise the devil. Gillet is a mathematician. His wife's asking the sum tells as much about their relationship, as does his patient answer.

Gillet has published a book, *The Rhythmic Universe,* which proves by differential calculus "that everything moves and grows and lives by little releases of energy all neatly spaced out." Gillet is untidy about the house, but he seeks to tidy up the universe, yet wonders if his having to teach school is not divine punishment for looking too closely into God's secrets.

The teacher who cares about his students has summoned Mackintosh for a talk about the facts of life, a subject which is not Gillet's forte. He asks his wife: "What are the facts of life, anyhow? Nobody knows." Bridie develops this theme by incongruity, then plays it in variations, which become increasingly ironic.

At fourteen Mackintosh knows more of biology than Gillet, and is far more at ease than the teacher, who does not know a bitch when he encounters her:

GILLET.   . . . The dog fish is oviparous.
MACKINTOSH. Yes, Sir. Like the shark. It is sometimes ovoviviparous too, Sir. In some circumstances, Sir.
GILLET.   Ovoviviparous? Oh, of course, yes. He does lay eggs, sometimes. I mean, she does.
MACKINTOSH. Please, Sir.
GILLET.   Yes?
MACKINTOSH. Is a dogfish that lays eggs called a bitch-fish?

Gillet learns that his book is a success, and while he telephones his publisher, the schoolmaster in a small Scottish town plans to change his way of living.

The Gillets are invited to the publisher's house. When they arrive at Miching Mallecow, they enter another world. It is sophisticated, and the bodies the babes encounter are vile, because they are infernal. Mrs. Hangingshaw, a noisome old woman, who wears a bird of paradise on her head and knits for the same purpose as did Madame La Farge,[4] welcomes "Mr. Giblet." The first meaning of "giblet" is garbage. Bridie's devils regard all men as rubbish.

The hero's name, Gillet, is Scots for a mare, that is, a spirit who sits on a sleeper's chest and thus produces a nightmare. Gillet's nightmare begins with the entrance of his publisher. Brewer is attired in Mephisthophelean red bathing suit and robe. His pool-wet hair is twisted in horns.

The Gillets meet other guests. Susan Copernicus is having an affair with Gerald Strutt. The adulteress admires Gillet's mind and body. Mrs. Copernicus, who believes men revolve around her, is the lust of the flesh and the pride of life.

Brewer, now attired in "dark blue-green shirt and trousers with a scarlet cummerbund," encourages the architect to show Margaret the striped stable Strutt has designed for the zebras. Stripes symbolize misdirected efforts.

Brewer's snare to trap the Gillets in adultery, Margaret's feigned interest in Strutt to make her husband jealous, and thus less interested in Susan, as well as most of the actions of other characters, are misdirected efforts.

Gillet, who is uncomfortable at the mention of sex, does not seem to recognize Susan's blandishments. Mrs. Hangingshaw, Brewer's mother, warns Gillet about having an affair. The old woman tells the truth to those whom she knows will not believe it, and uses verity to plant temptation in the hero's mind.

In the black and silver striped guest room, which reinforces the zebra symbol, the Gillets discuss the people whom they have met. Ironies arise from the couple's various misjudgments about others. Susan enters to entice Gillet to her room. Margaret is tempted to "stone" the adulteress with a hot water bottle.

The second act takes place two days later. Gillet kisses Susan, who is bored with the man, as she encourages his passion.

Margaret asks Mrs. Hangingshaw what to do about her husband's infatuation. The old woman gives bad advice.

Brewer, who has told his mother that Margaret will not succumb to temptation, tells Gillet his wife is an anachronism, which serves as a stepping stone to the diabolical view of the modern age.

BREWER. My good Sir, in the midst of all our free-winging birds of paradise,[5] our dear Margaret is a Dodo. I don't believe she knows that we are living in a new era.

STRUTT. New era, my foot.

BREWER. Darling Gerald, you should be the last to be contemptuous of these idyllic times. We have cast away the bonds of repression. We have tamed the crouching beast. We lead him by a pink ribbon to feed upon the lillies. We have sublimated our individual consciousness. We have the authority to do exactly as the spirit moves us.

STRUTT. Who says so?

BREWER. I say so. And it is the glory of our time that I have as much right to say so as anybody else.

SUSAN. It's not that, exactly, Jimmie. The need for freedom between the sexes is a matter of ascertained scientific fact. Isn't it, Robbie?

GILLET. Well, Susan, neo-psychology is not regarded as a branch of science by those of us who regard ourselves as scientists; but. . . .

BREWER. Tell me, Gillet, when will scientists begin to wear dog-collars?

GILLET. Dog-collars?

BREWER. And cassocks and albs and dalmatics and gaiters and mitres? They already hunt heretics. They already pronounce *ex cathedra* on this thing and that thing and the next thing. They are already the guardians and inspectors of human conduct.

The playwright is not offering science as a substitute for religion, but rather is showing that the forces of evil object to any form of order. Bridie's fondness for ambivalence is such that one can take Brewer's speech as an indication of the devil's love of science, because he has yet to tell the truth.

Margaret brings in Copernicus, who has come for his wife. The man Susan calls Puppy had followed Mrs. Hangingshaw's advice and treated her with sympathy and tact. Copernicus now follows his own inclination and hits her. Susan agrees to go with her husband to America. Margaret says, "All sorts of people advise you to do this and advise you to do that, and lay down the law about what's the right thing. I think we've got the law within ourselves if we only knew." Shortly after delivering this speech, the spokeswoman for Bridie's credo advises her husband about the kind of woman Susan is. Such ironies are interwoven so closely in the last act that one senses the nightmare is almost over. It is as if irony is the way back to the conscious world, where what the characters have learned can be applied.

The temptress suggests Brewer arrange an American lecture tour for Gillet, who does not yet see that this is one more ruse on Susan's part to drag him through the mud. In imitation of Copernicus, Margaret punches Robert. Brewer plays *Anges purs, anges radieux* from Gounod's *Faust*. Margaret does not appreciate the devil's pianistic wit. She tells Brewer that he is a baby who ought to be spanked. Gillet is immature. Those who live to make mischief and who enjoy the sufferings of others are immature as well. They may also be considered babes in the woods. Brewer counters with an accusation one could expect from the author of lies:

> BREWER. Madame, I have a good mind to vanish in flames through the floor. Alas, the door must serve! . . . I should have loved to make my own Hell for Mr. Gillet. He would have enjoyed it. But I bow to your superior expertise in Hell-making. Farewell.

Bridie attributes many of man's troubles to the lack of adulthood. The playwright, who could quote long passages from Barrie, was well acquainted with the Peter Pan syndrome. Here immaturity, which is the handmaiden of self-indulgence, is shown in a grevious dimension. It is a path into the woods where the soul may be captured.

IV   Mr. Bolfry

Noel Coward's *Blythe Spirit,* a light and bright piece of entertainment involving a seance, opened in 1941 and set an English record for a nonmusical with a run of 1,997 perfor-

mances. Bridie's *Mr. Bolfry* opened at the Westminster Theatre,
London, on August 8, 1943, and was soon retired. Bridie's work,
which includes a summoning of a spirit, is so far superior to the
Cowardy custard that comparison would be invidious. The
respective runs point out the fallacy of judging the merits of a
play merely upon performance records.

The critics reviewed *Mr. Bolfry* favorably, chiefly because the
cast, featuring Alastair Sim as McCrimmon and Raymond Lovell
as Bolfry, gave strong perfomances. Ivor Brown called *Mr. Bolfry*
"Manse and Super Manse."

Both Shaw and Bridie were labeled iconoclasts. Neither
dramatist seriously believed the icons would be broken, yet both
saw the need to point out the emptiness in traditional pictures
men took for granted as established images, and therefore
somehow true.

Bridie wrote of Shaw that he was "a deeply religious man."
The Scots Calvinist knew and respected the Irish Jansenist.
Bridie, in his essay on Shaw, criticized the dramatist's "judicial
attitude" in which both sides are made so stringent that one has
difficulty in discerning which position has the author's sympa-
thies.[6] In some instances Bridie was of similar inclination. If both
sides are depicted as strong as one can make them, the argument
may abate, but it need not conclude. It should not end, if man is
to grasp the message that his life is always a struggle. Bridie and
Shaw differ in means, because they differ in ends. Shaw is
sociological; Bridie is metaphysical.

Mr. Bolfry takes place in a Free Church manse in the Western
Highlands during World War II. Cohen, an agnostic Jewish
Cockney, and Cully, an Episcopalian who speaks with a public
school accent, have been billetted in the minister's house. It is
the Sabbath, which is kept in a most sober way by members of
the Wee Free Kirk. The "stricken hours" pass so slowly for the
soldiers that Cully reads from a book of sermons. "Indulge, my
soul, a serious pause. Recollect all the gay things that were wont
to dazzle thy eyes and inveigle thy affections. Here, examine
those baits of sense. Here form an estimate of their real value."
The homily serves as an exordium to the audience to ponder
their own beliefs and to revalue them, as they spend time in the
playhouse.

Bridie observed in several essays that West End theaters were
places where people passed time between dinner and a late

night snack at the Savoy. The observation is understandable, when one considers that his audience never accorded Bridie full marks for his best. Behind the flip pronouncement lurks a serious dramatic concept.

In *Mr. Bolfry* Bridie achieved the pacing he sought to take others into another world. The first two realistic scenes are structured to show passage of hours, when the clock is a means of measurement, and men do not know what to do. In the third scene, which depicts events in the world of the spirit, time stands still, for time and space are not limitations. Bolfry says, "Your scientific gentlemen have robbed you of Time and Space, and you are all little blind semi-conscious creatures tossing about in a tempest of skim milk."

The pace is made swift by argument, which leads to revelation, that results in fast action. Bridie sets a tempo that approximates dream. Nightmares of an instant seem interminable. Long and pleasant visions flash through the mind in what seems a moment.

Having stopped the clock, Bridie winds it again in the final scene. The conclusion is naturalistic, but it moves differently than the first scenes because of what the characters have experienced. It is as Mrs. McCrimmon says in scene 1: "with me the time passes without any help."

In the first scene Jean, the Reverend McCrimmon's niece, tells Cully of the religious hypocrisy of her people. "They don't worship God. They worship the Devil. They call him God, but he's really the Devil." This speech introduces a concept which is reinforced by the conjuring, during which powers who symbolize good and evil are invoked.

Jean, who is reacting to her strict upbringing, soon engages her uncle in religious debate. McCrimmon lectures on the evil of harmless things, e.g., "eating and drinking at unsuitable hours," He calls his opponent childish. Jean attacks her uncle by defining theological concepts in her terms: "Original sin means that a baby is damned to Hell Fire even before it's born. Election means that only a little clique will ever get into the kingdom of Heaven and the rest haven't a chance. Predestination means that it doesn't matter two hoots what you do, because it was all fixed long ago. It's all a pack of nonsense."

Mr. McCrimmon does not speak to her objections but follows Virgil's advice; he argues that Jean should believe an expert. He then tells a Jonahesque parable, which parallels the cycle of the liver fluke. When the minister says, "But I am wearying you, with my havers [poppycock]," the irony has several shades. McCrimmon's Olympian attitude is patronizing, and the remark is mere rhetoric. His response is nonsense. Yet it is nonsense with a purpose, which he proceeds to explain. The clarification sheds light on the play: "When I took you into a world outside this world you readily suspended what you call your reason and believed. . . . When Mr. Cully brought you back to earth and told you the story in another way, you believed it. . . ."

McCrimmon asserts that faith cannot be explained by reason, then appeals to reason in exhorting Jean to observe the world around her to see man as divided into the elect and the damned. To refute her disbelief in predestination he appeals to experience. Jean's oversimplifications are met by her uncle's evasions.

The parallel segments in which Cully kisses Jean and Cohen kisses Morag, the McCrimmons' servant show that Jean is more puritanical than the "savage," who accepts the cultic practices of the manse without question or understanding. Bolfry's noting of his summoners' private actions by way of tempting them to further lust indicates that he is more than a product of imagination.

To amuse themselves Jean and the soldiers decide to hold a seance. They use a book on witchcraft from McCrimmon's library and succeed in summoning the devil. Mr. Bolfry enters in the same clerical garb McCrimmon wears. The archdemon uses the same rhetorical style as the minister. The apparition is so like McCrimmon that the churchman says, "If you are as I think you are, a bad dream and the voice of my own heart speaking evil, I will tear you from my heart if I die for it."

Before the devil departs, Bolfry and McCrimmon confront one another before the others. As Bolfry drinks, he gives an example from engraving to show that man "cannot conceive of the Universe except as a pattern of reciprocating opposites." It is the opinion of an expert.

When Bolfry asks Jean what she believes, she says, "that the Kingdom of Heaven is within me." It is the reconcilation of this state with the presence of the Kingdom of Hell in man that brings happiness, says Bolfry. This is teleological fallacy.

Bolfry sees the seance as a play. McCrimmon provides the

"Personality;" but Marget McCrimmon, according to the devil, is "probably the key to the whole business." Bolfry's casting underscores that there are other people present.

The minister, even as those who are interested in demonology, is a seeker of power. In his desire to control the apparition, he insists that it is a dream. Bolfry wants power. He casts himself as part of the divine plan, thus espousing Manichaean dualism, a heresy which concerned Presbyterians in the days of the covenanting divines. The minister takes the ritual knife, inscribed with "Agla," a cabalistic symbol for power, and chases the devil out of the house. One wonders if this is an action of truth, for it is a deed which cannot be done.

The next morning McCrimmon attributes the visitation to the empty whiskey bottle, which he wants to believe he drank. He says that faith prompted him to strike the devil of his dream. Bolfry's umbrella "walks out" by itself.

Marget, her Faustian husband's Margaruette, exhibits the simple faith in God which is to be found in the heart of man. She looks within herself, and there she finds the answer.

MRS. MCCRIMMON. . . . Well, well, it seems you had kind of tuilzie with the De'il, after all. You're not the first good and godly man who did the like of that. Maybe you didn't kill him, but I'm sure you'd give him a sore dunt. And you're none the worse yourself.

It's a funny thing we should be surprised at seeing the Devil and him raging through the skies and blotting out the sun at this very hour. We're all such a nice kind of lot that we've forgotten there's nobody paying any attention to him with their fine plans to make us all the happy ones.

Will you be having another cup of tea, dear, now? You're looking quite white and peely-wally, and no wonder, dear me.

MCCRIMMON. I have nowhere seen such great Faith, no not in Israel.

MRS. MCCRIMMON. Drink you your tea.

Och, well, dear me, a walking umbrella's nothing to the queer things that happen in the Bible. Whirling fiery wheels and all these big beasts with the three heads and horns. It's very lucky we are that it was no worse. Drink up your tea.

V   Paradise Enow

Bridie leaned toward William Blake's vision. In "The Nero Concerto" the Scot states that "the Creator and the Destroyer may be parts of the same Godhead."

In the same book in which his artistic creed appears, Bridie included a one-act play that in light and humorous fashion illustrates how bedevilment may come from powers above as well as below the earth.

Ali, a Syrian merchant, provides a counterpoint of flattery to his wife's nagging. The motive for her shrewish behavior is jealousy of Miss Watson, the missionary. It is delightfully improbable that anyone should envy a woman who, from high mind to low tolerance, epitomizes all the negative qualities found in those who spread worthwhile messages in such a manner that those who hear them determine to follow alternate paths.

Miss Watson, who visits Ali's shop to buy an ashtray for her vicar, has a theological debate with the proprietor. In defending the Musselman paradise against the harp-playing afterlife, Ali argues that no one woman can possess all good qualities, and that therefore his heaven of houris makes more sense. To obtain those qualities he desires in a woman, Miss Watson suggests that Ali get a terrier. In this comic siege of the sexes, as most in Bridie works, the battle is concluded by the woman gaining her ends.

After Azrael, the angel of death, comes for the merchant, Ali discovers that a dog might be preferable to the virgins provided in Paradise. A bespectacled angel, officious as a civil servant and hearty as a games master, assigns carbons of Miss Watson to fulfill the new arrival's desires.

ANGEL.   . . . Wildness and the delirium of love. That'll be you, Miss Brown.
MISS BROWN. Oh, Lord!

The celestial ladies make Ali long for his wife. He even inquires about harp lessons.

Bridie's use of the animistic concept of incarnate evil is traditional, but his concern about whether certain dreams and inspirations came from the supernal or the infernal caused him to wonder if the Source of good and evil were one. The writer could not resolve this question, but his exploration of the subject led him to cast dreams into increasingly complex dramas to show that traditional answers to most questions are fraught with half-truths and myth.

CHAPTER 8

Spotlight on Miracles

WHEN a dramatist expends much energy in portraying the devil, it is human to wonder what he thinks of God. If one takes Bridie's *A Sleeping Clergyman* as a literal example of his concept of the Deity, the playwright could be considered a deist. The nodding divine is a device to make the audience ask what part God plays in the affairs of men. To show how God shapes human existence, Bridie recast an old dramatic form, the medieval miracle play. The dramas of the fourteenth and fifteenth centuries, which served as Bible histories, were written in the language of the people and made ancient stories more meaningful. They were plays for plain people.

Bridie also wrote moralities, in which he depicted the struggle between irreconcilable adversaries, with human souls wavering in the balance. In these plays mortals must make a choice between two ways of conduct, and the climax is reached when men reach a decision about how they will behave. Unlike his antecedents, Bridie's virtues as well as vices provide lively examples of character-drawing. Throughout his career Bridie worked with this genre, as his moral interludes attest. The traditional definition of the moral interlude is one of distinction: it is shorter than a morality and uses more humor.

Bridie's use of biblical material is consonant with those who made plays to be performed in pageant wagons. His allusions to the Scriptures flow through speeches of characters in a natural way. Mrs. McCrimmon's reference to 1 Peter 5:4 in her description of the devil is as right as her husband's final line, which is an appropriation of Matthew 8:10.

One must be thoroughly familiar with a source before he can make it more intelligible to others. Like his predecessors in the Middle Ages, Bridie was not above adding characters to the original story or expanding parts to add meaning for his audience.

93

His use of modern language and twentieth-century perspectives is the same technique writers used half a millenium before. Bridie contributed additional motivation, psychological insights, and made miracle plays a forum in which one requires the audience to consider the answers to profound questions.

One miracle of Bridie's best miracle play is his endowing the form with a new attitude of confidence. God is everywhere. He sends assistance to men, whom He loves, although they are obtuse, or may stray into the power of the devil. To enable men to carry out difficult tasks, which God intends for them to perform, He gives special aid, and, if they respond to this inspiration, they succeed beyond their dreams. *Tobias,* like the moral interludes of the Renaissance, reflects a new humanism.

I   Tobias and the Angel

Bridie was attracted to the grotesque and caricature. In *Tobias and the Angel* he created likable, rounded characters. These figures do much to make the play his best loved.

Tobias, a miracle play, opened at the Cambridge Festival Theatre on November 20, 1930. The cast, which included Tyrone Guthrie as Raphael, played to full houses for two weeks. The drama entertained Londoners for seventy performances at the Westminster Theatre, beginning, March, 1932. The play, which entered the repertory of the English-speaking world, has been produced by professionals and amateurs from Chicago to Johannesburg almost every season since it was first staged.

In his preface Bridie modestly describes the work as "a plain-sailing dramatic transcription of the charming old tale told in the Book of Tobit in the Apocrypha." This is only partially true. According to the biblical narrative, Tobit of the tribe of Naphtali was exiled to Nineveh. He observed the Law, but was blinded after burying a dead Jew. He quarreled with his wife and wished to die. At the same moment Sara longed for death in Ecbatana, because the demon Asmodeus had killed in succession her seven husbands on the nights of their weddings. Guided by Raphael, disguised as Azarias, Tobias, son of Tobit, drove away Asmodeus, married Sara, brought back to Nineveh ten talents of silver lent by Tobit to Gabael, and restored Tobit's sight by means of the gall of a fish caught in the Tigris. Raphael returned to heaven, and Tobit praised the Lord.

As Bridie's play begins, Tobias hands his blind father a stick. Tobit, who sees good in every misfortune says, "Isn't it lucky we aren't still in our fine house in Leviathan Avenue? I'd have broken the Chaldean vases and tumbled down the marble stairs, and bumped myself all over in the corridors." Tobias' response relieves the sentimentality: "We could have afforded a couple of slaves to lead you about."

The family that has come down in the world is supported by Tobit's wife Anna,[1] who is now a Nineveh char. Before Anna returns from the job that has cured her psychosomatic ills, Raphael brings food to the family. Although the humans do not recognize that their visitor is supernatural, Toby the dog does.

Mrs. McCrimmon's hens have not laid eggs during the devil's visit. Bridie follows the tradition that animals sense paranormal matters before humans do. In *Tobias* the dog's behavior is ironic, for the hero, who has said, "We of the new generation are all much more temperamental and highly strung," is not finely tuned.

Tobit sends his nervous son to find someone less fortunate with whom they can take "pot-luck." The modern phrase, which is here literally true, illustrates that in his use of contemporary idiom Bridie chooses carefully. His insertions of anachronistic materials have functions other than the provoking of laughter.

From his mention of caper sauce to his description of fellow Jews in casual understatement, Tobit is a middle class Briton. "I used, some nights, to trot round like an old jackdaw popping poor murdered Hebrews into holes in the ground. I thought it was the least I could do."

The accepting husband stands in contrast to the questioning wife. Anna asks the porter if he works for the government. When Raphael replies in the affirmative she presses to know the department, and learns that he works in "The Courts, principally." The divine representative, even as God Himself, has an ironic sense of humor. A number of lines are humorous, because men take the angel to be human. Laughter also arises from Raphael himself. The angel refuses to go swimming and says: "I have a slight abnormality in the region of my shoulder-blades. "

An overprotective mother and a materialist, Anna misjudges the characters of others. Bridie uses her preoccupation with worldly goods to show Depression audiences that there are worse things than poverty. The wife criticizes her husband for his charity, yet when Tobit is depressed, she cheers him. In Bridie's plays if a man attacks himself, his woman stops the attack and tries to rebuild his ego.

The idealist and the realist have produced a son, who is an amalgam. To reclaim a note owed Tobit, Anna convinces her husband to send Tobias to collect from a millionaire perfumer, Gabael. Tobias seeks a man who has succeeded in scent. Tobias succeeds with a stench.

The porter, who gives his name as Azarias, son of Ananias,[2] volunteers to accompany Tobias. Tobit gives his son guidelines for the journey. Since it is Pentecost, the celebration which honors Moses receiving the Commandments, the father's version of the Decalogue is fitting, and shows the playwright's ability to make ancient ideas come alive in a new way: "Don't forget the God, sonny, and He will do fairly by you as He does to all men. If He gives you any money, let the poor have some of it. If you can only give a little, give that and don't be ashamed of it. It is wicked to be ashamed about money, and very foolish too."

While Tobias and the angel rest by the Tigris, Raphael aids Tobias to overcome fear, which approaches phobia. The angel tells him how to catch a mud fish, and instructs him to save its liver and gall. As the angel tells his charge a fairy tale of a cure effected by using a liver, a bandit demands their money. Again Raphael instructs Tobias, who listens and fends off the robber with rhetoric.[3]

Bridie writes imprecations of the Middle East as skillfully as he does the Scots variety. "May your blood turn to dog's blood, you father of sixty dogs! Did you hear me tell you to go in peace? Your liver is too white to put beside that of a river dragon, for it is the colour of the dark flames of hell." The white liver is a traditional symbol of a coward. Tobias describes his own condition and foreshadows his encounter with Asmoday.

Withal this irony Bridie makes Tobias endearing by the hero's admission of weakness, even as he listens to his true source of inspiration and pushes on to do his appointed task. Tobias confuses this source by calling Azarias an "afreet," i.e., an evil demon of Persia. Like Anna, Tobias is a poor judge of character.

When the travelers arrive in Ecbatana, Tobias stands on Raphael's head to look over a garden wall. He sees Sara, a Jewish princess with a tongue as ill-fortuned as Elsie's, the representative of wrath in *The Sunlight Sonata*. Sara's attendant sings "The

Song of the Jackal," which is an apt if lengthy description of her mistress, who roams like a jaguar, sports like a kitten, and howls like a jackal. Bridie creates an entirely different Sara than appears in the Bible, which has a salutary effect upon the play.

As the girls play ball, they tell that Sara who is possessed by Asmoday, has buried seven husbands. The fighting females reveal that Sara is the image of Anna. The man who fears women, falls in love with Sara, the daughter of Raguel, Tobit's friend:

TOBIAS.   . . . She runs like an ostrich. She is as brave as a troop of cavalry with dragons' wings and heads like tigers. She has the heart of a rhinoceros and the gentility of a new-born lamb.

RAPHAEL. You have become quite the poet.

TOBIAS.   I'm inspired. I'm inspired. An Angel of the Lord has visited me. . . .

The inversion of traditional romantic description points up the contrasts in the personalities of Tobias and Sara. Suspense is maintained by the man's continual confusion with regard to what is divinely inspired.

After the suitor asks Raguel for Sara's hand, he has doubts and confesses his fear to the angel once more. Raphael tells him to burn the liver of the mud fish in the bridal chamber. The smell will protect him from Asmoday.

Bridie uses Reginald Scot's *Discoverie of Witchcraft*[4] for information about Asmodeus. This is the same source his characters consult to summon Mr. Bolfry.. Burning the symbol of cowardice to drive away the devil, the embodiment of man's ultimate fear is, in essence, Bridie.

After the brief wedding ceremony, the winged archangel in golden armor does battle with the demon. Bridie inserts an optional pantomime in which players act out the thwarting of evil in comic fashion. Asmoday with dragon's head and fish's tail is disgusted by the smoking liver. Raphael asks, "Don't you know me, Stinker? Don't you remember the College of Cherubim? Look at me, Asmoday!" The sequence is light, for there need be no serious contest between supernatural forces of good and evil in a play which devolves on man versus his inspiration.

Sara says she is grateful to Azarias for saving Tobias' life, but her husband becomes jealous of her regard for his angel. The chubby, immature, cowardly hero becomes boastful. Tobias shares these qualities with Jonah. The former acts upon his better inclinations, the latter does not.

When one looks at *Tobias* as a charming fairy tale, the plot has been resolved by the end of the second act. The third act explains the spiritual meaning of the Arabian Nights adventures. This makes the drama soar.

Sara tells Azarias she loves him. The porter reveals that he is Archangel Raphael. Many myths deal with human desire for a divine lover. Bridie uses a specific one. Sara quotes Genesis 6:2 when she says, "The sons of God saw the daughters of men that they were fair." She refers to the fragmentary legend of the Nephilim, giant demigods borne by daughters of men to "sons of God." Sara's flirtatious remark is ironic. When Azarias tells Tobit that he is a Nephthalite, the old man rejoices, for this is his tribe also. Thus, Tobias, her husband, is a product of this rare breed.

Raphael does not find Sara fair. "Your only admirable feature," he tells the woman, "is the magnificent impudence that impels you to make sheep's eyes at an Archangel six thousand years your senior."

Sara tearfully asks what hope there is. The answer the angel gives is that a woman may fall in love with a man's daemon in the "Pickwickian sense." This genius Bridie defines as "a creature by whose agency you write immortal verse, go great journeys. . . ." Raphael refers to Asmoday as a daemon. The spirit of inspiration can be good or evil.

The playwright believed that he was inspired by a Force he experienced and understood more fully in dream. It may be Bridie's reliance upon this Force that led him to say he was lazy. The power of the following dialogue shows that in conveying his vision he succeeded admirably. To accomplish this requires conscious effort as well as subconscious inspiration.

RAPHAEL. . . . Foolish women, of whom you are one, fall in love with daemons. Your excuse has been that a daemon of the inferior sort has tormented you since you were a child. He made you impatient with common men. He is now bound and in Egypt. There is no longer any more any excuse for you.

SARA. But I am still impatient with common men.

RAPHAEL. You must cease to be so. Often, at odd times in the future, you will see me looking out of Tobias' eyes. But you must look the other way and busy yourself with your household tasks. For I have pity on you.

You must study Tobias, and Tobias alone—his little oddities, his little bursts of friendliness, his gentleness, his follies. You must love him for those and for his little round fat body.

SARA. But how can I help loving his daemon?

RAPHAEL. You cannot love what you cannot understand. Love what you understand and you will understand more and more till your life is so full that there will be no room for any thing else—torturings and itchings and ambitions and shames.

When Tobias enters, Sara learns that her husband, who is now laden with dowery and the talents for which he undertook his odyssey, is of a poor family. She threatens to return to Ecbatana. The husband tears himself down and the wife builds him up.

Anna and Tobit await their son's return. She is convinced that Tobias is dead. Tobit knows her psychic sense is false and says, "You are possessed." Tobias and his party enter. The son, at Raphael's insistence, puts the fish gall in his father's eyes, and the cataracts disappear.

Raphael reveals his identity to the mortals. Tobit ends the play: "We have been visited." Audiences' continued and loving responses indicate that this is true. *Tobias* accomplishes the feat of making theatergoers believe they have witnessed a genuine spiritual experience.

II Susannah and the Elders

The History of Susannah in the Book of Daniel is as follows. Susannah, the wife of Joachim, a wealthy Jew of Babylonia, refused to lie with two Jewish elders, who approached her as she was preparing to bathe in her garden pool. They accused her of adultery with an imaginary youth, and she was condemned to death. Daniel convicted the elders of false testimony, and they were executed. The manner in which the playwright was to use this material came to him like a dream.

In his preface to the play Bridie states that the Bible story can be taken in a number of different ways.

It may be read as a plain story of a persecuted heroine and of the confounding of her persecutors. It may be read as a detective story. It may be placed among the more artistic reaches of pornography. It may be taken as a piece of character delineation. It may be regarded as comprising all these things with one or other feature predominating.

In the Argument of *Susannah and the Elders* the Reader indicates the path the playwright follows: "The old story says that these Judges who did this wickedness were false and evil to the bone; but who knows the heart of a man and what moves in that darkness? And is there any man living who has in him no tincture of goodness however unhappily he may do in his life?"

The Old Testament story is presented from a New Testament perspective. If judgment is the premise, justice with and without mercy provides the conflict. Kashdak's decision in court is an example of justice without mercy.[5] Daniel has the eye-for-an-eye concept of justice, which the Jews took from Hammurabi's law code during the Babylonian captivity. Susannah is merciful in her assessments of others, yet she comes to grief because she does not listen to the inner voice of inspiration. The woman is reasonable, but she is surrounded by radicals who tend to be irrational. More than reason is required to avoid becoming enmeshed in the world of the flesh.

Susannah and the Elders does not seek to show the spiritual heights of *Tobias*. The greatest miracle in the play set in the Babylonian suburbs, where Jedburgh justice flourishes, is that a fair trial does occur. The miracle Bridie seeks to make manifest is the realization in the minds and hearts of the audience that censorious man does not have the capability to make absolute judgments. He needs the final Arbiter.

As the drama begins, blue-bearded Kashdak is sitting in judgment of an Ethiopian, who has committed a crime of passion. The symbol of the magisterial office is the false hair, which is intended to make one think of the wife killer of the fairy tale. The magistrate is prejudiced against the dark defendant before the evidence is presented.

Bel-Kabbittu brings Susannah to see the court over which he and his friend preside. Kashdak is a puritan, who finds loose living more intolerable than murder. Kabbittu, a like-minded character, dons the blue beard and hears a case of blasphemy. Dionysos has been accused of speaking disrespectfully of Nebo and other gods. The Greek, who does not take the charge

seriously, tries to cajole the magistrate. Susannah pleads and does
charm the magistrates into releasing the prisoner. Kabbittu then
invites Dionysos, Susannah, and her husband Joachim to dinner.
Although the heroine has a shadowy premonition, she accepts.

Kashdak and Kabbitu share a house, but they cloak their true
inclinations.

I'm all for openness and freedom in speech on all sorts of subjects. All
sorts of subjects. And I think you will admit I'm as broad-minded as my
neighbor. But this modern fashion of speaking about the most—the
most *intimate* subjects as if. . . . You know I hate hypocrisy, and I like a
broad story now and then as well as the next man, but . . . there are
certain decencies, if you understand what I mean.

The irony of the hypocrites' conversation is predictable, but it
raises the question: Have these men lied to themselves and each
other so long, they do not know their own hearts?

The old magistrates contrast to Daniel, the young lawyer, who
speaks his mind fearlessly, although he is a member of a
conquered people in a foreign land. Daniel is a power-seeker.
His friends Shadrach, Meshach, and Abednego are sycophants.
These, Daniel says, "are easier to handle."

Daniel tells Susannah not to dine with the magistrates.
Susannah says she hopes he is not prophesying. Daniel answers
"of course not."

The heroine tells Joachim that ever since Daniel took up the
law, "he keeps laying it down." Daniel criticizes Joachim for
collaborating with the Babylonians.

DANIEL.   . . . You take the hands that spread blood and filth on the
holy places.
SUSANNAH. That was long ago.
DANIEL.   Long ago? And you are a child of Israel!
SUSANNAH. *(quietly and reasonably)* . . . Daniel, it's true that we are
in captivity, and it's true that we have lost our homes; but
we lost them because we were much fonder of talking and
arguing and quarrelling than of fighting to defend them. It
is true that Israel will go back to Mount Zion, because the
Lord has promised it. But I do not think we shall go back by
fighting, and I know that quarrelling and arguing and
hating is not the way. . . . The people of Babylon beat us

because they were braver and stronger than we were. And now that we are their prisoners, they are kinder to us than we would ever be to them. They are not fiends.

DANIEL. They are.

SUSANNAH. No, no, no. They are like all good soldiers. They are earnest, soft-hearted, sentimental, generous, stupid men until somebody makes them frightened or angry. And then the bad side of them comes out. Why do you want to raise the bad side of them? If you four are really Prophets of Jehovah, surely it's your duty to cultivate the . . .

DANIEL. You are not in a position to teach the Prophets of God their business. To begin with, you are only a woman. . .

SUSANNAH. So was Deborah. . . .

Daniel says that his name means "the Judgment of God," but Susannah's estimate, that he is an "insolent, evil-minded little prig," contains more truth, if reason alone is the criterion of evaluation. Daniel's warnings about the old judges prove true.

The Babylonians call Daniel Belteshazzar, i. e., the keeper of secrets. Bridie writes lines of sufficient ambiguity that one may hold that Daniel's secret is that he is not what he seems.

At the magistrates' dinner Joachim gets drunk. Dionysos is at his entertaining best. He professes a higher regard for women than Daniel, and as the Greek helps Susannah bring her husband home, he tries to arrange an assignation. She refuses to see the man who might tempt her.

After Joachim departs on a business trip, Kashdak visits Susannah. They discuss the case of the Ethiopian. Susannah points out the pitfalls of sentimentality, then she and Kashdak reveal things about themselves, which soften the state of Kashdak's soul. The magistrate may not see the lust in himself. That a woman of Susannah's perception does not recognize Kashdak's underlying motive points out how difficult it is to divine the human heart.

SUSANNAH. . . . I know it's terribly difficult for you. Day after day you must do your duty by a book of rules and forget that you are a man at all. And then suddenly your heart says to you, "I am here!" and you are astonished and don't know what to do.

KASHDAK. That is true. You know me, Susannah.

SUSANNAH. I think I do, Uncle Dick.

KASHDAK. How is it that you know me? I go about with a face like a
mask. I weigh my words, my thoughts, even. They all think
me a hard man. Dry and withered like leather. Kabbittu
says he has lived with me all these years and yet doesn't
know me. You must be very wise.

SUSANNAH. Oh, no. Men put on that mask because they are afraid
people will see them and laugh at them and hurt them.

Kashdak, who has invited Susannah to use his garden, returns
to his home, as does Kabbittu. They quarrel because Kashdak
believes his friend's motives are as lustful as his. Kabbittu tries to
prevent Kashdak fulfilling his desire to look upon Susannah
bathing.

Shortly after the heroine discovers the voyeurs, the major-
domo reports that Dionysos has been killed while trying to get
into the garden. The magistrates falsely accuse Susannah of
adultery with the Greek to cover their own actions.

The magistrates, who would pervert justice, appear in court
before a judge, who wants to "Keep those Jews quiet." Joachim is
convinced of his wife's guilt. The judge passes sentence while
Susannah prays "In Your mind alone there is justice and goodness
and right. O Everlasting Lord, receive my spirit!"

Daniel cross-examines the accusers, who say that they saw the
lovers under different trees. Kabbittu says it was a mastic;
Kashdak swears it was the holly-oak.[6]

DANIEL. Not the mastik tree or the oleander tree or the olive tree, but
the holly-oak, north of the pool. Go down to Hell, liar and
murderer!

In a play made colorful by natural imagery Bridie has the trees
function on a symbolic level. The mastic is a source of resin.
Kabbittu gets stuck in the situation with his friend. Kashdak is
the holly-oak. This is a compound masculine symbol. In Druid
myth both trees are associated with lust, The oak as a Jupiterian
talisman fits Kashdak, who tells Kabbittu, "We can take what we
like and no man dare call us to account."

At the magistrates' dinner Dionysos has sung a song that
describes Susannah's position: "Golden apple on the tree-top
blushing, /Too high, when the gatherers came and sought you."
Later that evening Susannah tells the cavalier: "You are trying to

set fire to a little oleander bush, by the roadside—only for the pleasure of seeing the flames leaping." When the oleander blooms, it produces poisonous flowers; but Dionysos, not Susannah, is the oleander. The heroine is the olive, the tree sacred to Athena and a symbol of chastity. The symbolism from a range of sources has a dreamlike quality, and the unraveling of it approaches solving a detective story.

The judge tells the defendant she has the right to become the plaintiff against her husband, who accused her falsely. Susannah declines. Again she shows mercy.

After the trial, Daniel, who exhibits no compassion, tells Susannah that she is "a compact of folly and danger." Daniel infers that although Susannah is legally innocent, she is morally guilty. Susannah has not listened to the voice of her inspiration, but Daniel is not a daemon. He is a stiff-necked man, whose prediction came true.

Daniel tells the judge that the old men perjured themselves, because "of the empty lechery that was in their evil hearts." Kabbittu admits the charge: "All the world has known me as a kindly, just respectable man. And so I thought myself. For I forgot how the exalted Anu had made us all. . . . The head ensues and cherishes honour, justice, pity, shame, a good conscience; the beast can be tamed but he knows nothing of any of these things." Kashdak tries to provide excuse for his sin. "It was not I but my hypocrisy that did this cruelty." If the old men do not give extenuating circumstances, they do raise doubt with regard to the degree of their culpability.

Meshach tells Daniel that God has spoken through him. Daniel hopes He did. Thus the play ends with sufficient ambiguity to leave spectators' heads whirling in speculations.

Early in the play Susannah says that facts never speak for themselves. "It's *people* who say whether a person is guilty or not." Decisions rendered in *Susannah and the Elders* lead one to conclude that God is the sole Source of absolute justice, for only He knows what is in the hearts of men. This is a recurring motif in Bridie's works.

The part of Susannah was played by Joan White, who appeared in at least six Bridie dramas during the decade. The first production of this play, by the London International Theatre Club, occurred on October 31, 1937, at the Duke of York's Theatre.

III   Jonah

Jonah 3 represents Bridie's final attempt to dramatize the predicament of a false prophet. Bridie says in *One Way of Living* that *Tobias* and *Jonah* are "about God and the relation of the individual man to Him." The design is grand, but when a protagonist does not know what he is talking about, a surfeit of his speech enervates. The circumstances in the three versions are not sufficiently potent to pull them out of lethargy.

While revising *Jonah and the Whale*, Bridie wrote to Amner B. Hall on September 20, 1931, that there was something wrong with the play: "I think it is that I think Jonah himself so very much funnier than other people do."[7] When a man does not heed divine inspiration, it is most difficult to cast him as a comic figure.

Jonah and the Whale opened on December 12, 1932, at the Westminster Theatre, London. Twenty-six characters in five scenes dramatized the Apocryphal story for forty nights.

In this production Bridie includes a women's club scene, which he did not use in later treatments. The ladies' adulation turns the prophet's ear to listen to human flattery. Susceptibility to vanity leads man to think he has power of himself. In this segment one of the women says that she has arranged for a performance of a play about "Man and His Inspiration." Had this material been developed, it would have strengthened the aim: to show man at odds with his inspiration.

When Bridie adapted the play for radio, he reduced the number of characters and simplified the scenes and sets. This condensed and softened version, retitled *The Sign of the Prophet Jonah*, was broadcast by the B.B.C. in 1942. It featured Ralph Richardson. To this script Bridie added a scene from the protagonist's childhood.

As a fat and unpopular little boy Jonah wants to be a prophet. When he wins a race, a girl believes he has predicted it. The child who cannot run well feels his winning is a miracle, for he wished his opponent would stumble, and the boy fell. The psychological insights are good in this incident, which shows Jonah as one who attributes to God things He does not do. It is what is not done and what does not happen that weakens the dramatic concept.

Bridie did not use the boyhood incidents in *Jonah 3*. He combined elements from the first two plays and added new

material. *Jonah 3* was first performed by the Unnamed Society of
Manchester in November, 1942. This was a more practical
production to mount, but it remained languid.

In the Bible Jonah is not the sort who lends himself to
humorous treatment. The Old Testament figure has sympathy
for a withered plant, but not for the population of a city. Unlike
Abraham and Moses, who beseeched God to spare people, Jonah
insisted upon punishment of the repentant. This is a neurotic
form of self-destruction. Those who choke themselves by using
other people's necks possess a guilt based on inability to function
in their social sphere. Man often attacks qualities in others he
likes least in himself. Jonah's own lack of faith prompts him to
attack the faithless of Nineveh; in this way he expiates his own
guilt.

The source has been given varying and contradictory interpretations. These arise from the several hands that revised the story
to suit diverse purposes. Bridie, who loved contradiction and
arguments on subjects vast, was drawn to the concept that
mediation entails the right use of privilege. And privilege
bespeaks responsibility.

The frame of *Jonah 3* is a conversation between the spirit of
Jonah and the Leviathan, who does not now recognize the man,
even as Jonah did not acknowledge the whale in life. This
exchange is in the Dialogue of the Dead tradition. Bridie uses
this device, popular in nineteenth-century Scottish poetry and
drama, in other works, e. g., *John Knox*.

The dialogue fades to flashback. The audience is whisked to
the days when Jonah was a small town prophet in Gittah-Hepher.
The pettish predictor, who believes he keeps the people in line
by his magnetism, does not know himself. Bridie casts Jonah in
the mold of a Calvinist clergyman who thinks that he controls his
"parish" by instilling the fear of God. The prophet may have
taken away smiles and bright clothing, but the people who abide
by Jonah's superficial religious mandates do so because of the
show he provides.

Jonah's debate with Bilshan, a foil who reasons, entertains the
villagers. Bilshan tells of prosperous Nineveh. Jonah, who has
used man's relationship to God to turn attention to himself, asks
his opponent, "Do you know that to be possessed by God is the
uttermost torment in the world?"

In private with Euodias Jonah admits to the woman who would

be his disciple that he is not much of a man. The false prophet attracts women, but he does not really want them any more than he wants to convert Nineveh. Jonah desires only to be the center of attention.

An angel and talking animals tell Jonah to go to Nineveh, but no voice mentions divine destruction. In short scenes we see the man called trying to escape his responsibility. Jonah boards a galley for Tarshish. On the ship Bilshan confronts him again. Jonah cannot bear such encounters. During a sudden storm fellow passengers throw the prophet who cannot pray into the sea as a sacrifice.

The whale gives Jonah a ride, and the great fish tries to educate him. The man disclaims as a lie the lesson on a planned world in which things "are like and yet not like." Jonah's reaction is like that of many early twentieth-century clergymen when faced with the controversy that arose between science and religion. When Jonah, who will not learn, meets the King, who considers Nineveh's religion myth, the prophet is given the opportunity to do God's work:

KING. . . . I believe in a purposive Universe. Myths—any kind of mythology is all very well, but it takes one's mind off the point. By the way, my Court buffoon the other day told me that a myth was a moth's sister.

JONAH. A moth's sister? . . .

KING. There was a truth in that Myths and Moths are destructive and destructible. A candle is lit. They meddle with the light. And out they go. You agree with me, don't you?

JONAH. I have nothing to do with myths.

Jonah harangues the people of Nineveh. He is the Scots pulpit orator who is carried away by his own words, and in search of a dramatic peroration forecasts doom.

As the prophet sits under his gourd and waits for the destruction, he knows his "Vindicator liveth." When he finally hears from the Angel that God is merciful, Jonah asks, "What must He think of me? It is horrible to think that the Almighty may have a sense of humour."

The protagonist, who sees wickedness in almost everything, does not confront evil, nor does Jonah, the humorless juvenile, grow within himself. The conflict requisite for drama is absent.

IV   The Dragon and the Dove

For his moral interlude originally entitled "The Niece of the Prophet Abraham" and later changed to *The Dragon and the Dove, or How the Hermit Abraham Fought the Devil for His Niece,* Bridie used Helen Waddell's *The Desert Fathers* as source, but the drama is the playwright's in thought and feeling.

The Dragon and the Dove was first presented by the Pilgrim Players at the Lyric Theatre, Glasgow, in August, 1942, and ran for over 200 performances.

The frame of the piece consists of a conversation between a Deaconess and an Abbot, who wait to see the Bishop of Edessa in 400 A.D. The flirtatious Abbot tells the coy female religious a story which illustrates that one fights "the Devil with the Devil's weapons." The frame provides an innocent parallel to the situation of the devil and Abraham's niece. The roguish religious lures the lady with a story. Their commentary enables Bridie to describe states which cannot be staged. It also functions as *mise en scène.*

The Abbot invites the Deaconess to see the story set down by St. Ephraem in "the sanctified theatre of your mind." The curtains part and reveal Abraham's hut, where the prophet and his niece Marie express Bridie's spiritual ideas.

MARIA.   . . . I think and think and I see that what you tell me is true, but I can't think of truths for myself.
ABRAHAM.   We don't think of truths. They are given to us if we wait. And if we cleanse ourselves from our passions.
MARIA.   But I have no passions.

By Socratic method Abraham shows his young charge that passions are alive in her, but that these can be controlled by holiness.

St. Ephraem, who had sent Maria to her uncle thirteen years before, has also sent a brother to the hermit for counsel. The monk Absolom is the devil in disguise. Absolom quotes from Scripture to lure Maria from the path of righteousness, and she follows him on a hellish route which ends at an inn of ill fame.

Abraham tells Maria an anecdote of an abbot who fed a lion that disobeyed him. The moral of the story, which parallels the situation of the prophet with the devil, is that "There is nothing in this world to be afraid of—except sin." Bridie continually uses parables to clarify events in the main action.

Abraham dreams of the dragon devouring the dove. As with other Bridie dreamers, the prophet does not know how to interpret his vision correctly. The frame characters then discuss Abraham's vision. When Abraham does understand the dream, he prays. Ephraem comes to the aid of the old man in his rescue of the dove. The instrument by which the devil came to Abraham's door is the same one who helps overcome the consequences of the wicked one's actions. Bridie uses this Blakean instrumentality to stress that only those who are tested and surmount temptation can be considered good.

The idealistic Abraham must disguise himself and become a man of action to reclaim Maria from a life of sin. The prophet learns to act and speak like a soldier, for his faith is so strong that he can assimilate a new personality. Abraham's efforts to pass himself off as a colonel provide some of the brightest comic moments of the play. The topsy-turvy way of showing what belief can accomplish reinforces the moral-theme. Bridie blends moral and theme as did eighteenth-and nineteenth-century dramatists, but his use of comedy to effect the combination is distinctive.

Abraham arrives at the Three Kittens of Bubastis, where his niece now works as a hostess. He foils the Landlady and a Knave. The prophet, as Tobias, frightens evildoers with rhetoric, for the devil's own are weaklings. To these Abraham will ask Ephraem to send missioners. There is hope. The uncle wins back his niece with kindness. "Don't distrust the mercy of God. Let our sins be as mountains, His mercy towers above His every creature. . . . There's nothing new about falling into the mire. The evil thing is to lie there, fallen. So bravely now return again to your place. The Enemy mocked thee falling, but he shall know thee strong in thy rising."

The Abbot says that God in His compassion so accepted Maria's atonement, "that after three full years He restored health to many at her prayer."

V   A Change for the Worse

To provide a full evening's entertainment at the Lyric, Bridie wrote *A Change for the Worse* as a companion to the well constructed *Dragon and the Dove.* He probably intended *A Change for the Worse* to be a companion to *The Sunlight Sonata,*[8] but the finished product was not staged until 1942.

A Change for the Worse is another modern rendering of medieval art in a tightly mitred frame. This verse drama demonstrates how pleasing role-transference can be in a fairy-tale fantasy. Gib and Tib, a poor couple, live on one side of St. Eloi's. Jon and Martha, a wealthy pair of burghers, live on the other side of the church. Vice, under orders from Satan, uses a metamorphosis stone to switch the couple's stations. When the puzzled Martha tells Vice disguised as a doctor of this transformation, the perpetrator advises her in such fashion that Dr. Mavor's low estimation of psychiatry becomes apparent:

> Calamy, laudamy, poultices, pills
> They are the stuff for bodily ills.
> Thingummybobs of a different kind
> Are the stuff for disorderliness of the mind.
> When with distresses your psyche is wracked,
> Relax. Think of nothing at all. Abreact.
> Associate freely, sublimate
> The origins of your anxiety state.
> Snap your fingers, my dear, as I do,
> At the tortuous twistings of your libido.
> Away with repression and up with the Id.
> Tell your medical man whatsoever you did.
> Trust the Unconscious. And that I suppose is
> How to get rid of hallucinoses
> And pseudopathomorphic psychomaticoses,
> And lie on a perpetual bed of roses.[9]

When goldsmith and fisherman change places, both couples are content. As St. Eloi observes, "Now Jon has health and Gib has rest/And everything is for the best. . . ."

The characters in *A Change for the Worse,* as those in *The Dragon and the Dove,* are drawn with the same broad strokes medieval artisans used for woodcuts. They are not, however, cartoons.

In his miracles and moralities Bridie combines humor, adventure, and spiritual insight. In general his manner is balanced. Without fail he shows good taste. In situations the playwright constructs, this is an accomplishment which borders the miraculous.

CHAPTER 9

Scene: Scotland

BRIDIE knew and loved Scotland and her people,[1] and he used his country as the setting for most of his plays. Moreover, the playwright was conscious of the desire for a national drama, and he wrote for Scottish audiences. He made plays for English audiences as well, because if national drama is to succeed, it must manifest values common to all human experience under its special national characteristics.

In the correspondence between Bridie and Moray McLaren, *A Small Stir: Letters on the English*, the authors attempted to determine what is English.[2] The elusiveness of the distinctions indicates how difficult delimitation of what is English or Scottish can be in the twentieth century.

In *British Drama*, Bridie doubts if the theater has ever reflected the lives of the audience who frequent playhouses. The way a dramatist sees his fellows is contingent upon what theatergoers will buy tickets to see.[3]

Since the London publication of *The Valiant Scot*, a 1637 play which treats the story of William Wallace, and uses burr that came from an English pen, one can trace the creations of genuine and spurious Northern accents for theatrical purposes. During the eighteenth century Scots authors under the spell of Burns manufactured dialect that bears slight resemblance to speech patterns of any sector of the population. This device is still used in variety and pantomime. In a land where accent is said to change every twenty miles, and different sections of small cities are distinguished by peculiar inflections, use of speech patterns serves to emphasize national and regional individuality.

Bridie writes a Scottish dialogue that is Celtic in flow. He selects a vocabulary that is genuine, but makes frequent linguistic accommodations for the general British audience. These concessions aid in conveying the Northern experience. He never yields when expressing Scottish thought.

Language, setting, history, and national consciousness are ingredients which contribute to the Scottish literary entity. It is the thought which is the essential part. A spirit of inquiry resides in practical souls, who are middle class—a designation of their morality rather than their economic status. The puritan heritage espouses individualism. The independent spirit can lead to conflict with the tradition that fostered this outlook. Existence is earnest enough to argue about, because it is strewn with metaphysical considerations with which one must reckon. For the transmission of Bridie's message, a Scottish locale is necessary. If one changed Bridie's settings, the works would not be the same. Where else but in a "town on an estuary of the Clyde" could a provost be unseated over a dog, or a man dream that new acquaintances were witches in league with the "de'il himsel'."

I   The Pardoner's Tale

The Pardoner's Tale (1930) is a one-act morality adapted from Chaucer's Canterbury tale. Bridie set his play in an eighteenth-century Scottish changehouse. In the dilapitated inn three Edinburgh bucks drink heavily: Elliot, a bully, Grant, an obsequious and treacherous rogue, and Philip, whom the author describes as a "debauched Galahad," discuss death. "Death's a man. There's nothing else in earth or sky could be so bitter bad," says Philip.

The old innkeeper, who waits for death, tells the youths, "Death's in this room." He gives the bloody history of the place and tells of a hidden box of money. Elliot discovers the cache, then plots with Grant to kill Philip. Philip overhears them. He pours the coins into the glasses. His companions stab Philip, then drink from the glasses fearfully.

Bridie's dialogue is a good approximation of Georgian Scots, without resorting to archaicism.

> PHILIP. . . . My father was a kind man, who prayed each night for Death to take him in a glen with four or five Whigamores at his claymore's point. The false thief, Death, chokit him with a bloody flux in a strange wife's house in Amiens. Lily-white maids and wee croodling weans that never did harm to any, the foul butcher clutches and slays and rots awa their bright beauty.

It is the attitude toward death—fascination with the grave and fear masking as bravado—that contribute to the distinctly Scots character of the piece.

II   The Tragic Muse

Bridie contributed *The Tragic Muse* to John MacNair Reid's *Scottish One-Act Plays* (1935), a collection whose *raison d' être* was to foster Scottish drama.

Bridie's farce is set in a Glasgow rooming house. A dance-hall hostess and a medical student converse in "och aye" accents, as does the landlady. A commercial gentleman who lodges in the house is prejudiced against the Irish, particularly his fellow roomer, who is using the bathroom. Mimi, the hostess, discovers Mr. Cavanagh in the tub, and screams that he is dead.

A reporter who lives in the house enters, and the stage directions call for the actors to *"become frankly fantastic and mechanical. MISS LUSK climbs the hat-rack and sits on a shelf at the top of it. She unrolls a newspaper bill announcing 'Murder Special' and begins to write."* In elevating the reporter, Bridie sends up journalism. The actors change accents and adopt an inflated journalese.

Susannah says the facts are never the facts. In *The Tragic Muse* the lodgers-turned-chorus illustrate this observation. Cavanagh, who has been taking a nap in the tub, walks out of the bath, thus invalidating the reports.

The piece, which resembles a vaudeville sketch, satirizes the fourth estate, with special emphasis upon the writing in the Glasgow papers, to which Bridie contributed features. *The Tragic Muse* is a rare instance of the dramatist's permitting local color to override larger considerations.

III   Storm in a Teacup

Storm in a Teacup bears out the observation that Italy is the country for men; America is the country for women; Spain is the country for children; and Britain is the country for dogs. The furor of the comedy is set in motion over a canine named Patsy. The play is more than a sentimental tale. It is a plea for justice which stems from concern for the individual and liberal political ideals.

Bridie, who had a gift for creative adaptation,[4] based this comedy on Bruno Frank's *Stürm im Wasserglass*. He took the continental zany plot from the German, wrote a new last act, and fashioned a distinctive Scottish comedy. The characters and their outlook on life made the story better in English than in German.

Bridie had collaborated with Frank on a scenario that was never filmed. He knew the author. Bridie also knew the proclivities of the British audience. Critics and theatergoers enjoyed Bridie's quickly written version better than Frank's, when *Storm in a Teacup* opened at the Lyceum Theatre, Edinburgh, on January 20, 1936. The play then went to the Royalty Theatre, London on February 5, and ran for over a year.

The storm occurs in Baikie, a burgh by the Clyde that is a microcosm for Bridie. The imaginary town, which derives its name from Lake Baikal, where the author spent vacations in boyhood, is the epitome of provincialism. It is a place of manageable size where the magnanimous and the petty, the rich and the poor, and other opposites mingle.

Mrs. Flanagan, a vegetable carter of Baikie, appeals to Provost Thomson to restore her dog that has been taken away because she cannot afford a license. Burdon, a reporter, McKellar, and his wife suggest that Thomson restore Patsy to Mrs. Flanagan, but the pompous politician remains adamant.

Bridie rarely misses an opportunity to perforate political conservatism, and *Storm in a Teacup* provides scope for satirization of the liberal's opponents. The first act closes with an ironic interview in which the provost tells the journalist of his concern for the individual, immediately after Thomson has sent Mrs. Flanagan away:

Of all the colossal impertinence. So much for her. Sorry to have delayed you. Where was I? . . . We must start with the individual before we can realize what Nationalism really means. It is only the realization, the sympathetic realization, the deeply sympathetic realization that each unit in the State is a living, breathing soul, each with his own aspirations, each with his own peculiarly intense perceptions of his own rights and his own wrongs. A leader must have that strange sixth sense that enables him to see into the hearts of his people—to feel in his own flesh. . . .

As the second act opens, Mrs. Flanagan and her pet are

"bandied about like a professional footballer's legs" in the newspapers. Victoria Thomson tells Burdon that the tumult is disproportionate to the incident. The man to whom she is obviously attracted counters: "Oppression is never a very small thing."

The angry crowds outside the Thomson house support Burdon's opinion. Skirving, the newspaper publisher and the husband of Thomson's mistress, proclaims the bruhaha "a storm in a bucket," but the third act trial proves that tiny tempests can alter lives.

The courtroom proceedings are enlivened by local types. Burdon, the defendant, is accused of stealing Patsy to stir up feeling against Thomson, whose political career is finished. The reporter is found not guilty. He will marry the soon-to-be-divorced Victoria Thomson. Bridie included a more traditional *gamos* in the engagement of McKellar and Mrs. Flanagan.

Mrs. Flanagan's attachment for Patsy required a strong actress to make the woman, whose dog has become a substitute offspring, engaging and pathetic. Sara Allgood's performance in the London production provided that strength. The actress also played the role in the film version, *Storm over Patsy*. The movie increased predictability. It became another instance of the film industry's choosing lesser Bridie works.

IV   The Last Trump

The Last Trump opened at the Malvern Festival, in early August, 1938. Bridie then revised the last act, but was not satisfied with it when the play opened at the Duke of York's Theatre, London, on September 13, for a few weeks' run.

The comedy is an example of what the ambitious dramatist tried to do rather than what he accomplished. Plot and subplot are difficult to cohere. Bridie's strands twine, but the play of ideas suffers as a result.

The play opens in a Glasgow nursing home where Buchleyvie, a greedy industrialist, is being treated for heart trouble. The patient has his nurse read the tea leaves, and her prediction is accurate in its peculiar way. This establishes the protagonist's superstition.

The aggressive builder of power plants badgers Dr. Gristwood. The young physician is no match for Buchleyvie, who carps: "I'm only a patient. The lowest form of animate matter."

Sir Gregory Butt comes in, fires questions at Buchlyvie, but ignores his queries for the truth. The industrialist is outclassed by the consulting physician:

BUTT.   You sit at the table and shovel down course after course of
              condimented, trucidated trash; and there's your poor
              tortured stomach, on bended knee at the foot of your
              oesophagus, lifting up its hands to Heaven and crying. "My
              God, what next?" You are like the heroes of our Augustan
              Age, sir. You should study their portraits. Pot-bellys at
              twenty and dead of old age at fifty. . . . And you take no
              exercise.

BUCHLYVIE. Have I got angina pectoris? (*He pronounces it to rhyme
              with "Dinah."*)

BUTT.   Angina pectoris, sir, is a Latin name meaning a pain in the
              chest. You know quite well you have a pain in the chest.
              I'm telling you what you don't know.

Butt assumes this manner to get Buchleyvie to change his ways. The patient will go to the Highlands to live.

Buchleyvie sends for MacPhater, whose property he has bought. The laird, who has lost his land and is about to lose his wife in the same hospital, refuses to sell the hill on which his observatory is located.

The electric company, which Buchleyvie is building on Mac Phater's land, is a symbol of power and wealth. The astronomical observatory represents knowledge; it also symbolizes the unattainable for Buchleyvie.

The traditionalist, who cannot take on the parvenu, explains that Schreiner, MacPhater's brother-in-law and a noted physicist, does important work in the laboratory. The climate of the area has restored Schreiner's health.

Tom Buchleyvie, a more pleasant version of his father, loves Jean, against his materialistic mother's wishes. Mrs. Buchleyvie learns of her husband's chronic condition from Dr. Butt, and responds in manner typical.

MRS. BUCHLYVIE. I don't know how you can take lunch after a tragedy
                 like this.

BUTT.   Don't you, ma'am? If I may give you a bit of advice,
                 talk about it for a bit, and then put it to the back of
                 your mind. You'll not help him by brooding.

Exchanges between the lovers provide contrast of youth's inability to comprehend mortality. They vary the pace of the play, but Tom and Jean[5] are of less interest than the situation that Butt inspires.

The doctor explains to his colleague Gristwood that Buchleyvie needs to be frightened. He tells an anecdote about a French Jew, which provides a parallel to what will happen to Buchleyvie. The doctors discuss the end of the world as Schreiner enters, thus giving him the design to frighten the heart patient to death.

Schreiner, who regards the world as "an infernal rotten orange," is the antithesis of Butt, who has a heart as well as specialized knowledge. The doctor dominates the bright first act. Butt's strength emphasizes Buchleyvie's weakness, as well as the debility of the play.

Act 2 takes place in the castle MacPhater has sold to the Buchleyvies, who have moved in with their entourage. The action retrogrades.

Tom and Jean discuss the merits of living together versus traditional marriage. It is filler, as is Mrs. Buchleyvie's conversation with her sister-in-law and the minister's wife. Bridie brings on the hypocritical women to put characters in place for the finish.

Schreiner tells the new owner an astrominical myth about supernovas which will destroy the world in less than a day. "Bullets of radiation" are the scientist's lethal weapon. Bridie foreshadows this event heavily, and prepares for the characters' acceptance of a lie by references to animal magnetism, horoscopes, and bizarre interpretation of the Apocalypse.

One faction goes to the chapel to prepare for judgment day. There they fall asleep. Buchleyvie, Tom, Jean, Dr. Gristwood, and the Nurse play poker. The prospect of cataclysm and gambling for high stakes stimulates Buchleyvie. He loses to Jean, who lays down a Royal Flush. She does not believe Schreiner's prediction, but has worn a poker face through the proceedings and wins over her prospective father-in-law with tough honesty.

The world may be coming to an end, but the characters do not change. Jean asks Gristwood if Buchleyvie will change. The doctor asks rhetorically: "Do you think anybody changes? Mr. Buchleyvie is a very characteristic person."

The static protagonist, who thinks he can still buy Schreiner at the end of the play, is not suited to participating in a conflict of ideas. The drama, which offers good thought in the beginning, becomes a situation comedy. Had Butt not led us to expect so much, we would not be as disappointed.

V   The Kitchen Comedy

The Kitchen Comedy, one of Bridie's infrequent excursions into radio drama,[6] was produced by Regional Programme on November 18, 1938, for the opening of Broadcasting House, Glasgow.

On a rainy November night three folk seek shelter in the kitchen of a country manse. Jessie, the minister's housekeeper admits Henry, a unionized tramp whose dialect is a mix of Scotch, Cockney, and Irish, as well as Victor and Annie, an engaged couple.

Metaphysical argument has been called the Scottish disease, and the discussion which ensues indicates its infectiousness. The speakers touch on the space-time continuum, the existence of an afterlife, spiritualism, and other topics.

Hughie, a simple-minded servant, enters, and Henry asks him, "What do you think we are here for, and what do you think is going to happen to us?"Hughie outlines his life and concludes, "I dinna ken." He describes exactly the states of mind of those who rely on science, religion, and their own conceptions.

VI   What Say They?

Bridie used the Book of Esther as a point of departure for *What Say They?* He covered his tracks so well that one needs to be told the dramatist's intention to see the biblical indebtedness.

In his preface to the comedy the playwright explains how the Scottish university resembles a little autocratic kingdom. Ahasuerus becomes Sir Archibald Asher, the Principal; Esther— Ada Shore; Haaman—Professor Hayman; Mordecai—Murdo Kaye. (Later Bridie changed the porter's name to Dan McEntee.)

The idea of the persecuted outwitting the powerful persecutors appealed to Bridie. He linked the idea to the Scots "tradition of the persecution of artists and the light-headed and light-hearted by the unco guid." But Bridie's conception is superior to his realization. In the Bible Esther delivers her people from destruction. The story of vengeance and persecution points up the triviality of the situation comedy.

Bridie dedicated *What Say They?* to Bernard Shaw. Bridie's title asks a question answered by the title of Shaw's *You Never Can Tell*, a farce with opened in London in 1899. The Scot, who looked like a pixie, had a taste for playing tricks associated with the cheerful mischievous sprite. From dedication to denouement *What Say They?* is a prank.

The jinks at the University of Skerryvore were first performed at the Malvern Festival in 1939. Bridie sat in the audience and enjoyed *What Say They?* as he had his own college years. He chortled at the fluffy movie version, *You're Only Young Twice*.

What reminds and amuses one of one's own experiences is not always as entertaining to others. In the first scene students welcome the Lord Rector. They are led by Sheltie, a lad not unlike George Windlestraw. While the students drink sherry in the Principal's library, Ada Shore enters. She is the niece of Dan, the porter, who is really Conal O'Grady, a noted Irish poet. Dan also runs the Plaza, a dance hall.

Improbabilities increase when Ada, who cannot type, becomes Asher's secretary. She is soon running things. The heroine tells Asher and Professor Hayman that Sheltie will sue for libel if he is suspended, as the hypocritical professor of ecclesiology has demanded.

When Sheltie hits a policeman during a raid on the Plaza, Ada again convinces Asher not to expel the youth. Later she talks Asher into giving Sheltie the scholarship Hayman has contrived to get for his son. Hayman's method is blackmail of the kind Groundwater employs in *The Sunlight Sonata*.

The students elect Dan the new Lord Rector. As Bridie mentions in his radio broadcast on J. M. Barrie, that playwright— whom Bridie regarded with suspicion—was made a Lord Rector, and this inspired the resolution of *What Say They?* Asher proposes to Ada, and the curtain closes on an insignificant entertainment.

VII   The Forrigan Reel

The Forrigan Reel opened at the Glasgow Citizens' Theatre on December 25, 1944. The ballad opera with Bridie's lyrics set to a folkloric score by Cedric Thorpe Davie was popular with war weary audiences who enjoyed the fantasy analogous to "The Cooper o' Fife," an old ballad. The piece was subsequently expanded for the London presentation at Sadler's Wells on October 24, 1945. Unfortunately, the printed text is this protracted version, which is a distortion of the original.

The wordy prologue establishes that Sir Brian Cooke's daughter Clarinda is ailing. Cooke and Phillips her swain, who is full of romantic sensibility, decide to take the girl to Scotland for her health. As the overture concludes, Old MacAlpin is discovered in front of his hut. The stage directions require that he resembles Pantaloon.[7] MacAlpin is a tinker who knows human nature as well as he knows the notes on a chanter and a fiddle. Mairi, who likes his son Donald MacAlpin, brings Mrs. Grant to the bothy.

The wife of the laird of Forrigan thinks she is a clock and that Donald is the devil.[8] Bridie satirizes psychiatry and its methods of treatment. The father fiddles while the son dances with Mrs. Grant, until Donald drops in exhaustion. The dance, which shows the passage of time, is an effective device, and the prancing cures Mrs. Grant. When the one who was afflicted sees her husband, she faints. The madness has been a means to get Mr. Grant's attention.

Mr. Grant brings his lawyer to make a settlement with MacAlpin, after the laird has hit Donald. Grant has the father sign a paper, which entitles the tacksman to a share of profits from future healings. The lawyer uses Latin to deter the rustic from going to the Lords of Session. The eighteenth-century comic gambit is suitable for a play set in the Georgian period. It also provides a parallel to MacAlpin's incantation as part of his remedy for Clarinda. Gaelic becomes a language of ritual.

Bridie uses Erse adroitly in the play. Words such as *amadan* and phrases such as *Mo chridhe! Mo thruaigh!* provide flavor, but do not obscure meaning. The Highlanders' dialogue has the lilt and flow of the old language. "The paleness of her" and many other expressions are direct translations from Gaelic. Bridie uses tangents as *cantrips* to charm theatergoers with talk. In places the dialogue sinks to *blethering.*

The English visitors arrive, but before Clarinda, who has been "bled . . . blistered" and "swallowed a Sahara of powders and drunk gallons of sewage at dozens of Spas," sees MacAlpin, too

many songs are sung. The lyrics do not further the plot. They
provide atmosphere, but this is established in the speeches.

Clarinda gives her symptoms, and the playwright gives menus
of good Scottish food, for proper diet and fresh air are of more
value than medicine to cure a psychosomatic condition. The idea
lurking in *The Forrigan Reel* and in other plays is that man makes
himself sick. He can also cure himself of most maladies.

Donald chants his "*Sian* against Harm." He sees immediately
that a firm hand is what his patient needs. He dances to make her
laugh. Be he tinker or therapist, a man's only power to alter
another's mind is that of suggestion.

Phillips becomes exasperated with the languishing Clarinda.
He slaps her. Clarinda considers the blow restorative. The same
impulse motivates men in their treatment of women in *Babes in
the Wood* and *Daphne Laureola*.

CLARINDA. Walter, it was not I who spoke to you those harsh and
wicked words. It was a simulacrum of your Clarinda. And
now you have rescued me by that sacred, sacred blow from
the Shadows as Orpheus rescued his Euridike, as Perseus
rescued the other young person from the clutches of the
horrid Dragon. . . .
PHILLIPS. It was Andromache, my darling.
CLARINDA. Was it? How clever of you to know! But you know
everything, my dearest.

In the Epilogue Mrs. Grant reinforces the premise that "half of
our camsteeriness / Is just pure, simple, undiluted weariness."

VIII   John Knox

Bridie originally called his play about the most romantic
chapter in Scottish history "The French Widow," but changed
the title to *John Knox*, because the Protestant reformer
overshadows Mary Queen of Scots in this historical drama, as he
has towered over Scottish life for centuries. That Bridie should
write a piece about the controversy which raises questions that
have yet to be settled approaches predestination.

Dramatists have attempted for almost two centuries to present
the events that led to Scotland's famed regicide, but the subject

is too complex for comprehensive treatment on stage. Rizzio, Bothwell, Lethington, and Lennox are but a sample of the complicated characters who lived during the turbulent time that radically changed the course of Scottish thought.

Bridie employed arresting theatrical technique, distilled Knox's theological views provided the requisite background to enable an international audience to follow the action, but the history remains richer than the drama.

Bridie's *John Knox* opened at the Glasgow Citizens' Theatre on August 18, 1947. The audience saw an important play, for it is the nookest antisermon ever done.

The playwright shows the misguided efforts of church and state, embodied by Knox and Mary respectively. The minister and the queen are miscreants, for Bridie reveals the feet of clay on which both factions stood.

Jerry, who represents foolish man, dances with both sides. Mankind puts faith in the institutions the protagonist and antagonist represent, rather than placing trust in God.

The frame of the play consists of conversation, comments, and reactions by three moderns, who provide odd parallels to the historic proceedings. Hector, a tipsy divinity student, Nora, a Leith prostitute and Jerry, a Mulatto clog dancer, meet in front of the National Gallery of Scotland in Edinburgh. The columned building in the classic style is of a design suited to the multiscened presentation, and conveys the idea that one will see portraits and tableaux.

Hector, according to Bridie's Notes on the Characters, "should be played by an actor with a personality nearly as strong as Knox's and Bothwell's."

Nora defends Mary throughout the play. The crowd in act 3 shout "Burn the hoor!" when the Queen of Scots appears, after she has become a prisoner.

Jerry, by direction "has a hotch-potch of all the accents of the world, but his voice is that of a West Indian negro." He recalls the blackamoors who served as jesters, and reminded the powerful of their own foolishness. That he is a West Indian indicates that the old world myths are perpetuated in the new. Jerry is garbed in striped pajama trousers. The costume functions as a symbol of misguided effort, as does the black and silver wallpaper in *Babes in the Wood*. Jerry keeps time to music from a gramophone mounted on a perambulator, a symbol of immaturity of inspiration. He dances to a particularly vehement speech by Knox. Rizzio plays the lute as Mary, her husband Darnley, and her courtiers dance the purpose. The Mulatto joins in with them.

Hector delivers a sermon at the beginning of the play which represents Bridie's viewpoint more than any utterance the Presbyterians or Roman Catholics make:

God that made the world and all things therein, seeing that He is Lord of heaven and earth, dwelleth not in temples made with hands; neither is worshipped with men's hands, as though He needed anything, seeing He giveth to all life, and breath, and all things; and hath made of one blood all nations of men for to dwell on all the face of the earth, and hath determined the times before appointed and the bounds of their habitation.

The ghost of John Knox appears. He and the other spirits who lived in the sixteenth century enact key scenes from the religio-political conflict, which is cast as a power struggle with Scotland as the prize.

Bridie arranges scenes to show the juxtaposition of the opponents' religious beliefs. The playwright also shows the flawed personal lives of the main characters. The eighteen-year-old Marjorie tells the forty-eight-year-old Knox that he is her God. The man who marries the girl is portrayed in such a manner that one is led to suspect he comes to believe Marjorie. Later in the play mention is made of Mary as "the woman and her boys."

Knox proposes a new government consisting of two estates: one, the prince and council, the other "God's Kirk." Knox outlines a system of elections and appointments, and although he compares the superintendants to apostles, the construct is merely one of governance.

To make his ideas realities, Knox's party commit acts of violence, as do the royal establishment in an effort to preserve the status quo. These developments lead to the confrontation between Mary and Knox. The crux of their discussion concerns who shall rule.

Mary is more human than Knox, who is, by turns, plain spoken, glib, courtly, venomous, but never lets his mask slip. This helps to convey his calculating fanaticism; it also makes him the more formidable adversary.

Bridie was criticized for the weak characterization of Mary, who is modeled to show the frailty-thy-name-is-woman motif. But the well-known historical struggle does not call for suspense which comes from the matched wits of worthy opponents. *John Knox* portrays men at odds with reality.

Before the audience is exposed to what the dramatist wishes to reveal in featured portraits, the author crowds the play with historical scenes, including a tableau of the assassination of Rizzio. These, as the informative choral sections, do little more than point up the intricacies of the persons and events that shaped the reign of Mary Stuart.

At the end of the play Knox and Mary sit together. The spirits tell what they believed they were in life.

> MARY. I was a King Crab. I thought I was born that.
> KNOX. You were born a grasping screaming little morsel of female flesh with an immortal soul somewhere in you, and you were born nothing else.
> MARY. That is true. And how were you born?
> KNOX. I thought there was a man sent from Heaven whose name was John, but I took the ordinary road for getting here. It was ill luck that I got a voice that could talk Kings off their thrones and I thought too much of it.

Knox observes that some men pretend to be gods, but they are not. In their selfishness both lost. Neither Knox nor Mary knew what love meant, and in failing to learn that, they knew nothing. The spectacular effects performed by a large cast and the tense moments provided by powerful speeches were designed to show the theatrical sham of a reformer and a queen who acted through life.

IX   *"Gog and Magog"*

Bridie's secretary, Lindsay Galloway also wrote plays.[9] He suggested that his employer and mentor write a piece about William McGonagall. The beloved Dundee poetaster inspired Bridie's "Gog and Magog." McGonagall, the prototype of Harry MacGog, was a weaver and self-styled Shakespearean actor, who had aspirations to become laureate when Tennyson died. A quatrain from "The funeral of the German Emperor" illustrates the quality of McGonagall's poetic disasters:

The Authorities of Berlin in honour of the Emperor considered it no sin,
To decorate with crape the beautiful City of Berlin;
Therefore Berlin I declare was a City of crape,
Because few buildings crape decoration did escape.[10]

The seriousness with which the versifier sought recognition for his miserable productions from Queen Victoria and other eminent contemporaries has comic-pathetic demensions. Such proportions are suited to Bridie's vision. The undereducated writer, a descendant of the obtuse pedant in comedy, is usually a minor figure. Bridie gives new importance to the artistic failure, who is a successful human. In the Scottish setting MacGog functions as the incarnation of national individualism.

The North is reputed to have more eccentrics than any other part of the British Isles. Scots sanction a spectrum of variant behaviors. Respect for nonconformity is linked to McGonagall's fame. He represents the peculiar conviction, executed honestly. Although his products are inferior, his way is admirable—or at least debatable. If a subject can inspire argument, it is worthy of Scottish attention. "Gog and Magog" opens with locals arguing.

CHARLIE: I don't admit a Universe at all.
HORNGOLLOCH: Then God A'michty, man, where are we to begin?
CHARLIE: Not at this stage of the discussion.

Briskett, the reviewer, enters, followed by Horace, a mechanic, whose pronouncements are more elegant than the phrases of the critic. Briskett is in Scotland to do a book on Smollett: "Sort of Chasing the perfervid ingenuity of the Scot to its lair." In conversations with Dr. MacKessock, Watts, and others, who exhibit Northern characteristics, such as the philosophical penchant and respect for the Deity, the critical hunter measures the "lair."

MacGog tells Briskett that the area is as backward as a pig's rump. The actor-poet tries to impress the visitor, who asks if MacGog is influenced by Eliot. The versifier identifies *The Wasteland* author as a Border man.

Briskett encourages the village doctor to unravel his umbilical theory, and at the raucous substitute for the Burns Supper, MacGog, the guest of honor, recites Shakespeare and one of his own poems. The patriotic jungle finds favor with the locals.

Briskett presents Harry with a pig-shaped balloon labeled Haggis. The amusement of the Englishman is to destroy the illusion of the Scot. The tatterdemalian tragedian possesses dignity in the insupportable situation, as he says to his host.

I do not grudge you your amusement. I have not gone through a hard life without, now and again, having to face up to mockery, from time to time the bairns and halfins in my audience have pelted me with vegetables and rotten eggs. That was a rude and uncultivated act, but it had honesty in it. I find little honesty in your behaviour this night.

MacGog and Briskett fight during a long denouement in the second act. The hero says that had they lived four generations back he would have put a dirk in the cirtic's thrapple. The Jacobite strain, which is first sounded in MacGog's doggerel, stresses the lost cause theme which Bridie develops in the third act.

The town turns to arms over the nodal theory of the universe. The umbilical controversy[11] shows the stupidity of violent acts. MacGog believes that the devil started the war. What began as a statement about the higher value of good manners than good taste becomes an unsatisfying apocalypse.

The opening night reviewers who saw the first production at the Arts Theatre, London on December 1, 1948, were no more amused by "Gog and Magog" than Queen Victoria was by McGonagall's verse. The play has not been published.

X   The Tintock Cup

The Royal Princess Theatre, the former home of Glasgow pantomime, became the playhouse of the Citizens' troupe in 1945. Bridie wanted to beat more commercial enterprises at their own game, and wrote a panto for his Group. In collaboration with George Munro, members of the cast, and others, he concocted *The Tintock Cup*. The Christmas season of 1949 was merrier for the effort.

Pantomime is an acquired taste. The standard recipe is a combination of satire, burlesque, music, and physical business. Every fairy-tale character has wisecracked his way into these shows, which are as much a part of British Yule as hard sauce for plum pudding.

As *The Tintock Cup* opens, performers Duncan Macrae and Molly Urquhart (who had appeared in *The Forrigan Reel* and other Bridie comedies), play themselves in search of a script. Amid local color and the broadest of lines, they satirize the form of the piece itself.

The second scene builds into a plot which is as thin as council house stucco. Druids, Maggie Blue, who has stolen "sweeties" from an ice cream shop, a warlock, an Italian laden with accent, all provide fun which needs explanation to those unacquainted with the Scottish stage.

Duncan Macrae, who had starred in Robert McLellan's *Jamie the Saxt*, recites a bit of verse which capitalizes upon self-conscious nationalism and relies upon egregious doggerel to make Northerners laugh at themselves:

> I'm Jamie the Saxt.
> Ye'll hae mind o my Maw and my Bairn—they was axed.
> For a that they ca'd me a bit of a fule.
> I won a the medals they had at the schule.
> I had Latin and Greek and I lippened what art meant
> In England they made me a Heid o Department.
> If y want ony mair ye can look at the play
> By Robert McLellan and Duncan Macrae.
> In Lunnon, whaur Woodburn and Alastair Sim is;
> There a statue pit up tae the Saxt o the Jamies.

In 1943 James Bridie, Paul Vincent Carroll, Dr. Thomas J. Honeyman, Guy McCrone, and others formed the Glasgow Citizen's Theatre. Despite the difficulties attendant with such an undertaking in wartime, they established a permanent, professional repertory company. The group has presented a significant number of notable world premieres.[12]

Had Bridie never written a play, he would be remembered in theater history for this contribution. The Citizens' enabled the dramatist to create a range of works. He designed the frame of "Red Riding Hood," a pantomime presented during the 1950-1951 season. Bridie also gave expression to serious ideas. He wrote his most powerful plays, *The Queen's Comedy* and *The Baikie Charivari*, sure that these experimental dramas would be produced.

CHAPTER 10

Backdrop: Satire of the Estates

S IR David Lyndsay's morality excoriated the spiritual and
temporal abuses so effectively that the Protestant reformers,
whom Lyndsay upheld in his *Satire of the Three Estates* (ca.
1540), realized the potency of the stage as a weapon. They also
saw that it might be used to their detriment. Soon after Knox's
supporters gained power, they inveighed against all theatrical
presentations. The early presbyters' worst fears were not
realized for four centuries. What kirkmen dreaded came to pass
in the last years of Bridie's career.

I   The Golden Legend of Shults

In his preface to *Susannah and the Elders and Other Plays*
Bridie names his sources and describes his method for *The
Golden Legend of Shults.* "In it I have canonised *Tyl
Eulgenspiegel* according to the Golden Legend formula and
added a bit of narrative of my own. I used a sort of revue
technique that hardens, as the play goes on, into a more
conventional dramatic form." Till Eulgenspiegel, a fourteenth-
century German, is the subject of satirical tales that began to be
published in 1483. The scapegrace, who pretends to be simple
and stupid, perpetrates knaveries against priests, nobles, trades-
men, and innkeepers. His stratagems show up the conduct of the
establishment. This is Bridie's manner of presentation.

The Golden Legend is a medieval manual of ecclesiastical lore.
Bridie uses the version published by William Caxton. In the work
that features mortality and piety Caxton states his purpose: "that
euery cristen man may be the better encouraged tenterprise
warre for the defense of cristendom." Bridie reverses this
parable about courage in dying to derive his theme. Living with
faith and freedom is superior to the panoply of the grave.
128

Bridie softened the protagonist to make him sympathetic and to show a world that deserves to be hoodwinked by "poly-tricks." This sphere is revealed in short scenes, some of which resemble expressionist experiments of Eugene O'Neill, but Bridie's differ in the employment of humor.

As *The Golden Legend of Shults* opens the main character, Davie Cooper, is caught cracking a safe. During the blackout the safe is turned. Its obverse side is painted with the wig and costume of a Scottish judge. The actor sticks his head and hands through the cut holes, in the manner of an old photography studio prop.

The judge recites Davie's long previous record, then sentences him to five years. The judge comes from behind the picture. The old man carries golf clubs. The safe swivels and becomes Davie's jail cell.

The judge gossips with his caddie. The jurist, who says it is a crime to put birds in cages, becomes ill. On his deathbed the elderly one persists in claiming that he acted justly in imprison-ing Davie. The doctor in attendance makes a speech about recovery and recuperation, then pulls the blanket over his patient's face. The nurse pays the physician's fee from the corpse's wallet. A chorus tells of the judge's harshness and gives a satiric eulogy on the medical profession.

The doctor and the chaplain observe Davie in prison. The reverend says he is a model prisoner. Davie is schizophrenic, the medical man answers. It is the physician who needs psychiatric care. Davie does not want to be released, because, as he tells the chaplain, it is hard to give up what you do well. The protagonist has learned to play the game of society, and the chaplain gets Davie a job as a traveling salesman.

Davie goes to Glasgow. Newsboys scream headlines of mayhem and foolishness. A street musician plays tunes that provide ironic counterpoint to exchanges which show urban degredation. A sailor and a prostitute come to terms, as the penny whistle sounds the reedy notes of "Love Is the Sweetest Thing."

As the second act begins, Davie is now a corset salesman riding a train to Shults. His fellow passengers are also commercial travelers, who tell how mean a place the small town is. They force Davie to play cards, and the ex-convict beats them at their

game. The game and its circumstances illustrate the premise of
the play. People get what they merit. The object of the game is
to spot the queen of clubs. The card stands for practicality and
commercial gain as well as a brunette.

When he arrives in Shults, Davie tries to be an upright man
and to conduct his business, but the citizens make it impossible to
attain privacy or dignity. He sees them in their homes, which
illustrate that there are prisons other than those with barred
windows.

Davie meets Annie, a waitress, who is the only decent soul in
Shults. As Davie rides the train out of town he says, "she's a bit of
a liar. But I'm a bit of a liar myself." Hiding under the seat of the
railway carriage is Adolf, one of Davie's old gang. The name of
the fellow confidence man is meant to evoke the image of Hitler.
Adolf and Davie drink and agree that Shults, like Carthage, must
be destroyed.

Newly printed counterfeit money enables Davie and his gang
to pose as a Mexican millionaire and his associates. The bitterness
of the satire becomes more palatable as the destruction of the
walls erected by those hypocritical souls, whom Scots call *unco
guid,* gets under way.

Davie as Mr. Monterey-Carrick buys the town from the
greedy, then pulls down the structures. Mid the rubble of Shults
Davie addresses the estates, who are dressed for a pageant to
dramatize spurious lore the protagonist has passed off to them as
local history.

> DAVIE. . . . . Whatamean tosay, there's some made one way and some
> another, and if those that's made one way would only let those
> that's made the other way alone, because how does anybody
> know what's going on inside a block's hied? How does he know
> himself.

The speaker's honesty causes the doctor to believe Davie is ill.
The citizens of Shults go on with their ceremony.

In the optional epilogue the people erect a statue to the late
Monterey-Carrick, who made the town royal and gay again. as
Annie and Davie read of the news in Hawaii.

Themes of man the builder, man the destroyer, and the cycle
of civilization are introduced in *The Golden Legend of Shults.*
Bridie would continue to explore these ideas in works of the

1940s. In discoursing on civilization Bridie throws light on the ending of *The Switchback*. In *The Golden Legend* archeologists are shown trying to piece together prior cultures from shards. In doing this they seek what cannot be found.

The Golden Legend of Shults is a step on a path which Bridie takes to set man on a new road of simple righteousness, but this way of living is as full of serpentine turns, when one encounters the old roads. These one must cross while striking out in a fresh direction.

The nonrepresentional trappings Bridie considered short-cuts to the telling of an episodic story were gathered together at the Perth Theatre, where the play was first produced on July 24, 1939. As the safe-judge-jail was set up. few realized the author was about to "ding doon" the whole establishment.

II Lancelot

Bridie wrote *Lancelot* in 1939, but it was not performed until October 30, 1945, at the Royal Princess's Theatre by the Glasgow Citizens' Theatre Company. The subject, if not the tone of the play, is consonant with *The King of Nowhere* of 1938. *Lancelot* is a step in the author's search for mythological sources to convey his estimation of the world's condition.

Bridie used Thomas Mallory's version of Arthurian legend to make a statement about the Nazi concept of breeding a super race. It was Bridie's method to take the conditions of another civilization, turn them round to examine, and find that on most important matters different cultures are similar.

The playwright, who says repeatedly that man should not try to interfere with God's providence, focuses upon one coupling to show that the attempt to achieve racial purity by an obscene act is senseless futility. Here the word "obscene" is used to mean repulsive, for that is the manner in which the antagonistic society uses the protagonist for its purposes.

Bridie chooses Camelot, an idealized society, to convey that warped ideas may be found in any place at any period. These are not the product of one man's mind, but are linked to the group in which the corruption occurs.

As *Lancelot* begins, Merlin, who represents science, states the social purpose: "I made the Age of Chivalry. That was only the first part of my work. I had created the time and the place in which the perfect man could be found and live and begin the new order of things. It is the bravest time since time began."

Merlin is a commentator. He is the key to the meaning of *Lancelot*. Merlin's ego is such that he attributes the shaping of an age to himself. This summons shades of Hitler, as does "New World," which is the New Order of the Third Reich. No one can singlehandedly create an era. Even the magician needs the help of others to make the hero a pawn in the game of eugenics.

Lancelot is depicted as a clean-hearted idealist whom Sir Kay labels a "school boy." It is Sir Kay, with his suggestions of promiscuity, who is immature.

Arthur, a Blimp-like figure, is comparable to Nestor in *The Queen's Comedy*. King Arthur presides over a tournie, during which Lancelot in Sir Kay's armor bests Sir Gawaine. Mid the panoply, Gawaine and Agravaine swear vengeance. Lancelot answers the war mongers. "In war the great and the simple, the high and the low, the knightly and the common, are seethed together in a pot. The end is victory, not honour, and honour is lost in the chase."

Lancelot is sent on a quest to rescue King Pelleas' kingdom from a serpent. Dream symbols proliferate. They reinforce the idea that the priest-king of Corbin is a hypocrite who is so blind to truth that he does not see his own duplicity. When first we meet Pelleas, he recites a lengthy prayer which reveals his low estimation of man: "Et quid faciat homo putredo ac vermis, quum ipsos quoque Cherubim verlare, ipso pavore, faciem suam oporteat . . . ?" Bridie writes "aye good Presbyterian Latin," as it was described in the seventeenth century, but the prayer is as long winded as the rest of *Lancelot*.

Lancelot is given drugged drink, and Pelleas weds the drunken hero to his foolish daughter Elaine. Merlin gives a speech which indicates that Bridie sees Nazism as chthonic religion. "Knighthood is the perfect state of mankind; even if nothing more were done it would survive long after you and I were dead—for ever. On this evening it is ordained by the powers of the air that there will be begotten in this palace the perfection of this perfect state, the perfect knight, who will be called Galahad and achieve the Grail and redeem the world by his greatness."

Bridie holds his Arthurian mirror in front of the Strength through Joy Movement. The reflection shows that Lancelot loses his strength through joyless sex.

When the outraged knight returns to Camelot, Queen Guenevere, Lancelot's ideal love, rejects him. The woman's jealousy, when she learns of Lancelot's marriage, makes her less than ideal. The perfect knight goes mad when she, who gave his life ideal meaning, proves to be human. Lancelot's love for Arthur's wife is a hopeless quest; as such it is unreasonable.

When Lancelot's sanity returns, he tells his son: "When I was a knight it was enough for me to fear God, to honour the King, to ride straight, to keep my body clean and to be courteous to my enemies. I thought that was enough." Abiding by established conventions in unquestioning loyalty is not sufficient, for it leads to disruption and disaster, as the playwright says more explicitly in *The Queen's Comedy*.

In *The Forrigan Reel* Bridie's heroine suffers from depression. Clarinda and Lancelot illustrate the same postulate: sometimes a person must loose his wits to be brought to his senses.

Lancelot kills a Ranger who has slain peasants for poaching. Gestapo tactics breed violence; the mad knight fails to distinguish the difference between killing men and slaughtering animals. Bridie uses a variation of this theme in his one-act play, *The Starlings.*[1]

Merlin tells Lancelot that he was drunk with belief, and thought himself different from what God made him. *John Knox* reiterates this idea. The exchange between the knight and the magician in the second act reads as though the playwright is arguing with himself about his own life and thought.

> MERLIN. The truth has as many faces as a nightmare. You must find your own truth for yourself. The Court you built in your mind has fallen to pieces. Before many days the bullies and strumpets will also break. Here you see the old bawd the first of them lost and tied in a rock. . . . Go back into the world and rejoice in your strength.

Lancelot returns to Elaine and Galahad. The boy is a symbiosis of idealism and violence; he says, "I should like to go and help the ragged man and cut off the heads of these people who are throwing stones." Galahad is his father's son.

Lancelot regains his sanity. He realizes that there never was a serpent in Corbin. Shortly after the protagonist returns to his responsibility(?), he is summoned to Camelot. The queen and the knight profess their love for each other. Agravaine, who has set up the trap, leads Arthur to Guenevere's room. The king discovers the innocent lovers, and decrees that both will die.

The souls of Lancelot and Guenevere speak in a *Colloque Sentimentale*. Guenevere, the realist, has told her romantic admirer to return to Corbin, but Lancelot has chosen the monastery, because, he says, we cannot be other than we are. This is Merlin's opinion. The knight, who has striven to be better than most, who has misjudged his peers by positing that they are nobler than they are, and who has been duped by others, is, even in the monastery, trying to be something he is not. Finally, Lancelot dies and is eulogized. As with most encomia, the praise is not true. Lancelot is not the noblest, gentlest, kindest knight. There are no supermen, even in the most perfect kingdom in Christendom.

III   The Holy Isle

King Lot and Friar Innocence are mentioned in *Lancelot*. When they are brought on stage in *The Holy Isle*, the characters speak thoughts the author had long pondered. Bridie depicts a community which abides by divine ordinance. These citizens are the antithesis of the denizens of Camelot and Corbin, who have warped their society by hellish ways.

The Holy Isle opened in December, 1942, at the Arts Theatre, London. The first set the audience saw was the palace of King Lot of Orkney at Kirkwall in 500 A.D.

Torquil, a sailor brings a map which shows the island of Ultima Thule—a description once applied to Scotland—which the natives call Ru-rhush. Grettir Flatface, a greedy business man, Friar Innocence, and Torquil undertake an expedition to explore and exploit the unknown land.

The Bishop, who sends Innocence to evangelize, preaches cant, that exemplifies how pietism and politics cloud true motive. The ecclesiastic speaks of "legitimate trade:" "An inalienable human right vested in those who have the God-given energy and public spirit to practise that activity. A world full of idle hands is swept and garnished for the entry of the Devil. Faith without works, says St. James, is dead. And the Church is fully conscious of the stream of life poured into the veins of its Faith by the beneficent labours of Commerce."

The travelers are taken to a guest house on Ru-Rhush where they are introduced to the inhabitants' logic, which makes more sense than the conventional kind. When Torquil finds that Lot's wife, Queen Margause, has disguised herself as a cabin boy in order to come with them, he is tempted to kill her, because he has a premonition the witch-queen will destroy the islanders. Torquil tells the friar, who responds, "It is evil to take human life without long and prayerful meditation." Torquil counters, "If I meditate I won't be able to do it."

Bridie strips the veils that shroud human motivation. Torquil attributes his desire to kill Margause to fear. Most people whom he has met in his travels have been good; then something or someone comes along to spoil them. Chief among the despoilers are systems. Torquil tells a parable of a place where potatoes were roasted.

Fried potatoes were invented. "Then two asses came to the conclusion that they ought to be done either one way or the other. Then they had a fight and everybody took sides."

Margause argues that without rules there would be chaos. Torquil, as other Bridie versions of Everyman, misjudges his associates. He thinks Margause will ruin the isle and Grettir and Innocence will help it.

She is the name of the chief decision maker for the island. The woman wears Chinese garb. The costume serves as a reminder that the ancient Chinese lived by a system of ethics rather than prescriptions springing from ritualistic religion. Her garment contrasts to Lot's saffron robes. Bright yellow is a dream symbol of emotional disturbance.

She explains how their community functions: "We have no government here. I have heard of governments. Their purpose is to keep the wicked in order. Here we try as far as possible to refrain from being wicked. Our reward is to have no government." She and her Ponderers advise wrong doers and deal with them by letting the punishment fit the offence.

When Margause asks She about the protective purpose of government She answers:

If a people cannot protect itself against Pestilence, Famine and War, I doubt if a government will protect it. We have no pestilence because we live principally in the open air and because we discourage visitors. We have no famines because we know if we do not sow and reap and bind and thresh and stow away, we shall starve. We have no wars, because we do not allow either gods or devils on this Island. The pebbles on our beaches are clean. Our cliffs are clean. And we give gods and devils to the mighty, cleansing sea.

Rather than outlining a Utopian government, Bridie points out defects in the existing order. For the playwright *perfect system* is a contradiction in terms.

To avoid being thrown into the sea, as was Mr. Bolfry, Margause tells She that they are teachers, The visitors give their conflicting views on the first things they will inculcate.

Innocence begins with the Adam myth to teach shame and guilt. Thus will he control adherents. Over the friar's objections She takes over the pulpit and tells how a god-man, i.e., a missioner, came before, and from his magic book the people heard: "Blessed are the meek, for they shall inherit the Earth." The people built churches presided over by The Meekest of All, who lived in a castle maintained by tithes. If this one and his assistants were not supported, they banged heads.

Innocence argues that he has the Truth, and that it "must be swallowed whole." In teaching the islanders, who wish to be as clever as She and the Ponderers, Innocence becomes the serpent of Eden.

Margause makes islanders her servants, although they have not had masters before. Grettir sets up a still for Heather Ale and opens copper mines. She "advises" the visitors to leave.

> SHE. . . . Your evil souls spread over my Island like the rust on the barley. . . .
> Long before my mother was born we killed the worshippers of the great Snake and tore down the altars where they had murdered our children. We broke our spears and slings and arrows and threw our gold into the sea. No rovers molested us for they feared the girdle of holiness that ringed our Island and the spirits of our dead watching over our fields. For ten generations we have kept the Island clean.

Bridie uses the hypothesis that the Minoans and the Celts both worshipped the Snake Mother. From the Minoans comes the myth of Europa—the figure who lent her name to the continent which gave birth to Western civilization. The parallel drawn between cults grown corrupt is an endeavor to show the real truth which all men possess in their hearts, if they look there.

Three years later the four visitors have gone native. King Lot and his party arrive. When Torquil is reunited with his former masters, he reverts to the old preconceptions. Grettir has become an alcoholic. Margause, more than the others, has accepted and learned the superior ways of the holy isle. The queen agrees to return to Orkney with her husband, because she has gained understanding. When Lot wishes to govern the island, Margause tells him, "The existing arrangements are admirable."

The Bishop chides Friar Innocence, because he has not administered the sacraments. The sacramental system is, according to Bridie, but another group of artificial objects organized into a network to snare man. As the curtain is about to close, the friar explains to his bishop what he has learned, and the playwright advises the audience what they are to gain from their stay on the holy isle.

INNOCENCE. Our Lord taught us the alphabet very simply, and when His disciples had learned that, He went on to teach them the mysteries. But we haven't learned the alphabet, have we, sir? We don't know how to live at peace with our neighbours. How can we understand the mysteries?

BISHOP. What you need is a sea-voyage.

[*He leads* INNOCENCE *through the doorway as if he were a decrepit patient.*]

INNOCENCE. I once thought I understood, but I'm not so sure now. I am not so sure.

The opening satire of *The Holy Isle* gives way to exposition of rich spiritual thought. Bridie does not tear down Kirkwall. He leaves it to give the blueprint for building of the temple of God within each person. The drama shows Bridie's profound grasp of Christian essentials, which are simply stated and set forth in a convincing way.

IV   It Depends What You Mean

It Depends What You Mean, An Improvisation for the Glockenspiel opened at the Westminster Theatre, London, on October 12, 1944. During the initial run of 189 performances theatergoers laughed at the satire which makes use of "The Brains Trust," a popular B.B.C. radio program. The film version,

Folly to Be Wise (1949), incorporated a farcical chase scene in a trailer, but the ramifications of the play are somber.

When the aim is to tell what is wrong with the world by a question and answer session held on a bare stage, the task is to arrange ideas and their interrelationshop. Bridie lays out lines to create an interesting game. To hold attention, the players' moves must be set at a tempo of a Gilbert and Sullivan pattersong. Characters play games to avoid detection when speaking in public, and thus they reveal themselves.

The Reverend Paris, an obsequious divine, asks the Prouts and their friend George Mutch to participate in a panel discussion to entertain the troops. The Brains Trust the clergyman moderates is comprised of representatives of the estates. The physician, poet, painter, politician, professor, and aristocrat are alike in that none of the "authorities" has satisfying answers to questions that range from the ridiculous to the profound:

> PADRE. . . . The next question. . . . reads as follows: "What is planning? . . .
> MUTCH. Well, it depends what you mean by planning.
> PROUT. We're asking what *you* mean by planning.
> MUTCH. Well, I mean, to say, isn't planning a sort of synthesis of correlated probabilities interdigitated into a sort of a—kind of a—well, *pattern*—with the ultimate idea of translating the resulting probabilities into some—some sort of concrete matrix? I should think that's perfectly clear. . . .
> PROUT. What it boils down to is, who is going to be boss? And you and I will have damned little to say to that.

The play takes a different turn when Private Jessie Killigrew asks if marriage is a good idea. The Prouts use a pantomime set and reenact their first meeting. In their dramatization of their romance they show the way of men's plans.

Prout wanted a woman who thought of others. Ironically Angela, who has put up with her husband's juvenile bad temper for fifteen years, now is thoughtful of his long-time friend, Mutch. But neither George nor Angela has self-knowledge, and therefore they can not know each other. Both are to blame for the condition of their marriage. The self-indulgent pair have neglected the duties of their state in life.

After the Brains Trust ends in turmoil, the participants adjourn to Prout's studio. Despite the answers she has been given, Jessie, who has said she has been lied to at home and who has seen how the "experts" operate, determines to wed someone practical. This is her solution.

Mutch, who wants Angela as a lover but not as a wife, is thrown out by the spurned Angela, who bickers with her husband at the end in much the same fashion as she did at the beginning. George puts the tea kettle on to boil, and although the stage directions indicate "this is the first time in years that he has ever done a spontaneously civil action," this is the illusion of marriage preserved.

In *Marriage Is No Joke* the hero is saved by a good woman. In *The Golden Legend of Shults* this idea is thrown out as a sop because of the playwright's conviction that the ladies in the audience wanted to have it so. In *It Depends What You Mean* the marriage is a joke. The opinions are japes as well, because the self-concerned do not know what to think, and the reactionaries do not have the answers.

V   The Queen's Comedy

Hitler has been called the fundamental trauma of the century. Men tend to describe in mythic or satiric terms that which is beyond human comprehension. In *A Small Stir* Bridie notes the tendency to diminish the hateful by making them small and ridiculous. Bridie uses serious and light approaches in writings that touch upon World War II. In *The King of Nowhere* he treats dictatorship as the sickness of grand delusion. In *Mr. Bolfry* the demon says that the devil and not Hitler started the war. Mr. Bolfry speaks of the necessity of altercation. In "The Nero Concerto," a 1942 speech, Bridie compares Churchill to Hitler. He casts Schickelgruber as clown, when measuring the two historians and painters. Bridie leaves the humorous figure to set forth ideas which aid in interpretation of *The Queen's Comedy*. He speaks of *The Marriage of Heaven and Hell* in terms of "reconcilliation of the contradictions" of Blake's arguments. Bridie's seminal essay explicates the spirals of thought that whirl through the mythic antiwar play.

The Queen's Comedy, A Homeric Fragment is the most profound play to come out of the experience of World War II, and possesses a universality that transcends its period. Bridie's source is *The Illiad*, Books 14 and 15. The drama that takes place under the sea, on earth, and in heaven is an episodic epic which dramatizes the line from *King Lear* printed on the title page: "As flies to wanton boys are we to the Gods: they kill us for their sport." According to Bridie Lear is the real fool in Shakespeare's tragedy. The deities Bridie puts on stage are the false gods that men worship. Those who honor them are fools, and their obeisance is as vain as bellicose action. To show the futility the playwright has no victors on Olympus or on the battlefield.

The work requires a thorough grounding in the classics for total appreciation of Bridie's material. The technical effects require speedy and effective staging, which makes unusual demands on a master producer. The greatest hurdle is the horrific ending. This more than any other consideration has contributed to the shelving of a masterpiece.

Tyrone Guthrie produced *The Queen's Comedy*, when it opened at the Lyceum Theatre on August 21, 1950, during the Edinburgh Festival. The peoples of the world needed this play, but when it was staged few acclaimed it. Guthrie succinctly stated the reason for its underestimation by critics and public. "What people *don't want* to understand, they don't hear!"[2]

Bridie wrote optional verse to be spoken while the scenes are shifted in full view of the audience. The drama may open with a statement about man the builder and destroyer, who is "At the behest of the Immortal Gods / Or anyone else who likes giving orders."

In the Introduction Thetis, who is knitting a seaweed jumper *à la* La Farge, asks Neptune about her son Achilles. The god-like hero has switched sides, and now Thetis supports the Trojans. Neptune built Troy, but the sea god wants the Greeks to win, because the Trojans have not repaid him.

Jupiter appears to Thetis disguised as an octopus. The eight-armed creature's tentacles are like the many arms of the Hindu Shiva, as the god appears in the *Mahabharata,* the Indian analogue of the *Illiad.* The supreme god of Greece assures Thetis that he has kept his promise to her, and that she must be patient and have faith. Christian echoes make speeches poignant. The mother does not believe him. The mortals who consort with deities are reminders that when men assume divine prerogatives, they encounter disaster.

Act 1, scene 1 takes place in a dressing station. Dr. Machaon and Nurse Hecamede tend the Greek wounded. An Orderly and

Infantryman, who speak in British slang of the 1940s, state how the Trojan War began.

> ORDERLY.   . . . We got an ideal to fight for, see?
>
> INFANTRYMAN. Never heard of it. It all come of a bit of square-pushing. One of them there Trojan Gussies pinched a General's Judy. What's you and me and that poor write-off over there got to do with that smooth Cissie and his little bit of Oojah.

Bridie puts Paris' abduction of Helen of Troy in the kind of language the explanation warrants to show the vapid reasons given for wars. The assassination of the Archduke Ferdinand at Sarajevo, which has been cited by some historians of World War I, or Hitler's tirades for *Lebensraum* before the outbreak of World War II, are no more satisfying than the pinching of a General's Judy.

Throughout the play the offhand tone of the conversation contrasts to the struggle in which mortals and gods are engaged. One irony of the twentieth-century permutations of Ulysses, Agamemnon, Nestor, *et al.* is that the belligerents, who are alike in believing that deity is on their particular side, make no more sense of war than do moderns.

In scene 2 Olympus, which by stage direction is to suggest "the Lounge of and expensive Hotel," is occupied by a jealous Juno. She plots to undo Thetis' work by using the cestus or magic girdle on the unfaithful Jupiter, to attain her own ends. The ox-eyed queen of heaven is abetted by a masculine Minerva and a feminine Mercury.

These depictions, which show inversion exists in the celestial realm as well as on earth, are indebted to a line from Herodotus. The historian reports that Queen Artemisia of Halicarnassus fought against the Greeks with such bravery at Salamis, that Xerxes looked at his Persians and said, "My men have become women, and my women men."

Throughout his mature work the author uses a wide range of veiled allusions: Those who grasp the references derive more from the play. Those who do not are entertained on another level.[3]

At the end of the second scene Bridie provides optional dialogue. The bracketed text indicates the playwright's aware-

ness that the sprawl of *The Queen's Comedy* was becoming too
great. The entrance of Bacchus and Apollo, which may be
omitted, shows that the various gods represent human states.
These conditions are ridiculed to show man the error of his own
ways, among which are his anthropomorphic conceptions.

Tipsy Bacchus says to the sun god: "Oh, look, look, look. Here
we come right into the middle of the intellectuals. There they
stand, cerebrating with a loud whirring sound and looking as
beautiful as rosy-fingered what-you-may-call-it." Homer's
"Dawn, rosy-fingered," is the most famous epithet in Greek
literature. That the god who presides over wine is too drunk to
remember the name of a fellow deity sums up the condition of all
the interfering, self-interested beings in the pantheon.

Bridie's original title for this play was "Old Nobility." Juno's
observation about Bacchus exemplifies the satire that inspired
the first title. "It seems hardly the occasion—when the whole of
civilisation is in jeopardy—for people of our class to stupefy
themselves with alcohol."

Minerva scolds Apollo for his support of the Trojans that kill
the Greeks, who cultivate science and art. Apollo's defense is
that Trojans preserve respect for the gods. Blind faith in
institutions is darkness indeed. At the end of the scene Hebe, the
cup bearer, and a Trojan chorus chant, "We can't do enough for
the gods." The line is as unnerving as mindless repetition of *Seig
Heil.*

In scenes that alternate between heaven and earth, self-
seeking politics, which have led to the atom bomb, the cycle of
life, the necessity of invention of gods, and other large ideas are
presented. Incidents in which the gods are featured are
particularly astringent, as the lying, unfaithful, infuriating
divinities engage in their petty intrigues.

In scene 3 the Orderly recounts his vision of a cold and cruel
Juno, who has told him, "Trust old Ma." The Scots psychic, who is
a democratic rationalist, represents the author. The Orderly
believes the gods are looking out for the Greeks, but he does not
take mortals' orders on faith.

The Infantryman does not believe in the gods, yet both
soldiers go to the same place before the final curtain, where they
learn how the gods regard them. When the slain mortals reach
Olympus, the Orderly asks for an explanation. In life he was

taught to revere authority and received answers from the clergy and the military, but he remains unsatisfied. The gods, however, who have discussed matters in the fashion of politicians who pass as statesmen, do not give answers. Such is beyond their capability.

Machoan asks the Orderly, "Are you saying we're better than the gods?" The Orderly replies, "Course we're better than the gods. We would need to be." In saying this, the Orderly has said everything about Jupiter's toy universe.

Jupiter wears a hood to indicate deception by a trusted one. Atop the hood he wears a large hat to signify his authority. In this guise Jupiter tells of his creation from chaos. The new myth to explain the formation of the universe is more frightening than old legends, to point out the fallacies of inadequate traditional notions.

JUPITER. . . . I soon found that it was easier to make a Universe than to control it. It was full of mad meaningless, fighting forces. I got most of them bound and fixed and working to rules and all of a sudden I felt lonely. I felt that I would rather my mother had given me a puppydog or a kitten. . . .

HECAMEDE. You have not answered us.

JUPITER. Were you asking questions? I am afraid I shall have to refer you to somebody who understands such matters. I don't pretend to understand them myself. But long ago I put a little swelling at the end of the primitive spinal cord of a sort of fish. I am happy to observe that in some of the higher apes, this lump has taken on extensive and peculiar functions. One of these functions appears to consist in explaining me and my little Universe. I have no doubt at all that these explanations are very interesting and stimulating. Perhaps, in time, these little objects will attain to the proper ties and activities of the Immortal Gods themselves. Who knows? I have not nearly completed my Universe. There is plenty of time. Plenty of time. You must have patience.

And now, if you will forgive me, I shall go back to Mount Ida. I have just thought of something else.[4]

In the sphere where wars are fought, this is the kind of diffident deity annihilators merit. Those who battle really seek

to usurp divine power, and in their contention devise their own
explanations, which are not true. There are no satisfying answers
for a world in which men kill their fellows.

VI   The Baikie Charivari

Bridie began writing a play which would show the ramifications of the quotation from the Book of Ruth: "Thy people shall
be my people, and thy God my God." While working on a draft,
he had a vision. This inspired him to do a different version. He
took the supernatural idea and used an interesting tale as another
frame of reference. The result was *The Baikie Charivari, or The
Seven Prophets*. The miracle play became Bridie's apotheosis.

The drama incorporates many thoughts hinted at or expressed
in previous works. It is a luminescent work which begins in the
red light of a hunter's or devil's moon and ends in the aura of a
man who has resisted the temptations of the postwar world.
Bridie puts new fire into old lamps to shed the proper light on
the way to God. This is a journey during which one encounters
good and evil.

The old recepticles are the characters from the Punch and
Judy shows. The title, *The Baikie Charivari*, exemplifies the
manner of the appropriation. *Punch, or The London Charivari* is
the source of Bridie's title. The playwright enjoins the audience
to recall the humor magazine, and thus to make the association
with the marionette that shares its name, to prepare them to
enter the world of Baikie.

The drama was presented posthumously on October 6, 1952,
at the Glasgow Citizens' Theatre. The Scots reviewers were not
prepared. They said the dramatist was "baffled," "interested
only in his personal amusement," and that certain characters
were "irrelevant."

The people of *The Baikie Charivari* are like interlocking
scrolls of Celtic design that seem at times to be mere involuted
lines when one regards the parts, yet make sense when the
observer sees the total picture. The seven prophets taken from
the puppet presentations represent modern views. Their attempt
to tyrannize the hero to accept these ideas is their deadly sin.
The Reverend Beadle (beadle), Robert Cooper (policeman),
Councillor John Ketch (hangman), Joe Mascara (clown), Dr. Jean
Pothecary (doctor), Lady Maggie Revenant (ghost), Mrs. Jemima

Lee Crowe (Jim Crow), all offer answers to Sir James Mac Arthur
Pounce-Pellott, who rebels against their solutions.

Pounce-Pellott, a descendent of Pontius Pilate,[5] is a former
district commissioner of Junglipore. He has returned from the
East after India has gained her independance. Mallaby goes to
the East. Pounce-Pellott sums up why he has come West to learn.
"The Wisdom of the East is that it is all no good." The hero
settles in Baikie to make a new beginning.

In the Prologue the De'il appears. He speaks to Beadle in such
a way that the minister believes God wishes him to shake the
protagonist's spiritual pride. It is this very self-esteem, Bridie
says in play after play, that enables men to accomplish positive
things. The hero whistles *"Lucevan le stelle"* from *Tosca* and
introduces himself while shaving. The Prologue ends with Judy
singing "The Flower Song" from *Carmen* as she bathes.
Throughout the play characters hum, sing, and play; as they
change their tunes the tone changes.

Pounce-Pellott at his toilet tells that he is the son of Grizel
MacArthur, who will live in a "chrysalis bungalow." The free
association technique used throughout the play provides clues to
layers of meaning. Grizel evokes Chaucer's "Patient Griselda."
Pounce-Pellott possesses cooperative forbearance, but this, the
playwright shows, is neither the essence of manners nor
intelligent kindness. MacArthur is the son of Arthur in Gaelic.
The pupa that was camelot is moribund.

The main room of Taj Mahal, the hero's residence, is
decorated with curios from the East and portraits of King George
V and Queen Mary. The Taj Mahal at Agra is a tomb. If the
bungalow in Baikie does not become Pounce-Pellott's
mausoleum, it does stand as Bridie's monument.

Ketch and Toby fix the broken space heater. They make a
mess round the electric fire. Man-made warmth and light leave
much to be desired. Ketch is an electrician and a communist
town councillor. As do all the characters, he wears several
hattocks. The political radical's reaction to the pajama-clad
Baby, the Pounce-Pellotts' eighteen-year-old daughter, is puritanical.[6] What man espouses and what his emotions betray are
different things entirely.

Beadle, Mascara, Pothecary, and Revenant drop in for tea, and
Pounce-Pellott asks their help in teaching him a new way of
living. The parable which the hero tells about the man who

consulted many doctors that gave conflicting opinions indicates
what Pounce-Pellott's reaction to the prophets' exhortations will
be.

Judy, the protagonist's wife, sees the visitors as oddities,
though her husband does not in his rational mind. He needs
assistance from his subconscious.

While waiting for Baby to come home from a date with
Mascara, a mediocre artist who uses his craft as an excuse for
hedonistic behavior, Pounce-Pellott dreams. The hero sees Jean
Pothecary, Lady Maggie, and Jemima Crowe as a coven of
witches. They dance widdershins. Mascara as clown beats the
drum for anarchy and summons the De'il. The author of disorder
preaches a sermon.

The Black Mass is a parody of the Mass. Bridie makes the
devil's speech a parody of a parody. Diabolic inversions become
port manteau compound images to show a ritual designed to
produce fear and awe as foolish. The trite homiletic opening—
Dearly Beloved: It behooves me on this solemn occasion to speak
a few words on Faith, Hope and Charity—becomes "Queerly
Beshoven: It bemoves me on this jollem oblation to squeak a few
worden on Graith, Rope and Parity."

The devil states the cardinal vices: graith—a prepared state;
rope—the means to maintain this order; and parity—the equality
of purchasing power, etc., the motive to maintain order. It is
ingenious foreshadowing of the temptations to be set before
Pounce-Pellott.

In the hero's dream of warning Baby receives the devil's mark.
The hellhounds leave with the spectral huntsman. The use of
Nordic myth serves as a reminder of the twentieth-century
Götterdämmerung. Pounce-Pellott wakens saying the words of
the Sign of the Cross. This indicates that he will surmount
coming trials. This dramatization of the subconscious has power,
irony, and mystery. As a dream vision for the stage it stands alone
in its complexity and in its effectiveness.

In act 2 Jemima Crowe visits the Pounce-Pellotts to offer her
host wealth for his memoirs on the decline and fall of the British
Empire. Mrs. Crowe is the lady literary agent of *Colonel
Wotherspoon* grown more sinister. Like the rest of the women in
The Baikie Charivari, Mrs. Crowe is different and stronger than
Bridie's other female characters. As he mulls the offer, Pounce-
Pellott speaks poetry that uses images of associative memory to

show the temptation has reached a deep level of his conscious-ness.[7]

Pothecary attempts to psychoanalyze Pounce-Pellott. The immature and ill-advised psychologist reduces every situation to component parts, but the Freudian starts from the wrong premises. Her approach contrasts to Pounce-Pellott's allusions to Oriental philosophies. Confucian ethics, which hold the family as central and the Taoist way of nature, which eschews artificial disciplines, are correct premises, but these have led followers in the East to wrong and negating conclusions.

Pothecary is unable to help Pounce-Pellott understand a violent world. The nonscientist spouts jargon in response to his painful questionings. Like the social scientist the psychologist makes a study of things already known. In trying to supply new information, and thus elevate these findings by expressing them in high flown language she distorts truth.

The woman wants an affair with her patient rather than his peace of mind.

POTHECARY. I'm afraid you're a bit of a philanderer, do you know?
P.-P. I wish I were. I can think of no more delightful hobby.
. . . No, I'm a lost child. I'm appealing entirely to your maternal instinct. . . .
POTHECARY. But you're a V.I.P. A V.I.P. can't be a lost child.
P.-P. He's never anything else.

During World War II Bridie was stationed briefly in Norway, then was put in charge of a hospital for mentally disturbed soldiers in Northern Ireland. This tenure in Belfast convinced him more than ever that catharsis in a drama does more good for a man than sessions on a psychiatrist's couch.

The Pounce-Pellotts give a dinner party which brings the seven prophets together. Cooper believes in protective govern-ment, like Queen Margause. He echoes ideas Bridie uses to expose Nazis Various estimates on the manner in which government should be conducted are alike in their repressive bent. Cooper, the social scientist, clashes with Ketch, the communist; Lady Maggie, the class conscious aristocrat; Mrs. Crowe, the politically self-righteous American agent; Mascara, the artist, whose only solution is to "let us alone;" and Beadle, the clergyman, who crusades for suppression. As the representatives of the estates demand to be heard and obeyed, the dialogue is structured to resemble the transcript of a trial. Bridie dramatizes the paradox that democracy involves the ambivalence of men and women hell-bent on being superior to their equals.

Judy says, "Perhaps there are no answers." She longs for the halceyon prewar days, when like Lancelot, she was content with prescribed values of a stratified society.

Baby tells the group, "You've forgotten what it is to be young." She expresses the pain and confusion of a generation that has inherited a war-torn world. "I've had too much of everything. I'm spiritually sick and perhaps you'd better wipe it up and say no more about it." Baby, who lacks emotional control, wants to cover things up; she is willing to leave the world in disarray. She needs help in arranging her life. The proper order must be demonstrated. This the dramatist does for the generation he seeks to reach by placing darkness in the middle of the play and surrounding it with light.

Pounce-Pellott is an example, not a cause, of the system. He is not the prime mover, nor does he see himself as a divinely appointed judge. Pounce-Pellott discerns as a man, and sees the foolishness in the ideas his guests espouse.

Earlier in the second act the protagonist says:

> To a vast, ancient land,
> Made ours by cunning and courage and force of arms,
> They sent me, Pontius Pilate, to teach and to rule.

In the culminating poem of the protagonist Bridie shows how easy it is for the hero to perforate the simplistic ways of the modern prophets, by casting Pounce-Pellott's rejection in nursery rhyme cadences.

> Your notions are confused and muddy;
> Your unbowed head is pretty bloddy;
> I find the skipper of your soul
> A little short of self-control

The irony of the lines, which play on William Henley's "In Memoriam R. T. Hamilton Bruce (*Invictus*)," is that the hero's only chance to find a new way of living is to realize that he is the master of his own fate and the captain of his own soul.

Midway through the poem Pounce-Pellot embraces his family. The gesture indicates the need for man to return to the societal base. The hero vows to be king and priest again. The individual will stand against the oppressive millstones that grind men. He tells the consequences of twentieth-century imperialism and in accepting worldly views that result in rejection of Truth.

> I have washed my hands of my God and killed
> Him
> I have sold Him for order.
> Therefore I must be punished.
>
> But, by the God I sold, I will not go quietly.
> Where is my Stick!

While a hurdy-gurdy cranks out "Rule Britannia" in a minor key, Pounce-Pellott takes his stick and kills six of the sooths. Revenant, who holds to the old class structure, is a revenant. He cannot murder a ghost, even in a ritual manner.

The slapstick is not merely an instrument to administer punishment; the noise it makes is also used to herald a change of scene. The clamor Bridie produces is a call for the improvement of the religious, governmental and social structures.

In the denouement Toby, the apprentice, who does not yet know who he is, asks to wed Baby. The De'il appears; although foiled for the time being, he does not know the final outcome. Pounce-Pellott has "killed all those fools who pretended to know," but knew no more than Pontius Pilate. The hero ends the play: "I must jest again and await my reply . . ./Good-bye."

For years Bridie was absorbed with a thought which may be expressed as: Jesting Pilate asked the Truth, but would not wait for an answer.[8] With the final speech of *The Baikie Charivari* the meaning of the jesting Pilate figure and much of Bridie's writing surfaces. Those who think they know the truth have not the truth. Those who know they do not know the Truth have the truth.

To live one's life and at its end not to see the meaning of one's existence disturbed Bridie. It may be said to be his great temptation. Yet he was often inspired and used his genius to accomplish more than most men. *The Baikie Charivari* is not a disillusioned cry that there are no answers. Rather, it is a mystic's vision in which the world of the senses and the world of the spirit, are brought together to show that they are one. The play is an acknowledgment to the Maker, Who has worked a wonder in the individuation of man, so that he can stand alone, if he must. The miracle of the play is man. Pounce-Pellott overcomes the persuasions of his age to seek the Truth that is ageless. Such a man is indeed a miracle.

CHAPTER 11

A Last Act

"ONLY God can write last acts," said Bridie, "and He seldom does." The playwright's final acts were often criticized because of the dimensions he added. In concluding a study of a writer who believed demonstration preferable to critical discussion, it seems fitting to indicate some of the other facets of this man of many parts.

From stage directions to imagery the dramatist exhibited a highly developed visual sense. In early childhood Mavor showed artistic ability. By the time he entered the university the artist realized his talent was "to shoot the boots off clay feet." Mavor's fine line realistic drawings were sufficiently skilled to have assured him a career in illustration, but he considered most of his "doodles" fit only for the wastebasket. "OH," as he signed drawings he took time to finish, sketched subjects from medicine, the Bible, and the stage. Dr. Honeyman watched his friend draw and observed that the process seemed accidental, but upon completion the work was ordered.[1]

Mavor seems to have produced series of pictures in spurts. The World Wars inspired him, and the vast difference in subject and technique manifest in the pictures that mark these events, show the change in thought, which living through the first half of the twentieth century produced. In 1916 Mavor drew two soldiers pouring over a dictionary under the watch of a woman at a window. The caption is lighthearted: "The Encyclopedic: 'Yes PAIN is the French for "bread" But you say MONGY. She'll understand yer.' "[2] This is the attitude one finds in *Some Talk of Alexander* and *Marriage Is No Joke*.

Bridie's watercolor, "Civilization, 1942," depicts a tired Glasgow woman in the foreground. A holocaust surrounds the industrial city. In the upper right portion is a wasteland. The

151

world view displayed in *The Queen's Comedy* and *The Baikie Charivari* is similar.

The Mavors sent outrageous Christmas cards, which the artist designed. In 1925 four names appeared under the season's greetings. In that year the father had said "Bingo! Full house!" when Ronald was born on May 13. Their second son had his nickname. Rona, determined to produce male children, had given birth to Robert on April 17, 1924.[3]

I   The Perilous Adventures of Sir Bingo Walker

Bridie could make children as well as adults laugh. His story for juveniles, *The Perilous Adventures of Sir Bingo Walker of Alpaca Square,* was published in 1931. At one time editors of leading magazines had made offers for his drawings, but Gilbert Rumbold illustrated the book.

The title character is an elderly Victorian gentleman. Bingo Walker is lonely, despite the solicitude of his Scots housekeeper. The rotund Bingo meets Charles, a boy with whom he conducts delightful conversations. Their talk of medieval adventure also satirizes contemporary life. With more than a tilt at *Don Quixote,* the companions help Alice Morgan, distressed damsel. To avenge Alice, Bingo and Charles trek Sir Isadore.

"Charles," said Bingo, "if I were to ride through modern London in full armour, it would excite comment. And Charles," he went on, "you may, if you wish, excite great multitudes to passion with your eloquence, but you must never excite comment." "Why not?" said Charles. "Because it is not done," said Bingo. "But if we did it, it would be done," said Charles.

Along the digressive way, with short jumps from fantasy to reality, the heroes meet interesting types, such as Dr. Heeney, an Irish country doctor. Characters inspire amusing incidents. These lead to the trouncing of Sir Isadore.

II   Mr. Bridie's Alphabet for Little Glasgow Highbrows

Mr. Bridie's Alphabet for Little Glasgow Highbrows (1934) originally appeared as a series of essays in the *Glasgow Herald.* The author revised the copy slightly between columns and hard cover. In the dedicatory section Bridie observes that the only universal Scots prayer is "God give us good conceit of ourselves." Glasgow highbrows he defines as "loveable little wretches with grave idiotic faces; practioners of derision, but terrified of the derision of others. . . ." The flight from A-asterisks to Z-zoom! is a gadfly journey which hops from the novel to the school essay.

The pace is leisurely, but the copy is brightened with illuminative sallies. Edward Shanks of the *Sunday Times* said that Bridie was one of the best essayists since Belloc and Chesterton. Here he is comparable in divigations.

III   Roger—Not So Jolly

Bridie put his son Ronald's name on the title page of *Roger— Not So Jolly*, a one-act play of 1937. Robert was going to a party, and the father proposed to his younger son they do a play. Bridie wrote a piece to entertain the boy who stayed home on the occasion. The collaboration proved prophetic.[4]

Mrs. Wilkinson is in a dither because her sullen ten-year-old Roger is to attend a fancy dress ball. Mother and sisters get him into a pirate garb, and the outfit inspires the lad to become piratical. The police arrive. An officer escorts Roger to the party, after which the boy is destined for the strap.

IV   Tedious and Brief

Bridie wrote a number of articles for periodicals which have not been collected in book form. He did prefaces for friends' books, program notes, and assorted ephemera. In *Tedious and Brief* (1944) the author gathered a selection of essays, poems, one acters, and incomplete works. He referred to such pieces as parerga. The book is small, because Bridie followed Saintsbury's dictum: "No great literature has ever been produced as a parergon unless it was trifling in bulk."

In this collection Bridie includes such things as a dialogue, "The Ear of Vincent van Gogh," which is written in French. Bridie uses Erse, French, Latin, Greek, pidgin Russian and Persian, as well as tongues he created for an Ethiopian and the people of the *Holy Isle*. Such display is not what one expects from a man who writes that he "has a morbid fear of pomposity in

himself." Contradictions or wheels within wheels spin through
the personality of Mavor. Bridie uses many of these in writing.

In "The Theatre" Bridie states the purpose of a play is to
create the illusion of a fuller life than one that contains longeurs.
These dragging hours are absent in dreams. The playwright's
task is to shatter brass clocks into pieces: "Then darkness,
whispering and the decorous unfolding of the blazing bright
rectangle in which things will be done . . . or informed with the
rebellious melancholy of Capricorn. The dream has begun. Time
is outside."

In "The Nero Concerto" the Capricorn tells what his dreams
are intended to convey. Bridie begins with a discourse on
Philistinism. Although Philistines are always with us, he concentrates upon the Nazis and Fascists, who like the Trojans in
The Queen's Comedy, destroy art and science. They worship a
destructive God, because they do not see "that the Creator and
the Destroyer may be parts of the same Godhead."

The end of art is spiritual. But some artists glorify God and
others the "Pride of the Eye and the Lust of the Flesh." The
contradiction leads to the estimate that the artist works for the
satisfaction of a spiritual appetite in himself for the "preserva-
tion, fulfillment or the enrichment of Life itself."

As he satisfies one appetite, man develops another. On an
ascending scale the artist begins with ego and grows to concern
for mankind: "higher still Mankind will be fused into all
Creation, and then we shall approach Knowledge." This state
will not come about until the selfish, physical "Pig Man" and the
selfless, spiritual "God Man" are separated, as St. Paul says, or
until they are blended, as William Blake predicts. Bridie thinks
that both may occur, but he leans towards Blake's vision. In this
blend is the meaning of Life.

The artist works to show the body is "a function of the soul
perceived through the senses." His labor is to sharpen that
perception, for he alone "can expound the soul in terms to be
understood by mortal man."

The public has the right to "expect" that the artist "will keep
Faith." Faith for Bridie is the acknowledgment of the power of
God and the reality of the divine order. As a human attribute, it
has definite intellectual content, which must be tested to
conclusive demonstration. One should not follow an orthodoxy
blindly. Such subservience jeopardizes faith.

Man may believe in that which he cannot prove. This is common to science and religion. Faith in a scientific principle is justified, when it is tested and its application leads to correct conclusions. The validity of faith in God and the right way of living is established by the results these beliefs bring.

Bridie concludes "The Nero Concerto" with an artist's prayer: "Establish the work of his hands upon him: yea, the work of his hands, establish Thou it." For James Bridie God did.

Notes and References

Chapter One

1. See Anna Jean Mill, *Mediaeval Plays in Scotland,* St. Andrews University Publications, no. 24 (Edinburgh, 1927). Miss Mill presents an illuminating collection of documents pertaining to early dramatic and quasi-theatrical entertainments.

2. James Bridie delivered "Ducdame!" a radio broadcast from Belfast, on April Fool's Day, 1941. The author defined the fool as a breaker of the Commandments, and the Scot like Solomon, whom he quotes, recommended "a rod for the fool's back." Bridie illustrated his position by including a Socratic dialogue. The use of the dramatic form to convey critical opinion has been favored by Scots for centuries, because they had slight opportunity to have their lines spoken on the stage.

In "Ducdame" Socrates meets a policeman. The deadliest sinner is the officer, whose job it is to create fear and terror. Socrates asks, "Have you not considered whether the search for good men might be nobler and more rewarding?" The truth seeker then asks if one cannot find wickedness on every street corner. It is easy to locate, as are fools. Yet without these bores life would be dull and unbearable for the wise.

3. Terence Tobin, *Plays by Scots 1660–1800* (Iowa City, Ia., 1974), treats the dramatic contributions of Northern dramatists at home and abroad during the Restoration and eighteenth century.

4. Harold William Thompson, *A Scottish Man of Feeling Some Account of Henry Mackenzie, Esq.* (London, 1931), p. 46.

5. James C. Dibdin, *Annals of the Edinburgh Stage* (Edinburgh, 1888), and Robb Lawson, *The Scottish Stage* (Paisley, 1913), consider Scots dramatic records and contributions during the nineteenth century.

Chapter Two

1. Sources of information about the subject's life include James Bridie's two autobiographies: *Some Talk of Alexander* (London, 1926), and *One Way of Living* (London, 1939). Winifred Bannister, *James Bridie and His Theatre* (London, 1955), provides much valuable

firsthand information obtained from the author. Mrs. Bannister includes a number of letters Bridie wrote to contemporaries.

The correspondence of Bridie is interesting and frequently delightful. Repositories of these letters are presently held by the Mavor family, the National Library of Scotland, Edinburgh, the Mitchell Library, and the University of Glasgow Library, Glasgow.

Interviews with Rona Mavor and Ronald Mavor, Summer 1973, provided much information about Bridie and his writing.

Newspaper accounts, a number of which are inaccurate, and other ephemera, e.g., program notes, contain biographical data. All of these sources have been used to piece together a portrait in mosaic. This writer merits a full-scale biography.

2. See Henry A. Mavor, *On Public Lighting by Electricity* (Glasgow, [1890]), a lecture at the University of Glasgow; *The Outlook for Young Engineers* (Glasgow, 1893), an inaugural address.

3. Francis Watt and Andrew Carter, *Picturesque Scotland* (Glasgow, 1883), p. 14.

4. *Some Talk of Alexander* had little chance for commercial success. Bridie told of his World War I adventures in an entertaining manner, but his experience was over ten years old when the book appeared. Bridie did not participate in a major theater of the war.

Well-told accounts of personal encounters, unless the teller is more famous than the author was in 1926, or unless the material is more sensational, are soon remaindered by publishers.

In this humorous chronicle the author assumes the role of raconteur. He features personal foibles and reviews follies of the era. Between each chapter he includes bits of his verse, then rambles on at a leisurely pace.

Mavor's account of the opera at Baku illustrates the general tone of the reminiscence: "Gucassoff, the tenor, was an Armenian. He was tall and slim with a hooked nose, and eyebrows that went up diagonally over his bald brow and almost met in the middle. He sang like a sucking dove in his love scenes and like a fierce tom-cat in his others. We called him Nyet, because the Russian version of 'Faust' begins with that word, and he uttered it with the most stentorian mew you can possibly imagine."

Bridie himself loved to play the piano and sing in a voice not even the kindest listeners ever praised. He used his knowledge of music effectively in his plays.

Chapter Three

1. *The British Drama* (Glasgow, 1945), Bridie's entertaining and provocative pamphlet, grew out of his tenure as Shute lecturer on drama at the University of Liverpool.

In examining the panorama of British accomplishment on the stage Bridie is more at home as an observer than as historian. He states that British drama should be a self-portrait of British feelings, but it is not. The author covers the early nineteenth century particularly well, and his comments are pungent because of phraseology: "The art of writing plays seemed to die and the macabre structure jerked its limbs without the help of a soul or a brain. The mangled masterpieces of the past were disinterred as 'vehicles' for the actor—much as they are today in the Film business. . . ."

Bridie compresses blocks of history, then gives his requisites for a good theatrical: "A play must have an interesting story; the clash of contending personalities, characterization; fun—to say nothing of all the traditional idiosyncracies that audiences have been taught to expect."

The author opted for decentralization of theater and considered London productions overpriced, overpaid gambles: "A gentleman whose only duty is to paint his face, disguise himself as a butler and speak a couple of lines for four or five hundred successive evenings is paid nearly ten times as much as a hospital sister."

Bridie was impressed with the Abbey Theatre as a truly nationalist group, and believed that Scotland with its heritage of racy, pithy, expressive speech was a good proving ground for experimental drama.

2. Helen L. Luyben, *James Bridie: Clown and Philosopher* (Philadelphia, 1965), pp. 97-98 ff., considers the influence of Ibsen on Bridie. Both authors use poetry and symbolism, but Bridie's inspiration and aims are vastly different.

3. Bannister, pp. 219-20, describes "The Pyrate's Den" as "a rollicking comedy about a Glasgow family adventuring in pirate waters." The program of this unpublished play credits the authorship to Captain Charles Johnson (adaptation by A. P. Kellock).

4. In *One Way of Living*, p. 25, Bridie states: "Accidia is my master Sin; but Accidia is in herself a composite character. The element of Accidia that ruled my life was sloth. Depression played its part but sheer simple physical sloth must be given the credit for building the admirable character it is my task to describe."

5. Luyben, pp. 35-50.

6. *What It Is to Be Young* was first presented by the Birmingham Repertory Theatre on November 2, 1929. The comedy, which was correctly labeled mediocre by reviewers, was produced by the Albion Players at the Athenaeum Theatre in Glasgow, shortly after it opened. Dr. T. J. Honeyman used the play as a fund raiser, because he knew local physicians would come to see what their colleague was doing on the boards.

In the prologue Father Time asks: "What is it to be young? It is to feel/Rebuff and glory and the bruising heel/Of brutal, careless Fact."

The prologue invites the audience to consider the facts of the case carefully. Bridie does not achieve his intention, and however long one reserves judgment, it is careless construction rather than "careless Fact" that beleagurers characters and playgoers alike.

The action takes place at the Anglers' Arms. The proprietor is Gryce, a professor of metaphysics turned innkeeper. General Dix and his family arrive. In the course of much conversation the Dixes and fellow guests, Captain Cochran and Miss Parker, plan to go to the Ex-Servicemen's Rally.

Dix discovers that Cochran has embezzled servicemen's funds that were placed in his trust. The general threatens to expose the captain.

While others attend the rally, Cochran, unwittingly abetted by Virginia Dix, steals Mrs. Dix's jewels and hotel silver plate. The thief plans to make his getaway in Dix's Daimler, but he is caught on the premises.

The general holds an inquiry, but Virginia lies to save the man with whom the eighteen-year-old heroine is infatuated. During this inquisition Mrs. Dix interrupts her prejudiced husband continually. She knows that the version which her daughter swears is not a dream is untrue. Gryce, who has said that a dream is "subjective reality," corroborates Virginia's fiction.

Depicting young love is not Bridie's forte, and although the dramatist successfully avoids the sentimentality to which the story lends itself, we are given little to indicate that Virginia will remember, let alone profit by the encounter. We know from the first act that Cochran is a thief. When all the circumstances are known, the captain remains an embezzler.

In his preface Bridie succinctly explains the flaw of *What It Is to Be Young.* The piece is "overcrowded with running hares." The "hares" are at their best when debating matters that do not further the main action. Gryce and Virginia discuss women. This spirited tangent with flashes of wit and engrossing argument shows that Bridie early used the elements for which he became famous.

7. "Up the close and doun the stair/But and ben wi' 'Burke and Hare.'/Burke's the butcher, Hare's the thief, /Knox the boy that buys the beef." The street rhyme succinctly tells the story of the West Port murders. Sir Walter Scott wrote to his daughter about the case. His attitude has something in common with Bridie's protagonist. For a consideration of Scott's views on the murders, see Edgar Johnson, *Sir Walter Scott, The Great Unknown,* (New York, 1970), II, 1094–95.

Interest in this case persisted. When antiquarian James Maidment's library was sold in the late nineteenth century, his collection of memorabilia relating to the Burke and Hare murders brought many more pounds than more savory rarities.

Edinburgh today possesses pubs named for the body snatchers as well as Deacon Brodie, Stevenson's prototype for Jekyll-Hyde.

The commemoration of crime occupied conversationalists at the Glasgow Arts Club. Bridie, who took part in these speculations, later used the case of Edward William Pritchard, a Glasgow surgeon, who, in 1865, poisoned his wife and mother-in-law with doses of antimony, as the basis for *Dr. Angelus*.

8. Dr. John Barklay, the actual assistant of Dr. Robert Knox and the author of medical texts, also wrote a melodrama based on Robert Burns' "Tam O'Shanter," which was presented at Edinburgh in 1825. Comparison of the prototypes with Bridie's characters shows the playwright's conception sprang from imagination.

9. All citations from Bridie's works are taken from the first or the definitive editions, which represent the final authorial intention.

10. James Agate, *Sunday Times*, October 31, 1931, p. 18.

11. Letter of Alastair Sim, cited in Bannister, p. 72.

12. Letter to Flora Robson, cited in Bannister, p. 90. See also p. 91 for other letters on *A Sleeping Clergyman*.

Chapter Four

1. Luyben, pp. 52–54.

2. James Agate, *The London Times*, June 12, 1934, p. 14.

Chapter Five

1. Jangalistan, like Junglipore in *The Baikie Charivari*, connotes "jungle." Those who seek to rule over others receive a chaotic mass of objects over which to hold sway.

2. Sir James Pounce-Pellott, who says he will be his own priest and king, is expressing the same thought. The individualism of Presbyterian tradition, whereby each man is his own minister, influenced Bridie, but the playwright carries the notion further in seeking greater freedom for man, who is overburdened by other men's repressive civil and ecclesiastical regulations.

Sir James Frazer, *The Golden Bough* (New York, 1951), pp. 10–12, provides an interesting analogue to the priestly king concept.

3. The source of Bridie's theme is Lao-tze's teaching on the difficulty of being rightly known. In the *Tao* the philosopher writes: "To know and yet think we do not know is the highest attainment; not to know and yet think we do know is a disease."

4. Letter to Stephen Haggard, cited in Christopher Hassal, *The Timeless Quest* (London, n.d.), p. 89.

5. Bannister, p. 131.

6. In all his writings which touch upon totalitarianism Bridie admonishes the English-speaking world that it can happen to them.

7. Dr. Ivy Mackenzie, an acquaintance of the Mavors, ran a private sanitorium. Mackenzie was pro-German. He served as a model for Dr. McGilp. Mackenzie's enthusiasm for the Third Reich was instrumental in Rona Mavor's visiting Germany in 1937. Her excursion was disillusioning.

Chapter Six

1. The plan of *One Way of Living* consists of dividing the subject's life into five year segments. These end with conversations between the autobiographer and spirits, who range from John Home to the Recording Angel. Sequences follow a general chronology, but events told in strict order Bridie finds uninteresting. Anecdotes, tangents— which in the instance of "A Lecture on Women" become like Laurence Sterne's and swell to a complete entity—Bridie considers more illuminating.

Bridie displays good critical judgments of his own plays in his second autobiography. For the author the facts are never the facts, and he conceals as much as he reveals.

Eric Linklater, in his article on Bridie in the *Dictionary of National Biography* (1951-1960), describes succinctly this autobiography, "which refuses, with charm and gaiety, to endow its subject with the importance he deserved."

2. See Bannister, pp. 114-116, for Bridie's correspondence with Flora Robson.

3. Luyben, p. 132.

4. Making the lover of the English noblewoman Polish is an example of Bridie's penchant to exasperate the audience. During the war years a number of Poles emigrated to Britain. As frequently happens with an influx of foreign population, prejudice grew. Bannister, p. 179, treats this bias and notes the German reaction to this aspect when Lucy Manheim's translation of *Daphne Laureola* was produced in Berlin in December, 1949.

Chapter Seven

1. Robert Louis Stevenson, "A Chapter on Dreams," in *Memories and Portraits, Random Memories, Memories of Himself* (New York, 1925), p. 163.

2. In *One Way of Living*, p. 267, Bridie quotes the review: ". . . The last play on the programme was *The Sunlight Sonata* by Mary Henderson. It was a somewhat extraordinary piece. In response to calls

of Author, Miss Henderson said that it was intended to be a propaganda play and was designed to combat synthetic productions from Europe and the United States." Although this is unquestionably the most bizarre notice of a Bridie play, a number of the critics who had actually seen his plays on stage were nearly as opaque.

3. It is difficult to give objective interpretations of dreams. The following selected sources have proven helpful in discerning Bridie's dream symbology: Patricia Garfield, *Creative Dreaming* (New York, 1974); Stearn Robinson and Tom Corbett, *The Dreamer's Dictionary* (New York, 1974); Elsie Sechrist, *Dreams Your Magic Mirror* (New York, 1968).

4. Allusions to the *tricoteuse* from *A Tale of Two Cities* and to Paul Dombey from *Dombey and Sons* are fitting when one is raising the Dickens. Bridie uses Dickensian label names, e.g., Hangingshaw, Brewer, etc.

5. The only bird of paradise in evidence is the stuffed one perched atop Mrs. Hangingshaw's head. The bird functions as a reminder that what looks like paradisial freedom may be a hellish and deadly enslavement.

6. See Luyben, pp. 33–34 ff., for a consideration of Shaw's influence on Bridie and pp. 23–25 for a discussion of Bridie on Shaw.

Chapter Eight

1. Eric Mavor considered that his brother had modeled Tobit on their mother. Rona Mavor believed that her husband had fashioned Anna after her own "anxious phases."

2. Azarias (Abednego) and Ananias (Shadrach) were Hebrew companions of Daniel. By believing they were miraculously delivered from the fiery furnace. See Daniel 1:7; 2:12 ff. The Babylonian name "Abednego" means servant of Nego, the god of wisdom, sometimes represented as the planet Mercury, i.e., the messenger. Mercury in *The Queen's Comedy* is the antithesis of Ararias in *Tobias*.

3. In *Some Talk of Alexander* Bridie dubs a character whom he met in his Persian travels "Asmoday," and recounts the tale of a bandit who was cowed by an indomitable Anglo-Saxon matron. The incident probably inspired the hero's confrontation with the bandit.

4. *The Discoverie of Witchcraft, wherein the Lewde dealing of Witches and Witchmongers is notablie detected, in sixteen books . . . whereunto is added a Treatise upon the Nature and Substance of Spirits and Devils* (London, 1584), is a condemnation of diabolism, rather like the investigations of Montague Summers.

5. Kashdak's remission is also an example of justice without understanding. The Ethiopian needs a translator, who interprets what he says to the court.

6. In the Book of Daniel the trees are the mastic and the holm.

7. The letter is in the University of Glasgow Library.

8. Bannister, p. 85.

9. Bridie was fond of poetry and used it generously in various genres. Comparison of serious verse, e.g., Maria's soliloquy in *The Dragon and the Dove*, with light lyrics shows that the writer's talents were better suited to the latter. Some of Bridie's best serious poetry is spoken by Pounce-Pellott in *The Baikie Charivari*, but it is the force of the character rather than the quality of the lines that gives the poetry strength.

"Hu-e," a 1943 poem that treats of Bridie's dejection and his rising above it, is interesting from the biographical standpoint. It is also challenging, because of Bridie's appropriation of Lewis Carroll's technique. "But as it was, a simple shubblegrub / Squattering stumblingly among the dub / Set my sad heart a-going Dub-a-Lub / With warm and pure affection."

Chapter Nine

1. Bridie's "The Scottish Character as it was viewed by Scottish Authors from Galt to Barrie" (1937) is one of those gargantuan topics few writers dare to publish, even in the *Papers of the Greenock Philosophical Society*. Character, a character, or the national character are about the same in the North, because of the esteem in which peculiarities are held, when they are related to the mind. A linguistic excursion into Scots words for characters, the apparent contradictions inherent in Caledonian sentimentality and other ideas are set forth to stimulate disputation. Neither side's answers can be definitive. Broad and annoying statements abound, e.g., that Robert Louis Stevenson is probably the only great sentimentalist who is not vicious and cruel as well. These thoughts provoke readers to revaluate their prejudices and perspectives.

2. Bridie collaborated with Moray MacLaren on *A Small Stir Letters on the English* (1949). During the war MacLaren was in intelligence, and the strain left its mark. Bridie, who was himself subject to depression, suggested the book to his friend as a rehabilitative gesture. The two cast their wide-ranging comments in epistolary form. The Scots discuss the differences between themselves and the English. The exchanges are literate, at times, wordy communications of the polite sort more popular generations before the book was published.

The accentual difficulties of English, writing, and ethnic peculiarities are punctuated with the occasional line of dash, e.g., "The great Englishman," writes Bridie, "is always a lunatic with a strongly practical side."

Bridie discusses the Scots anthropomorphic gods, who are arbitrary but interested in human affairs. The concept keeps people awed and apprehensive.

Bridie sees the funny side of Scots sentimentality, which he charactrizes as Wallacethebruceism, Charlieoverthewaterism, etc. The two authors gloss over government, love, drinking, and other topics, but the book does not create even the small stir noted in the title appropriated from the "Petition of the Cornishmen to Henry VII."

3. In his pamphlet, *British Drama*, Bridie states that the "study of native drama should provide a quick and easy synthesis of native life." This is, he acknowledges, as most theories admittedly wrong.

The practical consideration involved when drawing upon the Scottish experience is the slim chance that such a play has to succeed in London, which shuns the provincial. The Scottish presentation in 1945, Bridie says, would bring the author twenty-five pounds for a week's performance. The laborer who knows his hire to be worthy must still seek the London stage.

4. Bridie did an adaptation of Chekov's *The Proposal* for the Scottish National Players. He modernized a number of plays for the Glasgow Citizens' Theatre. The following list is incomplete, because scripts have been lost, and because Bridie did not sign all his efforts. Molnár's *Liliom* was staged during the 1943–1944 season. Molière's *Misanthrope* was not performed. Ibsen's *Hedda Gabler* was presented during 1946–1947. The same season Ibsen's *Wild Duck* was staged. Bridie's version added Scots flavor to this production and to *A Midsummer Night's Dream* in 1948. Shakespeare's lovers become sophisticates of the Noel Coward variety. Quince speaks broad Scots in this controversial adaptation done in modern dress. Bridie was working on an adaptation of Sophocles' *Oedipus the Tyrant* in 1950, but he died before he completed the work.

5. Jean's situation parallels that of the heroine in the Cinderella story Bridie used in *The Letter-Box Rattles*, a predictable, easy to perform comedy, which won the 1938 *News Chronicle* competition for a play to be presented by amateurs.

6. Bridie explains in *Tedious and Brief* that the limited market for radio plays and the penury of the British Broadcasting Corporation dissuaded him from writing radio dramas. He includes "Scheherazade Kept on Talking," a fantasy that might have been turned into a radio series.

Bridie also wrote "J. M. Barrie" and several other pieces for radio. His financial remuneration from films was better, and although he did the script of *The Paradine Case*, directed by Alfred Hitchcock, and other scenarios, his satire "Immortal Memory," a ten minute script about the life of Robert Burns, shows his attitude toward the celluloid business, that makes impossible requests.

7. Young MacAlpin dances in the manner of Harlequin, and one can stretch a correspondence between Mari and Columbine. Here the similarity ends. Using vestiges of Harlequinade in British comedy persisted for reasons of nostalgia until the postwar years.

8. Mairi accuses MacAlpin of being in league with the devil, because of the cure he has effected. She mentions the "wild white horses of Lannan Shi." Although the legend of the devil assuming the shape of a horse to deceive the unsuspecting is Scots, Mairi's reference to the white animal pertains to the soul. The white fairy horse takes the rider to his destination.

When Clarinda regains her senses she says, "I have not felt [a strange and pleasant sensation] since I went galloping on my pony. . . . I am feeling WELL!"

9. Bridie typed his own rough drafts, then had others prepare the fair copy. In his late years Bridie dictated a number of pieces, then had his wife read scripts to him before making corrections.

10. William McGonagall, *Poetic Gems* ([Dundee], 1890). This book was printed for the author by Winter, Duncan and Co.

11. In "The Umbilicus," a 1939 lecture to the Southern Medical Society of Glasgow, Bridie explains his use of this part of the anatomy in "Gog and Magog": "it is all that remains of the stem that bound us to the parental stalk. It is a reminder that we have been plucked and must sooner or later die."

12. Bannister, pp. 198–252, records the history of the Glasgow Citizens' Theatre. See also *A Conspectus to Mark the Citizens' 21st Anniversary as a Living Theatre in the Gorbals Street Glasgow* ([Glasgow], 1964).

Chapter Ten

1. *The Starlings* (1937) is a trialogue in which Pim, a protestor, whom Bridie stated was "a disguised self-portrait," Examphalos, a country squire, whom Ronald Mavor believes to be Bridie, and Cain, the gatekeeper, discuss extermination of pests. It is a parable of Nazi atrocities.

Bridie witnessed an incident in his garden that motivated him to write the piece. Rats had eaten the grapes. The Mavors hired a ratcatcher who promised to banish the rabbits after the rats. In the process he also shot a starling.

2. Letter of Tyrone Guthrie, cited in Bannister, p. 247.

3. In "O Philosophers!" a 1942 lecture to the Royal Philosophical Society of Glasgow, Bridie discussed Shakespeare's method: "And he had to deceive his patrons into thinking they were hearing a very different kind of play from that which he actually gave them." This was Bridie's practice also.

4. In his preface to *The Baikie Charivari* Walter Elliot calls Jupiter the "Unknown God of the biologists. The speech hushes the characters, Gods and men alike. It hushes the audience. It gives, shortly and ruthlessly, the picture of a creator, an author, driven by an urge not under his control, to engender a creation beyond his comprehension, but instinct with characters as important to him as he to them. This Unknown God speaks neither in wrath nor, certainly, in pity; but in some strange form of kinship, though remote and salt as the sea."

5. In a Note on *The Baikie Charivari* Bridie discusses the tradition that Punch derives from Pontius Pilate. The dramatist considers the Roman procurator a good man: "it was his misfortune that he was cast for the villain of the piece in a play where virtue was, mainly by his act, triumphant. That is, if we are to believe the Apostle Paul." Walter Elliot also discusses Bridie's use of the Punch-Pilate association in his preface.

6. Joe Ketch is the man who saved Baby when she went overboard from the *Brahmapootra*. The rescue, indebted to the violence Punch does Baby in puppet theater, takes on new significance. The name of the ship from which the infant fell means "son of Brahma," the creator in Hinduism. In the course of the play the young woman appears to be in danger of falling from the ways of the Son of God also. Of all Bridie's rescues, this is the most ingenious.

The incident resembles the rescue of little Eva in *Uncle Tom's Cabin*. The parallel leads one to see the communist as slave. The baby this "Uncle Tom" saves becomes shackled by the Peter Pan pathology. The stories within stories technique requires explication in a critical edition.

7. Pounce-Pellott speaks a soliloquy in which he wrestles with the temptation to write his recollections of India. The fragments he remembers of his life there are things which cannot be bought or sold. "What am I bid for the deodar and cherry." Deodars, East Indian cedars, are timbers of the gods. Cedars in Old Testament tradition are considered "incorruptible." The hero recalls "The dear smell of cedar, my darling brown people, / Moving, dreamily, nowhere . . . / O Karma . . . Om mane padme hum. . . ." The Sanscrit invocation to clear the mind or to reach oblivion functions the same way as the reference to a "bairagi." The Hindu mendicant "seeking the Way" stands for other approaches to find truth.

Pounce-Pellott determines to sell his memories for security to the "St. Louis Woman, with your diamond ring." The near quotation from W. C. Handy's "St. Louis Blues" jars one to consider the materialism of the West, after images of nature and spirituality from the East.

The protagonist ends his reverie with " 'And the karela, the bitter karela shall cover it all.' " The large umbrella-shaped balsam tree with elongated, warty, yellowish fruit, which shades Pounce-Pellott, evokes pictures of Buddha under the Bodhi or "Wisdom" tree, where he found enlightenment. The Indian apple also puts one in mind of the fruit of the tree of knowledge of good and evil in Eden.

Bridie uses comparative religious symbols to demonstrate the universality of the temptation to obtain gold. He also implies that in the Father's house there are many mansions.

8. Bridie uses the Jesting Pilate image in *The Christmas Card* (London, 1949). The melancholy fable approaches genuine sadness.

Sir James and Lady Watson live in Alpaca Square. Sir James has won his lady by rescuing her from Sir Isadore Waldteufel, i.e., forest devil. This demon is vanquished, but Lady Watson is possessed by another evil. She cannot laugh. Sir James sets himself to provoking mirth. He takes up painting to make his wife a Christmas present: ". . . Lady Watson . . . did . . . ask him where he had been and what he had been doing with himself; but, like Jesting Pilate, she seldom waited for a reply." In this atmosphere of indifference Sir James paints a picture in which he incorporates forgotten incidents and odd insights. Lady Watson takes her husband's effort to amuse seriously. She thinks he needs psychotherapy.

"Mary Queen of Scots at Fotheringay," a water color which resembles an expressionistic stage set, pokes fun at contemporary artistic styles, includes a depiction of John Knox upside down and a comic self-portrait of Bridie. The picture, which now hangs in the dining room of the Ronald Mavors' home, is like Sir James' painting.

The Watsons have little in common, and we are given to understand that lack of understanding will continue. *The Christmas Card* succinctly shows the deplorable state which exists when laughter is not possible.

Chapter Eleven

1. T. J. Honeyman, "OH! Did This," *The Scottish Art Review*, 3 (1951), 5.

2. The University of Glasgow possesses sixty-one paintings and drawings by O. H. Mavor. This is the largest repository of his art presently available to the public. The National Gallery of Scotland also holds examples of his work.

3. Robert Mavor served with the Lothians and Border Horse, and was killed in France in 1944. Bridie's poem, "A Thought," is a quiet threnody.

> Home are the Hunters from Olympus hill
> Bearing the body of the murdered bairn.
> Alas! our lochs are ponds; our glens are nullahs
> Our bens are molehills. Barren is our soil.

The imagery recalls *The Queen's Comedy*, which the author began writing to assuage his grief.

4. Ronald Mavor followed his father's professions. He became a tuberculosis specialist. He found the medical profession pretentious, and after careful consideration became a playwright. In his Heriot-Watt University lecture "Science and Art" in *Creativity and Innovation* (Edinburgh, 1969), the second generation physician-turned-dramatist noted that few doctors admit that treatment is "largely a matter of bluff." He decided to pursue spontaneity in art, which for Ronald Mavor includes writing, painting, and music, because "Change means creation, and creation is our only wall against death." Mavor's plays include: "The Keys of Paradise " (1959); "Aurelie" (1961); "Muir of Huntershill" (1962); "The Partridge Dance" (1963); *A Private Matter* (1972).

A Private Matter is set in motion when an interviewer stays with a family to do research for a book about their famous father. Mervyn, a Cambridge type of modest repute tries to ingratiate himself with assorted family members, who are less than infatuated with their forebear, a carry-on-chaps general. In the London production Alastair Sim played the writer. Mavor's most successful play to date may be said to be an example of *plus ça change*.

Selected Bibliography

PRIMARY SOURCES

1. Published Plays

The Amazed Evangelist. London: Constable, 1931. Reprinted in *A Sleeping Clergyman* (1934).

The Anatomist. London: Constable, 1931; 2d rev. ed., 1932. Reprinted in *A Sleeping Clergyman* (1934).

The Anatomist and Other Plays. London: Constable, 1931. Contains: *The Anatomist; Tobias and the Angel; The Amazed Evangelist.*

Babes in the Wood. A Quiet Farce. London: Constable, 1938.

The Baikie Charivari; or, the Seven Prophets. A miracle play. Preface by Walter Elliot. London: Constable, 1953.

The Black Eye, A Comedy. London: Constable, 1935. Reprinted in *Moral Plays* (1936).

Colonel Wotherspoon and Other Plays. London: Constable, 1934. Contains: *Colonel Wotherspoon; What It Is to Be Young; The Dancing Bear; The Girl Who Did Not Want to Go to Kuala Lumpur.*

Daphne Laureola. A play in four acts. London: Constable, 1949.

Dr. Angelus. A play in three acts. London: Constable, 1950.

It Depends What You Mean. An improvisation for the glockenspiel. London: Constable, 1948. Reprinted in *John Knox* (1949).

John Knox and Other Plays. London: Constable, 1949. Contains: *It Depends What You Mean; John Knox; Dr. Angelus; The Forrigan Reel.*

Jonah and the Whale. London: Constable, 1932. Reprinted in *A Sleeping Clergyman* (1934).

The King of Nowhere and Other Plays. London: Constable, 1938. Contains: *The King of Nowhere; Babes in the Wood; The Last Trump.*

The Last Trump. London: Constable, 1938.

The Letter-Box Rattles. A sentimental comedy. London: *News Chronicle* Publications Dept., [1938].

Marriage Is No Joke. A melodrama. London: Constable, 1934; 2d rev. ed., 1936. Reprinted in *Moral Plays* (1936).

Mary Read. A play in three acts. Written with Claud Gurney. London: Constable, 1935. Reprinted in *Moral Plays* (1936).

Meeting at Night. Introduction by J. B. Priestley. London: Constable, 1956.

Moral Plays. London: Constable, 1936. Contains: *Marriage Is No Joke; Mary Read; The Black Eye.*

Mr. Gillie. A play in two acts. London: Constable, 1950.

Mrs. Waterbury's Millennium. A play in one act. London: Samuel French, 1935.

Paradise Enow. In *One-Act Plays for the Amateur Theatre.* Edited by M. H. Fuller. London: George G. Harrap, 1949.

Plays for Plain People. London: Constable, 1944. Contains: *Mr. Bolfry; Lancelot; Holy Isle; Jonah 3; The Sign of the Prophet Jonah; The Dragon and the Dove.*

The Queen's Comedy. A Homeric fragment. London: Constable, 1950. 2d ed., 1952.

Roger—Not So Jolly, etc. With Ronald Mavor. London: Samuel French, [1937].

A Sleeping Clergyman. A play in two acts. London: Constable, 1933. 2d ed., 1934.

A Sleeping Clergyman and Other Plays. London: Constable, 1934. Contains: *The Anatomist; Tobias and the Angel; The Amazed Evangelist; Jonah and the Whale; A Sleeping Clergyman.*

Storm in a Teacup. An Anglo-Scottish Version, etc. London: Constable, 1936. Acting edition, London: Samuel French, 1937.

Susannah and the Elders and Other Plays. London: Constable, 1940. Contains: *What Say They?; Susannah and the Elders; The Golden Legend of Shults; The Kitchen Comedy.*

The Switchback. A comedy. London: Constable, 1931; 2d rev. ed., 1932.

The Switchback. The Pardoner's Tale. The Sunlight Sonata. A comedy. A morality. A farce-morality. London: Constable, 1930.

Tedious and Brief. Contains playlets; see below, nondramatic works.

The Tintock Cup. Written with George Munro and others. *Glasgow Evening Citizen,* December, 1949–January, 1950. The Mitchell Library, Glasgow, contains a bound copy of the newspaper printing of the pantomime. This version differs from the acting script.

Tobias and the Angel. London: Constable, 1931; 2d rev. ed., 1932. Reprinted in *A Sleeping Clergyman* (1934); 3d ed., 1961, with an introduction and notes by A. C. Ward.

The Tragic Muse. In *Scottish One-Act Plays.* Edited by John MacNair Reid, introduction by George Blake. Edinburgh: Porpoise Press, 1935.

What Say They? A play in two acts. London: Constable, Co., 1939. Reprinted in *Susannah* (1940).

2. Nondramatic Works

All of Bridie's major nondramatic writings are listed as well as selected articles and ephemera. Bridie was not concerned with keeping copies or records. This list is incomplete, although it is more extensive than previously published bibliographies of the author.

The Glasgow Herald, to which Bridie contributed frequently, is abbreviated *GH*. The letters which appear after page numbers in these newspaper entries refer to the columns.

"The Actor and the Cinema." *London Mercury*, 33 (April 1936), 619-20.

"Address at Anderson College Prize-Giving." *GH*, March 14, 1936, p. 9a.

"Affinity between the Professions of Medicine and Journalism." *GH*, January 21, 1935, p. 13d.

"Artists and the State." *GH*, October 5, 1949, p. 3b.

The British Drama. The British Way Pamphlet Series, no. 12. Glasgow: Craig and Wilson, 1945.

The Christmas Card. London: St. Hugh's Press [1949].

"Comedies and Tragedies." *GH*, June 24, 1937, p. 73.

"Cricket Match." *Spectator*, 184 (June 30, 1950), 880-82.

"Dramaturgy in Scotland." *Proceedings of the Royal Philosophical Society of Glasgow*, 74 (1949). Scots plays were "treacle baths" before the National Theatre Society was formed. Bridie covers the repertories and writers of his day.

"Entertainment Tax Criticized." *GH*, October 2, 1944, p. 2f.

"Equilibrium." *The London Mercury*, 39 (April, 1939), 585-89.

"Fifty Years of the 'G. U. M.'" *GH*, March 14, 1939, p. 8d.

"Film Talks Fail." *GH*, May 27, 1941, p. 3e.

"Foreword." In *North Light: Ten New One-Act Plays from the North*. Edited by Winifred Bannister. Glasgow: William MacLellan, 1947.

"Foreword." In *The Story of Glasgow Citizens Theatre 1943-48*. Edited by Jack Gourlay and R. C. Saunders. Glasgow: Stage and Screen Press Ltd. [1948].

"Foreword." In *Alfred Wareing: a Biography*, by Winifred Isaac. With forewords by James Bridie, Ivor Brown, Rt. Hon. Walter Elliot, and Sir John R. Richmond. London: Green Bank Press [1951].

"The Functions of a Workaday Critic." *GH*, November 10, 1932, supp.

"George Bernard Shaw." In *Great Contemporaries*. London: Cassell, 1935. Retitled in U.S. as *Men of Turmoil* (New York: Minton, Balch, 1935).

"Harry Lauder." *Spectator*, 184 (March 3, 1950), 269.

"Health Service a Swindle." *GH*, June 14, 1950, p. 5f.

"Home Rule for Scotland?" *Spectator*, 184 (June 9, 1950), 782.

"Letter." *GH*, May 4, 1948, p. 2f.

"Making Film Version of Tolstoy's 'The Living Corpse.' " *GH*, January 10, 1935, p. 8f.

Mr. Bridie's Alphabet for Little Glasgow Highbrows. London: Constable, 1934. This book is comprised of essays that originally appeared on the front pages of *GH:* "Asterisks," April 8, 1933; "Coward, Cavalcade, and Camels," May 6, 1933; "Thoughts on Barbarians," April 22, 1933; "Reflections on 'drink,' " May 20, 1933; "This Education Business," June 3, 1933; "Gossip," July 1, 1933; "Fights and Fighting," June 17, 1933; "Going on Holiday," July 15, 1933; "India," July 29, 1933; "Jellybellyism," August 12, 1933; "Kilcreggan," August 26, 1933; "Laughter," September 9, 1933; "Preamble to a Confidential Chat on Motives and Mankind," September 23, 1933; "Noah," October 7, 1933; "A Defence of Ostriches," October 21, 1933; "The Play," November 4, 1933; "Rhetoric in the Theatre," November 16, 1933, p. 2g; "Quibbling," November 18, 1933; "Russia," December 2, 1933; "Mr. Shaw," December 16, 1933; "A Rhapsody on Trees," December 30, 1933.

"National Theatre." *London Mercury*, 36 (September, 1937), 423-28.

Notes on a Shakespearean Production [Glasgow: 1947].

"On Humanity and Max Beerbohm." *GH*, March 1, 1930, supp.

One Way of Living. London: Constable, 1939.

The Perilous Adventures of Sir Bingo Walker of Alpaca Square . . . With . . . drawings by Gilbert Rumbold. London: Constable, 1931.

"Plays of Ideas." *New Statesman and Nation*, 39 (March 11, 1950), 270.

"Preface." In *Classic Crimes: a selection from the Works of William Roughhead*, made by William Nicol Roughhead. London: Cassell, 1951.

"The Public School." *GH*, October 1, 1936, p. 19f.

"Reminiscences." *GH*, October 11, 1923, p. 4d. Published under by-line O. H. Mavor.

"Review of Citizens' Theatre Returns." *GH*, June 10, 1949, p. 4e; June 11, 1949, leader.

"Rhetoric Needed in Theatre." *GH*, Jan 22, 1949, p. 4d.

"S.C.D.A. Efforts Sterile." *GH*, October 13, 1949, p. 4c.

"St. Andrews—Defends Scottish Writers' Use of English." *GH*, April 30, 1948, p. 2c.

"Scotland and the Theatre." *GH*, June 19, 1937, p. 13b. Transcript of a radio broadcast.

"The Scottish Character." *GH*, October 23, 1937, leader and p. 13c.

"The Scottish Character as it was viewed by Scottish Authors from [John] Galt to [James] Barrie." *Papers of the Greenock Philosophical Society.* Greenock: 1937. Reprinted in *Tedious and Brief.*

"Shaw as Playwright." *New Statesman and Nation*, 40 (November 11, 1950), 422.

A Small Stir: Letters on the English. With Moray McLaren. London: Hollis and Carter, 1949.

Some Talk of Alexander. London: Methuen, 1926.

"Sterilization of the Unfit." *Spectator,* 151 (November 3, 1933), 623.

Tedious and Brief. London: Constable, 1944. Contains: Ducdame: (playlet for radio); Prologue to an Unfinished Play; The Theatre (essay); A Change for the Worse (one-act play); O Philosophers! (essay); The First Scene (dramatic squib); The Open-Air Drama (dramatic squib); The Umbilicus (essay); The Three Tykes (poem); Country Matters (poem); The Scottish Character, etc. (essay); A Thought (poem); The Doctor's Back Garden (essay); The Ear of Vincent Van Gogh (playlet in French); The Prize-Giving (essay); Immortal Memory (film scenario); Scheherazade Kept on Talking (playlet for radio); J. M. Barrie (playlet for radio); Hu-e (poem); Prologue to King David; Paradise Enow (one-act play); The Fat Women (playlet); The Starlings A Play in One Act; A Fragment (dramatic squib); The Nero Concerto (essay).

The Theatre, A paper, etc. Glasgow, 1939. Reprinted in *Tedious and Brief.*

"Theatre in Scotland." *Spectator,* 148 (May 28, 1932), 758.

"Three Score and Ten." *Spectator,* 173 (December 1, 1944), 498.

"To Visit Hollywood." *GH,* April 18, 1946, p. 6c.

SECONDARY SOURCES

1. Book-length Studies, Articles, Reviews

BANNISTER, WINIFRED. *James Bridie and His Theatre.* London: Rockliff, 1955. Study of the life and plays of Bridie by a drama critic who knew him personally.

BENTLEY, ERIC. *In Search of Theater.* New York: Knopf, 1953. Pp. 42–43. Considers "Gog and Magog" and treats Bridie as a playmaker who is attempting new structures in each vehicle rather than a failure at well-made constructs.

BROWN, IVOR. "Bridie; review of his Five Plays." *New Statesman and Nation,* 7 (May 5, 1934), 674. Consideration of *A Sleeping Clergyman and Other Plays.*

——. "James Bridie: General Influence." *The Prompter. The Bulletin of the Citizens' Theatre Society,* 61 (March, 1951), 3. Appreciation of the playwright's contribution.

COOKMAN, A. V. Review of *The King of Nowhere. The London Mercury,* 38 (May, 1938), 62. Commentary by a puzzled critic.

CRAWFORD IAIN. "Auld Nick and Mr. Bridie." *Theatre Arts,* 34 (July,

1950), 25. Asserts that the struggle between God and the devil brings out the best in Bridie.

DIACK, HUNTER. Review of *Dr. Angelus*. *The Spectator*, 179 (August 8, 1947), 173.

GERBER, URSULA. *James Bridies Dramen*. *Swiss Studies in English*. Bern: Francke Verlag, 1961. Survey of major works.

GREENE, ANNE. "Priestley, Bridie, and Fry: The Mystery of Existence in Their Dramatic Works," Ph.D. dissertation, University of Wisconsin, 1937. Chapter 3 treats of Bridie's metaphysical concerns.

HARDACRE, KENNETH. *James Bridie: Tobias and the Angel*. London: Notes on Chosen English Texts, 1960. Study guide for students of the play.

HERRING, ROBERT. Review of *Daphne Laureola*. *Life and Letters Today*, 61 (May 1949), 167-69. Adverse criticism.

HONEYMAN, T. J. "OH! Did This." *Scottish Art Review*, 3 (1951), 2-7. Consideration of Bridie's drawing. Illustrated.

JEFFREY, WILLIAM. "James Bridie." In *The Oxford Companion to the Theatre*, ed. Phyllis Hartnoll, p. 96. Rev. ed. New York: Oxford University Press, 1957. This article concludes that good dialogue cannot hide Bridie's weakness in dramatic structure.

JENNINGS, R. Review of *The Anatomist*. *Spectator*, 147 (October 17, 1931), 488. Favorable appraisal; discussion of actors' performances.

KERR, WALTER. Review of *Daphne Laureola*. *The Commonweal*, 52 (October 6, 1950), 630. Consideration of the New York production.

KRUTCH, JOSEPH WOOD. Review of *A Sleeping Clergyman*. *The Nation*, 139 (October 24, 1934), 486-87. Perceptive consideration.

——. Review of *Tobias*. *The Nation*, 144 (May 8, 1937), 544.

LARDNER, JOHN. Review of *Daphne Laureola*. *The New Yorker*, 26 (September 30, 1950), 52. Posits that Dame Edith Evans saved the play.

LEWIS, THEOPHILUS. Review of *Tobias*. *America*, 97 (January 25, 1958), 496. Stresses elements of fantasy.

LINKLATER, ERIC. *The Art of Adventure*. London: Macmillan, 1948. Pp. 25-43. Treats his friend's conceptions of drama.

LOW, JOHN T. "The Major Plays of James Bridie." M.Litt. thesis, University of Edinburgh, 1964. Analysis of most popular works which provides many details of plot and staging.

LUMLEY, FREDERICK. *Trends in 20th Century Drama*. Rev. ed. London: Rockliff, 1960. Pp. 221-23. Brief notice which cites Bridie's obvious merits and faults.

LUYBEN, HELEN L. *James Bridie: Clown and Philosopher*. Philadelphia: University of Pennsylvania Press, 1965. Textual criticism of selected plays to analyze three stages of Bridie's philosophical growth, viz., innocence, disillusionment, and resolution.

MC LAREN, MORAY. "Edinburgh Festival: Theatre." *The Spectator,* 185 (August 25, 1950), 241. A friend's generous assessment of Bridie and his place in the development of his nation's drama.

MCLAUGHLIN, R. "Bridie's Scottish Facetiae." *Theatre Arts,* 35 (November 1950), 42–43. Clever investigation of Bridie's use of local color.

MARCEL, GABRIEL. *"Le Théâtre de James Bridie." Etudes Anglaises,* 10 (1957), 291–303. Perceptive consideration of Bridie's thought.

MARDON, ERNEST G. *The Conflict Between the Individual and Society in the Plays of James Bridie.* Glasgow: William MacLellan, Embryo Books, 1972. Bridie questions accepted values in his plays. This study was interdicted by Winifred Bannister.

MARSHALL, MARGARET. Review of *Daphne Laureola. The Nation,* 171 (September 30, 1950), 295. Seen as a study of the female's survival struggle.

MENON. K. R. *A Guide to James Bridie's Tobias and the Angel.* Singapore: India Publishing House, 1956. Elementary aid for students studying the work.

MICHIE, JAMES. "A Question of Success." *English,* 17 (1968), 98+. Analysis of the dramatist's best facets.

NATHAN, GEORGE JEAN. Review of *Daphne Laureola.* In *The Theatre Book of the Year, 1950-1951.* New York: Knopf, 1951. Pp. 31–32. Severe criticism.

PEAKE, M. "Portrait of James Bridie." *The London Mercury,* 39 (April, 1939), 584a. Biographical account which notes leading works.

POLLOCK, J. Review of *Jonah. Saturday Review,* 154 (December 17, 1932), 644. Notes its faults.

POPE, HENNESSY, JAMES. Review of *Daphne Laureola. The Spectator,* 182 (April 1, 1949), 483. Concentrates upon performers' renditions.

"Portrait." *Bookman* (London), 86 (September 1934), 289. Biographical highlights sketched.

"Punch on the Clyde." *The Times Literary Supplement* (July 24, 1953), 474. Notes Bridie's ambiguity.

REDFERN, JAMES. Review of *It Depends What You Mean. The Spectator,* 173 (October 20, 1944), 359. Unfavorable notice.

SALTER, WILLIAM. Review of *Mr. Gillie. New Statesman and Nation,* 27 (March 18, 1950), 299. Notes its perspicacious characterizations.

SPEAIGHT, ROBERT Et Al. *Since 1939: Drama, The Novel, Poetry, Prose Literature.* London: Phoenix House, 1949. P. 38. Mention of Bridie's existence; exemplifies the tendency of contemporaries to undervalue the playwright.

STOKES, SEWELL. Review of *Dr. Angelus. Theatre Arts,* 31 (November 1947), 47. Discusses authorial intention.

TOBIN, TERENCE. "James Bridie's One-Act Plays." *Delta Epsilon Sigma Bulletin,* 19 (March, 1974), 26–32. Textual consideration of selected curtain risers.

VERNON, GRENVILLE. Review of *A Sleeping Clergyman*. *The Common-weal*, 20 (October 26, 1934), 618. Notes its panoramic proficiency.

VERSCHOYLE, DEREK. Review of *Tobias*. *The Spectator*, 147 (March 19, 1932), 409. Mentions Bridie's new concentration upon character rather than caricature.

———. Review of *Jonah*. *The Spectator*, 149 (December 16, 1932), 861. Makes just comment on play's long-windedness.

———. Review of *A Sleeping Clergyman*. *The Spectator*, 151 (September 29, 1933), 401. Traces the growth of the author.

———. Review of *The Black Eye*. *The Spectator*, 155 (October 18, 1935), 606. Unfavorable consideration.

WAKEFIELD, GILBERT. Review of *The Anatomist*. *Saturday Review*, 152 (October 17, 1931), 499. Concentrates upon the electrifying presentation of the controversial protagonist.

———. Review of *Tobias*. *Saturday Review*, 1953 (March 19, 1932), 196-97. Includes suggestions for improving staging techniques.

"War Office Objection of Medal Incident." *GH*, October 17, 1933, p. 9f. See also July 29, 1933, p. 8d; July 21, 1933; p. 11e; August 1, 1933, p. 11c. Treatment of furor which arose over action in *A Sleeping Clergyman*.

WEALES, GERALD. *Religion in Modern English Drama*. Philadelphia: University of Pennsylvania Press, 1961. Chapter 4 treats Shaw and Bridie in relation to man's temptation and fall; this consideration provides inspiration for Helen Luyben's treatment of the daemonic in Bridie.

WILLIAMS, H. Review of *The Anatomist*. *Theatre Arts Monthly*, 17 (January, 1933), 24. Deals with development of tension in the drama.

[WORSLEY, T. C.] Review of *The Baikie Charivari*. *The New Statesman and Nation*, 44 (October 18, 1952), 448. Notes the symbolism of the drama.

———. "The Last Bridie." *New Statesman and Nation*, n.s. 44 (October 18, 1952), 448. Treatment of the mature work of the playwright; focuses upon *Meeting at Night*.

2. Selected Biographical Newspaper Articles

For twenty years James Bridie was frequently written about in British newspapers. The following entries are listed to aid future biographers.

"Appointed Chairman C.E.M.A. Scottish Advisory Committee." *GH*, November 27, 1943, p. 2f.

"Bridie Ill." *GH*, January 29, 1951, p. 5a.

"National Theatre (Glasgow)." *GH*, November 24, 1938, p. 13e.

178

JAMES BRIDIE

"Opens Glasgow Book Exhibition." *GH*, November 17, 1938, supp.
"Profile." *The Observer*, August 20, 1950, p. 15.
"Receives C.B.E." *GH*, June 13, 1946, p. 6b.
"Resigns as Arts Council Scottish Chairman." *GH*, July 30, 1946, p. 2g;
    August 17, 1946, p. 2e.

3. Selected Obituaries

Americana Annual, 85 (1952), 85.
British Medical Journal, no. 4701 (February 10, 1951), 303-4.
Glasgow Herald, Death, January 30, 1951, p. 3f: Portrait, January 31,
    1951, leader, p. 4a and c; Funeral, February 2, 1951, p. 3e.
Illustrated London News, 218 (February 10, 1951), 209.
Lancet, 260 (February 3, 1951), 281.
New York Times, January 30, 1951, p. 25.
Newsweek, 37 (February 12, 1951), 53.
Theatre Arts, 34 (February 1951), 35.
Time, 57 (February 12, 1951), 85.
Wilson Library Bulletin, 25 (March, 1951), 274.

Index

179

Nephilim, 98
New Testament, 100
New Thought, 62
New York, 24, 34, 71

Observer, The, 82
O'Casey, Sean, 24
Oedipus the Tyrant, 165n4
Olivier, Laurence, 53
Old Testament, 100, 106, 167n7
Old Vic Theatre, 53
On Public Lighting by Electricity,
    158n2
O'Neill, Eugene, 24, 129
Outlook for Young Engineers, The,
    158n2
Over Soul, 62

Pantaloon, 120
Parsifal, 35
"Partridge Dance, The," 169n4
Pasteur, Louis, 28, 32
"Patient Griselda," 145
Paul, St., 55, 154, 167n5
Perth Theatre, 131
Peter Pan, 17, 86, 167n6
Peter, St., 93
"Petition of the Cornishmen to Henry
    VII," 165n2
Phoenix Theatre, 38
Picturesque Scotland, 20
Pierrot, 54
Pilate, Pontius, 57, 145, 148, 149,
    167n5, 168n8
Pilgrim Players, 108
Playboy of the Western World, 24
Pollockshields, 19
predestination, 88, 89
Presbyterian, 69, 90, 123, 132,
    161(5)n1, n2
Priestley, John Boynton, 18, 44, 60
Pritchard, Edward William, 161n7
A Private Matter, 169n4
The Proposal, 165n4
Protestant, 15, 52, 53
Puck, 19
Pulcinella, 54
Punch, 54, 144, 167n5
Punch, or The London Charivari, 144
Puritan, 70, 112, 145
Pygmalion, 64

Quincentenary Year Book, The, 21
Quintessence of Ibsenism, The, 23

Ramsay, Allan, 16
Reformation, 15, 17, 52
Regional Programme, 118
Reid, John MacNair, 113
Renaissance, 94
rescue, 41, 50, 61, 64, 65, 68, 69, 139,
    167n6, 168n8
Restoration, 16
Richardson, Ralph, 26, 47, 105
Riefenstahl, Leni, 53
Rig-Veda, 49
Rob Roy, 17
Robson, Flora, 32, 65, 66, 161n12,
    162(6)n2
Royal Army Medical Corps, 22
Royal Princess Theatre, 126, 131
Royal Theatre, 56
Royalty Theatre, 114
"Rule Britannia," 149
Rumbold, Gilbert, 152
Ruth, Book of, 144

Sadler's Wells Theatre, 120
St. Andrew's Society, 18
"St. Louis Blues," 167n7
St. Kilda in Edinburgh, 16
St. Serf (Sydserf), Thomas, 16
Saintsbury, George, 153
Salamis, 141
Samson, 56
Sarajevo, 141
satire, 38, 39, 41, 44–45, 46, 61, 62, 63,
    77, 78, 79, 82, 120, 126, 127, 137,
    139, 152. . . . of the estates, 78, 79,
    113, 128–50
Satire of the Three Estates, etc., The,
    15, 128
Savoy Hotel, 88
Schiller, Friedrich, 23
"Science and Art," 169n4
Scot, Reginald, 97
Scotland, 24, 44, 54, 134, 159n1;
    dramatic history, 15–18, 157(1)n1,
    165n3
    literature, 39–41
    setting, 111–27
Scott, Dr. J. C., 20
Scott, Sir Walter, 17, 40, 47, 160n7